THE SOCIETY FOR THE COMPLETE EXTERMINATION OF *ETHAN FROME*

BY

D. J. PHINNEY

To Sharon

OTHER BOOKS BY D J PHINNEY

RED CAR NOIR SERIES

The Anaheim Beauties Valencia Queen
The Cigarette Girl on the Tango

PROLOGUE

"How you react to *Ethan Frome* tells how you feel about yourself." My wife gazes from Alioto's toward sails on San Francisco Bay. She offers me a mint. I face her sapphire eyes and shake my head, rejecting her idea or her candy. I'm not sure which.

I ask, "How many men read Edith Wharton?"

"You did, Allen."

"Fifty years ago, in high school, when they forced me."

She sets her glass down, strokes my palm, and invites me toward her kiss. On her breath I taste the cabernet we've shared. She closes her eyes, smiles.

I yield to temptation.

Our waiter interrupts. "Sir, your check."

We Uber home, and my mind returns to high school. They'd made us read *Ethan Frome,* the year they'd licensed us drive. What on earth had they been thinking? Besides ensuring none of us ever named a kid Zenobia, I have no clue. But once our Uber driver drops us at our doorstep, my wife's comment on *Ethan Frome* lures me upstairs into our attic. There, in a squashed-down cardboard box, I find a book report I wrote.

I got an F.

I haven't read the thing since 1969.

If you never did have *Ethan Frome* inflicted on you, read it.

<u>**Book Report**</u>
<u>***Ethan Frome* by Edith Wharton**</u>
Prepared by Allen Daniel Martin
for Mrs. Winchcombe
Sophomore English
January 10th, 1969

There's this dude named Ethan Frome. He lives in Starkfield, Massachusetts. He's married to this battle-axe, Zenobia, who's not into him. When her cousin, this chick named Mattie, moves in to help do housework, Ethan totally digs Mattie, who always wears this hot red scarf. Don't ask what's hot about a scarf. I can only guess. Ethan also likes to dream he's like this hot-snot engineer, as if being an engineer might make him groovy.

One day Zenobia, who goes by Zeena, bails to Bettsbridge, Massachusetts. If you check *Rand McNally's Atlas*, Bettsbridge and Starkfield aren't in it. But while this hypochondriac Zeena's off consulting with some quack in this fake village, Mattie's homing in on Ethan. She serves him munchies on Zeena's china. But Zeena's cat knocks over this dish. So to fix a stupid broken pickle plate, Ethan needs to make a glue-run. First, they stash the pieces together on the top shelf of the china cabinet, hoping the old lady will never notice.

Except, she busts him. The next day, Ethan strolls in with his glue, and Zeena's there. Sure enough, she's found the dish and fingers Mattie. Zeena tells him she's made her mind up. Mattie's gotta go. Ethan and Mattie are seriously bummed.

The ever-brilliant Mattie cooks up this scheme to crash their sled into this elm tree. In their death, she says they'll always be together. But Ethan's such a loser he even messes up their suicide. Mattie winds up in this wheelchair, and Ethan becomes lame. (Let's make that *lamer*. Ethan Frome was lame throughout his stupid book.)

Rather than go to engineering school, Ethan ends the book caring for two whiny old broads, and Mattie's bitchier than even Zeena. I found this book to be depressing. So, unless you're into downers, there are better books that should be taught in high school.

So there you have it. Aren't you "bummed" you never read it?
Maybe you could read my story instead.
It's better.
Honest.

CHAPTER ONE

HITCHIN' A RIDE
PASADENA, CALIFORNIA: FRIDAY, AUGUST 28TH, 1970

The Society for the Complete Extermination of *Ethan Frome* met Friday evenings, in secret, in my eighteen-year-old mind. I pictured Ethan Frome and Mattie Silver on their sled, gathering momentum, zipping toward Edith Wharton's elm.

Had Ethan been a man, he'd never crash into a tree. I saw him waving his middle finger, flipping off Miss Wharton, veering from Starkfield's sled run to careen into a chasm longer and more cavernous than my imagination. Down I let him spiral, thousands of feet down. Ethan and Mattie screamed for one whole minute and several seconds before they met an end that seemed too perfect for two narcissists who'd forced entire high schools to read their dreary little love story. Punji sticks, sharper than those amazing Ginsu knives, waited to impale them on my mental canyon floor. There, a provident earthquake, followed by an avalanche, were set to remove all traces of *Ethan Frome* from high school.

Sorry to say, my one-man "Society" neglected to convene the last Friday of August, 1970. Evidently, Ethan Frome had launched his own preemptive strike. I'd fallen racing scaffolds, and I'd landed in the hospital. In my agony, the Society had completely slipped my mind. My more immediate goal now was escaping from the hospital. My busted arm had placed me in their orthopedic wing. There, on the third floor of Huntington Memorial, I found big Mandy Richert from my homeroom.

She was a candy-striper.

She was staring through my doorway.

She was—waving.

My heart sank. *Crap, not her! Please, God, not Mandy.* I shut my eyes. I barely knew her, but I didn't want to hurt her. I scanned my *Reader's Digest,* trying to block out Lawrence Welk tunes droning from hidden speakers with wires I couldn't find to snip. I willed my plaster cast to hurry and harden around my arm so I could split.

"Allen Martin!" She burst in through my doorway, hand creeping toward a face round and puffy as a catcher's mitt. "What happened to your arm?"

"I broke it."

"Poor guy." She sounded almost sympathetic. "How?"

I mustered my kindest leave-me-alone voice. "I fell." I was sitting in my hospital gown. Too short, even for me, it let their antiseptic butcher paper irritate my butt. *Hmmm.* How to make Mandy go away...?

I'd start by being friendly. This wasn't her fault. Sarcasm usually got me into trouble.

"Howja fall?" Mandy asked.

"We were racing scaffolds."

"What?"

"On the track. At La Cañada High."

"Scaffolds?"

"Those things we stand on to paint the high school walls and windows. If you unlock those little wheels at the bottom you get a chariot. Two stories high. Think *Ben Hur*, except on stilts."

Mandy paused. "You were racing? You and who?"

"Don't ask."

We raced Fridays after work. Four painters per scaffold served as "horses." Each scaffold became a "chariot" pulled in a race around the track. Being small, I was a jockey. I should have known this was unsafe when my coworker, the Jabberwocky, drove the other scaffold. But painting schools got boring. A mundane summer job mixed with turpentine and thinners had warped my juvenile mind. I liked to dream up entertainments between brain-deaths from paint fumes, starting with kumquat wars. Kumquat wars had lasted through July, when all the kumquat trees on campus had been stripped bare.

Next, I'd invented *Tape-O*, foot hockey with a masking tape roll. Tile walls surrounded the showers in our high school locker room. Openings on each side provided goals to be defended. We scored a point for kicking the tape roll past a goalie in the gym showers. Fat cumulus clouds, steaming through our showers, made it hard to see the tape roll when it skidded past our sneakers across bath tiles like those plastic pucks in air hockey.

It was good fun—until "Momma," the high school principal, busted us, outlawing the emerging sport of Tape-O on the spot. The scaffold races had started after Momma'd changed the shower locks. I dared not mess with "Momma." She could seriously fire me, and I'd never save up for college with no job.

Mandy stared at me, tapping her huge foot on the Linoleum. "Well anyways, it's neat to see you at my hospital."

"Sure," I said.

Mandy didn't own the hospital, but she sure seemed glad to see me. If a girl was jazzed to see me, why *her?*

She paced the room, Saint-Bernard large. Her candy-striper dress stretched in too many wrong places. Huge white crepe-soled shoes squeaked as she walked on checkered floor tiles. She'd been humongous since junior high, five-foot-eight in seventh grade and called 'Girlzilla' by laughing boys who these days never called her, period. Boys in German class were so mean they were calling her *"Die Hindenburg"*.

Although Mandy hadn't grown, she claimed an inch or two on me.

"Howja get here?"

"The Jabberwocky drove me in his Plymouth."

"He couldn't stay?"

"He was pissed. My blood messed up his seat covers."

"They're just Naugahyde. And over a sixty-three Plymouth Valiant? Puh-leaze!" She plunged her fists into her candy-striper skirt pockets. "I mean, it isn't like the Jabberwocky can't sponge a vinyl seat cover. Here's a tip. Don't play Scrabble with the Jabberwocky. Ever!" Mandy cocked her head. "Howja think he got his name?"

"I dunno." I shifted on the examining table paper, hoping her question ended her inquisition.

It didn't.

"He cheats at Scrabble. I'll bet he pushed you off that scaffold, Allen, didn't he?"

I closed my eyes. The plaster cast was getting hot. My right arm throbbed. I didn't care about the Wocky, cared less about his nickname, and desperately wanted to get out of here. I spun my Class of '71 ring inside a tray beside my bed. Left-handed, this took some getting used to.

"When he tried to tell us 'slithy' was a real English word. Leta Hertz and I named him 'Jabberwocky' at Palm Crest Elementary."

My ears perked. "Lovely Leta?"

"Stop it. She's my friend, Allen."

Of course. Leta Hertz could be anybody's friend. She was a "piece," a knockout, the star of every boy's wet dreams. But if Leta was a Corvette, Mandy Richert was a Buick; dependable, old-fashioned, extra-wide.

"Slithy's not a word?"

Mandy glared through sad brown eyes. "No." She shook her head. "Except in Lewis Carroll's poem."

"Shucks." I scratched my neck. "Say, how 'bout 'brillig'?"

"Quit it!" said Mandy. "Please, don't make me sound like I'm your mother."

"My mother never speaks to me."

"I'm sorry," Mandy said. "I was supposed to cheer you up. Can't a candy-striper do that?"

I flashed a grin I might have flashed were I auditioning for the Brady Bunch.

Mandy grimaced back. "You were serious?"

"'Bout what?"

"Your mother."

I shivered. Why had I brought up my mother? I stared in Mandy's eyes. *Could I trust her?* I'd been burned by other girls. Like Heather Fairchild, my "girlfriend,"—before she'd gotten the first boob job in La Cañada High School history and dumped me. Seemed her uncle was this cutting-edge plastic surgeon. Before I knew it, Heather'd anointed herself Radio Free La Cañada. Every confidence I'd shared she'd propagated at warp-speed throughout our high school. I'd vowed never to trust a girl again.

"Let's talk about the scaffold." I worked Mandy's sympathies. She nodded when I explained how the Wocky had pushed my scaffold when we'd rounded the north goal post, and then the right rear leg had buckled.

"Glad you bled all over the Jabberwocky's Plymouth. Good job, Allen."

"Thanks." I nodded, oddly grateful.

I hadn't planned to chat up Mandy. But I was willing to play along, hoping she'd drop a couple clues on how to break out of this hospital without my having to call my mother. Half the times I called my mother, she never bothered showing up.

"Hey. You're frowning. I'm s'posed to make you cheery. Don't be a sourpuss."

I scowled. I *liked* being a sourpuss.

"And why race scaffolds? I'd figured you'd be running," Mandy said. "Don't you run cross country?"

I was flabbergasted she'd noticed. La Cañada High School offered two sports in the fall. For athletes, there was football. And then, for fat jocks, there was—football. According to the football coach, cross country was for weenies.

"You like to race, Allen?"

"No."

"Then, why do you bother?" Mandy asked.

I shifted my weight. My ribs felt tender. I racked my brain for clever comebacks, staring at her, the way I'd learned in fifth-grade staring contests, where the kid who blinks first loses their Hostess Twinkie.

I couldn't beat her. Clearly, Mandy was a staring-contest black belt. I blinked and swallowed hard. "You wanna know?"

"You think I'd ask if I didn't care?"

"When you run—" I checked her eyes again. "When you run, it's like you vanish."

"Vanish?"

"You know—when life gets weird, I run. And then I'm going at a different speed from all of La Cañada. One minute, people see me; the next moment I'm gone. Better than smoking marijuana. Cheaper too."

The dimple on her left cheek was wider than the other. "You get tired, Allen?" she asked.

"Runners get used to feeling pain."

"You sure?" Mandy leaned forward.

"Scout's honor."

"I never figured," Mandy said. "Is there someplace you run to—while you're running away from everybody?" She straddled a vinyl chair, and foam puffed out between its cushion seams.

"Flint Peak." Instantly, I wished I hadn't told her.

"Where's that?" Clearly, she didn't share my apprehensions.

"It's like—this mountain."

"Well, duh."

"Where Glendale and Pasadena come together. There's this radio tower there. It's got these big red blinking lights. And giant rattlesnakes sometimes."

"Can you show me?"

"The rattlesnakes? Not now."

"Why? Are they sleeping?"

I gave her a look. "I'm in the hospital, Mandy."

She plunged her fists into her side. "Suppose I spring you?"

"Tonight?" I pondered Mandy's latest offer. "You can do that?"

"Not really. But I—get off at six."

"You're not supposed to."

"Ya gonna tell?"

I shook my head, astonished she'd take the risk for *me.*"

"Six o'clock." she said.

I slowly nodded back. Ethan Frome would have to croak some other day.

CHAPTER TWO

THE LONG AND WINDING ROAD

PASADENA, CALIFORNIA: FRIDAY, AUGUST 28TH, 1970

From Huntington Memorial, we cruised California Boulevard to the stoplight at Orange Grove, where the Rose Parade runs on New Year's. We sped north on Orange Grove Boulevard toward the Pasadena Art Museum. It's that black building you see behind the Rose Parade on television. My teachers made me go inside it for this field trip junior year. This room there holds this giant herd of Degas ballerinas. Every New Year's Day, the Rose Parade hangs a right by that museum and marches east into Old Town Pasadena.

If the Rose Parade hung a left instead of a right on Colorado, they could march one-hundred yards to Suicide Bridge, which has another name, although nobody in La Cañada knows just what it is. The bridge on Colorado has been called Suicide Bridge for as long as anybody can remember.

Its construction date, 1913, is stamped into its concrete. It was once a part of old Route 66. It shows up on TV reruns; Tod and Buz in their Corvette speeding across its arches, high above the Arroyo Seco. Tonight, fluted lampposts threw silhouettes down slopes. Shadows zigged and zagged through palm trees, through laurel sumac and poison oak, past a busted power pole sticking straight up like a skewer. The canyon sent back echoes from the quail beneath the sycamores, huddled in clumps around the boulders in the arroyo bottom.

Suicide Bridge looked like a bitchen place for Ethan Frome to die, but I was too sore at the moment to explore the possibilities. Riding home with Mandy, I had to stall to give my Mom time to get drunk and go to bed.

Plus, I was talking, a rare treat.

Mandy shook out her hair and punched her Volkswagen into third. "Can't believe your mother doesn't know you broke your arm yet."

"Why tell her? Hospitals don't care after you show 'em your insurance card. Besides, she doesn't listen."

"She doesn't listen. She doesn't talk. She a mannequin?"

I fumbled with my arm sling. "Mom's just angry."

"At you?" Mandy's smile would be cute if she were thinner.

"At men in general. Mom's reading Betty Friedan's *Feminine Mystique*."

"Oh." Mandy hung a right from Colorado to Linda Vista. The gears ground. The clutch engaged. Her eggnog-colored Volkswagen lurched out into traffic. She rolled her window down, then rolled it up when the wind drowned out her voice. "What about your dad?"

"Don't know where he is." I shook my head.

"He's your dad, Allen. Come on."

"Mom doesn't tell me."

Mandy sighed. "Sooooo—he's not—living with you, I take it."

"Not recently. He left a year ago before I started running."

Mandy gave me a look. "Does your whole family run away?"

"When we're not invisible."

She nodded.

I was shocked she even listened. I wasn't usually so candid. My arm ached. It hurt less when I talked. She concentrated on driving, which permitted me to ramble.

I turned to Mandy, whose brown eyes held a warmth I hadn't noticed, like I could trust her. I was surprised to feel comfortable with a *girl*. I told her how we'd sneak into the weight room after paint crew, a year ago, after Snooge had ripped off the master key from John the janitor.

"Why so secret?" Mandy asked.

"Guys laugh at me."

"They do?"

"What? Do I look like some big weightlifter?"

Road noise from Linda Vista Avenue underlined her silence. Since Mandy hadn't answered, I explained how after this workout I'd jogged home after sunset, and for some reason, once I'd gotten there, our whole house had seemed chilly.

"So what happened?"

I rubbed my chin to keep my thoughts off my sore arm. I was beginning to think I liked talking to Mandy. "When I walked into the kitchen, it got chillier," I said. "Mom was staring at the counter as if her Princess phone had bitten her. She'd been crying. She held a martini glass half-full of cabernet."

A long breath. I was giving up my secrets.

"Mom glared at the telephone like she'd kill it if it moved. I poured some orange juice. Her kitchen felt as cold as her refrigerator. Mom's head swiveled like a Barbie doll's. Then she lowered her Foster Grant shades and informed me that Dad wasn't coming home."

"Allen, how awful!"

"Yup. As if she'd washed him down the sink without a care. She sipped her wine and asked. 'Can I just be alone, Allen?'"

"So I'm like, 'You okay, Mom?'"

"'I'm fine,' Mom rattled back in a voice that said she wasn't. 'It's just....' She grabbed her glass and left the room."

"How sad." Shaking her head, Mandy signaled to change lanes.

"Mom was so calm. And I'd been pumped when I had strolled into her kitchen. Now I felt more like the Michelin Man if some dude slashed his air valve."

Mandy shifted the Beetle into third. The gearshift groaned, and the Volkswagen charged up Linda Vista. She faced me. "What'dja do?"

"Went for a walk, but started running. Hang a left at Lida." I rubbed my arm cast near the break. "We got a half an hour. I can show you."

From Linda Vista, Lida Street switch-backed east toward Glendale; two miles of non-stop up I must have run a thousand times. The slope started through a neighborhood of ivy-covered bungalows. West of Wellington Street, Lida wiggled up the San Raphael Hill slopes past a brick wall hiding acres of expensive stucco boxes. The hills upslope were bare. There'd been this fire my sophomore year. Rye grass and poison oak erupted from black ashes.

Mandy shifted into first. The Volkswagen chugged uphill. A big blue Buick Riviera roared around us. Mandy's Beetle coughed and sputtered.

"I feel weird about this, Mandy."

She shook her hair out.

"Because I'm riding in your car. We're supposed to *run* up Lida." My side coiled in sympathetic pain. "Every time I run this hill, Coach Neal's at the summit in his minibus and t-shirt with sweat moons beneath his armpits, staring at his stopwatch, raising his sunglasses and frowning. I've never seen the summit without him there."

"Why's he make you run uphill?"

"He found 'Lida' my freshman year, after our La Cañada cross country team finished fourth in CIF. But we placed second in Rio Hondo League. San Marino, the State champion has won our league for years. Coach Neal keeps reminding us we're losers."

"He's such a jerk."

"He's trying to help us. So he came up with this strategy. For home meets, we run a two-mile course above Verdugo Park. It's called 'The Hill.' It's so steep it should probably be outlawed.

We run up Sunshine Drive which is like racing up a staircase. Once Sunshine tops out, this other hill, Polaris Street, is even steeper, burning your legs until, no street leads any higher."

"Then what?" Mandy asked.

"What goes up must come down. You don't run down Hillside Drive. More like you fall down."

Mandy giggled.

"You're like this out-of-control school bus rolling downhill without brakes. You put one foot before the other, and you pray you never stumble. Gravity does the rest, pulling you faster-faster-faster while you throw your legs in front of you and try to keep from falling, from crashing into asphalt, from auguring into parked Oldsmobiles. You try not to collapse on legs that wiggle like rubber bands. If you're in shape, you sprint down Hillside Drive in total terror. If you aren't in shape, you walk."

Mandy seemed to catch my drift.

I explained to her Neal's strategy; how every day we'd practice Lida. San Marino's runners might defeat us on a flat course, but nobody could touch us on "The Hill."

I pointed past a yellow curve sign. "See that stop sign at the saddle, Mandy? Hang a left. Park by the cable across the fire road."

The Volkswagen rounded a bend gouged through thirty feet of granite where tree tobacco and monkey flowers squeezed up through the rock fissures. A flat spot at the saddle was surrounded by wild mustard plants. Mandy followed tiretracks to the pad.

"This it?" Mandy scrunched her parking brake.

I popped my door, stepping into wind. "Up there." I pointed to a ridgeline stretching two miles south, following power lines that fizzed above our heads. Overhead wires shot up an escarpment on t-shaped steel trusses to a radio tower, red and white, like someone had built it out of candy canes.

"There's Flint Peak," I said. "It's like where I sort stuff out."

"Like when your dad left?"

"Yup."

"Can we go up there?"

"Tonight?"

Mandy nodded.

I wasn't sure about showing her my place. But in a town full of rich people, you needed places you could be human. Maybe Mandy needed a place too.

"We can't drive there. I mean—even if I cut the cable, there's this washout on the fire road a half a mile up. We'll have to run."

"We could walk."

"It's steep, Mandy."

"I can make it."

I eyeballed Mandy's candy-striper shoes. "You'll wreck your shoes, you know. It's cold out."

"I got gym shoes in the trunk. What do you wear when you run up there, Allen?"

"My gym shorts."

"Can't be that cold." Mandy popped the Beetle hood. She had her gym shoes on before I could say no. "Let's see those rattlesnakes."

How could I tell her I had lied about the snakes?

The fire road to Flint Peak was filled with gullies. I had to watch where we stepped so Mandy didn't twist an ankle or step on alligator lizards when they wriggled from the shade. I led Mandy to the fire gate. The padlock seemed as rusty as the cable between the posts. I stepped across the wire rope.

Mandy followed.

Although my arm throbbed, I was used to climbing hills. I charged upward in strong steps. Mandy fell behind.

"Wait for me."

I had no choice given that Mandy had the car keys. I paced in circles by granite boulders where this storm had washed the road out. I stared at chunks of mica shimmering in sunlit gullies. Mandy huffed like a freight train. Her face was redder than a blood orange. She'd only climbed a hundred feet and bent to catch her breath.

"Sure you wanna do this?" I asked, hiding my impatience.

Mandy nodded.

What was her obsession with climbing this stupid mountain? She was gonna have a stroke. How would I call an ambulance out here with no phone booths for miles? I slowed my pace. She panted. Yet I was proud that she kept moving, as if she understood now, what it's like to be a runner, to hear your pulse pound in your temples, to feel it throb inside your neck, to feel your legs burn, feel them tighten. "Mandy?"

A breath—a breath—a breath. "I'm okay, Allen."

"You sure?"

She nodded. She moved slow, but she kept walking.

Her pluck impressed me. "It's not so bad up near the ridge. It flattens out. Then it gets steep."

"Worse than this?"

"Yeah," I said. "But short."

Mandy chugged and didn't stop. Sumac and toyons yielded to greasewood and Spanish daggers. The road flattened and smelled of skunks where a fire trail slipped east toward Pasadena. The sun faded. Yucca shadows curled through weed-filled canyons. The sun blazed tomato red, and then it fell behind a ridgeline where the twilight shadows lingered.

Mandy inched up the road, tortoise slow. Veins pounded in her neck, but her breath had found a rhythm.

"Lookin' strong there," I said.

She grinned.

"You're gonna make it."

The road grew steeper. She didn't stop.

"Look! The lights are turning on," Mandy said. "Up on the tower." Three red lights crackled. The highest one was blinking.

"This the steep part?" she asked.

"Keep moving."

"I gotta stop, Allen."

"We're almost there."

Streaks of sweat ran through the dust that caked her forehead. Mandy clumbered up the road.

The fire road turned the corner, circling Flint Peak. Glendale and Scholl Canyon spread out to our right. San Gabriel and its valley rolled out to the east. Across the first ridge, Eagle Rock turned on her nightlights. Los Angeles stretched beyond, skyscrapers grasping toward stars, distant fingers of blue and orange climbing from the city. Behind Downtown, the Harbor Freeway glistened south toward harbor lights and tank ships bearing miniature white blinkers. Beyond, the silhouette of Catalina Island cast reflections on the Santa Barbara Channel.

"My God."

"Nice, huh?"

"Oh my God. I never knew." She kept climbing. "Can I see more from the top? I wanna see." Mandy acquired a second wind, scurrying up the fire road so fast *I* was panting.

"Oh my God. Omigod. Omi...."

At the peak, wind whipped through Mandy's hair. I stumbled up behind her and stretched my legs to keep them warm. She didn't shiver. She paced around the radio tower, pointing. "There's Mount Wilson. Look! Allen, There's Griffith Park. There's LAX. I can't believe this."

She grabbed my arm cast, and my arm roared out in pain.

"Ouch!" I pulled away.

"Whoops!" She touched her lips. "Allen, I'm so sorry."

Crickets scritched from canyons while I nibbled back my pain. "I'm okay."

"You sure?"

Neither of us spoke. Above the distant groans of traffic came the evening scent of sagebrush. Twilight faded into darkness. Streetlamps twinkled from dark ridges. Colorado Street, Glendale Boulevard lit up in phosphorescent lines. From Hollywood, a searchlight leaped from the back of Griffith Park and sent a sword of light circling through a violet-colored sky.

One by one. Ten by ten. A sea of lights filled valleys until the basin fired with bright electric glitter.

"You cold?"

She nodded.

"We should go."

"I'm not quite ready."

I tossed a stone. "It's easier going down." I helped her up. She seemed lighter than I'd expected. We walked downhill by moonlight.

I heard her breathe above the crickets, and I liked having her with me, but it felt scary to know I'd shared my secret place.

Even Heather Fairchild had never been here.

"So according to the quadrangle maps, that tower's on "Flint Peak?" Mandy asked more questions going down than coming up.

I nodded. "Except nobody I know calls it Flint Peak. Just those USGS dudes somewhere back east who draw the topo maps."

"What do people here call it?"

"The ugly brown hill with the tower."

Mandy was kind enough to laugh, which made me worry she might like me.

I wiped sweat from my chin. "So now you know about my hideout. I like to stand up there at night and feel the wind against my ears like I'm Zubin friggin' Mehta, directing my neon symphony. 'Hey you! Yeah, in Burbank. Turn those sparkly lights on.'"

"Burbank obeys you?"

"Just somethin' I like doin'."

"Does your symphony, like—play music?"

"I usually tell 'em to shut up. I like things quiet when I'm sortin' out the hard stuff, like my family."

"Or Heather?" Mandy asked.

I stiffened. "Why'd you ask?"

"She talks. It's a small school."

"About me?"

"Well, yeah."

"Like, what's she say?"

"It's not like everyone believes her. I mean she's been this total creep-ball since they pumped her full of silicone."

"What's she say?"

"Says you're queer."

My stomach tightened. "You mean like—gay?"

"Says you never kissed her."

"So, I'm shy." I gave a shrug.

Still Heather's lies hurt like a swift kick in the nuts and made me want to crawl beneath a rock. I'd heard rumors too. How Heather Fairchild was getting it every night from Garry Jackson in the back of Garry's Mustang up Angeles Crest Highway; how Garry was such a stud Heather always begged for more. Even if Garry didn't like you, he never kept these things a secret.

Had it only been two weeks since Heather'd dumped me?

Mandy walked beside me, mesmerized by the view, and my mind fell into its well-worn rut of pining over Heather. I'd thought I'd loved her. Each night I'd nodded off with Heather's face etched on my mind. Her chipped tooth I'd always liked, her flowing auburn hair. Then, everything had ended.

Heather traded up.

Why did women seem so sexy once they'd dumped you?

She was a transfer from Connecticut, a debutante from Darien, a year behind me at La Cañada High. Until the previous June, when I'd discovered Heather, I'd scarcely even known women existed.

Then, like Aphrodite, Heather'd tiptoed from her seashell and swapped her goddess garb for bellbottoms, a cameo choker, a Doors t-shirt. She worked Saturdays in the Montrose Theater ticket booth on Honolulu Avenue, wearing this scarf across her forehead, like a nickel-arcade gypsy. Except on Heather, scarves looked foxy, and she wasn't reading fortunes.

I'd been jogging home from a time trial on Coach Neal's crummy "Hill." My chapped lips tasted salty from my sweat. I'd shaved four seconds off my time, even beating Ivan Alphabet. By all rights, had I been capable of pride, I would be gloating. But L.A.'s smog gnawed at my lungs. A pebble was wedged in my Adidas. I had a blister.

I'd stopped by the Montrose Theater to dump the pebble and snag a Pepsi. The marquee for Saturday's matinee said *Easy Rider.*

I grinned at Heather. "One adult."

From her ticket cage, she studied me, the way a pitcher on a baseball mound scopes out a rookie batter. She was calm while I wiped sweat. I hadn't caught my breath yet, and my temples pounded.

"Do you always breathe that hard?" she asked at last.

"Sorry, I've been running. We had a time trial at Verdugo." I bounced up on my toes to look athletic.

"Don't be sorry," she said. "D'you know your shoulders are way cute?"

Not sure what to say here, I said nothing. Heather had zipped me a no-win question, a trick I'd soon learn she excelled at. If you agreed you had "cute shoulders," you were "totally stuck up," and if you disagreed....

"I paint schools."

Heather seemed impressed. "Don't you go to La Cañada?" Her tone betrayed she knew, plus it was obvious, with "L.C. SPARTANS" stenciled on my gym shorts. She gazed up at me with brown eyes peering beneath her black silk scarf.

"Yeah," I said. "You too?"

She nodded. The cameo on her choker nodded with her. "You know my brother? Jack?" She rubbed her freckled forehead. Red hair cascaded around her cheeks and feathered to her shoulders. She smiled from one side of her mouth while the other side stayed blank. "My brother says you're bashful, but you're smart."

"So you're Jack's sister?"

She snapped her gum, exhaling a spearmint-flavored sigh, as if struggling to save this conversation. "Um, yeah!" she said. "I'm my brother's—uh—sister."

"Sorry. Stupid question. I'm Allen."

"I know," she said. The other half of Heather's mouth curled into an imp smile, almost omniscient, like Mona Lisa flirting with the boys down at the Louvre. Heather's smile made me feel like she almost read my mind, as if she actually enjoyed whatever she'd found in there to read.

"I'll need a dollar, Allen."

"Of course."

Then, I realized—*crap!*—I'd stashed my money in my gym shoes. The only cash I had on me was drooling with Adida juice. "Cute" shoulders deflated. Why didn't gym shorts come with pockets?

She smiled, as if she had a thing for *eau-de-dirty-socks* or didn't mind when it was lathered onto other people's money. My dollar squirmed as Heather watched it dry.

"Kill it, Allen. Ish! It's moving."

I stretched my hand and flattened it.

"Hey! No. Let's put your dollar on top," she whispered. "My boss licks the bills at night to wet her fingers to count the money." She giggled.

I laughed. Easier than gagging.

Heather counted out four quarters. "Buy me a tub of popcorn. Oh, and Allen...." She smiled again. "Wait five minutes. I get off then." She popped her gum and winked. "I can get you in for free."

"They let you do that?"

"You'll have to sit beside me."

Yesssss! I was amazed Heather wanted to sit by *me.* Maybe nobody had clued her in cross country was for weenies. She liked my *shoulders.* When you're five-foot six, and all you do is run and study, you don't turn down opportunities when they're foxy.

We split a tub of buttered popcorn in the theater. While Peter Fonda and Dennis Hopper were scoping out America, I scoped out Heather, hoping my jock odor, those stains beneath my armpits, and my stinky dollar bills didn't offend her.

Somehow, Heather didn't mind. I soon concluded she'd seen *Easy Rider* half a dozen times. I couldn't scope out Heather because she was scoping *me*.

By Fourth of July we were an item; holding hands, picking out china patterns at Ivers' Department Store. Heather scheduled our rendezvous on weekdays after work. We met between the Waterford crystal and the Royal Doulton china. I punched out at three from my paint job, skipping Tape-O to see Heather. It took me seventeen minutes to sprint from La Cañada High up Michigan Avenue to Foothill Boulevard to Oakwood Drive.

There, Heather waited, drumming fingers on "her" china. I clocked in at seventeen past three, "Ivers' Standard Time," she called it. There, squeezing my paint-stained fingers, she'd tell me her preferences in crystal, while I gazed at her luxurious frost-pink lips, hearing her talk. She talked a lot. I feared one day she might go silent; ask about *my* day.

Happily, she never asked. What could I say about my day? I painted toilet stalls. I patched concrete cracks in basements and painted them over with gray enamel. Even janitors outranked me. But I was saving up for college. What do you talk about when paint fumes are killing off your favorite brain cells, and your job is to sand graffiti and paint partitions?

Still, each stall became a masterpiece completed in Heather's honor. After power-sanding limericks through the battleship gray topcoat, through a mustard-gas green layer to a crusty sheet of metal, I primed and rolled each surface, then brushed out roller marks with my bristle brush. I alternated strokes up-down, left-right before repeating the process for that extra coat of paprika needed to cover the battleship gray, the mustard-gas green, and the rust. With each completed stall, I imagined Heather nodding, as if I had redecorated one of seventy-three toilet stalls inside her palace. Then, I removed the masking tape beneath each painted partition, revealing an inscription:

ALLEN MARTIN + HEATHER FAIRCHILD

To see this, you had to slide under the stall, flat on your back, usually through a puddle of someone's urine. Our names were on each stall, in three-eighths-inch capital letters outlined in bold mustard-gas green.

By July 21st, my eighteenth birthday, Heather had named our children. There'd be four of these, she said. Delilah, Dahlia, Dusty, and Destiny. She lifted the bottom seam of her faded Woodstock t-shirt and tapped her belly button, with which, she assured me, she'd dial in our offspring's genders.

I bristled. "Whoa! Time out. We never talked about four girls."

"It's a woman thing." She adjusted the cameo on her choker. "I can't explain it to you darling. You could use a course on women."

"On women? You want me to take a class?"

She flashed her sideways smile. I'd be studying under Heather. Her class was titled "Woman 101." This was my present for my birthday. She'd teach me all I'd need to know. "Everything about women—and then some," she assured me.

It soon became apparent the "Woman 101" curriculum was focusing exclusively on Heather. If you liked women (meaning Heather) you had to like the Association. You could *not* like Jimi Hendrix or Janis Joplin. I scribbled in my three-ring binder, that Heather's favorite ice cream flavor was Rocky Road, that Heather's favorite actor was Robert Redford, that Heather thought the fabric pills on my t-shirts were disgusting.

I bought new t-shirts. I read fan mags on Robert Redford. I bought Association eight-tracks and memorized the lyrics until I wondered if I could mold Heather into someone who could cherish me. Each morning, before the mirror, I sang into my razor, imagining Heather Fairchild on the far side of the glass. She asked me if a time might come when I'd grow tired of her. I, of course, whispered, "Never, my love."

One day she failed to show up for my lesson.

I was blindsided. I hadn't seen it coming. Sometime during the summer while we'd been picking out her china patterns, she'd grown prettier. Her hair had filled out. Sun had bleached it Ann-Margret red, and when she'd come back from "vacation," she was "stacked."

On my lesson day, I saw her with Garry Jackson from the football team, upstairs in the cashmere section at Ivers'. Garry was buying her a sweater, "to show those tits off," for her birthday. Besides remodeling her breasts, Snow White had dumped her dwarf—me, and had traded up for Garry, her new prince. Since preschool, I'd been a wimp. Now, Garry rubbed it in. To make things worse, Garry's old man, who had more money than Elvis, had bought Garry a new cherry-red 289 Mustang.

Garry was clearly signing up for "Woman 102."

That evening, I tried to call her. Her mother told me on the phone Heather "didn't wish to talk," but I was "a nice boy for a Jew." Her mother told me Heather truly hoped we'd still be "friends."

I dropped the phone, kicking it. I'd never wanted to be a "nice boy" or a "friend." Who'd decided I was Jewish? I *wasn't* Jewish. I was an atheist. Still my long Italian nose left people wondering. I didn't cry. I had to run my workout. I had to return the crystal unicorn I'd bought for Heather's birthday. And after that, all those names on all those bathroom stalls in high school....

Crap!

They'd need a paint-over before Momma changed the locks.

"You've sure been quiet, Allen. You okay?" Mandy interrupted the private pity party I'd hosted over Heather. A moon rose over Pasadena. Mandy sounded sympathetic.

"My arm hurts," I said, hiding my real reason.

Ahead, I saw the fire road cable with Mandy's Volkswagen behind it.

"I like talking to you," Mandy smiled wide. "Is that okay?"

I paused. This was a compliment. I didn't want to hurt her.

I liked talking to her too. I just didn't want to say so. Here was my dilemma. Mandy wasn't popular. Not that I was either, but still....

"Look, we can't talk like this all the time. I'm sorry." My voice trembled.

"Well, what's your problem?" Mandy reddened. "You embarrassed to be seen with me?"

"I'm just—not ready for a girl thing."

"You got that jacked-up by Heather?"

I nodded.

As though she felt my pain, Mandy's eyes turned sympathetic, while her mind assembled thoughts in the tempest behind her pupils. "Well then—" Mandy said "—I have a duty to girls in general. Don'tcha think you should have one of us in your corner?"

Not sure where she was headed, I didn't answer.

"Allen, we have some stuff in common. I haven't told you about *me*."

She was right. This whole trip up here, I'd monopolized the talking.

"I won't tell about myself until you ask, Allen."

I'd been a creep. I knew it. "You're right, Mandy. I'm s-s-sss—" the word stuck inside my throat, like I was trying to remove a tennis ball wedged behind my teeth "—sss-s-sorry."

"Really?" She seemed all happy.

It felt freeing just to say this. Perhaps that *Love Story* Erich Segal guy had gotten stuff all wrong. Heather'd had opinions. She hadn't cared much for the "s"-word. To Heather, being *privileged* meant never having to say you're sorry. I'm not sure Heather knew much about love, but what do I know?

But now, I *was* sorry. If you were sorry, you had to promise to do better, to try not to repeat whatever stupid thing you'd done. I *hated* making promises. Keeping them was painful. I dreaded making any promise to Mandy.

"I want you as a friend, Allen, the way we were when we first got here."

Mandy had a point. Not many girls were such straight shooters. Maybe Annie Oakley Junior here deserved a second look.

"Okay. But just you, Mandy." I faced the tower. "And—what we talk about up here stays on this mountain. Dig?"

She slid into her Volkswagen and revved the engine. I wasn't sure what she'd do next. I half thought she'd cruise off and leave me standing by the fire road, but when Mandy popped the door lock open, she grinned.

"Deal," she said. "Your secrets never leave this mountain."

"Yours don't either," I said. "They never leave Flint Peak."

Her smile widened.

Privately, I was glad we'd cleared the air as the two of us sped north toward La Cañada.

CHAPTER THREE

I'LL NEVER FALL IN LOVE AGAIN
LA CAÑADA-FLINTRIDGE, CALIFORNIA: WEDNESDAY, SEPTEMBER 2ND, 1970

Run, you faggot dwarf!" Garry hollered from the bleachers. I warmed up with Ivan Alphabet around the La Cañada High track. "Don't disappoint me, dwarf, I bet twenty bucks on you." I was practicing with Ivan just to see if I could run with my arm wrapped in a cast up past my elbow. Garry annoyed me. This was a warm-up. If stupid Garry and Pudge McMasters were betting money on this lap, I'd make sure that Garry lost. I'd settled things with Pudge when we'd fought back in second grade. Garry had been taunting me since preschool.

Ivan glanced at me. "Ignore him. Garry drives that Mustang ragtop cuz his puffed-up head is so huge it won't fit in a sedan."

I smiled and kept running. Ivan and I weren't bosom buddies, but we went back to second grade when Ivan had moved out west from Queens. Most of Ivan's friends were Jewish, but we still shared some traditions from Paradise Canyon Elementary

School that weren't Jewish. The most sacred of these had been "The Sacrament of Wax Packs" held on the final day of school at Paradise Canyon every year.

We'd sit Indian style beneath the jungle gym, unwrapping baseball cards for hours, dividing a full carton of Topps wax packs. With mouths wadded with gum, we'd guzzle down bottles of Bubble Up. The soda covered up the gum taste. Topps gum tasted like cardboard, assuming you could chew it to begin with. Ivan would wear his Giants t-shirt. I'd wear my Dodgers ball cap. We'd sing. "Mine eyes have seen the glory—" delighting in bad harmony "—of the burning of the school. We have tortured—" a Marichal and a McCovey flipped into Ivan's pile. "—every teacher. We have broken—" Koufax, Drysdale, Maury Wills landed in mine "—every rule." Ivan made up verses, and I sang along off key, shaded by guardian eucalyptus rows towering over our playground. We divvied up the cards. He took Giants. I took Dodgers. The rest were cut between us to be traded.

We'd done this every year on the final day of school. Seven days, each spaced exactly one school year apart, had been the happiest seven days of of my pathetic prepubescence. My Dodgers' baseball card collection had been the envy of my neighborhood....

...Until just weeks ago, I'd sold them to buy Heather's crystal unicorn.

I'd watched little Vinnie Skinner strap his shoebox to the bike rack above the rear wheel of his brother Richard's Sting Ray. Vinnie had whooped and pulled a wheelie, spinning gravel across my shoes. Every Dodger that had suited up since the team had moved from Brooklyn was in that shoebox. Every Dodger from Hank Aguirre to Don Zimmer.

They'd been sorted out by seasons, secured with comfy rubber bands to their teammates and wrapped up in wax paper to keep them warm. I hadn't even said goodbye. They were seriously *gone*, sold to Vinnie Skinner for forty bucks.

I chewed my lip. This had been a heavy price to pay. I'd just watched half my childhood ride away on Vinnie's Schwinn. But Heather, I'd convinced myself, was worth it.

And now, not only were my baseball cards past tense, but seventy-three bathroom stalls with our names on them required my attention. I emptied three bottles of Testor's model paint into the trash. I scoured the pigment out with turpentine, refilling each glass bottle with Dunn-Edwards enamel, paprika, same color I'd been dealing with all summer. I'd managed to lift a pint from the supply room.

At ten p.m., I parked my Yamaha 60 where nobody could find it, in the bushes in Oak Grove Park across the chain link from the high school. I grabbed my bike bag and carried it past picnic tables and fire pits. It took forever for the Michigan Avenue stoplight to turn green. At last, I could get busy with my mission.

I'd done the math. I had ten minutes per stall. The clock was ticking. There were only two nights left to get the job done. Snooge had warned me the janitors were changing locks on Friday. After that his bootleg skeleton key was worthless.

Tonight I'd have to work non-stop through five a.m. It was my only chance to finish work on schedule. I had six hours, enough time tonight for thirty-some-odd stalls. My operation was straightforward. I had to sneak through every door and slide beneath each stall on my paprika-spotted beach towel. Thirty strokes with coarse sandpaper, twenty with the fine. I'd clocked it out. It took me nine minutes and 30 seconds per stall.

With the precision of James Bond, I prepped each toilet partition. I opened the glass jar from my pocket. I pulled my half-inch bristle brush from my bike bag for what usually took two coats. Because I'd mixed the paint with spackle, it went on extra-thick in just one coat.

By five a.m., I'd finished bathroom stall number 30. The spackle had worked better than I'd expected. You'd never see the words I'd painted over. I was cruising. To stay on schedule, I worked beyond my time limit.

Men's bathrooms were easy. Women's bathrooms scared me spitless. I had these nightmares of a teacher walking in on me. There were more stalls and fewer urinals—*no* urinals in fact. Women's bathrooms took forever. I checked my watch. Five-thirty-five. Two more stalls remained for me to finish 40 stalls. Daylight crept around the doorframe. I had to hurry. After sunrise, God knows what sweet thing might walk in on me and call the cops.

Now, every noise, every squeak curled up my spine—a teacher, some girl, I didn't care.—I was too terrified. I worried about some female slamming open the steel door, and I'd be busted—squished like some masher against the corner of her bathroom, while she let out a chilling scream that Edvard Munch could never replicate. Or I'd be sitting with my paintbrush and my feet above the toilet so nobody could see my hairy legs.

Then—footsteps. *No way!* This couldn't really happen! At six a.m., what were women doing walking around my high school? There was one out in the hallway. With that pissed-off high-heel rhythm, a block away. I knew exactly who it was.

Momma!

A key turned in the lock. I jumped and grabbed my spattered towel. Balancing on the toilet, I pretended not to breathe. I saw sandpaper on the floor. I didn't dare retrieve it.

Shit!

I didn't say this, but I thought it extra loud. So loud it surprised me Momma didn't hear me think. Crouched on the toilet seat, I squeezed my spattered towel against my armpit, teddy-bear tight, holding my breath, praying Momma wouldn't see me or, worse yet, perhaps decide to take a dump inside my stall.

Her footsteps filled the ladies' room. She bent down and grabbed the sandpaper, crumpling it in her fist. She lit a cigarette.

Silence.

For as long as it took Momma to suck down one Virginia Slim, my too-brief life unreeled in my mind. I already saw the headlines: LA CAÑADA BOY CAUGHT PEEPING. I tried planning my escape. But with more stuff than I had hands for, a towel, a paintbrush, paint, I couldn't even run away. The paint jar and the sandpaper on the floor would tell the tale. I was *so* busted. Even Momma would know exactly who I was.

She hacked her smoker's cough. I managed not to move.

Then Momma ran the sink forever. I heard this whoopee-cushion sound. Momma was *farting*—in slow motion—like this went on for thirty seconds. It filled the bathroom up with rotten-egg scents worse than any cesspool. Any moment I was terrified my eyeballs would start melting. I held my nose to keep from gagging, terrified I'd feel my brains, or what was left of them come melting through my nostrils.

She turned the faucet off. The plumbing thunked.

Momma flipped the lights.

Slam! The door closed.

Whew!

I heard her walk away.

A whiff of putrid air refilled my lungs with toxic gas, reinflating me like a beach ball but with pure hydrogen sulfide.

I coughed it back. I gasped and somehow managed to find air.

I waited five long minutes as Momma's clicking heels faded, willing them to carry her to someplace far away. I left the lights off just in case, not daring to turn them on. I waited ten more minutes, until my heart returned to duty. Then, I finished off the toilet stalls by Braille in the dark, until the dawn came glaring in beneath the doorsill.

More than half the stalls were finished.

So far—so good.

The next night, I took precautions. Supply shopping was in order. I found these go-go boots, just like Mrs. Dunlap's, at the Bargain Box, a thrift ship. I even bought a checkered maxi-skirt to drape around them. As I touched up every stall, I dropped the boots in front of the toilet. I slid the dead bolt on the stall and dropped the skirt around the boots. You couldn't be too careful. By four a.m., the stalls were finished, except those in the gym where Momma'd already changed the locks.

I'd get these later. They were the only eight stalls left.

Right now, I had a score to settle with Momma.

I left the go-go boots with the maxi-skirt in the faculty lounge bathroom. It seemed a bitchen place to store them until I needed them. When I slid the dead bolt on the stall shut and slid under the partition, it looked just like Mrs. Dunlap had camped out on the toilet.

I wondered who'd have the gall to interrupt her.

Ivan Alphabet's real name was Ivan Alexandrowycz. Everyone called him Alphabet for short. The welcome mat on Ivan's doorstep was eighty inches wide. Ivan's mom had ordered it from a catalog house in Cleveland. The doormat didn't fit on the Alexandrowycz family doorstep. The "wycz" flopped off the concrete and got lost beneath her fuchsias. Still, it offered lots of real estate if you had to wipe your shoes, even if reading the "wycz" was problematic.

Besides the trading of baseball cards, Ivan was responsible for a custom that began in our senior year. Before races, some guy always came to take the runners' names. It helped them figure out who'd won (while all the winners were off puking.) Ivan called these people "clipboard weenies."

He hated them, worse than I did. You'd be waiting for your race. Nerves were firing in your belly, and then some freshman showed up. He usually had a crew-cut. He *always* had a clipboard, and it took this guy forever to write our names down.

"Your name?"

"Ivan Alexandrowycz."

Things went downhill after that. We were pumped full of adrenaline, each wound up tighter than a Superball. Then some guy wasted ten minutes trying to write down Ivan's name. Ivan swore clipboard weenies had cost him six or seven races. While some guy scribbled on his clipboard, Ivan freaked. He paced. He gyrated. He clawed dirt to burn adrenaline. Soon, Ivan crossed over from psyching up to psyching *out*. By the time the starting pistol fired, Ivan had lost his edge.

At the Crescenta Valley meet, Ivan took action.

"Your name?"

"Alphabet. A-L-P-H-A-B-E-T." Ivan glared like he might eat the freshman's clipboard.

"That's a reaaally funny name." The freshman giggled.

"Deal with it." Ivan scowled. "I have a race to win."

Snoogey gave him "S-N-O-O-G-E."

Rusty Howard gave him "B-O-O-B-O-O."

The Jabberwocky signed up as "the Jabberwocky."

I was the only dude who gave my real name.

The clipboard weenie scrawled our names down. And then the gun went off. The time had come for us to do our job.

Which was to *win.* Once Ivan had given his name as Ivan Alphabet, Ivan ran the best race of his life. He came in third, not fourth, the way he did when he psyched out. As usual, Jabberwocky won. Booboo came in second. Snooge fought it out with me and kicked for fourth.

I'd never had a kick. Everybody knew this. I was the official Indy pace boy. No matter how hard I ran, I hit a wall. Teammates hung on me for tempo, then beat me in the sprint while my sides cramped in giant knots. I'd cross the mile in exactly four minutes fifty seconds—every race. If I didn't, it was time to fix your stopwatch. It was a good time, enough to leave Crescenta Valley or any other team in the dust—any team but San Marino, the C.I.F. champions. Except all my teammates knew, if they let me set the pace, they could beat me in the last 400 yards.

I crossed the mile and a half at seven minutes fifteen seconds, exactly the same pace I'd run the mile at. Then, the pack scattered. The Jabberwocky tore ahead. Like the world's fastest toothpick, he dashed the last eight-eighty, throwing elbows, spit and cusswords at anything in his way until he'd guaranteed nobody beat the Wocky.

Booboo finished next. Booboo ran like a gazelle. He didn't even look like he was trying when he beat you.

Ivan Alphabet always looked as if he'd lost his large intestine. He grabbed onto his jersey as if his sides were falling out, and his chin hung as though it had dislocated.

I never saw Snooge until the last 400 yards, when he shot past me. I finished right behind him at nine minutes 40 seconds. I'd be staring at Snooogey's jersey. I always stared at

Snooge's jersey. I always finished at precisely the same pace I'd run the mile. I grabbed my "stick" with that disgusting "5" in Marks-a-Lot at one end. After you finished, your "stick" helped scorekeepers write down where you placed. Mine proved I'd finished *fifth*. I finished *fifth* in every race. You'd think after a while they'd remember.

It wasn't really a stick. It was a tongue depressor. Still, they should have written my name on it, since I got it every week. I walked across the infield, folded over like an envelope. My legs tried to buckle as I tottered toward the bathrooms or the dumpsters or the bushes or whatever I found first, so Coach Neal couldn't see where I threw up.

While I was puking, the other team trickled past the finish line. I never saw this. It took forever for the pain to leave my side, until my pulse no longer pounded like two jackhammers in my skull, until I felt like I could stand up and not blow over if someone sneezed, until the world blurred back into focus, and my throat burned.

Somebody with a microphone called out the winners as usual. Except our names today were seriously better.

"In first place—from La Cañada—Jabberwocky."

I raised my chin, walking in a circle. I was dizzy. At least my legs moved.

"In second—from La Cañada—Booboo."

"Woo-hooo Booboo." I recognized the Jabberwocky's voice somewhere in-between the throbs that flooded my temples.

"In third place—Alphabet—from La Cañada."

I tried to laugh, except I hadn't caught my breath yet. Some reporter from the *Valley Sun* was writing down the names.

"In fourth—from La Cañada—Snooge."

"Hey Snoogey!" Ivan hooted.

"And in fifth—from La Cañada—*Alien Martian.*"

Snickering. Laughter. "Yuk-yuk. Haw-haw." The *La Cañada Valley Sun's* ace reporter wrote me down as "Martian." *Crap!* I dropped my head. I wanted to just vanish. That stupid clipboard weenie had given me a nickname.

Coach Neal rubbed it in. "Martian," he laughed out loud. "Alien Martian. The name fits you real good." He spat a loogie. "You're so damn alienated you might as well go *live* on Mars, you freak. Every race, you start out well, and then you choke. Get some courage. Get some *cojones.* Get some *balls,*" Neal said. "Maybe then, someone'll want you as a friend."

I stared down at the dirt and walked alone toward the team bus, wondering why the hell I put up with this torture. Coach didn't hate me. It was Neal's way of training us to win. Part of being on the team was putting up with the abuse. Every coach at La Cañada was some ex-military hard-ass on a mission to shame us into winning. I didn't have the balls to tell Neal I didn't run to win, but ran to vanish the way I longed to vanish now.

The big story when high school opened was Jimi Hendrix. He'd suffocated in his vomit on September the 18th. In my running shorts, outside the teacher's lot, I overheard my English teacher, Mrs. Zinicola, express surprise they'd lowered the flag.

"For some dead rock star?" Mrs. Z asked.

"Wasn't a rocker," Momma said and looked away.

Mrs. Z nibbled her ring finger and pinky.

"Some kid died in Vietnam." Momma smoothed her tailored suit. "The *Valley Sun* says he was a student here at La Cañada High."

"What was his name?"

Momma shrugged. "Mike somebody," she said.

"How did he die?"

"I don't remember. Somebody shot him I suppose."

"How very sad," said Mrs. Z.

"You get used to it," said Momma. She swiveled on her shiny black high heels and walked away.

I felt a shiver, and my gut knotted. *Poor guy was somebody I knew.* His name was Michael Patrick Arthur. Guy lifted barbells with the older kids two houses north of mine. Mike used to drive his blue Camaro every morning up Oak Grove Drive. He'd park his Chevy in the Senior Lot behind the chain-link backstop. Penny Clark would be there waiting with her Beatle boots and books, smoking a cigarette. All of us had figured they'd get married. Then Penny ditched Mike for some rich dude with a law degree from Princeton and a medical deferment. Mike bulked up, lifting more weights. Someone told me he could bench three-hundred pounds for twenty reps.

Mike signed up with the Marines and said he wasn't coming back. We never heard from Mike again. None of us thought he really meant it. But now the flag was flying half-staff "for Jimi Hendrix" we kept hearing. Seemed like nobody remembered Mike at all.

Coach Neal, who'd never heard of Jimi Hendrix *or* Mike Arthur, looked at my arm cast as he strolled across the track. He scratched his head. Then he spat beside his Pumas and dug his spikes into the cinders. Seven a.m. My balls were freezing. The sun was barely waking up.

"You can still run, right, Martian? Even with your arm busted like that?"

I nodded, and I shivered.

"Good."

End of conversation. Coach Neal blew his whistle. We lined up barefoot on the grass inside the oval. There'd be an hour of 440's before first period started. For 60 minutes, we'd run around in circles.

I stood behind the Jabberwocky outside the fifty-yard line. The whistle blew. We took off. My arm felt good, even though the cast was heavy. I dropped my wrists. Best to run your quarter-miles staying loose. My head circled in an easy rhythmic motion. My running music, *"Born to be Wild,"* rumbled through my mind. My breathing kept the rhythm. I'd be fine.

Running numbed my broken arm. I finished my first quarter in official pace-boy time. Seventy-two seconds—and a half. There'd be twenty-nine more quarters, but I'd checked into my groove, grateful my injury from the scaffold wouldn't sideline me.

The freshman-sophomores ran next. While the Varsity caught their wind, the Jabberwocky paced in little circles. The Wocky liked to do things when he wasn't running laps. Usually he brought a javelin or discus; he liked to throw things. This particular morning the Wocky'd brought a football.

He'd brought three of them, in fact, propped each up on a kicking tee on the thirty-yard line and drilled one through the goal posts. The football sailed between the uprights like he'd shot it from a rifle.

"Whoa-hoa, great punt Wock!" Our jaws dropped in admiration. The ball bounced against the cinders and it caromed off the chain-link. It wobbled to the track curb.

The Jabberwocky grinned and shook his hair across his shoulders.

Coach Harron, the football coach sitting in the bleachers, pretended not to notice the Wocky's "field goal." The Jabberwocky moved his tee a few yards toward the center of the field and kicked the second football straight between the posts. He raised his arms straight-up above his head.

"Good punt," we cheered again.

The Wocky grinned. His long locks flowed in the breeze like in those posters for the *Hair* musical. He danced a shuffle and drilled the final football between the posts from 40 yards. Strutting to the track, he refilled his arms with footballs.

I caught my breath. I liked this little drama.

It was no secret. Varsity Football lacked a punter. The first-stringer had blown his knee out. The second-stringer sucked. Even the first-stringer on his best day had never nailed one from the 40. But Coach Harron had a policy. If you wanted to play football, you got a U.S. Army Airborne Ranger regulation buzz-cut. A flag tattoo was good for extra credit.

With the Wocky kicking field goals, Harron faced a new dilemma. Either he had to bend his rules, or he'd lose games thanks to "The Policy." Now, everybody saw, if not for Harron's stupid rule, their unproductive football team might win.

Except, Coach Harron never bent rules. Harron might have been a redneck, only God forgot to give the man a neck. "You disgrace the game of football," Harron shouted from the bleachers.

The Wocky slouched past Harron and flipped him off.

"That your IQ there?" Harron called.

The Wocky kept on walking. We lined up on the 50. Coach Neal blew his whistle, and we ran another lap.

I wondered how long this adventure might continue. We could feel the tension build between the Jabberwocky and Harron. They were like two opposing charges, one's hair Jim Morrison long, the other's Frankenstein short. The Wocky drilled another football between the goalposts from the 40.

Harron rose. He stomped down from the bleachers. His footsteps pounded on the track. He was evidently ticked. He stormed across the cinders, veins popping from his temples. You could see his flat-top wiggle. His "Airborne" tattoos throbbed against his forearms.

A whistle. I had to run. I hated missing this argument. Harron was only getting started when we finished our quarter mile. The Wocky launched another football. He strolled downfield to retrieve it, twirling his new football on his finger.

Harron was shouting at Coach Neal. "Get your faggot off my field." Harron spat when he got mad. You needed a face shield just to talk with him, especially with those f's. Coach Neal tried to calm him. "Not so loud, Richard. They hear you."

Neal blew a whistle. The varsity ran.

It was hard to run a quarter when you were laughing. Rounding the south goalpost, our eyes were glued on Harron. Stomping on the cinders, he was screaming.

"Get him off my field."

"It's not your field, it's my track."

"Get him off. It's a field. It's full of grass."

The Jabberwocky inhaled like he was sucking on a joint. Coach Neal blew his whistle. The freshman-sophomores ran.

Harron whispered, gyrating like a traffic cop on speed.

"What's he talkin' about?" Ivan's voice.

"Discipline," said the Jabberwocky. "Biggest word in Dick Harron's vocabulary."

On queue, Harron roared the word "DISCIPLINE," as if invoking some hard-ass god. "Your boys need discipline—and haircuts." Harron's words echoed from the walls behind the bleachers. "Discipline—discipline—haircuts."

"Bull!" Neal's voice dropped to a whisper. But we heard it all the way across the field. "They win. That's all I care about. This isn't the Army, Richard. It's a high school."

Little puffs of dirt rose where Harron stormed from the track.

Neal blew his whistle. The varsity sprinted a 440. Clearly, all the dust had yet to settle.

Before third period, the football players huddled around the snack bar on the east side of the student cafeteria. They cut in line, trading wisecracks while we waited to buy sodas. I laid low. I wasn't ready to trade insults with the jocks. Not when the Jabberwocky had rattled their cage this morning.

I was trapped inside the snack line between bubble-gum-pocked handrails. I was afraid of what I'd stick to if I moved. The kid in front of me had farted. Someone punched my back. Then—I saw Garry.

I stood rigid. I breathed shallow.

He was holding Heather's hand. Heather hand-fed Garry from her little bag of Fritos, like she was nurturing a duckling. And Garry's shirt had little fabric pills. The ones on *my* shirts had disgusted her. How come with Garry, Heather didn't care?

My heart sank. I felt it crawl behind my stomach. I didn't need this. Not on my first day of senior year. I was finally getting used to being dumped by Heather, when Garry came along and rubbed things in.

Garry grinned. Life must be sweet when you can walk around your high school with your mouth open, while pretty girls walk up and feed you from their snack bags. He looked so smug, like he *deserved* this. I glared at Garry, and my stomach twisted. Didn't Heather know what she was doing?

For a second, I met her eyes, the ones I'd stared at for half my summer when she'd liked me; back when I'd thought there was a soul behind those eyes. For one summer, she'd made me feel like I wasn't such a loser. I missed her. I wanted to know *that* Heather still existed; the good Heather, the one before the boob job.

Then she caught me. Her jaw fell, like she knew what I was seeing. Sheer terror—as though she'd landed on a tightrope without nets. She could *fall* in La Cañada. There was a caste system. We were the "La Cañada *Spartans*," after all. And our caste system had been imported intact from ancient Sparta with all three castes: hoplites, freemen, and helots.

For a transfer from Connecticut, Heather had figured this out quickly, doing an end run around the entire high school food chain. But what went up came down. A food chain was still a chain, and she was chained to Garry Jackson. There was no way out—but down.

Our cruel system enforced the desired order. The caste system in La Cañada could put a Brahmin prince to shame. On the top rung, the hoplites were robed in big gray "Spartan Men's Council" windbreakers. Their elite club of well-heeled seniors all played first-string varsity football. God had elected them to serve as "Spartan Men" at La Cañada, while other males were predestined to serve as Spartan something-elses. They were a service club, they claimed, tasked with protecting the senior lot from lower life forms who dared to park a car in their domain. They didn't like us. Hoplites had ways of getting even. But they were kind enough to share their Spartan manhood with their women.

The hoplites, perched atop the La Cañada Spartan food chain, considered themselves cousins of the Trojans of USC. Our "LC" cheers were SC ripoffs. Our fight song matched SC's; even the lyrics went "Fight on for old LC." Our high school looked like USC, (if it were overrun by midgets) except SC boasted blacks. Of course, our students were all white.

Beneath the hoplites, the marching band, the drill team, and JV football, were, on occasion, allowed to share the field with their betters. Freemen drove old Datsuns, not the Mustangs or

Corvettes that made you eligible to park your car in the Senior area. They wore letter jackets, not lordly gray, but SC cardinal red and gold. Freemen tended to be careful not to break the hoplites' rules. They played the "La Cañada Fight Song" as if it were written for La Cañada and didn't question being a scaled-down "University of Spoiled Children."

Below the freemen, the rest of us had jobs. It didn't leave much time for after-school activities. Painting toilet stalls didn't carry the same cachet in La Cañada as playing safety on special teams or playing oboe in the band. Only losers and plebeians admitted to having jobs. We were the helots, the bottom caste who needed jobs to pay for college, given that we didn't have rich parents. Hoplites needed helots to flip their burgers and bake their pizzas. Hoplites needed someone to look down on.

Yet, beneath we low plebeians, remained another life form, "untouchables," girls cast off by aristocratic boyfriends. Such girls gave the helots someone even *we* could sneer at. I'd sanded their names and phone numbers off so many bathroom walls I was sure all La Cañada knew their phone numbers by heart. You didn't date them. Polite people never spoke with them in public. They were tarnished, no longer virgins. Rumors said they had diseases from the pick-up boys they met down near Olympic Auditorium.

I raised my gaze toward Heather. She shivered as though she knew which way was down. Garry'd warned her. I sensed the nerves behind her shudder. For the moment, she rode high with Garry Jackson in his Mustang, *but only for as long as she pleased Garry.*

Her eyes narrowed like closing curtains. Her irises choked off remnants of the Heather I remembered. Pupils shrank to tiny dots almost too small to let in light. She smiled, then walked away on Garry's arm.

As luck would have it, Mr. Harron taught my third period class on Government, where Garry and Heather had been assigned to sit together. Checking the seating chart, I hated it. I'd been assigned to sit behind them. I sighed. This was *not* a good arrangement.

Mr. Harron hadn't asked for my opinion.

From the doorway, I scanned the room. This might be a long semester. The world globe on Mr. Harron's desk looked old enough to vote. He evidently didn't know that Abyssinia had changed its name, and Tanganyika and French West Africa were long gone by 1970. But it was tough getting excited about American democracy taught by some Nazi who'd just assigned me to sit behind my ex and Garry.

Garry Jackson shifted his fingers from Heather's bracelet to her knee.

Heather preened a fuzz ball from her cardigan.

It was cashmere. I'd watched Garry buy that stupid scarlet sweater up on Ivers' second floor the very day Heather had dumped me. She'd pretended not to see me. I'd pretended not to look. Garry never wasted time pretending.

It was obvious what Garry saw. Heather never seemed to mind. Each sweater she'd tried on at Ivers' had seemed tighter than the previous. At last, it had looked like she'd shrink-wrapped her bogus boobs inside a sweater so tight her nipples might have punched right through the wool.

Garry'd bought it for her. It matched her lipstick and his Mustang. Now, she wore it just for him. She wore it 'just-for-him' a lot. Below her cameo choker, she unbuttoned the top three buttons. Garry licked his lips.

Heather straightened her denim skirt.

You saw from Garry's pants how much he loved it. When he thought Heather wasn't watching, he scratched his not-so-little friend until she grabbed his roving fingers and returned them to her knee. Garry snickered at her glare. But Heather needed Garry's status. He was a senior, varsity football. Being a junior, she couldn't dump him or trade up for someone better.

Which made me sick. I'd treated Heather with respect. I'd tried to make her happy. Hadn't I adored her? Now, she was *verboten*. It made her foxier than ever. I couldn't stand it. She was eroding any confidence I had left. She even showed up to hate me in my fantasies.

She was whispering things about me in front of Garry as I stood there. "Allen never wins a race. Like, he always finishes fifth. I mean *always*. He's such a wuss."

That was so unfair even I knew it. I could have lied about my finish. Everybody else did. It wasn't like people went to cross country meets to check if you were lying. Besides, she'd never seen me race. I'd had to tell her how I'd finished. Now, she used my honesty against me.

Garry snickered, as if he could match my time.

Had life been fair, I imagined we could race for Heather's hand. Garry would never make it up the Hill. There was just too much of Garry to haul up Sunshine Drive. And coming back down Hillside—well, he'd just have to walk. Lucky for Garry he didn't need to win at all since he played football.

Heather giggled. "He has a girlfriend," she whispered to Garry.

"Thought you said he was a faggot."

"He is. But—Allen has this friend. You know that lez job in your French class who wants to be a nun?"

"Mandy Richert?"

My stomach twisted up in little knots.

"*Die Hindenburg?*" Heather smiled a very vicious grin. "I saw him riding in her Volkswagen," she whispered.

"Noooo! Allen and Mandy? What a freak show!"

Coach Harron cleared his throat. I saw the clock. He scowled at *me*. I hurried toward my seat. Garry and Heather moved their desks. I tried to walk between them. Garry took Heather's hand. She stuck her chest out. Even the chip on Heather's tooth had that authoritative jut that somehow made it clear I was a loser.

"Go around, not between us," Garry said.

Heather smiled too, at exactly the same angle.

"Dickwad," Garry said.

"Dickwad," Heather whispered, lowering her gaze.

I stepped back. I needed to sit down. My arm throbbed beneath my books. I breathed in deep and walked around.

The bell rang.

A foot flew out from Garry, and I tripped. Textbooks flew out from my arms. I landed on my cast. I heard a crack. And then my arm ached. It hadn't hurt that much the first time.

"Problems, Mister Dickwad?" It was Harron.

Students snickered. Heather laughed although she didn't move her chin.

"No sir." I lied. My arm was throbbing like a gong.

"Sit down."

I rubbed my arm.

"I said sit down."

"I think my arm...."

"Gee coach, my arm hurts too. Can I go see the nurse?" It was Garry.

The class burst into laughter.

Harron massaged his chin, staring at me.

"Some day—Dickwad." Egg pieces strafed from Harron's teeth. "That your *real* name?"

"It's Martian, sir." Garry's voice. "Some kinda Jew name."

"Some day—Martian," Harron paced. He turned and glared at me, eyes shooting darts. "You know your type won't last five minutes in Vietnam," Harron said. "Some day, when you're drafted, your DI'll take one look at you—" Harron took a breath and flexed his Army Airborne forearms "—he'll take one glance at *you*, Martian, and he'll puke."

Chalk squeaked across the blackboard while Harron wrote the names of all the secretaries in Richard Nixon's cabinet. The class was mortuary quiet except for Garry and Heather's snickers.

I found my seat. Lucky for Harron I didn't own a gun, or I'd be waiting for the chance to pull the trigger.

After a lecture that lasted longer than my entire summer vacation, I shot from Harron's classroom like a bullet when the bell rang. My arm was throbbing. Garry and Heather were whispering behind me. Heather was holding Garry's hand. I could *sense* it, just as sure as every hair behind my neck rose to attention and zeroed in on Heather's thoughts. Heather was giggling. I tried to hear what she was saying, but her voice dropped, and I heard nothing.

My arm pounded like a sledgehammer. I shouldn't have run before first period. My body needed rest, needed its energy to heal. I'd been sapped, even before Coach Harron had launched his tirade. I wanted to paint a metal sign, nail the damn thing to my forehead. "MY NAME IS ALLEN, DON'T CALL ME MARTIAN, FAGGOT, ALIEN, OR MISTER DICKWAD." But that would amuse the very people I didn't feel like entertaining, and I was beginning to wonder who I was, myself.

Just then, Mandy whirled around the corner. She lugged a locker-full of books under her arms. She smiled. Her eyes brightened like a puppy seeing its friend, as if she hadn't gotten the memo it was okay to be my friend up on Flint Peak—*but not here*. No way was it cool in La Cañada. I wasn't sure exactly where I'd learned this, but somehow the lords of bitchen-dom had hard-wired my brain. To have friends, you needed money, sex, or drugs, and I had none of these. Neither did Mandy. We were freaks. We had to fly beneath their radar.

"Hi, Allen." I was scared to death she'd wave and drop her books.

Not now, Mandy! I shut my eyes. My heart shriveled in my chest. I wanted to pull in my head and arms and burrow inside me like a turtle. *And not here, Mandy! Please no!* I could talk to her off campus, in the hospital, or on Flint Peak. But not in front of *them!*

Mandy smiled. "Allen what's up? Something wrong?"

All I heard was Heather whispering, *"What a freak show."* Without her uttering the words they broadcast through my skull as if the hair-antennas rising behind my neck were tuned to Heather.

I whispered "Hi, Mandy" with so little of my mouth actually moving you'd have to watch the instant replay to determine if I'd spoken. I felt my arms scrunch in my sleeves until I felt like half a freak show, the little half, of course. The big half stood in front of me, looking puzzled.

Somehow, my silence let Mandy know our meeting on campus was off-limits. Her face scrunched. Her smile lost half of its air, like on those blow-up toys after they've floated on backyard pools for half the summer. No wonder I had no friends. If you were "nice," you couldn't have friends. Only "the cool," were worth befriending. Mandy wasn't one of them, nor I.

But it seemed Mandy had forgotten to read the rule book. And deep inside me, I wished I'd never read it either.

CHAPTER FOUR

AIN'T NO MOUNTAIN HIGH ENOUGH

FLINT PEAK, GLENDALE, CALIFORNIA: THURSDAY, OCTOBER 1ST, 1970
(253 DAYS TO GRADUATION!)

Knowing half my high school believed me to be Jewish, I felt entitled to at least one Jewish holiday. So I cut school on Rosh Hashanah. All the real Jews got it off. They had to go to temple.

And I didn't!

I woke up early to see the sunrise from Flint Peak. There was so much to sort out while I was running up the fire road. For instance, my sucky life. Heather had dumped me. Dad had run off. Mom never spoke to me. Coach Harron had informed my class I'd die in Vietnam. Their laughs had hurt me more than my sore arm.

I hadn't broken it again. Only a contusion, although the doctor said my fracture hadn't healed yet. Still it hurt like hell. The doc had told me to go easy. Yeah right. This was high school. Easy wasn't on the menu, especially if you ran cross country, even more if you looked Jewish. I decided, like the Jews, I had been born for persecution.

And feeling pain. I was a stoic. You didn't run cross-country unless you excelled at hiding pain. I'd been hiding pain so long pain had become my anesthesia, helping me forget I was a dickwad.

Why was it all the glory went to football? Even when they lost, they got steak dinners, pancake breakfasts. Cheerleaders brought them donuts. A runner's only prize was loneliness. They shot a gun off. You ran your race, then went and puked behind a bush. They even made you give your tongue depressor back.

I passed the fire road that forked down to Pasadena by the slopes of Whipple yuccas that never bloomed. I picked my pace up. The road got steeper, and I wanted to feel pain. The only time I felt alive was when I ran. It didn't matter if I sucked. I was alive. I had my pain, and with it, there was meaning in my life.

I'd been chosen to feel pain like Ethan Frome.

I spent the morning of Rosh Hashanah sitting underneath my tower watching dump trucks hauling trash up to Scholl Canyon. This was a landfill in the gullies at the end of Glenoaks Boulevard. Trucks meandered from the scales to haggard piles of garbage that sent odors wafting toward my lookout. Every hour, herds of bulldozers started up the canyon and bladed garbage into layers packed over with fresh dirt. Full trucks blew their lonely horns. Empty dump trucks scattered. By the scales, new trucks stood in line to take their places. It occurred to me while the tractors bladed dirt across the garbage—here was a bitchen place to bury Ethan Frome.

By afternoon, the trucks were fewer, and I was getting hungry. October sunshine basted me with the final sprays of summer. I picked burrs from my Adidas and wiped my forehead on my sleeve. I unscrewed the plastic cap and squirted water from my boda, chasing it with an apple pop tart and two prepackaged honey servings which was the only food I'd salvaged from the pantry leaving home. I hadn't even started to do my thinking.

What was I here for? Or was that a stupid question? Was it just to feel pain, to help Coach Neal win a trophy? I had no clue. Even "love" had turned out to be painful. The word was like some synonym for dope, or getting laid, or never having to say you're sorry, or all three if you could swing it. It seemed so pointless. And even clipboard weenies saw me as an alien; "Alien Martian," which I could handle given other possibilities. In the *Baseball Encyclopedia*, there's this pitcher named Mulcahy known to posterity as "Losing Pitcher Mulcahy." Honest! Look it up. There are worse names than "Alien Martian".

Still, why did I have to be an alien? And why was I so lonely? Shouldn't aliens get a robot like that "Gort" thing in the movies, zapping death rays from its skull in *The Day the Earth Stood Still*. I could use one of those babies. I'd seen the flick so often the command *"Gort, klaatu barada nikto"* was seared into my memory. Except—there was no Gort, no matter how badly I wanted one. I had to sort things out myself. La Cañada was so screwed up, Ethan Frome's home town of Starkfield now looked seriously attractive.

So here I was on my day off. All the Jewish kids, like Ivan, were in temple for Rosh Hashanah, and I sat up here alone.

"What do you do on Rosh Hashanah?" I'd asked Ivan.

I'd asked the previous Monday while we'd been stumbling up Lida, just in case some teacher might ask me. I hadn't clued in Ivan I had plans to swipe his holiday.

"It's like our New Year's celebration," Ivan told me. "Actually, it's the whole world's New Year."

"Even for atheists like me?"

Ivan nodded.

"Bitchen! So what do they make you do—give 'em money?"

"They blow a *shofar*, a ram's horn. They read stuff from the Torah. You get ten days to straighten up, or else you might get blotted out of the Book of Life."

"Whoa! No lie?"

Ivan shrugged. "They say it's supposed to make us better people. Sometimes you have to score some *mitzvah* to balance your accounts."

"What's that?"

"This good deed, this commandment you follow to fix things. Maybe you're kind to someone other guys aren't nice to."

We hadn't talked much after that. We had reached the crest of Lida, and I was reminded of when I'd ridden up Lida with Mandy in her Volkswagen. Coach Neal was at the summit with his stopwatch and his spray bottle. We'd turned right and headed home on Figueroa.

A long horn moaned and echoed from Scholl Canyon. The last dump truck left the scales down the access road. The final furrows of dirt were bulldozed over garbage. Reflections of sunset glistened off Pacific waters.

Mitzvah. Ivan's word bubbled up inside my brain. It was bouncing off the walls alongside *klaatu*, and *barada*. I'd never heard of any *mitzvah*. But then again, what was a *nikto?* I scrounged for ideas. Any clue was worth a look. After the episode in Harron's class, I was desperate for *something*. A *mitzvah* sounded like a place to start.

At dusk, I was surprised to see an eggnog-colored Volkswagen roll up to the bottom of my fire road. Mandy slammed the door. She had her shoes on and started running.

Running?

She was running up my hill.

She ran slooooow. But she was running. Like a bicycle in loooow gear, she shuffled up the trail in front of little puffs of dust. I was amazed. Last time, she'd walked up. Mandy set her jaw. She masked pain like a master. She was every bit as good at hiding pain as I was.

And most amazing—Mandy didn't stop. She chugged along the road like that *Little Engine that Could* in that old book inside my toy chest. She fixed her chin, as if carrying toys the way that engine in the story did. Maybe children would get bummed if Mandy failed to climb the grade. I never had seen anyone run so slow.

I wondered when she'd stop.

She didn't. She kept approaching. Her face folded around her pain in a frown, as if she'd swallowed a giant lemon. Sweat glistened on her forehead and darkened her cloth headband. I heard her breathing. Her footsteps pounded up my mountain. I feared she'd have a heart attack, a stroke, or something worse.

Past the hillside of Whipple yuccas that never bloomed, the path grew steeper, and Mandy rolled forward like a tank. She didn't slow. I was almost feeling proud. Her fists tightened. Sweat streaked through the dust on Mandy's legs.

I yelled, "Keep your arms low, Mandy. It's easier."

She dropped her arms.

"Open your fists up. Smile, Mandy. It saps less energy."

She tried to smile. Clouds of gnats must have landed in her teeth. She turned the corner, the hardest part. She kept coming–coming–coming.

"Come on, Mandy. Come on, come on."

She slowed.

I screamed. "Come on. You can make it. I know you can." I clapped my hands, trying to telegraph my energy. She raised her chin.

"Almost there."

She kept running.

"You're gonna make it."

Running.

She landed in my arms, a puddle of sweat. She soaked the front of my faded Spartans t-shirt. She was panting. Her heart pounded in her chest like it was trying to get out. She leaned against my shoulders; I braced my legs to hold her. I felt her awkward strength. Her breathing slowed, found a rhythm, *Panting–panting.* Sweat poured across her face.

"You okay, Mandy?"

"I made it." She was nodding in my arms. *Breathing, breathing.* "I—" *breathing* "—made it."

"Don't sit down. Walk it off."

She staggered around the tower, catching her breath, wiping her sweat. Shaking tightness from her thighs, she basked in joy as if the clouds above had parted in her honor.

I didn't see her clouds, but I felt some of Mandy's joy after she'd orbited the tower and re-docked inside my arms. Her heart hammered like a sledge. Blood thumped through her wrists. Her cheeks pulsed against my temple. Her circulation throbbed against my arm cast. She was grinning. She seemed so happy. I hoped if I held onto her long enough, some of Mandy's "happy" might rub off into me.

Minutes later, she caught her breath. "Can I sit down now?" Mandy asked.

"Sure."

The sky darkened on the horizon. I felt a chill, not from her sweat. Nobody had ever touched *me* except to hit me. I'd held another human being. I hadn't felt alone when Mandy'd leaned on me. *I hadn't felt afraid.*

"I finally made it," Mandy said.

"You've tried to run up here before, Mandy?" I stared at her. Her eyes were smiling back and almost beaming.

"Every night. I've been coming here a lot—" *a breath* "—since you showed me."

I turned. *Had I just heard her right?*

"Usually after dark," she said. "I was afraid I'd be embarrassed."

"If *I* saw you?"

She nodded.

This felt strange. I wasn't used to people caring what I thought. I wasn't used to holding other human beings. Except with Mandy, it felt okay. She seemed happy, like we could share each other's space, each other's feelings, each other's victories. She seemed so—human, so vulnerable. She had this secret strength that had propelled her up my hill. *Our* hill. We'd shared it now.

When she sat down, I felt cold and missed her warmth, her heartbeats. But now, I knew Mandy had an inner strength.

"Mandy?"

"Yes?"

"Does it bother you I'm up here?"

She seemed surprised. "Why should it?"

"I dunno, it's just...."

"Hey." The way she said this reassured me. Just a little 'hey,' seemed to underscore her friendship. She didn't mind. Like she was glad to share our mountain.

"Mandy, do you know you're *really* strong?"

She nodded. "I never thought so." She smiled as if suddenly she thought so.

"Lots of guys would never make it up this hill, even football players."

Mandy chuckled. *Strong!* I almost heard her thinking the word. *Strong!* Strong enough to beam her friendship through my force field.

The moon's reflection cast long shadows across the chaparral horizon. We walked down the road together, listening to the night. It was our hill. We'd each conquered it. Now, we'd conquered it together.

As the sun set on my day of ditching school on Rosh Hashanah, I had this feeling teaching Mandy how to run might be my *mitzvah*. After seeing her run tonight, I was certain I could help her, if I only had the courage to be her friend.

CHAPTER FIVE

LOVELY LETA

LA CAÑADA HIGH SCHOOL:
MONDAY, OCTOBER 5TH, 1970
(249 DAYS TO GRADUATION!)

A llen?"

Plop! My physics textbook tumbled from my locker into the stuffy third-floor corridor of La Cañada High. I peeled its open pages from the sticky concrete floor. "Allen?" It was Leta Hertz's voice.

I grabbed my calculus book, returning it to the chaos in my locker. The book I needed was somewhere near the bottom of the pile. Simple things were hard with your arm stuck in a cast. Sure enough, there was *Beowulf,* underneath the stack, wedged between *Julius Caesar* and *Canterbury Tales.* My English Lit test was tomorrow for Mrs. Zinicola. I hadn't started *Beowulf.* Just this morning I'd learned the Cliff Notes were sold out. *Crap!* How did you study without Cliff Notes? The only option left was—read the book.

I jerked the paperback from underneath, avoiding another spill. The first fifty pages of *Beowulf* were folded over backward. I pounded the book against my locker wall to flatten out the pages and tossed it into my bike bag beside my battered three-ring binder.

"Allen?" It was Leta's voice again; probably some other Allen or Allan or Alan or Al she wanted. A big problem in my high school was there were waaay too many Allens. It was hard when they were popular—and I wasn't. There was Alan (Pudge) McMasters who played fullback on the Varsity. And Allan Parker with the Paul Newman eyes over in drama. There was Alan Smithee, Junior. Alan Junior drove a Porsche. His old man worked in Hollywood. He was *the* Alan Smithee.

I didn't dare to turn around. It had happened all too often. I heard my name, turned; and there was Alan McMasters, or Allan Parker or some new Alan I hadn't known existed. The young siren I'd thought had called my name snickered, "Not you," while I crashed into rocks, dissolving into the smallest smithereens.

I slinked away, sticking one arm through my bike bag. I grabbed my motorcycle helmet I never wore during school hours that made me look exactly like Speed Racer the cartoon guy. I walked the way you walk when you're scared on city streets, passing classrooms, crossing the bridge to the stairwell behind the library, descending concrete steps toward the gymnasium.

Past the gym, there was this cage for all the motorcycles. It was supposed to keep your bike from being stolen, except it didn't. Luckily, my Yamaha 60 wasn't something you'd want to steal. The best defense against thieves was to own nothing thieves might want. Except gas caps were a problem. Mine got stolen all the time. I kept a spare cap in my bike bag just in case.

Leta caught me by the cage. "Allen Martin. Stop!"

I turned. "You mean me?"

She caught her breath.

I braced to answer. What did Leta want with *me?*

She wore this coral cardigan, probably one from Ivers' Garry Jackson had passed over to buy a tighter one for Heather. Except Leta's sweater fit her. It didn't crinkle around the buttons. And her hair looked like she'd stolen it from one of those Breck shampoo ads on the backs of my mother's magazines.

Rumor had it Leta *was* a Breck shampoo girl. If you could find last April's *Redbook,* Leta's face was on the back. Now, Leta was facing *me,* and she wasn't on any *Redbook.*

"Allen, I have a question." She dug her fists against her hips.

I stiffened. I felt a second reflex. *Not now!*

"Please." Leta smiled, pulling her sweater across her skirt. She was the type of girl who didn't really want to be a fox, which made her so much sexier for not trying. Besides blue eyes, she had a figure no plastic surgeon could improve on. Add a teaspoon to her breasts, and they'd be—too Betty Page, but you didn't want to subtract anything either. Even her face was flawless as if her fairy godmother had sponged off any moles or zits and installed them on some less fortunate classmate.

"Sorry, Leta. I didn't think that you meant me."

Leta nodded, then, flushed as if aware that I was nervous.

"So your question?" I flipped my hair, trying to look calm. In my mind, the Beatles chanted in the background,

Luh – vlee – Leee – taah – mi-ta – maid....

I knew full well John Lennon's meter maid was *Rita*, and not Leta. It was this thing that—happened, this involuntary reflex. I imagined any moment she'd unbutton that coral sweater just to tease me with a little bit of....

Luh – vlee – Leee – taah – mi....

"Do you like Mandy Richert?"

"Huh?" Like soap bubbles, the Beatles popped and disappeared. I blushed.

Leta waited for her answer. "I need to know."

"You—need to know."

Leta tapped her foot. "She's my friend."

"Oh." Things were hardening in my pants, and now my balls ached. Leta was Mandy's friend. She had to know. This was complicated. Her patience was exasperating, and I was leaking.

I had no answer. I wasn't ready to trust a girl right after Heather. I saw a problem near my zipper. I moved my motorcycle helmet.

"Kinda," I said. "I mean—Mandy's nice."

Leta looked down at my helmet. She looked away. "That's a start."

She said this like she wanted to hear more. Like this was so important she'd excuse my masculinity.

"I mean—she's good to talk to. Mandy's a good listener. And she's strong," I said.

"Do you *like* her?"

What kind of question was that? Were we supposed to be an *item?* Mandy was a friend, but she was tall. Maybe three inches taller than I was, and that was in her flats. She was Amazon material. And she was heavy. Mandy and I together might almost pass for Laurel and Hardy. Our deal was we talked. That was all.

Except Mandy wasn't quite as big as Ollie. Not lately. She was thinner since she'd been running. Still she was kind, just like Ollie. And that stuff about the *mitzvah*....

"Should I like her?"

"She likes you. Mandy's such a sweetheart."

She likes me? Somebody likes ME? This was getting complicated. It dawned on me I had something here to lose. No girl liked *me.* Not even my mother.

"I heard she wants to be a nun."

"Is that like some sort of felony? I didn't say you had to marry her. Just—be her friend."

Confirmation. Mitzvah? Oh crap! This couldn't happen.

"Aren't *you* her friend?"

"Mandy likes you."

What did that mean? Especially Mandy Richert. Hadn't Leta just confirmed Mandy planned to be a *nun?*

"I trust her," I said. "I'm not sure I can explain it. I'm not in love with her. But I—trust her. That's not true for many people. I mean like—let's see now." I counted up one finger in my mind. Okay, she was the *only* person I trusted. Why had Leta done this? If I didn't play my cards right, I'd lose Mandy, the only female on the planet who even liked me.

"Treat her right," Leta whispered. "She trusts you too."

My head whiplashed with surprise. I'd never thought anyone trusted me. Nobody trusted anybody at La Cañada High. It was like this unwritten rule. *Thou shalt not trust thy neighbor.* Wasn't that in the Bible? It should be if it wasn't. It was a darn fine rule to live by if you hated getting burned.

Now, Mandy had to ruin things by liking me. She'd even had the nerve to talk to Leta. Perhaps Leta was Mandy's friend. I'd heard this more than once. *That's* why Leta was asking questions. She wasn't sure about me and was protecting her best friend.

This was complicated. This was really *really* complicated.

I sighed. "Okay, Leta. I'll be nice. I mean, why would I wanna hurt her? I like Mandy."

"Promise?"

"I promise. Cross my heart."

"Good." Leta tipped her head as though she wasn't quite convinced. "And hope to die?"

Whoooooooa! I paused.

She rolled back on her heels, her blue eyes narrowing. "Stick a needle in your eye?" She had a way of saying this like she'd gone and bought the needle.

"I promise." I hoped to end this inquisition.

"I had to know." Leta sounded satisfied. There was even a kitten smile, one that barely cracked a dimple, the kind Ivan Alphabet used to flash those times we'd shared a Bubble Up. But that was back in grade school, before Ivan was competition. Still, Leta acted like we'd made some sort of bargain. She studied me. Leta's gaze fell on my cast, and her head tilted.

"Your cast looks kinda lonely," Leta said. "Can I sign it?"

"Lonely?"

"There's nothing on it. It's like—white."

"Oh." I looked down. Sure enough, the thing was white. Other than paprika speckles that had spattered from my paint roller, the plaster was as white as the day the doc had cast it, barring the sweat stains on the dirty sock that crinkled up inside.

I was excited. Leta Hertz would sign my cast. Only, there was this—spot—behind my motorcycle helmet, which was the only thing I had to hide the obvious embarassment.

I raised my arm. I moved the helmet. I hoped my sling could block her view. I prayed she wouldn't notice what went on below my belt. I leaned over. She was gorgeous. Even the pressure on her Flair pen had a certain sensuous touch. I felt it through the plaster. Leta wrote:

Allen,
Keep your promise!
Leta Hertz

The cashmere touched my arm. It felt so soft. I smelled her breath. I even smelled her Life Saver. *Lime!*

Her hair tickled on my arm as it swooshed across my shirt. And then she paused.

She was staring.

A wet spot bigger than a baseball!

I froze. I wanted to evaporate.

She clicked her Flair shut and returned it to her purse.

"I'm—sorry." My voice shook like I'd just backed across her puppy. Could I have crawled into a storm drain, I'd have done so in a heartbeat. Why'd *this* have to happen? Why did I always look so stupid?

Leta snapped her purse shut. She flipped her hair across her shoulder. "Don't be sorry. Just keep your promise. Mandy really likes you. And Allen, despite rumors to the contrary, Mandy isn't queer. And—" Leta whispered "—you aren't either."

CHAPTER SIX

EVERYBODY'S TALKIN'

VERDUGO PARK, GLENDALE, CALIFORNIA: FRIDAY, OCTOBER 23RD, 1970
(231 DAYS TO GRADUATION!)

Our cross country meet against Duarte finished no different than our meet against Temple City; a perfect race. La Cañada swept the top seven places. Except Coach Neal was unhappy. Our times could not beat San Marino. The next three weeks would be sheer hell until that cup was in the trophy case.

We'd had no pep rally. No cheerleaders or song girls came to praise us. While seven exhausted runners struggled to catch our breaths, Coach Neal ranted, berating us for racing like old ladies. The clipboard weenie wrote down the results.

RESULTS: DUARTE HIGH V LA CAÑADA HIGH

1st	Jabberwocky	La Cañada	9 minutes 17 seconds
2nd	Booboo	La Cañada	9 minutes 35 seconds
3rd	Alphabet	La Cañada	9 minutes 37 seconds
4th	Snooge	La Cañada	9 minutes 39 seconds
5th	Martian	La Cañada	9 minutes 40 seconds

Total points

15 points	La Cañada (W)
50 points	Duarte (L)

To get your score, each team added up the places of their first five finishers. The low score won, like in golf. The sum of one through five equalled fifteen. Rattfink finished sixth, and Psycho seventh for La Cañada. But you didn't add the scores in for your sixth and seventh runners. Duarte's eighth through fourteenth place finishes added up to fifty. A 15-to-50 score was the best a team could finish.

As usual, I'd finished fifth. Snooge had outkicked me at the finish, and I'd ended my race staring at Snooge's jersey. There was nothing else to look at after Snooge had sprinted past me. I was seeing Snoogey's jersey in my nightmares.

But my race was over—for this week. The clipboard weenie handed me tongue depressor number five. I bent over to kill my pain. I tried not to throw up. And when I finally felt my blood refill the vessels in my brain, the clipboard weenie made me give my stick back.

The Duarte runners were finishing. They ran slow, but didn't care. The Duarte freshmen cheered for their Varsity as if conquering "The Hill" was an achievement. For me, it was a job. I came. I ran. I finished fifth. Coach Neal called me a loser. Coaches on other teams had wondered out loud why he yelled at us. Hadn't his runners just cleaned up 15-to-50 against their team? But San Marino was the only team that mattered in our league. San Marino had never been defeated.

What was odd was there were coaches from other high schools at this meet, a coach from every Rio Hondo League team.

"'S goin' on?" I asked the Jabberwocky. "These guys checkin' out our times?"

"Don't think so," said the Wocky.

"Whatcha mean?"

"Wouldn't they have stopwatches if they cared about our times, Martian?"

Of course. Where were the stopwatches? And why was Temple City's coach here? We'd creamed Temple City last week. It seemed totally bizarre. San Marino's race was scheduled in three weeks, and even *their* coach had no stopwatch.

Another starting pistol. The freshmen ran. All the coaches clustered on the north of Sunshine Drive. They watched the freshmen climb the Hill while we stood across the street. Except the only freshmen running up the Hill were La Cañada's. The ones from Duarte turned around after walking halfway up. Seeing the coaches, runners turned back and kept trudging up the grade. The rest didn't care. One kid even shrugged his shoulders.

The coaches nodded. The Bell Gardens coach waved his arms and bellowed. "It's not cross country. I can't make my freshmen run this course. We don't have any hills like this one in Bell Gardens we can train on."

"Or Temple City. It's not fair," piped in Temple City's coach.

Even the guy from Duarte seemed convinced, when they had plenty of hills to practice on in Duarte.

"Only wusses can't run uphill." Coach Neal spat into the grass. "This is cross-country. It tests endurance. This isn't some lollygagging sport for lazy...."

That did it. San Marino's coach now called the question. The coaches' hands arose in unison to vote against the Hill, except for Neal's. His eyes narrowed. His face was redder than a plum.

"Your guys are hamburgers." His voice rose. "Your guys are wimps."

The other coaches folded their muscled arms across their polo shirts, shaking their heads. They grinned and slapped each others' backs once they'd agreed. The coach from San Marino hiked his slacks up with his thumbs and strolled across the park with his companions.

Ivan Alphabet walked up to us. "'S goin' on?"

Booboo raced toward us. "They just outlawed The Hill." He'd jogged by to loosen down. He'd overheard.

"No way. We're racing San Marino in four weeks. It's a home meet," Ivan said.

"Guess where?" said Booboo.

"Here. The Hill. It's our turn this year."

"Lacy Park," said Booboo.

"What? That's San Marino's course."

"Easy, Ivan."

"You're full of shit, Booboo." The Wocky for once had lost his cool. "If it's true, it sucks the big one. Don't fuck with me, Booboo."

"Lacy Park."

"Bullshit."

"Lacy Park."

You could see from Neal's face, Booboo was right. Neal was stone-faced. The freshman-sophomores finished their heat. The Duarte freshmen had turned around. La Cañada runners sprinted past them.

Neal spat. He shook his head and spat again.

The other coaches chuckled. The San Marino Coach smirked. Car doors slammed. Turn signals flickered, and the coaches were on their way.

The rest of us stood stunned. The Hill had just been *outlawed*. All Neal could do was stare and cuss, and no one listened. San Marino was in four weeks. We had to race at Lacy Park, where no team had ever beaten San Marino.

After my embarrassment over the incident with Leta, I wore a second pair of shorts to school to guard against humiliation. I hated this. The lines looked stupid where they grooved against my slacks. Still, I had to take precautions. It wasn't cool creaming your pants. Not in high school. I was grateful Leta hadn't spread the word.

I kept the promise I'd made to Leta out of gratitude. I'd even shared my lunch hour with Mandy on occasion. We might as well be public friends. Let Heather spread her cruel gossip. There were just 230 days to graduation.

Heather's gossip about our friendship had lasted no more than a week. Heather's scoop on Mrs. Dunlap preempted any talk of us. Mrs. Dunlap had quit her job. Heather had it on authority Mrs. D had gotten pregnant. (She wasn't married!) Heather promised more details at eleven.

And now, Momma had just figured out it wasn't Mrs. Dunlap who was camped out on her faculty lounge toilet. "It was a pair of empty go-go boots—and a maxi-skirt," said Heather. "And Momma found paint speckles on the maxi-skirt."

Crap!

The paint speckles were paprika. Momma was evidently livid. Heather said there'd been an "accident" when the toilet was out of service. Heather's gossip made the rounds. Momma had "piddled in her petticoats!"

Piddled?

I heard it first from Ivan Alphabet when we were practicing up Lida. He clearly hadn't seen the speckles up the right side of my arm cast. I crapped a giant brick. I nearly left the brick on Lida. Whoever's clothing matched the paint speckles was sure to get expelled. After her "accident," Momma had no sense of humor.

My arm cast had to go. Its plaster was already frayed around my wrist from all my running. I could paint over the speckles, but I'd be covering Leta's signature, and after painting it, the plaster wouldn't breathe. The cast was heavy and had mildewed around my arm. It smelled like some small animal had crawled in there and died. And it itched. Even my coat-hangers no longer cured the itching. Still, I was grateful it was sunset. No one would see me after practice.

That evening, when I got home, I found the tools.

After my mother went to sleep, I filled the bathtub. I grabbed my father's pruning shears from the garage. At least my old man wouldn't miss his tools the way that I missed him. I soaked my plaster. The doc had warned me not to get my cast wet. But I also wasn't supposed to get expelled.

The saddest part about the cast was Leta's signature. It faded and swirled away, a cloud of ink. But the paint-speckle evidence was fading. The cast softened around the edges. I grabbed the shears. It was hard to cut through plaster with one hand. I propped the pruning shears against the tub and pressed down hard. The stainless steel blades nibbled with effort through my cast. This was easy near the wrist, but it got hard up near the elbow. The cast was thick there, over five-eighths of an inch. The shears weren't cutting it.

Maybe a tree saw. There was a new one in the garage behind Dad's golf clubs. I had to find it without waking up my mother. Still, the old lady wasn't speaking to me. This made things pretty easy. I drained the tub, with paper towels across the drain to catch the plaster. A five eights-inch thick tube of arm cast bounced around my elbow. It looked silly. But I was gonna saw it off.

I pulled some pants on and went outside to find Dad's saw in the garage. Once I'd found it, I saw a light on in my mother's bedroom window. That's what she called it now. *Her* bedroom, as if Dad had never lived there. I saw her silhouette behind *her* draperies by *her* dresser. Did she watch me? Her draperies never parted. She never looked in my direction.

Screw her. The saw blade echoed between the house and the garage while I sawed. I'd use a chain saw if I'd had one just to find out if she cared. It took me 40 minutes to cut my cast off with one hand, gouging deep into the plaster until I found a pair of aircraft shears and clipped along the score line. I swept the tiny plaster pieces and hosed the shavings down the driveway. When I'd finished, her silhouette remained in profile on her draperies, casting a shadow fifteen feet across the lawn.

I tiptoed into my bedroom.

I slammed the door.

She didn't even bother to come downstairs.

By Thursday, Mom hadn't noticed my cast had been sawed off and had been absent from my arm since Tuesday night. I found her sitting on the sofa reading *The Sensuous Woman*. I wandered through the living room.

"Hi Mom."

I did not expect an answer, which is why I always greeted her. Mom stared down at her book as if she'd just glued in her eyeballs and was afraid they might fall out if she looked up.

Today she had a question. Perhaps the glue had finally set. Her gaze lifted.

"Allen?" She sounded nervous. "Do I look pretty?"

"What?"

"Am I attractive?"

What difference does it make? I wasn't quite sure what to say here. Talk about a no-win situation.

Not that Mom was ugly. She looked okay as mothers went. But what did she really want? I closed my eyes. When I opened them, she'd put shades on, wandered to the kitchen and refilled her martini glass with zinfandel.

"You okay, Mom?"

"What do *you* think?"

"I think you're lonelier than hell."

She glared at me as though I'd stolen her last bottle of zinfandel. "Don't say hell, Allen. I didn't raise that kind of boy." She looked away.

The way Mom said this made it sound like she'd disowned me.

"Oh."

Chugging her wine, she poured another inch to refill her martini glass, staring into the liquid as if she'd seen her own reflection, not pleased with what she saw.

She poured the contents down her throat. She ran upstairs, slammed the door.

It was weeks before she spoke to me again.

CHAPTER SEVEN

MAKE ME SMILE

FLINT PEAK, GLENDALE, CALIFORNIA: NOVEMBER 2ND, 1970
(221 DAYS TO GRADUATION!)

I watched the sun drop like an orange into a far ocean horizon from my spot beneath the tower on Flint Peak. Out of nowhere, Mandy came running up our fire road. I hadn't thought I'd see her. She seemed stronger and ran faster with longer strides. She'd been building up endurance. She didn't drag her feet, although clearly she was struggling, muscling her way along the hillside.

I was thrilled. I'd missed seeing her at our tower. I'd missed the safe feeling I got whenever we sat together talking. We shared here. We smiled without the pressure to look cool; talked things out, like how we felt when Michael Patrick Arthur died. I'd forgotten how it felt to have a friend.

Footsteps thundered like a mare's. She turned the bend beyond the hillside that was dotted with Whipple yuccas. Her breathing had found a brutal rhythm. She clenched her jaw. Closer, closer. Her breath called out in cadence. She was climbing, a steady gait. She balled her fists, tightened her arms, plodding upgrade, dropping her head, and then raising it once she'd seen me.

Mandy stooped beside me at the crest. Dust caked her t-shirt. Sweat poured off her forehead and washed streaks down her neck. Hands on her knees, she caught her wind before shaking the breeze through her hair—and smiling as though God had watched her climb.

I'd never seen her smile so wide. She was a runner, and she liked it. "How'd you get here?" I asked. "Didn't see your car."

She sat beside me in the clearing, needing time to catch her breath.

"From Glenoaks," Mandy answered. "That other fire road from Pasadena. You should try that way. It's pretty where you wind along the ridge above the golf course." She stretched her calves against a rock, struggling to breathe steady. "And not as steep."

"Glenoaks is kinda far from where I live."

"Where do you start from, Allen?"

"From my mom's house on Indianola. It's a long run, but it gives me time to think."

"Like an hour?" Her hands slid to her hips. "Each way?"

I nodded.

"Oh." She stared across Scholl Canyon, then stared at me the same way. I felt awkward, as though Mandy'd been poking around inside my head. "You okay, Allen?" She was quiet.

I couldn't fake her out, and didn't want to. I picked a burr from off my sock. Flicking it into the breeze, it helicoptered in spirals into a clump of laurel sumac. I tossed another one behind it. It winged across the canyon.

"What's wrong, Allen?"

"Nothin'."

"You're awful quiet. Whatcha thinkin' about?"

"Ethan Frome."

"Yeah, right." Mandy straightened. "That book sucked."

"Well, we agree. But lately, I've been wonderin' why I hated it."

"Does it matter?"

"Yeah," I said. "Maybe it hits too close to home."

I didn't tell her of my Society for the Complete Extermination of *Ethan Frome*, although I knew my club could use another member. A society with one member seemed a total waste of time. What could you do with just one member, except feel sorry for yourself? Perhaps as Groucho Marx said, any club that would accept me as a member wasn't worth joining.

"Like your family?" Mandy asked.

She knew half of it.

"Except, *my* family runs away, Mandy." I lowered my voice to hide the shrillness. "Ethan Frome stays home trying to be nice to his wife, Zeena. Only she treets the guy like dirt. Never once tells him she's sorry. Won't let Ethan say he's sorry when the cat breaks Zeena's pickle dish. They're stuck in ruts, like that sled run that finally smashes him and Mattie into the elm and leaves them crippled."

"How would you change things?" Mandy asked.

"I dunno. Maybe I'd make Ethan Frome *good* instead of *nice*. Have Ethan walk up to his wife and tell her to make her own damn breakfast, get out of bed, quit being a lazy hypochondriac. Show empathy. Problem today is, men are either such nice guys they're useless, or they're bad-asses who marry some sweet girl and beat her silly."

"Did you ever think that Ethan should have run away with Mattie?"

"Maybe. But my whole family's been runnin' away for years. I say if Ethan wants to die, I'll help him figure out how to do it."

"Like how?"

I wasn't sure if she was serious. It was a guy thing. You didn't share this stuff with girls. "Maybe his sled runs off a cliff." I checked for her reaction.

Her quiet eyes locked on mine. She was listening.

"He's angry." I clenched my fists. "And powerless," I said. "I'd kinda like to see him grow a spine. That's what I hate about Ethan Frome. He never pursues the stuff he wants. What kind of failure even fails to commit suicide?"

Mandy folded her legs. Her heels pressed against her gym shorts. She picked little granite pebbles from her knees. For a moment, my stomach tightened. Did she think that I was strange? Lights below us twinkled on. Mandy turned to me.

"Did Leta—talk to you?" she asked.

I nodded.

"I didn't mean for her to do that," Mandy said.

"It's okay. Leta was kind. I'm fine with you and Leta."

"I'm still sorry."

I turned to face her. "Don't be." Something soft in Mandy's voice wedged beneath my armor. It was the first time I remembered someone telling me they were sorry. She even looked sorry. It felt weird when someone told you they were sorry.

"Do girls scare you, Allen?"

She'd read my mind again.

"Yeah," I said in reflex. "After Heather."

"You never kissed her?"

I shook my head.

"Why not?" Her head tilted.

"I dunno. I just thought...."

"Girls scare me too," Mandy said.

"Girls scare each other?"

"We can be cruel. That's part of why Leta and I became friends at Palm Crest Elementary."

"What happened?"

Mandy faced me, pupils narrowing. "I can't tell you."

"Is it secret?" She wasn't usually this opaque.

Mandy nodded. "I don't gossip. You wouldn't trust me if I told you. At least you shouldn't."

I took a breath. *Should I trust her?* I'd heard Mandy trusted *me.* Would she trust me if I lied; if I didn't share my thoughts? I searched her eyes. "Okay, Mandy. This doesn't leave Flint Peak. Remember how Harron wished I'd die in Vietnam?"

"He's a jerk."

"I realized this morning—" I took a breath "—-in six months, they draw my draft number. I can die like poor Mike Arthur."

"Don't you have to be eighteen?"

"I *am* eighteen, Mandy. They held me back in first grade."

"No way."

"Said I was too skinny."

"That must have really sucked."

"Big time." I rubbed my eyes. Didn't help that bigger kids used to whup me every day. Where 'd you think I first learned how to run?"

Mandy looked up.

"That whole summer, I was dreading even more *Fun with Dick and Jane.*"

My throat tightened. I felt like I was ripping open wounds. "I'd learned to read, to write, learned addition and subtraction, and then the principal calls me in and says I have to do it over. Over! I mean she tells me this in June. If they'd wanted me to grow bigger, couldn't they stuff me full of chocolate while I stayed home where I could play between forced-feedings? All the parents gossiped like they knew I was retarded. In September, I got treated like I was."

"Howdja handle it?"

"I cried in my backyard. It was the only place where nobody was looking."

"You didn't pray?"

I took a breath. "I'm an atheist. We don't pray."

"Aren't you Jewish?"

"Italian. Some Ellis Island guy couldn't spell Martini."

"So they shortened it to Martin?"

"You got it."

"Does it bother you I want to be a nun?"

I shook my head. "Not in your case. Just don't preach. I'm not cut out for religion. Nothin' personal."

A long breath. Her lungs inhaled forever. She touched my wrist. "Don'tcha think you should have one of us in your corner?"

"Sure. But I'm a skeptic. I live by Occam's Razor. When life hands me a question, I seek the simplest explanation. I don't multiply hypotheses. I shave off unnecessary assumptions. Like the whole idea of God."

She touched my shoulder. "William of Occam was a Christian, a Franciscan who sought God's grace when the church was selling *dis*grace."

"How'd you know about William of Occam?" I asked, stunned Mandy had heard of him.

"He wrote a pamphlet proving Pope John was a heretic," she said and rubbed my neck.

I relaxed. The gentle kneading of her touch softened my edge.

"He couldn't do that if he disbelieved in God," Mandy said. "It's like we're looking at the seashore—" she pointed toward the harbor. The lighthouse beacon from Point Fermin seemed to vanish across the water. "—-and you don't want to believe that somewhere there's another seashore. Then suddenly you know there *has to be* another seashore."

"How?"

She kneaded harder. "Because, silly, if there wasn't another seashore, all the water would drain out. Something needs to hold it all together."

I folded my arms. I was starting to feel chilly. This discussion made me feel like I was drinking from a fire hose. A haze spawned velvet clouds that gathered across the evening.

"Allen, *this* life we're living is our miracle. Just accept it. Occam called his life a gift, even in prison. We didn't earn it. Allen, I know your life can feel like a burden...." Her voice cracked, like Mandy was afraid that she might cry.

"You okay?" I asked.

"No."

She stretched toward me like she'd been hoping I'd hug her, and so I did. I felt her tears, her heartbeat and the rhythm of her breathing. She seemed tenderer than I'd expected.

Mandy cleared her throat. "When I was really, really young, my mother died from lupus complications. Something I'm still afraid to talk about. But it happened." She started weeping. Her eyes were teary. She lowered her voice. "I never wanted to go to church again. All those saints and catechisms they made us memorize. As if being forced to memorize things somehow made them true."

"Does dogma give them power or does power create dogma?"

"I'm not sure. But it sure let them off the hook. It let them miss the point and blame us for stuff that didn't matter. Didn't Jesus say you'd know who his disciples were? They'd be the ones who loved one another. And nobody loved me."

"What'd you do?" I asked.

"It helped a lot to learn of Occam's razor," Mandy said. "So I could will myself to love—what Jesus wanted from his disciples, the simplest truth of all."

"That took courage."

"And all the while I prayed there'd *be* a god to share my days, 'cause if there wasn't, there'd be no reason to love."

"But you want to be a nun."

"Someone has to, Allen. Churches are full of selfish clergy who love no one but themselves. But someone has to love. Even in the church, someone has to find the courage to help others to love. Tell me, what's the use of churches that aren't helpful?"

We sat in silence. I imagined being that hurt and turning my pain toward helping others. Night filled with haze. She'd never shared like this before. I felt confused. Fog snuffed out the traffic noise and tucked in all the crickets. We held hands until the night had closed our wounds.

"It's gettin' cloudy," I whispered. "Ready to head down?"

Mandy nodded.

I touched her wrist. "Let me teach you how to run."

"You can't tell me how to run."

"Just listen to me, Mandy. I watched your climb. You've got guts. But you run tight. You work so hard. It saps your strength. Loosen your arms up, Mandy. Think of Occam's Razor."

Mandy smiled, although she seemed reluctant. For a moment she lowered her gaze as though I'd hurt her pride.

"Listen, I just thought I could show you."

She looked up like she was swallowing her ego. "Okay," she finally whispered.

I helped her up. We ran the road together. Her arms tightened into fists. "Mandy, relax your fingers. All that energy in your fists won't help you run. Open your hands. Drop your arms. Occam's Razor."

Past the hillside full of yuccas we ran together. Our arms dropped. Footsteps found the hillside's rhythm. The puffs of dust behind our steps were scarcely stirred. "That's it, Mandy, minimize the energy you spend. You wanna flow just like a wind along the canyon. Try not to bounce. Let the mountain pull you forward."

She clenched her jaw. Her pace grew longer, and she surrendered to the mountain.

"Now, smile, Mandy. Your neck relaxes when you smile. Just use your legs. Nothing else'll move you forward. Think of legs. Send your strength down to your legs."

She seemed to hear me. Her neck loosened. Her stride grew stronger. We ran the fire road in silence. The damp October air glided across our faces. We reached the trail fork to Pasadena, and her unnecessary motions were shed beside the road as if removed by Occam's Razor.

I followed her, though she took the long way home. The lights of Pasadena shined below us. I was glad to hear her breaths. We continued across the ridge, beyond the toyons, to where the sumac and the scrub oak clung to granite with gnarled fingers. Then, we wound into the darkness of the canyon.

She wasn't panting when we reached her car. Her arms were loose, and she was smiling. I'd taught her to relax. She looked stronger, now she'd learned to let the mountain pull her forward.

"Allen, I can't believe we ran so smooth. That was soooo cool. Like flying. We were soaring to Pasadena."

I gloated. "After a while you find ways to run more simply," I told Mandy. "I run waaaay too many miles to make it hard."

She reached her car door. Our eyes met. Awkward silence cut the evening. Buzzing rural streetlights were muffled behind fog. I walked away. I stooped to tie my shoe.

"Allen?" she called.

I turned.

"Allen, don't you need a ride?"

"Uh, yeah, I guess so."

She laughed. "You *guess* so?"

Mist condensed across my forehead.

"It's—kinda late?" She tilted her head. "And it's like—raining?"

She was right. If I ran, I'd be running into a storm. It would be ten o'clock before I reached my doorstep. Not that someone waited—or cared.

She popped her car door, and I slid in beside her. The engine grumbled at the cul-de-sac and lurched forward as she wheeled a tight radius across the asphalt. She let the clutch out. My shirt squeaked against the vinyl in her car seat. The gears scraped. The car lurched forward onto Glenoaks.

It drizzled as we descended toward Pasadena. I was grateful for the ride, but "Vee-dubs" felt so cramped. Their windshields were squashed down, like on Gemini space capsules that floated while carriers plucked them from the ocean. I'd heard Volkswagens floated too. Their doors sealed up so tight the air inside them pulsed in rhythm with their engines. But none of us had tried to float a Volkswagen so far. It was a rumor. I counted myself a skeptic.

Mandy clicked on her high beams. Light cones vanished in the mist. A stop sign. She let a car pass. I was glad I wasn't running. Wipers swooshed away the rain that spattered in gusts against our windshield. Taillights vanished. The cloud engulfing us made the car feel even smaller.

She was focused on her driving. Streetlights glowed from fluted poles, casting reflections in the Linda Vista gutters. We passed a playground. Slides slicked with rain flowing through puddles beneath the swing sets.

Mandy broke the silence at the traffic light. "Allen, what happened to your arm cast?"

My nerves tightened. The stoplight reflected red against wet asphalt. I took a breath. Why was she asking me this now? I was too weary to explain.

"I cut it off."

"You *what?*"

I told her how I'd autographed the toilet stalls last summer, how I'd touched up all but eight of them where Momma had changed the locks. How Momma had almost busted me in the ladies' room at dawn.

"What's this have to do with your arm cast?" Mandy asked.

I took a breath and closed my eyes. "You know those go-go boots that showed up in the faculty lounge bathroom? The ones that Heather says made Momma piddle?"

"So what about them?"

"I put 'em there."

"No way."

"They were my decoys."

"What on earth?"

"So nobody busted into my stall while I was painting—I was storing them for when I finished up the women's rooms."

Mandy sighed, drumming her fingers on the steering wheel.

The stoplight changed to green. She shifted into first and let the clutch out. We continued toward the high school. I hadn't talked for several minutes while she processed what I'd told her. It was pouring. The wipers struggled across the windshield like drowning swimmers. Debris poured out of the culvert where Linda Vista turned into Highland. Mandy swung right onto Berkshire.

I checked her gas gauge. "I'll buy you gas, Mandy." I pulled three bucks from my running shoe. "There's a Richfield Station on Woodleigh." (My way of changing subjects.)

She hit the blinker and hung a right. We forded a gutter filled with oak leaves. She drove beneath the Richfield canopy, scrunched the parking brake and stared at me. Turning the engine off, she touched my arm. "Need any help, Allen?"

I unlatched my door beside the pump island. Raindrops banged against the canopy. I was grateful to be dry. I paid the attendant and waited for him to leave.

"Help with what, Mandy?"

"To finish the paint stalls—in the girls' gym." The canopy light reflected off diagonal lines of drizzle.

I shoved the nozzle into the gas tank. "You'd help me touch up toilet stalls?"

"You got the paint?"

A smile filled my face. I nodded, almost too eager. I hadn't dared to ask for help, but Mandy'd volunteered. It was almost like the rain had been turned off.

I strolled inside and bought some coffee for us to share. A hundred pounds had just been lifted from my shoulders.

We cruised up Indianola Way to get the paint.

The doors were open at the high school. The lights were on in the gymnasium. Basketballs bounced against the boards and rattled ceilings above the lockers. I guarded the door outside the girls' rooms while Mandy slipped inside. I listened to rainfall for an hour that felt like half a year.

At last, she walked outside, smiling. "Your turn, Allen." She handed me the paintbrush. The women's room was done. It was my turn to finish the men's stalls. I'd honed the process to a science. I stirred some spackle into my paint jar and slid my beach towel beneath the stalls to catch the paint drops before they splattered onto the tile.

It was pouring again. Mandy waited inside her Volkswagen for me to finish. It was time to get to work.

I crawled beneath the partitions and painted, lying on my back, covering the markings in record time. Gym shoes squeaked above the ceiling. The odor of paint mixed in with turpentine, reminding me of summer. The smell saddened me, like saying farewell to dreams that never came. The names were covered as though there'd never been a Heather, or painting stalls, or scaffold races. Even the cast was off my arm. Still, I felt reborn. I had a new friend, Mandy, who cared enough to help me. She'd been the Bonnie to my Clyde.

I couldn't wait to join her in her Volkswagen.

I wrapped my brush inside my rag and screwed the lid back onto the paint jar. A happy sigh. I tugged my drop cloth.

It was stuck.

I panicked, jerking it harder. It didn't move.

I blocked my heel against the partition base and pulled the drop cloth with all my strength to slide it toward me. My injured arm was throbbing. The cloth yielded to my pain. Two Converse sneakers and high white socks rode the beach towel when I tugged it, like they'd been laced on by Aladdin, and he was surfing my magic carpet. Long hairy legs cast a shadow. I didn't dare to look outside.

Someone's throat cleared. Hairs behind my neck stood at attention.

A gust of air swooshed past my chin while I lay helpless on my back. The stall door banged above my head. A sneaker pressed my chest. He towered over me with folded arms and a head shaved bald for football—like Mister Clean without the earring. His Spartan Men's Council windbreaker was zipped up to his chin.

A grin engulfed the face of Garry Jackson.

He was figuring his advantage. His eyes kachinged like those cash-register eyes in old cartoons. He nodded, as though calculating just what he could extort. To my horror, I recalled that Garry's dad was an attorney.

"Well if it isn't little Alien Martian." His sneaker twisted on my chest. "Those paint drops on your towel, and on your paintbrush, and—what'd the student bulletin call that color on your toilet stall—'paprika?'"

My eyes kept saying yes.

"The spots on those go-go boots in the faculty lounge bathroom—weren't they that color too?" Garry gloated like he was Perry friggin' Mason. I wanted to puke. "Isn't it true? Oh Allen, you disappoint me," Garry mocked.

I was sooo busted. To make it worse, I'd just been busted by Garry Jackson, who was Teflon. And I was clearly Velcro. That Spartan Men's Council jacket gave him that extra dose of smugness.

His sneaker crushed down on my chest. "You owe me, pal," said Garry. "I could rat you out to Heather. She'd tell half of La Cañada, and you'd be expelled." He booted my side. "Keep that in mind, Martian." A quick kick bruised my balls before he ambled from the bathroom, turning the lights out as he whistled *"Instant Karma"* in the dark.

I limped out of the bathroom, still in pain.

I didn't sleep. Mandy had driven me home in silence. When she'd asked me what was wrong, I hadn't told her. From the time I'd left the bathroom, my mind whirled with apprehension. What was my problem? How was it Garry never got in trouble? What was it football players had that nothing stuck to them?

And what did *I* have that everything stuck to me. I'd done nothing—except paint over some graffiti, free of charge. And all Garry had done was pick the perfect time to take a leak.

He was charmed.

I was cursed.

And now, I *owed* him. Did God think Garry needed leverage? Wasn't stealing my girlfriend enough to put me in my place? What else would he extort? I was sure I wouldn't like it. Garry was Teflon; a *teflocrat*; a *teflonista*.

And I was a *velcroid*, a human being made out of Velcro. After Heather had met Garry, I'd been peeled off like a leech. And now, things stuck to me that shouldn't.

Martin's First Observation:
There are two types of people; velcroids and teflonistas. Teflonistas never have to say they're sorry.

That's how things worked in La Cañada. The teflonistas, the fortunate ones and their mascots went through high school without a clue that anything could be their fault. To make things worse, cluelessness was reckoned as a virtue. As a velcroid you'd be punished for any teflonista's trespass, while teflonista's looked down at you and sneered. The only point of our existence was to stand around on-call to serve as whipping boys and boost the teflonistas' self-esteem.

I knew Garry'd waste no time before he pressed his new advantage.

I didn't know he'd call the marker in so soon.

CHAPTER EIGHT

JAM UP AND JELLY TIGHT

LA CAÑADA HIGH SCHOOL:
THURSDAY, NOVEMBER 5TH, 1970
(218 DAYS TO GRADUATION!)

On Thursday, I met Mandy during lunch. We had two bucks to split between us. It didn't buy much, but we shared. I didn't care for cafeteria food, but there was nothing else on campus. Still, I liked eating with Mandy. We complemented each other. She had strength that I could lean on. Some days she even leaned on me. A perfect symbiosis bound our friendship.

The sheet-cakes that were served up in the high school cafetorium never did taste any better as they aged. Twice a month, a brand-new sheet-cake would appear behind the glass; carrot or pound cake, you were never quite sure which. After fifteen minutes, the center of the cake would be devoured. Inside pieces received frosting and sold out on the first day. The rubbery perimeter did not get any frosting. Pieces remained on sale for weeks, until they hardened into squares that were so tough even the weevils refused to eat them.

Not to worry. The cafeteria ladies placed old cakes behind the glass until enough geologic time elapsed to petrify them solid. Perhaps some unwitting freshman might buy a square of ancient "ton cake," and some starving little child in Biafra might be comforted. Weeks had toughened up the cakes until a cold day in November, someone bought *all* of them. I searched the cafeteria to see who. Momma would *never* sentence those ton cakes to the dumpster.

Garry took his station by the door.

He had an arsenal. Cake squares were piled like grenades on Garry's yellow cafeteria tray. Pudge McMasters took the other door, armed with twice as many cake squares. Garry caught my eye. He sent one spinning my direction.

I ducked. "Ouch!" Too late. He'd nailed me on the shoulder. He sent a second cake toward Mandy and caught her butt. *Garry you jerkwad!* Mandy shrieked. These things were harder than old hockey pucks. Food flew in all directions. Hostess Ding Dongs, chicken surprises, lasagna pudding, grape jelly sandwiches were torn in half and flung.

"FOOOOOODFIIIIIIIGHT!"

The room erupted with more chaos and confusion than a battery of two-year-olds launching Gerber bottles in unison. Bowls of broccoli, orange Jell-o, applesauce splattered across my chin. Linguini landed in my hair. A plastic glass bounced off my ear.

A ton cake skidded toward me across the linoleum. I picked it up.

It wasn't broken. I stared at Garry, glared at Heather.

Yeah! Heather! Sweet revenge.

She was wearing that scarlet sweater Garry had bought her the day she'd dumped me. She wore that stupid cameo choker that wasn't choking her enough. Her fake boobs jutted at an angle. I wanted to hurl my cake and pop one, just like those balloons that you throw darts at for school carnivals. Except Garry had just nailed Mandy and I needed to pay back Garry. I wound up. I aimed at Garry. Like Don Drysdale of the Dodgers, I threw....

...A fastball, a brushback pitch, inside and near the letters. Heather screamed. The ton cake sizzled between Garry and Heather's chests. Broken glass. A maze of cracks spidered across the window. There was a square hole in the center. The cake square sailed into the hallway.

Someone blew a whistle.

Screeeeeeeeeee! Screeeeeeeeeeee! Screeeeeeeeeee!

Teachers ran in like SWAT teams. Heather pointed out the perps. If her boyfriend would get busted, she'd make certain he had company. Coach Harron grabbed me. I felt his hand. I smelled egg salad on his breath. "Let's go, dickwad." Harron jerked me. A piece of tuna hit my lip. *No fair, Harron! Late hit.* Hadn't they whistled down the food fight? Harron grabbed the arm I'd broken.

He twisted it.

Don't show pain. I clenched my teeth. Seething, I saw lights behind my eyes. *Don't show pain.* I ground my teeth like I was biting a phantom bullet. More faculty surrounded me like hyenas around a carcass. Harron twisted my arm up to my neck. I was escorted to one corner while students cleared the cafetorium, Harron pressed me onto a bench, then cleared the intercom and told Momma I'd started the foodfight. Then he split. The bell rang, leaving just three of us in custody; Garry Jackson, Pudge McMasters, and me.

I never knew if Garry Jackson meant to be funny or just stupid. The truth was hiding beneath Garry's big wide grin. Only Garry could take a true-false quiz and answer every question *wrong*. The science teacher had seemed convinced Garry had done this to be clever. He'd told Garry he was amazing, an *idiot-savant*, and had awarded Garry the only perfect score. It just proved Garry was Teflon. He was so much more than lucky. He was charmed. (In Mrs. Zinicola's class, when a vocabulary test word was *euthanasia*, Garry had written down the answer "little Chinamen." Mrs. Z. had laughed out loud, giving him credit for his answer.) He was the archetype teflonista. He could cruise and not get bruised. He could lead and never bleed.

I *hated* him.

To make things worse, Garry's allowance exceeded the GNP of Panama. His rich attorney father had litigated more than one Corvair case. He could buy Pacific Islands and give one to Garry for his birthday.

Garry smiled. He *knew* that he was Teflon.

I sat across from Pudge and Garry on a bench covered with slop. Hundreds of students' lunches were smeared against the floor, splattered against the masonry, dribbling down glass windows. After my episode with Garry in the bathroom stalls last night, I had a premonition things wouldn't go well.

My gut twisted.

Garry's smile hardened. He glowered at me. "You threw a ton cake at my girlfriend. I saw you aim, Martian."

My gaze lifted. I bit my tongue.

"I should ream you a new asshole. I should rearrange your face. I should tell Momma about...."

Blackmail. "I'm sorry."

"I could crush you."

"You'd never catch me."

"Catch you?" Garry said. "I could flatten you in first gear. You and your Yamaha 60 would be stripes along the highway."

"Try it without the Mustang."

Garry didn't get it. He had money. He had privilege. He had a hot girl, Heather Fairchild. I understood his logic.

Thud! Doors swung open. Momma's high heels click-click-clicked across linoleum. She slipped in a puddle of lasagna but tottered back up into balance. She cleared her throat. She folded her arms across her chest and gave the Momma-glare. Clearly, she was furious.

"Which one of you boys is responsible for this—this...."

Pudge McMasters looked at me.

Garry looked at me, folding his arms. His eyes kachinged, the way they had last night. I almost felt his foot, like it still pressed on my chest. Garry stood stone-faced, almost Buddha-like before me.

Garry and Pudge's gazes zeroed on Momma. "Didn't you hear Coach Harron on the intercom?" asked Garry.

Momma jerked a thumb at me. "He started this?"

Garry nodded. "He broke your window." Garry and Pudge talked like *victims.* They didn't smile. They didn't laugh. They just looked Ozzie Nelson righteous and pointed toward the window. I could almost feel Ozzie's newspaper crash down on my head. *(Bad velcroid!)* Garry zipped his Spartan Men's Council windbreaker which was so spotless it almost looked as if he'd worn it as an alibi.

"Thank you," Momma told Garry. "You two are excused."

"B-b-but...," I stuttered.

Garry was gone in seven seconds.

My heart sank. Why me? Why did life suck for velcroids?

Momma frowned. The cafetorium looked like the inside of a dumpster. Did Momma really think a single kid threw several hundred lunches? Movie sets after pie fights had never been this dirty.

Momma looked down at her wristwatch then at me.

"Start scrubbing," Momma said. "I'll be coming back at three o'clock to check your progress." She swiveled on her stilettos and pointed to a sponge. "You'll go home when this room is spotless and not one second before."

It was a big room. My heart sank to somewhere below my stomach and burrowed in beneath my small intestine.

Momma grinned with her teflocratic smile. Then, her heels click-click-clicked straight out the door.

The sponges had their value when I'd try to wipe the floor, but they were worthless when I'd use them on the windows. They just smeared stuff on the glass, until the panes fogged up with peanut butter, or mustard, or three-day-old spaghetti.

I felt helpless. By one-thirty, I had barely make a dent in all the mayonnaise and ketchup-covered crap that filled the lunchroom. I'd computed I'd be cleaning here through early Sunday morning. Hundreds of portions had been thrown. The room looked like a salad bowl. It wasn't fair. But I didn't get to argue.

To keep from going crazy I tested out my theory, assigning literary characters as either velcroids or teflonistas. My list was only starting. Assignments were as follows:

1. *George F. Babbitt – teflonista.*
2. *Wright's Bigger Thomas – velcroid.*
3. *Steinbeck's Joad family - all velcroids.*
4. *Shakespeare's Julius Caesar – a teflonista who gets traded to the velcroids.*
5. *Fitzgerald's Jay Gatsby – ditto.*
6. *Zeena Frome – teflonista.*
7. *Ethan Frome – the archetype of all velcroids.*

By two o'clock my pants were filthy. They reeked of mustard and Heinz ketchup. Food caked my arms up to my elbows. My knees ached on hard linoleum. The aroma of rancid milk permeated the room.

I'd filled two trash cans. I was working on the third when John, the janitor, poked his head inside the doorway. "Jeezuz Christmas. Momma pin this mess on you, kid?"

I nodded.

John looked at me with sympathetic eyes, velcroid to velcroid. He looked like Popeye, only smiling between two jug-handle ears. "You're pretty talented, Jackson Pollock." He lit himself a cigarette. "It'd take me weeks to finish throwing this much food. But I'm—just the janitor." He ran his fingers through his hair and rubbed his chin, deep in thought. "Your parents buy you all this food?"

He smiled like he was kidding, but I said, "No."

"Momma always pulls this crap. She picks on one kid at a time. As if the whole thing is his fault. Then she punishes her scapegoat while she waxes all self-righteous. She's a bully."

No shit. I thought but didn't say.

John grabbed a push-broom from behind the multi-purpose stage and cut a swash through the mess, three feet wide. It piled twelve inches high in front of the big black nylon bristles. I grabbed a trash can. I didn't waste any momentum John had generated. He squeegeed puddles of food from the floor into my trash can.

"Take this can out to the dumpster. I'll have more piles when you get back."

I raced outside. John the janitor had just come to my rescue.

My heart lifted. It boosted itself from somewhere below my kidneys, clawed its fingers into my lungs and scrambled back into its perch. Things were on track now. I was a key cog in a well-oiled machine that now sent garbage to the dumpsters at record rate.

John was a wonder. He was a janitorial science virtuoso. When I returned, he had three piles of garbage waiting for my trash cans. I reloaded them and hurried them to the dumpsters behind the bleachers. When I returned, John was mopping down the walls.

"You're good," I said. "More like amazing."

John raised a finger to his lips. "Keep your voice low. Momma hears us, I catch hell."

"You're not supposed to help me?"

John kept his finger by his lips. "Ssshh. That woman hates me. She treats us like appliances and seems to think we live here. It never once occurs to Momma that we might want to go home at night. And I don't have all morning just to stand around and watch you. No offense, kid."

I said, "No offense taken."

John smiled. I trusted John a whole lot more than Momma. I grabbed a mop and joined him, wiping down the walls and baseboards. Working with John, you almost wished you could grow up to be a janitor.

At three o'clock, when Momma's footsteps warned us of her approach, John stepped outside and lit a smoke while Momma checked up on "my" progress. I grabbed a rag and sponged the floor in sweeping Cinderella arcs.

Her stiletto heels resounded through the doorway. I wanted to take up a collection and buy that hag a pair of jackboots. She wore a brown skirt that might have flattered her had it stretched beyond her ankles. Her plain wool jacket could have been picked up at an Eva Braun garage sale.

Momma surveyed the cafetorium from above her wire-rim glasses. She stared at it like an art gallery to which she'd appointed herself head docent but had forgotten to buy the art. She ran her hand beneath a window and blew breadcrumbs off her palm. She had a knack for looking comatose when she spoke to those she disciplined. "Keep working. I'll have my janitor keep his eye on you."

High-heel noise echoed off the walls as Momma strutted out the door. She didn't goosestep, but she resounded like a one-woman SS battalion. Her nylons sagged off knobby ankles that grew like burls on baby redwoods. She was a whole lot worse than Garry, a holy terror to all velcroids. I hoped to heaven Heather's gossip about her piddling was true.

A half-hour later, John returned with some Comet, buckets, ladders, and enough paper towels to dry a Boeing 707. He mixed in water with ammonia that smelled like half a gallon of cat piss.

"Momma gone?" I asked.

John nodded. "Her Lincoln Continental just went home."

"Good. I hate that pompous, self-congratulating witch." I shook my fist toward the door extending my middle finger.

John cleared his throat. "Keep your words sweet, kid. Some day you just might have to eat them." His gaze met mine.

I nodded.

"Let's fix that window."

He brought a glass pane from his closet, a bucket full of putty and two pairs of leather gloves to protect our fingers. I hammered out broken glass and scraped the edges with a putty knife. John set the pane in while I puttied around the edges.

"Perfect." He wiped our fingerprints off the window.

I painted over the putty and admired our latest handiwork.

John handed me a bucket.

For an hour we wiped the windows from the ceiling, working down. Ammonia burned our eyes and scorched our lungs. We worked at light-speed, trying to finish before the ammonia melted our eyeballs. Soon the windows became clear, the smears of grease and condiments filled a pile of paper towels below our ladders. John turned the lights on. The last smears blotted through our towels. I threw the rags out. The place was spotless. It smelled industrial-strength clean.

I turned to John, and we both nodded. We folded our arms in unison. I turned the lights out. We put our tools back.

John locked the doors, and we were done.

"You want a smoke?" John asked outside, shaking a Camel from his pocket. He mellowed as though he'd earned this simple pleasure. He lit a match and found a picnic bench inside the Senior area. He stretched his arms and propped his boots against an oak.

I shook my head. "Can't screw my lungs up. I'm a runner."

"No joke. A runner?"

Like he's impressed?

"Cross country," I said.

John nodded and inhaled. For five minutes we relaxed. It was "Miller time." He said we'd earned this. He puffed his cigarette. Soon, John cupped his ear. Something was squeaking.

Peep-peep-tweep.

"Hear that, kid?"

I nodded.

John leaned sideways.

Peep-tweep.

He turned his cupped hand toward the gym like a radar dish. He jumped up. Leaping forward, he pointed toward the doors. "Let's have a look."

I followed John across the concrete. How could a small man take such enormous strides? He ran a bee-line toward the gym, hurdling a fiberglass picnic bench. I bounded alongside him. John homed in like he had twenty-twenty hearing. "There!" He pointed at something quivering beneath a bush. "There he is. Lookit!" John cocked his head. "Hey. Lookit that."

Peep-peep-tweep.

The tiny sparrow was no larger than my thumb. His matchstick leg had splintered when he'd fallen from his nest. His beak looked pliable, like that weird plastic they use in yellow rubber duckies. Baby pinfeathers sprouted through puffs of bird fuzz.

Peep.

I craned my neck. Shadows of empty nests loomed above me on the arches below the eaves of the gymnasium. "He must have fallen," I said. "Look, his leg's busted. Poor guy."

John nodded, scratching his forehead. "Can you crawl in there and fetch him?"

I snaked beneath the pyracantha. Thorns barbed into my shirt, nudging me forward through the bushes. I reached out, scooping the sparrow up and carrying him through the brambles.

"Gotcha, fella. Relax."

He seemed so terrified I felt as if I held a ball of nerves. He didn't peep. I cradled him, careful not to twist his leg. One foot was hot on his good leg. The injured one was cold. I shimmied forward with the bird cupped in my fingers.

"Whadda we do with him?" I asked John. "Thought you weren't supposed to touch them."

"That's not true. Trust me." John folded his Popeye arms. His seasoned smile reassured me this wasn't his first bird rescue. "He needs our help. 'S fix his leg up. Get some Scotch tape from the library." John pulled a key from off his key chain.

I followed orders.

I bounded upstairs, rifled some tape from the librarian's unlocked cabinet. *Electrical tape. Perfect!* I locked the door and dashed downstairs.

When I returned, John cradled the chick. It wasn't shaking in John's care. The bird studied us through darting black-bead eyes. He looked naked with so few feathers, innocent and helpless, but John.s voice appeared to soothe him. "Easy, little guy."

Peep-peep-tweep.

"What's he doing here in November?" I looked at John as though he understood the secret lives of sparrows.

John shrugged. I wrapped electrical tape and paper towels to splint the leg. It looked bizarre, but held his leg on. The bird lay still. John cupped the bird inside one palm where he was resting.

"He still breathin'?"

"Kid, he's sleepin'."

I smiled. "Should we put him in his nest now?"

John nodded.

John had a putty can in his closet. We filled it halfway up with Kleenex. A ladder in the gymnasium closet got us to the roof. We scurried up the rungs with the sparrow in the putty can hooked to the key chain that jangled from John's belt loop.

He wrapped his arms around my ankles while I crawled out on the arched roof and set the sparrow inside a nest below the eaves.

The bird was sleeping when I left him. I hoped his parents would come feed him. I left a few grapes from the food fight in case they didn't.

According to John, a fledgling sparrow needed food every six hours, which meant I had to feed the poor bird every night. I wished his parents would show up. But tonight I couldn't risk it. He needed me. Without me he might die.

Mom never noticed when I woke. Even at two a.m., the noise inside the kitchen didn't wake her. I rinsed out a Schilling spice bottle and pureed a tablespoon of blueberries with some lasagna. I wasn't at all certain birds would eat this. That's all I found inside the fridge. I worried all the way to school. Here was this little guy who needed me to feed him to get well. I wasn't sure why I'd signed up for this, but somehow touching him, we'd bonded. He was my family.

I named Ethan. He was a velcroid, just like me.

CHAPTER NINE

UP THE LADDER TO THE ROOF

LA CAÑADA HIGH SCHOOL:
MONDAY, NOVEMBER 9TH, 1970
(217 DAYS TO GRADUATION!)

You named him what?" Mandy leaned against her egg-nog-colored Volkswagen so hard its left fender sank an inch below the right one.

"Ethan," I said. "Like Ethan Frome." I folded my arms. Grinned.

"Thought you hated Ethan Frome."

"I did. But now, I like him."

"And they say girls can't make their minds up?" Mandy sighed.

"Ethan's a velcroid." I explained to her my theory our high school had been divided into velcroids and teflonistas. "Ethan needs me. I kinda like it. Wanna see him?"

"W-where is he?"

"Under the eaves of the gymnasium." I pointed.

"Oh." Mandy shuddered. "Isn't that kinda—like unsafe?" She tilted her head sideways.

I shrugged. "I'm a painter. You get used to being on roofs. I need to feed him, anyways. C'mon, I'll show you."

She seemed nervous, but she followed.

I'd discovered Snooge's master key still unlocked some janitor closets. A stroke of luck. I'd found this out the morning after we'd found Ethan. Perhaps the janitors saw no point in changing locks on their own closets. Perhaps it ensured Momma had no access to their space, which might explain why all their Playboy pinups hadn't yet come down.

Mandy followed me up a long wrought-iron ladder inside the closet that extended from the concrete up a vent shaft to the roof scuttle. Odors of turpentine and cleaners became less pungent as we rose. I climbed the rungs like they were monkey bars, a trick I'd learned from painting. Thirty feet. I was up in fifteen seconds.

Mandy climbed slower. She seemed too cautious. Her arms shook the whole ladder. Her fists tightened around the rungs, and her forearms swelled and quivered. She didn't look down. She looked up. Her face craned toward me on the roof like she was hoping I'd assist her from the ladder.

I reached a hand down through the trap door. She almost cut the circulation to my arm, she gripped so tightly. She was trembling when I pulled her to the roof. She didn't say so, but it was clear Mandy was terrified. She shook and gasped ten-second breaths.

"You okay?"

She breathed so hard I thought she'd panic. "I'm okay."

"Mandy, don't work so hard. Occam's Razor. Remember?"

She dropped a knee against the scuttle curb and wiped rust from off her fingers. She wasn't shaking but still seemed anxious.

I crawled out across the roof deck. "Over here," I said. "Let's talk to Ethan." I took her hand. Mandy scooted feet-first behind me. She inched forward with cautious motions, as though the height of the gymnasium roof still scared her. I stopped beside her, hoping to calm her.

I remembered how nervous I'd been when I'd started painting eaves. It took a while to get a feel for roofs. She didn't seem as nervous if I moved the same way she did, sitting upright like a crab with your feet planted in front of you.

Peep-peep-tweep.

We inched forward. My feeding bottle and my eye-dropper were in my pocket. I'd filled the bottle with my blueberry-lasagna. Ethan wolfed it down like candy. John had asked me for my recipe.

The sad part was Ethan's deadbeat parents hadn't surfaced. Maybe they'd flown south. Poor little Ethan was abandoned, just like I was. He needed me. I pushed the dropper into his beak and squirted food into his mouth. He gulped. A lumpy bite worked its way down Ethan's throat. He tried to turn inside his nest, but Ethan only turned one way having just one working leg that he could push with.

"He's cool!" Mandy waved at him. "Hi, Ethan, I'm Mandy." She waved again. I lay beside her and gave her a chance to use the dropper. We watched another lump of food work from the beak down Ethan's throat.

I put my fingers to my lips. "*Ssssh!*"

Peep peep peep.

"He likes me, Allen." Mandy smiled baby-sparrow wide.

I grinned too.

He was starting to grow feathers.

We talked for hours on the roof of the gymnasium after feeding Ethan. The sun set over the Foothill Freeway and was replaced by lines of taillights. Floodlights on the football field glowed against the dusk. The Spartan Marching Band played Sousa marches, practicing for Friday; a private band concert. Nobody even knew we listened.

We held hands, like we were children riding together on the school bus. Something about it made me feel at home. But Mandy sensed a tension, perhaps stiffness in my grip. "You seem—preoccupied," she said. "What's on your mind, Allen?"

"San Marino," I told Mandy. *She was so easy to talk to.* I'd learned to trust her. I didn't have to put up force fields. She didn't talk a lot. She listened. And when she did, Mandy accepted me. I was content to sit and watch the night awaken.

"You'll do fine, Allen. You always do. Isn't your team still undefeated?"

"Only so far," I said. "San Marino's different. They're like State Champions; tops in C.I.F., the King Kongs of Cross Country."

"That was last year."

I shook my head. "They've been number one for decades. You should see their trophy case. It's like their coach plans to collect the entire set."

"So? Ruin his day."

"You don't get it. At La Cañada, nobody gives a flying Frito about cross country. But San Marino? It's San Marino's national pastime. They got this one guy—this José Lopez."

Mandy looked at me, head cocked.

"He's like the top guy in Peru. They imported him as an ASF exchange student to run cross country. I mean the guy trains in the Andes two miles above sea level. His lungs are huge. He's an Olympian. Put him at sea level and he's turbocharged; probably runs a quarter-mile on one breath."

"Oh." Mandy swallowed. She was beginning to understand.

"And—we have to race at Lacy Park. They've never lost there. We were supposed to race the Hill, but it got outlawed. Lacy Park makes you feel like you're this English pony at Ascot.

"Allen, please."

"You run in circles on the grass till you get dizzy. All these old San Marino biddies who raise the money to import guys like José Lopez come over from the Huntington to watch cross country. They sit at tea tables in flowered dresses and place bets on all us runners. Even the cheerleaders at San Marino High show up to boo us."

She squeezed my hand. "Can I ask you a question?"

"Sure."

"What do you look at when you race?"

"I—I dunno."

"Yes you do." She squeezed my hand a little harder. "What do you look at when you're racing?"

"The Wocky's jersey," I replied.

"Maybe you should look at something else."

"Like what? I mean his jersey's right in front of me big as a movie screen. I can't exactly look behind me."

"What if you look *beyond* the Wocky. See what's out there."

"No one there but José Lopez."

"Then you need to look at *his* jersey."

"I'd need binoculars," I said.

"Focus on some one in front of Lopez. Make somebody up."

"Who?"

"Ethan Frome. Pretend he's running in front of Lopez."

"Sure, Mandy."

"Just do it. Imagine you're passing Ethan Frome. It'll help you beat the Wocky. I want to see you beat the Wocky."

I shook my head. "The Wock's my teammate. He's—well, you dunno how good he is. Just 'cause some Peruvian guy is better."

"I'll be there watching you."

"What?"

"What time's your San Marino meet?"

"Three o'clock. You're still in class."

"It's trigonometry. I'll ditch. Besides, who cares about arctangents?"

"Mandy...."

"Allen, I've never seen you race."

It occurred to me, at that moment, I preferred to race in private. I liked when nobody showed up to my races. Not that there'd be much to watch if we were racing on the Hill. She'd see me take off from the starting line. She'd wait nine minutes and 40 seconds and watch me choke at the last minute when Ivan and Snooge kicked past me. But Lacy Park was even worse. She could see the whole darned race.

"Maybe, I want you to win," she said. "Maybe, for once you need to finish higher than fifth."

"It's not that easy."

"I'm trying to help you. You need to help your team beat San Marino."

I felt uncomfortable. I hadn't asked for her help. I didn't like finishing fifth, but then again, I'd gotten used to it. It was cozy; my place in the scheme of civilization. Finishing higher might upset the natural order. There could be unintended consequences.

I changed the subject.

By eight at night, the marching band had finished their rehearsal. Mandy and I observed them from the roof as they dispersed. Two sophomores waited for rides, their band-hat shakos beneath their arms. When floodlights blinked off from the field, the night seemed so much darker. Even little Ethan had stopped peeping.

A car door slammed, a Corvair screeched off with two sophomores and their tubas, and all was silent.

"Allen?" Mandy sounded upset.

"What Mandy?"

Crickets screeched below.

"How do we get down?"

"Same way we got up."

"I'm scared of heights."

"But you got up here."

"I know. I can go up. Just can't climb down."

I sucked in a deep breath. "Well, what do you wanna do? I can't just leave you here. What am I supposed to do, call in a helicopter, Mandy?"

"Allen...."

"Why'd you come up here if you're scared to climb back down?" I paused. I didn't want to sound self-righteous.

"I'm sorry." She looked dismayed. "I just wanted to see your bird."

"Just climb down one step at a time. It's not that hard."

"I can't."

"And you thought men were impossible."

"Allen my forearms. They're all cramped."

I felt her arms, and they were tied up like a pair of Gordian knots.

"I'll help you," I said, not sure how I'd do this.

I strolled over to the hatch, and it was locked.

Locked?

"Uh-oh." I rattled the hatch. "Oh no!" I shook it. She must have closed the thing behind her. I never closed it. I didn't know it was....

...self-locking.

I gulped.

"Crap, Mandy were screwed."

"What, Allen? What's wrong?"

"You closed the hatch."

"I wasn't supposed to?"

"No-oooo! Now, we're stuck up here."

"Oh!"

The sound of Mandy's 'oh' thudded across the roof like a basketball trying to bounce after it's flat. She looked at me in horror. "I'm so sorry, Allen. I didn't know. What do we do now?"

"I'll think of something." I sat down, not in my best mood. Below us, north of the gym, concrete flatwork ringed the library where the janitor had found Ethan after he'd busted his leg. The pyracanthas were too thorny and too low to break our fall. On the west side—hard asphalt. On the east side, steps and concrete. To the south, 30 feet below the south eave of the gym roof, a swimming pool was gleaming full of water.

My mind raced with calculations. I'd jumped 30 feet before. Wasn't a ten-meter platform even more than 30 feet? And all those Acapulco diver dudes who wore those Timex watches. They jumped off cliffs, and it didn't seem to kill them.

I'd seen the Wocky do it on paint crew. But I was too chicken myself. Except I had to get us down, at least get *me* down.

I snapped my fingers. "I got it. You won't even need your arms, Mandy."

"How?" She sounded doubtful.

I pointed toward the pool. "I'll show you."

She shook her head. "Allen, you're crazy. That water's fifty feet...."

I scooted down the roof slope, feeling my heartbeat in my throat.

I held my nose.

I closed my eyes.

And then I jumped.

For a moment I felt suspended as I plummeted toward the swimming pool. It was almost like *Butch Cassidy* where they fall down in slow motion. I opened my eyes and watched the pool zoom toward me, and I whooped.

Sploosh! Pool water engulfed me in its wings, and I descended to the bottom of the deep end. Pressure squeezed against my eardrums. Water filled my nose. Air from my pants bubbled upward. I popped my head up from the surface, feeling a stinging on my back. "Come on down, Mandy."

"Are you crazy?"

I shook my head. Water splashed out from my hair. "Just do it. Or spend the night up there. Your choice."

She stood rigid, as if pondering her decision. I'd seen gargoyles that weren't half as stiff as Mandy.

"Allen," she said. "I'll make a deal."

"What?" This was *her problem*. She'd closed the hatch. She was the one afraid of heights.

"What deal? Just jump."

"I'm afraid of heights. You're afraid to finish higher than fifth place. If I jump, Allen, you have to beat the Wocky."

"I can't beat him. He's scholarship material."

"Make the promise."

She pouted on the roof, looking sadder than even Ethan. How did I get into these messes? Did any good deed go unpunished? Mandy was even better than Lovely Leta at wangling promises.

I could lie. But I had never lied to Mandy.

If I did, I'd be—like Heather.

"Promise me, Allen. Cross your heart. Hope to die."

"Okay."

"Stick a needle in your eye?"

"Okay," I lied.

My throat collapsed. I could almost feel my nose grow.

Mandy screamed. Mandy leaped....

She did a bullseye in the deep-end, toes cutting the water without a ripple. When her head popped to the surface she was laughing.

We were soaked. The only towels I saw were on the deck and waterlogged.

She shook her hair. I looked away from nipples pointing through her blouse. Her pants bloated around her legs. She paddled toward me, throwing her knee up on the pool deck.

"How do we dry off?"

I shook out water on the pool deck like a dog shakes out his fur. I snapped a wet towel toward Mandy. "Let's run." She took off chasing me across the field around the backstops where the baseball diamonds backed up to Oak Grove Drive. She was running like an ocelot. Minimum motion. Smooth as glass.

She had learned her lesson well. Occam's Razor.

I'd never seen a girl run quite as fast as Mandy. It was scary. She ran as fast as I did. She chased me for twenty minutes until I noticed we were dry. I wished I'd never shown her Occam's Razor.

Mandy's Volkswagen wouldn't start. We didn't care. I drove her home. My Yamaha 60 whined like a small gas-powered lawnmower. It ran slooooow, but it felt good to feel her arms around my waist.

And then it dawned on me. I'd kept the promise I'd given Leta to befriend Mandy.

But how would I keep my promise to beat the Wocky?

CHAPTER TEN

BALL OF CONFUSION

LA CAÑADA HIGH SCHOOL: TUESDAY, NOVEMBER 10TH, 1970
(213 DAYS TO GRADUATION!)

I was never really sure whether the game against the football team had been the Jabberwocky's brainstorm or Coach Harron's bright idea. I hadn't even known about it until we suited up for workout, pinching our noses to keep from smelling whatever lived in Snoogey's locker. Coach Neal was at some coaching workshop down in San Diego. I'd expected we'd be running to Verdugo Park and back.

The Wocky strolled into the locker room with a box of beat-up football pads. He was grinning. He had something up his sleeve. He dropped a junior varsity jersey in front of every runner's locker, Booboo's, Ivan's, Snooge's, Psycho's, mine.

"'S up Wock? Neal want us runnin' in pads or somethin'?" I asked.

He shook his head.

"Then, what?" said Ivan.

The Wock threw pads at Ivan and a second set at me. "Getcher pads on. We're playin' football."

"What?" we said in unison.

"Football," Wocky said. "You know that sport with the pointed ball? I made a deal with Coach Harron. We play the football team in football.

"Tackle? Today?"

The Wock nodded. "They win, I get my hair cut."

"What's the point?" said Booboo. "Go ahead and cut your hair."

"*We* win—we get the cheerleaders," the Wocky said.

"Cheerleaders? No way. You must be smokin' dope," I said.

"You're crazy," said Snooge. "I haven't played football since junior high."

"Cheerleaders, Snooge. Think cheerleaders. Trust me, I got this wired. We beat the football team, and those fatsos'll be ashamed to go to pep rallies. What kind of football team loses to cross country?"

"Yeah!" I loved it. I hated pep rallies and cheering for football "heroes" while no one ever mentioned we existed.

"We haven't beat 'em yet," Snooge reminded us, in a voice filled with more caution than I liked.

"I have a plan—" the Wocky said "—to win."

"To what?"

"To beat those egocentric blimps. You need a dictionary, Booboo? Win. It means you score more points than they do."

"Count me out." said Booboo.

"No, wait a minute," I said. "What's your plan, Wock?"

The Wocky whispered, "Endurance."

Our six jaws dropped in unison. It suddenly seemed possible. We were spellbound. How come we'd never even thought of it? While the football team ate donuts, and drank Gatorade, and talked to cheerleaders and listened to Harron call us weenies and bark out the word "discipline," while they lathered themselves with privilege, we ran twenty miles a day.

Endurance.

I faced Booboo. "We can do this, guys," I whispered.

"We have discipline in spades. Four years of torture with no Gatorade or cheerleaders or donuts." Talk about "Spartans," Coach Neal might even have invented the term himself.

Booboo looked at me and smiled. "Endurance."

It was brilliant. I led the team in chanting the word "endurance," until the Wocky had to tell us to calm down.

"Listen up," he said.

The Wocky laid it on the line. "I bet my hair we can stick it to Coach Harron just this once." If we beat his team in *football*, you think the school renews his contract? He embarrasses us. Insults us. You want Harron to get tenure?"

We shook our heads in unison. We felt exactly like the Wock did. Except we hadn't bet our hair and Wocky had. He had stood up for us. This was more than just a scrimmage.

This was more than even cheerleaders.

This was—revenge. Nobody even had to say the word.

Harron had squished our egos. Harron didn't like us. Coach Harron was eating crow in 60 minutes.

I remembered how that man had called me dickwad more than once, the day he'd told our class I'd die in Vietnam, the day he'd twisted my sore arm after I'd thrown a piece of ton cake. I wanted this jerkwad. I wanted that man *out* of La Cañada.

"So whadda we do, Wock?" It was plainer than white yogurt we were pumped. Four years of insults. Four years of slander festered to the surface.

"Every play—" the Wocky whispered "—we make 'em run. We make 'em play against our strength. We lateral. We sweep. We pass. Anything we can do to make their hearts pound. Make 'em pant. Make 'em sweat. Make their sides ache."

"You mean they chase us?"

"Just like Keystone Cops," the Wocky said. "We play keep-away. We tease these guys. We make 'em think they'll catch us. Make 'em work. Wear 'em out. The last second, dash away. And if we get stuck on fourth down, I kick a field goal."

It was genius, and nobody kicked field goals like the Jabberwocky. Cheerleaders! I almost saw them getting on our team bus, calling our names out, cheering for *us!* Finally giving us the respect we'd need to face San Marino at Lacy Park.

"Listen I've had it with these turkeys." I spoke up. "I wanna beat these Pillsbury doughboys. Aren't you pissed at how we're treated?"

We were pissed.

"Then get your pads on. Kickoff's in twenty minutes. We don't show up, then Harron's right to call us pussies."

We dressed in silence, saving all our energy. If the Wocky had stuck his neck out, we'd stick our necks out to support him. From the silence that passed between us you could almost feel the anger that had jelled since freshman year against Coach Harron's primadonnas.

Somebody whistled.

Garry Jackson and Pudge McMasters had donned their jerseys. Garry called out, "You ready for us —l-l-ladies?"

I smelled the grass cuttings. The football field was freshly mowed and watered, and we walked along the track behind the Jabberwocky. Coach Harron strutted along the sidelines, glaring across the gridiron, figuring his football team would teach us all a lesson. His Army Airborne tattoos throbbed with expectation, and his flat top wiggled at the prospect of--at last--winning a game. He hadn't won a game all season. Here was his chance to win a scrimmage and force the Jabberwocky to shave his flowing hair.

Harron led the football team in jumping jacks. His team excelled at jumping jacks. It was one thing, besides haircuts, they were good at.

"Atta boys," the Wocky mumbled. "Jumpin' jack your eyes out. Do several thousand. Use up your stamina. Wear yourselves out before the kickoff."

The rest of us walked quietly. We had no energy to waste. It was game time, and none of us were any good at football.

Our pads stuck out like wings on scrawny shoulders. In position, we looked like seagulls in formation.

"Just remember," the Jabberwocky whispered. "Endurance."

The word echoed in my brain. I mumbled it like a mantra to stop flutters in my stomach. I sucked at football. Half my football pads were sliding down my legs.

I pulled them back up, tightening a strap.

We won the coin toss. Poetic justice.

Someone kicked the ball to Ivan. Ivan picked it off the grass and threw a lateral to Booboo. Eleven players raced toward Booboo, who waited.

Then he lobbed the ball to Psycho, and when two tackles tracked him down, he lobbed to Rattfink, who swept around the left. Rattfink handed off to me, and I zig-zagged to the rear, hearing football players puffing just to breathe. I handed off to Wocky. We were cornered at midfield. He lateraled to Booboo, and the ball went out of bounds.

First and ten.

The football players were panting.

"Great work. Don't let 'em catch their breaths," the Wocky called. "No huddle. Same play. Same line-up. Razzle-dazzle." He clapped his hands.

Booboo centered.

The Wocky faded right, and just before they tackled him, he passed to Snooge, who flicked the ball to me.

I swept left. I jogged slow. I let Pudge McMasters get close, then I gunned it.

Touchdown.

Six-zip. Cross country.

It felt sweet, but it was too early to celebrate.

The Wocky kicked the extra point, and we had seven.

Like the world's meanest toothpick, the Wocky glared down-field and landed a kick into the coffin corner. We swarmed downfield like gulls. Garry Jackson scooped the ball up. We jumped on top of him, weighing him down like a cloud of little backpacks. Garry stumbled for ten yards before collapsing from exhaustion.

First and ten. The football team huddled to catch their breaths.

I had no idea why Stan Cunningham threw the football on first down. Too big for us to tackle, Stan could have walked the ball downfield. Instead, he threw a pass.

From nowhere, the Jabberwocky leaped in front of Pudge McMasters, jumping kangaroo-style, snagging the football, mid-air. He ran backward, holding the ball up, taunting half a dozen linemen, who chased him downfield. The Wocky spun, and McMasters slipped and fell.

Wock swept around him, dashing sideways.

He flicked to Snooge.

"Endurance," the Wocky yelled while Snooge zigzagged back and forth, until five linemen surrounded him like arms upon a starfish. Booboo raced between them, allowing Snooge to fake a handoff. They chased Booboo. Snooge whirled and got away. Snooge handed to Ivan, who handed off to Psycho, and we played keep-away for a minute and a half. Finally Psycho flicked to Ivan, who walked the ball into the end zone.

The football team bent over from exhaustion.

Cheerleaders. We could almost see them getting on our team bus. Harron paced up the sidelines. He was pissed. I imagined our cheerleaders having to learn our names so they could cheer for us when we raced San Marino.

Harron blew his whistle. He stormed onto the field. "I thought you cross country weenies played football—" Harron said "—not some candy-ass brand of keep-away. This is bullshit."

Booboo centered the ball while Harron talked.

Wocky kicked.

The football sizzled past Harron. Had it passed closer it might have peeled an Airborne tattoo from Harron's forearm. The ball shot between the goalposts.

"Fourteen-zip," the Wocky whispered.

Harron's head sank. "Damn it."

Psycho ran downfield to get the ball, kicking his heels like a leprechaun on speed.

The Wocky shook his hair and stared, flipping off Coach Harron, twirling the football on his middle fingertip and grinning. He tossed the ball to Booboo who lined up to center.

Veins in Harron's neck began to bulge.

Screeeeeeee! Coach Harron whistled a time out.

For five minutes, football players argued with Coach Harron. Lots of whispering. It was clear they weren't too happy. The discussions became louder. Players voiced objections.

"Shut up." Harron's voice. He glared at all his players until their chins dropped.

They caught their breaths and lined up across the scrimmage line while Harron calmly strolled off of the field toward the locker room.

Booboo centered.

Ivan placed.

The Wocky kicked the ball.

And then, the football team emptied their benches.

Though there were twenty of us, seven varsity, seven J.V.'s and six freshmen, only eleven of us at a time were on the field. There were *fifty* on the football team. Out of shape, but still outweighing us, all fifty stampeded onto the grass.

We stared back like eleven deer in headlights.

They hollered like Comanches, surrounding us and charging. After the Wocky kicked the football, nobody was near the goal. I wriggled free and ran downfield, picked the ball up and walked it into the end-zone.

Then I saw.

The whole football team had piled on the Jabberwocky—fifty football players had stacked up on his knees and on his elbows. Arms and fists and elbows swung in all directions. The Wocky squirmed and screamed. "My finger! You wrecked my finger."

Coach Harron was nowhere to be seen.

No one saw except the football team and us. No one knew who hurt the Wocky. Horror filled my veins. I saw why players had objected. They had to do what they were told. If they rebelled, they might not letter this year in football.

I ran downfield and helplessly yanked on football players' pads, trying to pull the bodies off the pile. A hand smashed against my lip. An elbow stung my temple. Someone knocked me across Ivan who had a gash across his forehead.

At last a football player whistled between his teeth, and guys climbed off.

The Wocky moaned.

My heart climbed up my throat.

When the last guy crawled off the pile, the Jabberwocky was unconscious. The rest of us had our own wounds to attend to.

The Wocky's scalp was bleeding. They'd torn out several pieces of his hair. Both the Wocky's eyes and half his nose were swollen shut. They'd torn his finger from its socket. It was bent out of position, dangling where it would never flip Coach Harron off again.

Kurt Hansen strolled over to the Wocky after the Wock began to move, spitting beside him. For all I knew, Kurt might have aimed and missed. He yanked the Jabberwocky from his back up to his feet using his hair. A hush had descended onto the field.

We crowded around the Wocky, and he was wobbling. Booboo and I had to carry him between us. He was silent, and limping. His hand was turning black.

Ivan's face was washed with blood. Snooge's forehead had a lump on it. My lower lip was swollen like a strawberry.

The football team walked slowly to the locker room. Kurt Hansen whispered to Psycho. "Better keep your mouths shut. This little scrimmage never happened."

I lowered my head. glancing at Ivan, and he stared back at me. San Marino was in ten days. The Wocky's right knee puffed above his shin, swollen the color of eggplant. I worried whether the Wocky could even run.

And then we knew there were no cheerleaders or pep rallies for us. There was no cosmic referee to blow the whistle or call penalties. We were trapped like Ethan Frome in a whole high school run by Zeenas.

We were velcroids. And they were teflonistas.

The one bright spot of my day was feeding Ethan. I scooted toward him across the gym roof, glad for a comforting evening breeze. The fuzz that had once covered him was filling out with feathers. I kept looking for Ethan's parents, but they never came to find him. He was my step-bird. I hoped someday he might fly.

Gulps of blueberries and spaghetti wormed down Ethan's throat. He was excited and seemed especially glad to see me. I felt like Ethan read my mood and saw I needed cheering up.

Peep-peep-peep.

"Thanks, Ethan." His chirp sounds made me happy.

I screwed the lid back on his food jar and scooted across the roof, waving goodbye, wishing Ethan could wave back at me. He was my little island of sanity in a world I didn't fit in. I wished that I could join him in his nest.

But I couldn't. My arms were cold now. I scrambled toward the roof hatch, closing it behind me and scurrying down the ladder. I grabbed my bike bag and wandered toward the motorcycle cage.

Crap!

Some jerk had ripped off another gas cap from my Yamaha.

I grabbed a spare from my bike bag and replaced the stolen cap. I kicked the starter and rode away, feeling my bruises from my pads, and hoped the Wocky could still run against San Marino.

CHAPTER ELEVEN

TURN BACK THE HANDS OF TIME
LA CAÑADA HIGH SCHOOL: FRIDAY, NOVEMBER 20TH, 1970
(203 DAYS TO GRADUATION!)

Race day. I hadn't eaten anything since breakfast. My stomach gurgled in its ritual self-digestion. I stared into my gym locker like it was ninety inches deep, found my honey tube, and in 30 seconds sucked out all its contents. Temples throbbing, heart nerves twitching, I struggled to relax.

San Marino.

In my mind, I'd run my heat a thousand times. Even in my dreams, I'd never pictured myself winning. It was hard to imagine myself even finishing fifth. That Peruvian, who'd placed second in the Pan American Games, was headed for the Olympics. José Lopez was unstoppable. I had to beat Ivan Alphabet or Snooge to finish fifth. I'd promised Mandy I'd beat the Wocky, and nobody beat the Wocky, except for Lopez.

Nobody.

And Mandy was coming to watch *me*.

Instead of going to the pep rally and cheering for Harron's blimp fleet, she had to drive to Lacy Park to see me prove I was a liar. I'd never beaten the Jabberwocky since I'd met him in sixth grade. I had as much chance at the Wocky as a basset hound at Indy had of catching Bobby Unser on a straightaway.

I wished I hadn't told Mandy where the race was. Her interest in my races was flattering but annoying. If I hadn't given Mandy that stupid promise I'd beat the Wocky, she'd probably still be on that roof, and she'd be leaving me alone.

The bell rang. Seventh period. *Crap!* In ninety minutes, our meet started. Seconds ticked off in my temples. My head ached. I'd lied to Mandy. My whole season was on the line. Compressed into nine minutes and change, the two-mile race loomed before me like that whale that had swallowed up Pinocchio.

Monstro. That was its name. Monstro the Mighty Whale. My thoughts funneled into a whirlpool of nerves. I closed my eyes, seeing ribs inside the roof of Monstro's mouth, feeling gastric juices sear my throat. *Don't psyche out,* I kept repeating, which had the opposite effect, like trying not to think of Monstro after he'd swallowed me. The stench from whatever life form grew inside of Snooge's locker washed over me and jarred me to reality.

Lockers were slamming all around me. Seconds ticked off in my temples. Ivan Alphabet sucked a tube of Sue Bee honey down for energy. The Jabberwocky, whose bandaged knee was swollen bigger than a volleyball popped pain pills until his eyes glazed over so cloudy I couldn't read him. I was afraid he wasn't with us. Booboo paced back and forth, flapping his shoes against the concrete.

I pinched myself. *Focus.* My knuckles tightened. My knees whitened, prickling into a moonscape of tiny goose bumps.

Neal strolled into the locker room, shaking his head. "Hey, listen up, guys. We got a problem."

"Problem?" Our heads jerked up in unison. Like our meet wasn't enough?

"What now?" sighed Snooge.

"No team bus."

"Hunnnh?" we groaned in eight-part harmony. Here was the biggest meet of our lives, and our Director of Student Activities, in all his wisdom, hadn't even booked a bus.

"Doesn't Conrad know Lacy Park's in San Marino?"

"He says this week's a home meet," Neal said.

"What a dipshit!"

Clearly, the running gods had joined the other side, outlawing the Hill, taking away our bus, appointing Conrad the Dipshit our Student Activities Director. To get to Lacy Park, twenty runners of all sizes would have to pack into Neal's Volkswagen Minibus like circus clowns.

After unbolting Neal's van seats and hauling them to the locker room, our arms cramped. We were so wound up, even the Wocky was stone silent. We donned our uniforms like businessmen, pulling sweats across our silks. No words passed between us as we packed into the van.

I was on the bottom, lying on my back. A carriage bolt dug deep into my shoulder.

Focus.

Booboo farted. No one laughed or groaned.

Focus.

I closed my eyes to keep from staring at Psycho's armpit. I breathed as shallow as I could. Snooge's running shoes smelled worse than Booboo's farts or Psycho's body odor. I closed my eyes. I didn't want to stare at sweat stains.

The Volkswagen engine grumbled. Neal's minibus rolled onto Oak Grove Drive. I felt the Foothill Freeway on-ramp; the rumbling of the axle beneath my head from I-210; the California Street off-ramp; a stoplight I couldn't see; a light; another stoplight. I felt acceleration and braking underneath me through the curves as Neal navigated the streets of Pasadena.

A left-turn signal. Lacy Park. Twenty minutes until our race. There was no time to find Mandy.

My temples pounded, bulging in and out with every heartbeat. I jogged to loosen up, trying to laugh, trying to smile, studying the course, three oval laps around the grass at Lacy Park, before we lined up at the starting line.

We waited.

Focus.

Puke rose in my throat. Thirteen runners lined up beside me, twitching like anxious fingers on triggers. I looked at Lopez.

Bang!

When the starting pistol sounded, it seemed a gallon of adrenaline detonated to power my legs across the grass at Lacy

Park. I exploded through the heat, fighting a river of sharp elbows. Adrenaline. I had to stretch it through nine minutes and a half. I couldn't run my usual time. *Don't think about time. Just run into the pain. Occam's Razor.*

My reputation as "official Indy pace boy" had preceded me. San Marino runners hung on me like fruit flies. After a half-mile, Lopez sprinted forward. I let him go.

Lopez was gone.

The rest of us crunched together. I conceded first place to Lopez and fought to place distance between me and twelve runners behind me. Sweat washed across my eyes. Gnats collected in my throat. I didn't hurt. I had to hurt more. My only chance was to out-ache them. My stride lengthened. My arms numbed. Tendons in my legs burned.

"Go, Allen!"

It was Mandy. I couldn't nod. I needed every ounce of strength to run my race. I hurt like hell, except I smiled. *Occam's Razor. Occam's Razor.* We hit a small hill. I lowered my fists, attacking. I trained on hills. I loved hills. I used them to my advantage.

Break out. Build some distance so they can't pass you in the kick.

My sides throbbed, as if that vacuum nature abhorred was in my stomach, sucking all my guts into its dust-bag. My neck pounded. Breaths behind me seemed more distant. I'd opened a lead. I wasn't pace boy. I passed the hillcrest. *Advantage me.*

I had to use it.

"Go, Allen!"

I let the grade carry me forward while it lasted. We passed a lily pond. Ladies in flower-prints from the Huntington with teacups blurred before me. I dropped my head. Greenery spun past my eyes. I ducked around a tree, passed some colored plastic flags, leaning forward, almost falling, running until my arms ached and tingled from no blood, until my head spun. My legs, my arms, my hair flapped in the wind.

I breathed faster. Air seared my throat. I circled my head and dropped my wrists, reaching, trying to run beyond the pain. I blinked my eyes and stared at Lopez, a hundred yards in front. I stretched my stride. Sweat poured into my eyes.

I had no kick. My only chance was to escape from the pack—now.

Now!

I passed the mile. I was dying.

Where was Wocky?

By all rights, I should have heard him, and I didn't.

"Go, Allen. C'mon. C'mon. You can do it. You can do it." Mandy cheered for me. I could feel Mandy loaning me her strength. I pressed the straightaway and felt like when I'd jumped over the pool. A surreal calm engulfed me.

I had to push. I had to widen my lead. If I didn't, the others would out-sprint me in the kick.

Lopez faded out of sight.

After a mile and a half, the Wocky hadn't passed me. I reached down in my gut to pull out all the strength I had, to keep my place for every yard, widening my lead, adding distance ahead of those who lagged behind me.

My side ached. My head spun. Footsteps faded behind me. I tried to think of my advantage. I had no cast now. My arms felt light. I ran faster without a cast.

Tendons ached in my left leg. Back muscles wrenched. Sides knotted and cramped. I breathed faster, harder. My vision blurred in gray-green spirals. Smog burned in my lungs.

Footsteps.

Sweat flowed across my face. I saw the chute. Far up in front, Lopez hit the tape and won.

Footsteps.

Booboo zipped past me.

Footsteps.

Ivan Alphabet wiggled past me, elbowing, thrashing toward the finish line.

More footsteps pounded.

"Go, Allen. Goooooo, Allen."

"Martian, move your ass," yelled Neal.

Breathing.

Breathing.

I leaned forward.

Breathing on my ear.

I didn't dare look back. *Run into the pain. Make yourself hurt. Hurt. Hurt. Lean forward.*

"Go, San Marino. Go, San Marino."

"No, Allen, no."

"Martian, you weenie!"

David Prentice from San Marino stretched his legs and thrust his chest out, elbowing in front of me in the chute to grab my stick.

I thought I'd beat him.

Maybe we'd tied.

Prentice grabbed stick number four and ran away, waving my stick over his head.

"YOU HAMBURGER!" Neal exploded. "My grandmother could beat you with a walker."

I got the next stick, with horrible number five. *Dreadful, awful, horrible, terrible, abysmal number five.* Coach Neal crawled all over me. "You hamburger! You weenie!"

Five.

My sides collapsed. Crowds spun around me.

Five.

My head buzzed.

Mandy called my name.

I gotta puke, Mandy. Just go away and let me puke.

I found a bathroom. Thank God for toilets. I slipped into a stall. I put my head between my knees and writhed in agony.

Fifth place.

I slid the latch shut on my stall door. I placed my hands across my head. I wanted to sink into the toilet bowl and flush myself away. I imagined myself funneling down a counter-clockwise vortex. My finish replayed in my mind. *Booboo and Ivan sprinted past me. David Prentice from San Marino stuck his chest out and grabbed my stick.*

I didn't want to talk to Neal....

...or Mandy....

...or anybody.

I opened my stall door.

David Prentice stood outside. "Nice effort man. You ran better than we expected." He shook my hand.

"Thanks." I smiled politely and tiptoed outside from the bathroom, wiping my hand off on my shorts when no one saw me. I almost wished he'd flipped me off. I was pissed that he was gracious. But then again, he could afford it. I'd just handed him the victory.

José Lopez bounced in his Adidas. San Marino cheerleaders kissed his cheeks. They passed out laurel wreaths like candy. Their coach wore one, over his suit. All San Marino's runners had them. Even old ladies in flowered dresses pranced around like those pompous Grecian Urn ladies in *The Music Man*. An entourage of girls in chiffon dresses giggled past me.

I'd lost the race. Thanks to me, San Marino was ecstatic. I saw the headlines:

LA CAÑADA TEEN CROWNED WORTHLESS LOSER.
JOINS RANKS OF GUTLESS WEENIES.

There'd be my name on the centerfold of the *La Cañada Valley Sun* on a ready-to-tear-out dartboard with my face on it.

The race results were posted on their gazebo on blue posterboard.

RESULTS: SAN MARINO HIGH VS LA CAÑADA HIGH

1st	Lopez	San Marino	1 pt	9 minutes 7 seconds
2nd	Booboo	La Cañada	2 pts	9 minutes 27 seconds
3rd	Alphabet	La Cañada	3 pts	9 minutes 28 seconds
4th	Prentice	San Marino	4 pts	9 minutes 30 seconds
5th	Martian	La Cañada	5 pts	9 minutes 30.1 seconds

6th	Casey	San Marino	6 pts	9 minutes 37 seconds
7th	Nelson	San Marino	7 pts	9 minutes 38 seconds
8th	Snooge	La Cañada	8 pts	9 minutes 41 seconds
9th	Baccellia	San Marino	9 pts	9 minutes 48 seconds
10th	Jabberwocky	La Cañada	10 pts	10 minutes 2 seconds

Total Points

San Marino	27 pts
La Cañada	8 pts

I'd blown the race. I'd blown the entire cross country season. From hero to zero in zero-point-one seconds. I was surprised they hadn't circled my name in fat red Marks-a-Lot with arrows pointing to my name and spelling "Loser."

I clenched my stick trying to rub out the number five. Before they asked for it, I broke it into pieces, mincing it with my fingernails. I shredded woodchips into splinters, ground splinters into sawdust with my shoe heels. I pestled splinters into powder.

Someone asked me for my stick back. I pointed to the sawdust and said they'd have to make a new one or glue the old one back together. The freshman-sophomores were running. The meet chairperson panicked.

Somewhere beneath my pain, even my anger felt pathetic.

They cut a new stick out of cardboard from a "San Marino Spirit" poster.

I didn't even watch the final race.

After the frosh-soph race was over, and we'd been swept by San Marino, Coach Neal locked the slide door on his minibus to keep us out. He burned rubber out the parking lot and squealed off through San Marino. We stared out at the asphalt by the bathrooms at Lacy Park. Getting home would be on us, now. We could walk home, we could hitch-hike or we could run.

I looked at Ivan. He and Booboo started running. Mandy walked up and rubbed my shoulder. "You wanna talk?" she said. "Need a ride?"

I shook my head. "I wanna die."

"Allen?"

"Leave me alone."

I shook my head and walked away, sucking back tears. I didn't deserve her sympathy or ride.

She slammed her door and cranked the engine, puttering off in her Volkswagen. Part of me wanted to be with her. Most of me didn't.

The Wocky limped across the lawn beside me at Lacy Park, past tea tables and gazebos and girls in flowered dresses. One called us names and stuck her tongue out. I wanted to flip her off, afraid if I didn't, the Wocky would rip her tongue out.

He didn't. I didn't either. We jogged along Virginia Road. The twilight made us shiver in our running silks. We climbed the grade to Old Mill Lane, which ran downhill to Pasadena. At Oak Knoll, we hung a right and passed the Huntington Hotel.

Pinehurst, El Molino, Glenarm. Streets wound through Pasadena. Lincoln Continentals and Jaguars drifted past us. Georgian homes with colonnades loomed beyond wide circle driveways. Deodars and cypresses guarded mansions. My sides ached. But I deserved this. I was a loser.

And for once, I had to slow down for the Wocky.

His leg had swollen huge. There was a welt, big as a grapefruit, beneath the bandage. His thigh had darkened to a bloody shade of brown. With every step, his leg wobbled. I wondered how it held together.

"Screw him," the Wocky screamed when we ran downhill on Glenarm. "FUUUUUUUUCK HIM. Fuck that bastard, Harron."

I didn't answer.

The Jabberwocky was loaded up on painkillers. "Fuck that asshole," he said again.

We found our rhythm. Running together, it was almost like our souls touched, and I took some of his pain. We breathed in unison. Our footsteps found a cadence. For a moment, my anger and self-hatred were forgotten, and I felt as if the Wocky and I were friends.

"Feel like crap?" I asked.

He nodded. "You?"

I nodded back.

"Course you feel crappy. You ran your ass off, Alien."

"I lost, Wock."

"Bullshit, Alien. You ran the best race of your life."

"Still lost."

The Wock glared at me. "Who cares?"

He shook his head back and forth like a bobble-head doll, scolding me. "This high school's totally whacked out, Martian. Don'tcha see? Harron and all his football-heads can't even take a joke."

I let him ramble. He unloaded like I'd pulled back on the pull cord on a chainsaw and let him uncork all the hatred he'd bottled up since seventh grade. Every put-down, every slam, every broken heart. "Judy Whitmore, Susan Angard, Candy Reinhart with those hooters."

"Candy was a babe, Wock. I mean seriously hot."

"No lie," he said. "Shame she moved to La Crescenta."

We followed Glenarm—to Fair Oaks—to Bellefontaine—to Orange Grove Boulevard, and somehow it soothed me knowing our high school was "whacked out." To hear the Jabberwocky say it lent my worldview credibility. Velcroids. Teflonistas. It fit my theory.

Halfway up Orange Grove, I remembered my ride with Mandy. I hoped she didn't hate me, but I'd been too self-absorbed to talk. I remembered our first evening, when we'd climbed Flint Peak together.

The Wocky interrupted with more chatter.

At Colorado, we hung a left. My footsteps and the Wocky's marched in cadence, keeping better time than the Spartan Marching Band. I turned to him. "You look serious."

"Serious as a heart attack," he said.

"'Bout what?"

"'Bout this novel I'm gonna write," he said. 'Bout La Cañada. 'Bout all the social climbers and jocks who screw us over. Gonna call it *Awful-Awful Time* after those milkshakes at John Henry's. Neal'll be in it with his minibus and stopwatch."

"No kiddin? How 'bout Conrad the Dipshit?" I asked.

Wocky nodded. "He'll be in it. Coach Harron'll be there big time. Dumber than a chainsaw. Moron couldn't read an M&M and pass a test on what he'd read. I'll kill him off, Martian. Maybe I'll kill myself off too."

"Am I in it?"

"Don't know yet. You wanna be?"

"Just don't kill me off."

The Wocky laughed.

It was the first time I'd heard the Wocky's laugh sound sick. "What the hell," he said. "I can't run, Alien. My knee's wrecked all to hell."

He seemed so bitter. I was starting to feel uneasy.

He exhaled a long sick Norman Bates-ish laugh. He stopped running and started limping. He tore the bandage from his knee. "Check this out." He slipped his knee out, then slid it back into its socket without a pop. "I mean I'm screwed. It's a wonder I can walk. He grabbed a eucalyptus nut and tossed it off the bridge. "Thanks to Harron, I get no scholarship—no college—no student deferment."

"How 'bout your parents. Can't they help?" We stopped walking.

Wock glared at me like I'd dropped out of a spaceship. "Parents?"

"You know, those old farts who hang around your house."

"Might as well shave my hair off and sign up for Nam," said the Wocky. "Least Garry Jackson knew the score." The Wock still giggled.

"Whatcha mean, Wock?"

"They call it euthanasia."

"I get it. Youth-in-Asia. But you're four-F with that knee."

"Don't bet on it," said the Wocky. "Not when your draft board is in Hollywood. Bunch of old guys think they're John Q. Friggin' Wayne." More weird laughing. The Wocky sounded higher than a kite.

It started misting.

"Listen, Alien," he whispered. "I gotta stop. Can't keep goin'." His eyes glazed over. "My knee's screamin' like Janis Joplin."

"You okay, Wock?"

"I gotta take this wicked shit. Why'n't you just run on ahead?"

"I'll wait for you."

"Nah, don't. Martian. It's raining. The way my knee hurts, I'll hitchhike. Go on without me."

"I'll wait."

He stopped smiling, as if his painkillers had died.

"Go!" He waved me forward.

I stood beside him in the drizzle.

"Damn it, Martian!" He glared at me with rage and flipped me off. "Fuck you, Alien. Get outta here. Fuck you all to hell. Fuck La Cañada. Fuck Coach Harron." His eyes glared with crazy hatred.

The fury in his eyes could scare the pants off Vincent Price. I dashed up Linda Vista, sprinting through the rain. But it was lonely after that, and cold after the sunset. Gusts from the Arroyo made my cheeks flap in the rainstorm. I stared ahead, running through pain, counting the miles past the Rose Bowl to La Cañada. Rain bleared across my eyes. I told myself, soon as I could, I'd get the Wocky on my Yamaha.

When I got back and climbed up the ladder to the gym roof, Ethan was gone.

CHAPTER TWELVE

BRIDGE OVER TROUBLED WATER

LA CAÑADA HIGH SCHOOL: FRIDAY, NOVEMBER 20TH, 1970
(203 DAYS TO GRADUATION!)

Ethan was gone!

I had his blueberries and pasta in my eyedropper. I'd brought him special fennel seeds I'd found on sale at Thrift-T-Mart.

Ethan was missing.

Not now.

"Please—" I whispered "—not now."

It was dark. I crawled down-ladder. I found a flashlight in the janitor's closet. I scoured the wet pavement, the pyracantha where we'd found him on the day we'd fixed his leg.

I imagined whatever lived in Snooge's locker had come for Ethan, oozing through the locker vents after we'd all gone home from school, swallowing him like the Blob in that ancient Steve McQueen flick. My stomach was wrung in knots, washrag tight.

"Ethan," I called out, listening for little peeps. "Ethan!"

Rain splattered against the pavement.

Maybe a cat had found him.

"ETHAN!"

I searched the bushes again, crawling through mud and listening, flashlight shaking, hoping by chance he might have limped somewhere to safety.

No sparrows. I circled the gym.

Thunder.

I climbed the ladder. I checked again in Ethan's nest.

It was empty. I was the only breathing soul out on the gym roof in the rain. Nobody from high school was in sight.

I didn't believe in God. Mandy knew I was an atheist. But if there was a god (just in case), I had to tell him I was pissed. I shouted from the roof.

"WHAT HAPPENED TO MY SPARROW OR DON'T YOU CARE?"

Silence. It figured. God must live in San Marino. My words muffled into clouds that engulfed the Foothill Freeway.

"WHY DO YOU HATE ME, YOU STOPID GOD? YOU ONLY CARE ABOUT TEFLONISTAS."

No answer. I waited, daring lightning to strike me dead. Blood pounded through my neck. Rain splashed into my eyes. I wanted to spit at God, to throw something and hurt him. I screamed until my voice squeaked, and it was dark, and the moon had crawled halfway across the sky, peeking through clouds. I climbed downladder into the gym. Hearing my shoes squeak on the floor, I locked the gym doors behind me.

Ethan was gone. I'd never know how he had died. After yelling, the inside of my throat felt rough as sandpaper. Then I remembered. The Wocky! I had left him on the bridge.

When I ran out to the lot to find my Yamaha 60, my gas cap had been stolen, and all my gas. There was rainwater in the tank. I kicked the starter. My Yamaha wouldn't start.

My teeth chattered. I was too worn out to care. I pushed the bike to Oak Grove Drive. I had no more extra gas caps. I was stuck here in the rain, having to walk my cycle home. It would be midnight before I reached my doorstep.

On Monday, the Jabberwocky missed second-period English. His beat-up Plymouth Valiant was still parked in its stall. Wocky hadn't called in sick. None of us had seen him. I told Mrs. Zinicola I was concerned.

"Let's just think positive," she reassured me with her Mary Poppins voice, engulfing me in a cloud of cinnamon Lavoris. "We have class now. *Alice in Wonderland.* Have you read last night's assignment?" She straightened her *faux*-pearls and smoothed them out across her turtleneck. "Wasn't it fun?" Her Pepsodent smile flashed wide enough to make even Doris Day uneasy.

Lightning flashed through the windows, followed by a roar. My stomach kept on tightening. I'd been the last to see the Wocky. He'd said he'd hitchhike. Maybe by now, he'd been picked up by Charles Manson. Wock could have overdosed on painkillers, or passed out from his injuries. It wasn't like the Wocky to disappear on us.

The last thing I cared about right now was *Alice in Wonderland.* I took my seat. Mrs. Zinicola read from Chapter

Nine, about some Duchess and how she planned on banning pepper, vinegar and chamomile from her kitchen.

My stomach churned. Worried about the Wocky, I was afraid to raise my hand and get hosed down with Mrs. Z's positive thoughts. I usually liked Mrs. Z. She was a bright spot in a dull school. But today I found her sunny ways annoying.

She wore rose colored glasses (real ones) to school, and it was raining. She had a closet full of miniskirts with hearts on them. Her pink Corvette (the Pepto-Bismobile) matched Barbie's and Ken's sports car. Even her purse was blemished with flocks of smiling bluebirds who suffocated beneath transparent vinyl.

Where was Wock? I was the only kid in class who seemed to worry. Lightning flashed. Thunder rumbled, and Mrs. Z. ignored it. She'd come from some region of Italy that must have been too sunny. Take Mattel's Barbie, add too much pink frosted lipstick, a bouffant, and you had Mrs. Zinicola in her Stepford-esque high heels, oblivious to horny boys who drooled from front-row seats, watching her legs stretch from her high heels up her miniskirt. Happy boys. Happy faces. Happy suffocating bluebirds. I imagined she wore a bra with smiley faces on each D-cup. Only her ragged fingernails, gnawed bloody to the quick, revealed Mrs. Zinicola had more than Wonderland on her mind.

Ivan had told me her husband had some sales job in Burbank, signing up Hanna-Barbera's sponsors for the Saturday cartoons. When he wasn't locked in board meetings with Yogi Freaking Bear, Mr. Zinicola popped by in his Jaguar for a nooner.

I was in no mood to think of Alice, or the Duchess, or Yogi Bear or any other happy creature in the Zinicola universe. I kept imagining nightmares happening to the Jabberwocky. A hit-and-run, a murder, kidnappers cutting off his ears.

"What did you think of the Mock Turtle?" asked Mrs. Z., re-straightening her pearls across her turtleneck and facing me.

My mind raced beyond the looking glass. I kept thinking about the Jabberwocky, while Mrs. Z.'s tits jiggled below her sweepstakes-winner's smile. She lifted her rose-colored glasses and glared beneath them.

"I—didn't read it," I answered.

"Oh," she whispered, nibbling her nails, before returning to read *Alice.*

"That's the reason they're called lessons,' the Gryphon remarked: `because they lessen from day to day.'

"This was quite a new idea to Alice...."

The bell rang. I grabbed my books. I walked past Mandy and slinked outside. Six periods of guilt and worry remained to fill my school day.

Lightning flashed. I dashed to my next classroom through the deluge. My worries about the Jabberwocky lingered.

As soon as the tardy bell rang for our seventh period work-out, we could feel Coach Neal storm behind our locker benches. "Where's the Wocky?" Odors of strange life forms emerged from Snooge's locker and soured our nostrils. "Where's the Jabberwocky? Booboo, Martian, Ivan, you guys seen him?"

We shook our heads.

Neal's running shoes padded across the concrete when he paced. We were exhausted. I hadn't slept the past two nights. I was worried, and I didn't have the answer Neal wanted.

He scowled. "Run Lida," he barked. "Run it twice." He grabbed his car keys.

Groaning, we laced our shoes. We had no heart to run at all, and it was raining. Having lost to San Marino, we took our punishment in silence. League Finals were in a week, at San Marino. One last chance. But with the Wocky out, we knew we had no prayer.

I hadn't seen the Wocky since he'd told me to get lost. None of us had. Running south on Linda Vista, we all compared our notes. Booboo told us how the Jabberwocky had missed his first period class. Snooge said he'd missed third period. Maybe he'd taken some time off, gone to the beach, up Angeles Crest, the movies, maybe space aliens.

We hoped.

But it was pouring. You didn't cut class when it rained. Muck filled our shoes. Rain soaked our hair. We splashed through Linda Vista's gutters, pushing the Wocky from our minds. Cars sprayed mud. At the stoplight, Snooge hung a right to run up Lida. I was the last runner who'd seen Wock—on the Colorado Street Bridge.

Suicide Bridge.

My mind spiraled with fear.

We passed the bungalows on Wellington, the ticky-tacky subdivision up Lida Street. I kept my mouth shut, not wanting to talk about the bridge.

Suicide Bridge. Not the Wocky. Suicide Bridge was nuts. Wock was the best natural athlete in all of La Cañada. Only losers jumped off bridges. I lowered my chin, climbing the steepest part of Lida with my shoes so full of water they felt like dumbbells.

Coach Neal didn't meet us at the saddle, a rare occurrence. So rare, we tried to remember the last time this had happened. We came up blank. We began to even worry about Coach Neal. A flat tire? Maybe his minibus had slid off from the road in all this rain.

We turned right on Figueroa, ran down Chevy Chase to Highland to Linda Vista, feeling the rain come down in sheets across our faces. Then back up Lida once again. We found no coach at Lida's saddle. Not that we needed Neal spritzing us. The storm was so intense it felt like running through the gym showers with clothes on.

Figueroa, to Chevy Chase, to Highland Drive again, to Dover.

When we returned, we saw the Jabberwocky's Plymouth still in the lot. It was clean from all the rain, as if he'd washed it for a change. We hoped the Wock was goofin' on us with his morbid sense of humor.

His locker had been emptied. His combination lock had been cut off with a hacksaw while we were running. Snooge and Psycho found the filings.

We didn't find the Jabberwocky.

I used a phone book and called his house. The phone rang 37 times. I slammed down the receiver.

No answer.

I tried to push thoughts of the Wocky from my mind.

Except I couldn't. I walked my Yamaha around Devil's Gate Dam to the gas station on Woodbury in the rain. I filled the tank and rode my Yamaha to the crest of Suicide Bridge. I had to check.

I'd never sleep until I did.

Numb and worried, I parked my Yamaha 60 on Linda Vista. I walked above tall concrete arches feeling the storm blast almost hard enough to blow me over the railing. Cold gusts punched up the Arroyo. The *Arroyo Seco*, they called it, Spanish for "dry gulch." It wasn't dry now. It was flooded. Wet hair whipped against my eyes. Wind chilled the tips of my ears. Lights along the bridge reflected in streaks across wet pavement.

I found a slope and snaked downhill, Adidas skidding through muddy weeds and into the Arroyo. Muck oozed through my shoes. I slipped and started sliding, landing butt-first on a rock, almost falling into the river. I wiped the mire from my hands. Brown muddy turbulence roared past me, tumbling Dixie cups and branches. If Wock had jumped, his corpse could be anywhere from here to the L.A. River to Long Beach Harbor. It occurred to me I was nuts to even look for him.

I checked uphill. There were gouges in the grass where I'd slid down. My pants were coated with dead sycamore leaves and clay.

"Wocky...." My voice echoed down the canyon, muffled by rain.

A streak of lightning answered.

I searched for footsteps. Any sign he might have spent time in the canyon. "Yo, Wocky...."

No answer. Thunder echoed.

I walked beside the floodwaters, fat mud sucking on my shoe heels, thunder ringing in my ears.

I searched the slope above me. I studied the bank across the river. Lightning flashed. Any evidence of footsteps had been covered up by mud. Clumps of laurel sumac whipped back and forth behind the rain gusts. Rain funneled into my ears, dripped down my legs into my shoes.

For a moment, I thought I heard the Wocky's voice echo, "Fuck you....," fading like the howling of coyotes. It was only wishful thinking. All I heard was thunder. I searched the canyon again for evidence the Wocky had come down here.

Nothing.

A bolt of lightning lit the sky electric black.

I scrambled back up through poison oak, grateful I hadn't found a corpse. Rain hammered against my arm, soaking my shirt, washing the mud beneath my feet from underneath me. I fell, hoisting myself up with a rope of poison oak until my arms hurt. My freezing nipples poked through my faded cotton t-shirt. Brambles cut my thighs. Grit oozed between my toes. Gasping for breath, I slipped and skinned an elbow. When the rain paused, I crabwalked to the top of the slope, panting. My hair flopped down my forehead. I wiped mud across my cheeks.

I puffed to catch my breath.

"Martian?"

My head jerked.

"What the hell you doin' out here, Martian?"

I sat, wheezing in the grass to catch my wind. Coach Neal towered over me, hands on his hips, eyes betraying exhaustion, staring at me as if he'd kick me down the slope.

I caught my breath. "Looking for Wocky, Coach."

"You crazy?"

"No, I'm worried."

He softened. "Me too. Been drivin' around lookin' for him for hours. I even cut his locker open."

I scrambled to my feet, meeting Neal's gaze. "He wasn't acting right last night, Coach."

Coach stared back at me.

"After we reached this bridge coming home last night—" I gulped air "—the Wock told me to run ahead. He told me to get lost and go up Linda Vista without him. Said he had to take a dump...." Another air gulp.

"Martian, I saw your Yamaha. You scared the hell outta me."

I nodded. "Sorry."

Then we both looked off the north side of the bridge, the side I hadn't gone down, and saw....

...The body.

There he was, impaled on an abandoned power pole that had broken off ten yards up the canyon. I must have seen that broken pole a hundred times. He was impaled on the tip, 60 feet below us. Limp arms and legs dangled like a broken marionette as if someone had skewered a pole straight through its heart. His La Cañada jersey was a bloody shade of brown. The Wocky's hair, what the football team hadn't ripped out of his scalp, flopped loosely across his face like Spanish moss.

My heart filled up my throat and deflated in slow motion. Numb, I had to do something. The Jabberwocky was *dead.*

Call the cops. Emotions spiraled, anger, guilt, an odd joy I wasn't the only kid in pain. I feared at any moment I might jump the bridge myself as if the Wocky's suicide had just cleared away the railings.

"Holy fucking shit," Neal whispered. "Jeezus H. Christ, no!" Neal shivered like a paint-mixer, his face ghost white. Sixty feet below the Wocky's body dangled, shaking like a weather-vane in a wind gust. His faded maroon running jersey flapped and dripped with rain.

"No!!!"

I sprinted. Pounding rain, taillights shining across wet pavement, thunder and lightning searing a black sky. Short of breath, temples throbbing, I sprinted across the bridge. *Find a friggin' phone booth.* I dashed between cars to the telephone at Colorado and Orange Grove.

I dialed 911.

Then I puked into a trash can.

In minutes, two black-and-whites were headed my direction. Sirens. A prowl car skidded to a halt. A balding cop in uniform ordered me into the back seat. I jumped inside, sniffing back tears, still tasting vomit in my throat. The vinyl upholstery smelled like I was riding inside a cigarette.

The car door slammed behind me. More sirens. Whirling blue lights. Windshield wipers slashing. The squad car fishtailed onto the Colorado Street Bridge. Cops from the other squad car set barricades and cones. Strontium flares hissed. Wet asphalt reflected sizzling scarlet sparklers.

The car braked to a stop. Guilt pumped through my veins. I could have stopped the Wock if only I had cared more. I should have talked him out of it. *Could've-would've-should've.* He'd never race again, or kick his field goals, or shake his rebel hair out.

Two Pasadena cops swapped wisecracks in the front seat. I wondered what they thought was funny. Their voices came through the holes in the wire screen in front of me.

The driver unhooked his police radio.

My mind was swimming. Numb. I caught the letters "D.O.A." and then some static. I heard "Suicide Bridge. Skewered...."

Static.

"Eleven-forty-four. Need a fire truck, a meat wagon and a coroner ASAP."

"What's your twenty?"

Static. I caught my wind. Things were coming into focus.

"North side of the bridge."

"They're on their way."

Static.

"Ten-four. Out."

The driver hooked his radio and jumped outside. My door was locked. I had no handles.

His partner glared at me through the screen. "Tell me what happened." He had a jaw shaped like the front blade on a bulldozer.

Panicking, I reached for the door handles that weren't there. Giving up, I explained to him the Wocky and I had run home together after our loss to San Marino.

"Keep talkin'." The cop grabbed a clipboard, clicked a ball-point pen and scribbled.

I explained how the Wocky had said he had to take a dump and had told me to run ahead without him.

"Tell me what happened again."

"Weren't you listening?"

The cop gave me a look.

I retold the story. This time it seemed Dick Tracy didn't trust me.

"You feel any remorse?" He clicked his pen repeatedly.

"What?"

"You didn't like him that much, did you?"

"We weren't close but...." *Holy crap!*

"Do thoughts of violence ever cross your mind?" He asked questions as if he thought I'd shoved the Wocky off the bridge. "Where were you headed? Why did you stop? Why didn't you wait and run together?"

Shades of Billy Joe McAllister and Tallahachee Bridge. I had no answers. The cop suspected *me*. A mountain of guilt had already crushed me before his bogus accusations.

"My God, you think I pushed him? Like I just threw him by myself, way out on that power pole, like I'm the Incredible friggin' Hulk."

He frowned. "Just stick with what happened."

I repeated my story, worrying now I was the prime suspect, knowing Coach Neal, Coach Harron, the whole La Cañada football team, the whole damn town could be in jeopardy if I told this cop too much about the cruelty inflicted on the Wocky. I hated being the keeper of dirty secrets.

A hook and ladder truck arrived. Its ladder didn't reach the pole. Firemen rappelled down canyon slopes with nylon cords around their waists. Men lowered harnesses from the ladder and lifted a fireman into position. He clipped a harness beneath the Jabberwocky's arms and tightened straps.

They slid the Wocky from the power pole. His body hung beneath the harness almost fetal-position tight, pale and whiter than a cocktail shrimp that had been dipped into red sauce, then pulled, ever so gently, from its giant tapered toothpick.

I gulped back sorrow. In my memory I saw the Jabberwocky the day he'd walked into the locker room and revealed his grand scheme to beat Harron's team in football.

He'd been smiling. I still heard his voice say, "Cheerleaders."

Using the ladder as a crane, they moved the Wocky and the fireman until the two of them were lowered into a clump of laurel sumac.

A coroner came. An ambulance. It all happened in slow motion. Traffic backed across the bridge. Honking horns and sirens competed with driving rain. Lights glared from the pavement in wet red and white spirals. Lines of headlights reflected off the water.

The cop's partner wandered by, shaking rain from his police cap. After a pow-wow, he jumped into the front seat of our prowl car.

He asked more questions. "You do drugs?"

"What?"

"I asked if you do drugs."

"No. Maybe a beer sometimes. Nothin' to get excited about."

"Don't get smart, kid. I don't have a lot of time to fight with pukes. Answer the question or you'll wind up at the station."

"Don't I get rights? I just saw the body. I called you right away."

His partner glared at me. "Smart-ass huh? How'd you know right where to find him?"

"I didn't do this."

"How the hell'd he wind up on that pole out there?"

"Don't know, sir. I called you. I don't call cops on myself."

"You push him? He on drugs? Was it a suicide?"

Suicide. The word turned my spine into ice. "I dunno. I didn't see him jump." Tears clogged up my throat. "I just left him here last night. Just left him here. I didn't—He was alive then. I just left...."

The other pair of cops questioned Coach Neal, who argued loudly demanding to know why I was sitting in their squad car.

The driver revved up the engine in the prowl car. Wet tires squealed across pavement. The wipers kept time like funeral drums. "We need to take you to the station, kid—" the cop said "—for questioning."

I felt my heart fall through the car floor onto the pavement.

They released me at the station, not telling me what they knew. Someone mumbled beneath their breath what the coroner had suspected. Drugs. Acid plus painkillers. The coroner had known from Wocky's eyes.

And all along, all I had seen in there was anger.

Could've-would've-should've.

Voices spoke behind the counter. "Another La Cañada rich puke like that skinny kid that called us." The cops were talking now. "Lose the weenie. Get him outta here. Tell the coach we'll call him back."

I heaved a huge sigh of relief. My heart restarted. I had to watch what I said. "Yes, sir. Thank you, sir." Cops glanced at me sideways as I walked, eyes riveted forward, out their station doors.

I found Coach Neal in his van, still in the parking lot. His engine rumbled in the rain like it was shivering to stay warm. He yelled from the window of his red Volkswagen Minibus. "Get in, Martian."

I popped the door, jumping inside. My wet running shirt squeaked across his off-white upholstery.

"Thanks, Coach."

Neal eased out of the police lot, peeked across his shoulder, merged into a long parade of taillights. He pounded fingers on the radio in time with saccharine lyrics from Karen Carpenter singing *"We've Only Just Begun."* I was amazed Neal didn't catch the irony. By the second verse I felt like I was riding with a robot. How could Neal be so calm when he'd just lost his first man? Wocky was *dead!*

We turned from Walnut onto Orange Grove, onto a surface street called Rosemont, past palm trees and crabgrass and old rain-drenched bungalows. It was on our ten-mile workout. I'd often run it with the Wocky. Runoff splashed inside the wheel wells. Rain sheeted across the windows, leaked around the door handle and soaked up through my armrest. Behind the windshield wipers, the buzzing neon rosebud above the Pasadena Rose Bowl glowed in the dark.

Like a temple, the Rose Bowl sat in front of us. Its Parthenon-high columns rose above wet concrete. The green words "Rose Bowl" shined in humming neon script that was reflected back in puddles on the pavement. I imagined people cheering for phantom athletes inside, like they were running a track meet for ghost runners.

Neal pulled his minibus off the pavement into a parking space.

The wipers kept time with the Carpenters. Neal's forehead touched the steering wheel. He cursed beneath his breath, squishing his eyes shut, pounding the dashboard. Putting on his sunglasses, he faced the Rose Bowl stadium. We both bowed our heads.

Then we wept.

The next day, yellow plastic tape surrounded the Wocky's Valiant. I hadn't told a soul I'd found Wock's corpse. County Mounties had found nine tabs of acid in his glove compartment. A pink one-pound box, half-full of S&H sugar cubes, had also been discovered beneath the driver's seat. I watched in silence from the balcony near Mrs. Zinicola's third-floor classroom, trying not to scratch beneath the Calamine lotion I'd puttied over a rash of poison oak that bubbled from my forearms after my scramble down the Arroyo.

Nights without sleep had left me certain at any moment zombies would eat my flesh and make me join the living dead. I glared at freshmen gawking through the Wocky's windshield. Had I felt better, I might have eaten one for breakfast. Then, Mrs. Zinicola's Stepford-esque high heels click-clicked behind me. She unlocked her classroom door. Her bracelets jangled like alarm clocks while classmates filed into her class without a whisper.

Gossip of pending drug busts had spread out across our campus. It was rumored County Mountie dogs were sniffing down our lockers. Toilets in the hallways had run non-stop all morning. Even during class, the plumbing groaned and shook beneath us.

I fought to stay awake. I scratched a blister on my arm where poison oak erupted through flesh-toned Calamine. I stared at the hookah-smoking caterpillar that was thumb-tacked to the wall. The cardboard bubble caption—"WHO ARE YOU?"

Mrs. Z. chewed on her nails and paced across the classroom, ricocheting between the blackboard and the door. The Wocky's empty chair sat like a giant open sore.

The bell rang. Mrs. Zinicola cleared her throat.

"We've had a terrible thing happen, but we all have to move on." Mrs. Zinicola stared beyond the Wocky's empty seat. "We have class now," she said, after a thirty-second breather. "Let's just think happy thoughts." A gratuitous smile. "Have you read last night's *Alice in Wonderland* assignment?" She didn't ask if it was fun and didn't straighten her fake pearls, but let them dangle from her cowl neck like a Cheshire cat's grin. Nor did Mrs. Zinicola seem as sunny today. Her toothy smile looked so brittle I was afraid we'd see it shatter. There was lipstick on the tips of Mrs. Zinicola's teeth.

She wore another purple miniskirt, a new one with red hearts. I imagined her as Queen of Hearts in Wonderland. Maybe she wore these things on purpose. (Maybe for *Animal Farm,* she'd wear purple miniskirts with pigs on them.) Today, when her breasts bounced, I lacked the focus to pay attention. My Papermate Flair pen spiraled on my notepaper from lazy purple hearts to even lazier purple pigs, and I drifted into a slumber as deep as Alice's. It was pleasant and so sooooooothing. I thought of wabes and mome raths and fields of slithy toves....

"Sentence first. Verdict afterwards," Mrs. Zinicola barked from the aisle, followed by, "Off with their heads."

Her alarm bracelet jangled in my ears. I shook awake, touched my face. *Whew! Close call.* My head was present and accounted for.

She stood beside me. "Are you still with us Allen?" She drummed her fingers on my desk. I noticed her nails, so badly nibbled they were bleeding.

"Oh. Sorry, Mrs. Z. I just don't feel...."

"Don't feel what?"

"Uh...."

"Tell us how you feel, Mister Martin, because you haven't felt like reading *Alice in Wonderland* for weeks."

"Uh—no. I guess I haven't."

She offered a sympathetic smile. "Tell you what. I'd like you to write an essay on how you *do* feel to help me understand why you haven't been participating."

"What?" I didn't need no stinking essay assignment. She didn't know I'd found the Jabberwocky's body. I hadn't shared that. I gulped. Actually, I felt a whole lot more like Alice in Wonderland than Mrs. Zinicola might have imagined. Except, in my version, it seemed one of the characters had died. The Jabberwocky. I wondered if the Dormouse might be next, or the Mad Hatter, the White Rabbit, or even Alice. Except, Alice was a new girl, and Allen was just a velcroid. I wasn't sure how to explain the difference to Mrs. Z. And Alice had a knack for "outgrowing" all her problems. In my world, my problems outgrew me.

"I'll expect to see your essay tomorrow morning before class." Mrs. Zinicola swiveled on her heels.

The class snickered.

I groaned.

Mrs. Z. returned to lecturing.

I pulled two lined sheets of paper from my pale blue three-ring binder and scrawled with my purple Flair pen.

HOW I FEEL
BY ALLEN DANIEL MARTIN

When a classmate commits suicide, here's how it feels, just in case you really want to know:

It starts with this crappy little schadenfreude inside you. Secretly, you almost feel happy, knowing somebody hurt worse than you do. Which feels bitchen, in a sick way, to know you're not the only person who bleeds here. At least—in your case—you're still standing.

Then it hits you in your gut like a ninety-nine-pound dodgeball that there's now one less teammate to shoulder the burden. One less happy-friggin'-merry-worker rolling the giant wheel and bitching and struggling alongside you. And when the next dodgeball runs over you, it weighs more than the first, and after thumping across your chest, it reminds you the same amount of work still needs doing, after you've finished all your guilt trips and your pity parties.

You cry—when no one's looking, of course. When you're sure no one's listening, a couple of tears leak from your heart, before you plug things with epoxy and you superglue the holes shut. When you get home, you smile, and you put on your happy mask, never letting on how you're secretly afraid—that you might be the next kid off the diving board.

The next day, you smile, and you walk outside the door to go to school or go to work or wherever the hell it is that you go to every day. And other than that, Mrs. Z, nothing changes.

Except you're sadder, you're lonelier, and <u>so</u> much more jaded. What sucks about a suicide is how after the damn thing's over, you're a coward. You know in the bottom of your soul that you still don't have the balls to feel someone else's pain.

And so you put on that happy mask and whistle.

The bell rang.

I slid my essay into the center of the pile that weighed down Mrs. Zinicola's in-basket. I walked past the Jabberwocky's vacant desk. I never thought I'd ever see a chair quite so empty. I was puzzled Mrs. Zinicola had said so little.

I fastened on my happy mask and whistled.

"Allen?" The unmistakably lush voice of Leta Hertz purred out my name while I was staring into my locker.

I turned.

She whispered, "Allen, I think we need to talk."

I froze. I didn't like how she'd said, "talk."

She smiled, just enough to unthaw me from my funk. She tossed her Breck-shampoo-girl hair. Her voice hadn't sounded happy. She wore the coral-colored cashmere she'd worn the day I'd crossed-my-heart-and-hoped-to-die if I wasn't Mandy's friend.

I shut my locker.

Leta narrowed her eyes and gripped my arm. "We need to talk, Allen. I'm not letting you wiggle out of this."

I knew I was depressed when Leta Hertz could touch my arm and my manhood was too weary to salute. On normal days she left my dick as hard as Japanese arithmetic. Not that either of us wanted this. It was sort of like a health screen, like before school starts, when that doctor in the boys' gym makes you bend over, spread your cheeks and has you cough that little cough. He pats your butt and, every autumn, tells the clipboard weenie you're healthy. But things weren't healthy since the Jabberwocky's suicide.

I followed Leta past the faculty lounge, beyond the portable classrooms to the tennis courts. Tennis balls were boing-ing in the background.

"Allen," Leta said. "What's going on?"

"Whaddya mean?"

"With you and Mandy. Mandy doesn't think you like her. She's worried sick. With all that's going on, she needs a friend."

"I didn't say I'd fall in love with her."

"You said you'd be her friend. I didn't think that you were like the other snobs in La Cañada." She glared at me. Eyes hard as sapphires drilled into my soul. "Our class has learned the price of everything and learned the value of nothing. Allen, I could have sworn that you were different."

"Of course I'm different. I hate different." I hooked my thumbs into my pockets, trying to rock back on my Desert Boots and not fall into a puddle.

Leta winced, as though her eyes might pool with tears at any moment.

I swallowed hard and met her level stare.

"Do you have to keep it all inside you, like Ethan Frome?" Leta said. "You haven't said boo to Mandy since she came to see your race. The most amazing girl in high school thinks you're cool, and you ignore her. Like Lily Bart in *House of Mirth*, you have no inkling what you want."

"My bird died."

"Oh puh-lease. Don't shut Mandy out. She liked Ethan."

I sighed. "It's more than just the bird, Leta." I scratched a blister on my wrist that was itching something crazy. "You heard about the Jabberwocky?"

Leta nodded slowly.

"Last night, I was the kid who found his body."

"No way."

"But you don't know that. I didn't tell you, Leta. Don't tell anyone, okay?"

"Oh, how awful!"

"Yeah," I whispered. "Oh, how awful."

Leta lowered her chin. I sensed an ache behind her eyes. Her blue eyes clouded. Her pupils widened and I was staring into a well. Something deep beyond her eyes seemed to remind me of myself. How could a former Brack shampoo girl look so scared?

"Then talk to Mandy," said Leta, clearly a woman on a mission. "Allen, she likes you."

"I'm such a loser. I'm not good enough for Mandy."

"Bullfrog, Allen." She glared at me, eyes narrowing to slits. "You heard me. Mandy misses you. And you're *not* good enough for Mandy, now that you say so. I'm not either. But she thinks we're good enough for *her*—and she misses you and—" her voice was wobbling like an eight-track that was busted "—-Allen, y-y-you promised me."

Leta turned and walked away, hiding tears. Her voice kept wobbling like the noises from those tennis balls. "P-p-p-promised."

I hid tears too. Coach Harron strutted past us. I pulled my hand inside my shirtsleeve and flipped him off.

I felt so tired, I didn't even watch Leta walk away. She never even saw me flip off Harron. But with the Jabberwocky dead, I had to do it in his honor. We'd been through too much together, even though the Jabberwocky had pushed me off the scaffold.

Then I put on my happy mask and kept whistling.

For seventh period, before practice, Coach Neal called us from the lockers into a classroom. He closed the door. Neal asked us to sit down. He held his breath almost a minute. I timed him on the wall clock, watching the secondhand start ticking by the spit-wad near the seven, and when he breathed, it had almost reached the six.

I now noticed—Coach Neal wore a suit. I'd never even seen him in a necktie. He put his head between his hands. Staring at the floor, he looked uncomfortable. He faced us, trembling, looking at each of us with red eyes like he'd been crying.

"They found the Jabberwocky's body," Neal whispered.

We sat stone silent. Most of us had heard.

"Some say it was a suicide. Cops think he was on drugs. Frankly, I don't give a damn exactly how he died." Neal's voice cracked. "The only thing I care about is—now he's dead. I wish to holy heaven I coulda stopped him." He'd made it this far without losing it, but the latex started melting on his happy-mask. "Coulda stopped him." He paced Herman-Munster-like in his freshly-ironed suit to the center of the room and cleared his throat.

"In two weeks, you guys run C.I.F. finals. I'll be there cheering. I hope you run your best. But I won't be able to coach you guys the way you've gotten used to, like you deserve. I failed

Wocky, failed all of you." His voice cracked. "I have to get away. I need to think through my priorities. I know it's shitty to just leave you after you've all worked so hard. Frankly, you deserve a better coach."

Our jaws almost fell from off our faces. It was the first time I felt sorry for a coach.

Coach Neal cleared his throat. "But still, despite me, you've earned the right to run in C.I.F. a week from Saturday. You'll never run together—as a team again—in cross country. So run your hearts out, okay? This life ain't no dress rehearsal. How you prepare for it and practice is up to you."

He turned and walked outside, closing the door behind him softly.

We stared at each other. We had no clue what to say.

An understanding passed between us. *We were on our own. And yet, we were on a team.* Maybe the Jabberwocky was dead. Maybe Coach Neal was busted up after the Jabberwocky's suicide. But as teammates, we owed it to each other to run our best.

It wasn't about winning now, but honor.

We suited up.

We ran in silence for twenty miles.

We dressed back in our street clothes, and no one said a word.

We put our masks on. Snooge whistled. We wondered when they'd bury the Wocky, knowing next Saturday morning, was C.I.F.

As luck would have it, Forest Lawn scheduled the Jabberwocky's funeral before the final game the football team would lose to Temple City. The game explained the empty folding chairs at the Jabberwocky's burial. That, and Coach Harron had made no mention of the Friday sunset eulogy, after he'd promised us he'd announce it during the seventh period pep rally. The decision had been Conrad's, we were told after the bell rang. "It wasn't the right moment. Pep rallies should be peppy."

At the graveside, we waited in silence, the only sounds being the traffic on the Freeway, a few sparrows and the distant whine of leaf blowers. There were six teammates as Wocky's pallbearers, his mother, Coach Neal, two skinny guys with shovels, several curious underclassmen and a fat rent-a-preacher in a robe who looked like Dracula might look were he to drain all of the blood banks in Los Angeles.

The air chilled as the sun set. We folded our arms and rubbed our goose pimples. Klieg lights on the horizon lit up silhouettes of lawnmowers. In this section of the cemetery, all the headstones were planted flush, to make it easier for the lawnmowers to drive over the graves. The rent-a-pastor rose, waving his Count Dracula robes, moaning like a door-hinge in one of those Alfred Hitchcock mysteries.

"Shalllll weeee praaaay?"

"Okay!" Psycho squeaked back in this weird falsetto voice.

Rattfink clenched his fists to keep from giggling.

The harder I tried to keep from laughing, the more I couldn't hold it in, until my eyes bulged, and my cheeks felt like frog throats ready to explode. We had a duty to look solemn, but Rattfink's laughter proved contagious.

The rent-a-preacher prayed for freaking ever.

We tightened our stomachs, to hold in chuckles that squeaked out through our noses and shook our shoulders. I touched my stomach. My diaphragm quivered like a trampoline. We closed our eyes to keep from smiling, to keep from seeing each others' faces, to contain ourselves from busting out with out-of-control laughter.

The rent-a-pastor was stuck in auto-preach. We'd come to show respect, but even the Wocky could never tolerate this never-ending eulogy. We imagined him nudging the lid off from his clunky hardwood coffin, begging Reverend Rent-a-Prayer to cool it.

The Jabberwocky's mother sat in a lawn chair like an ice sculpture. She must've paid the preacher by the word. He droned on for ten more minutes, until our chests ached and quaked in unison, our cheeks quivered, and even Booboo and Ivan Alphabet fought off lip farts.

Fifteen minutes.

"...and dearest Heavenly Father, we beseech thee to bestow thy richest tender mercies upon the departed soul of theess thy beloved...."

Twenty-five minutes.

Psycho's falsetto "okay" squeaked like chalk across my mind, the little voice crying out, "Help me," in *The Fly*.

Please say amen. Please?

Raspberries and lip farts puffed in unison.

The preacher stopped.

"Knock it off," he thundered. "This is a funeral, Goddammit."

Our diaphragms could no longer hold back.

Booboo, Snooge, Ivan, Psycho went off like human whoopee cushions. Wock's mother glared across the grave pit. Coach Neal shook his head. I tried to sound like I was crying, and I was, but my emotions were so confused I couldn't steer them. The gravediggers shook so hard the dirt was flying off their shovel blades. They roared and banged their tools against the grass.

"AMEN!" shouted the preacher, interrupting his own prayer. "AMEN, DAMMIT."

We blushed. The laughter drained, carried away, now, by the gravity. We stuffed our hands into our pockets and hung our chins.

The Wocky's mother closed her eyes and shook her head.

Coach Neal spat.

Silence. Even the sparrows and the finches stopped their chirping.

I felt the tears, too late to redeem my rudeness. The Jabberwocky, who'd pushed me off the scaffold and broken my arm, cheated Mandy playing Scrabble and flipped off every kid in La Cañada High School, the Wock, who in the end had cheated himself out of a life, would never get the chance to make things right.

We lowered the Wocky's casket into a long rectangular hole, and the shovel guys covered his coffin up with six feet of gray dirt. It took less time to fill the hole than the preacher had spent praying. We listened to the lonely scrapes of spades.

And then we walked across the lawn to Neal's minibus.

We felt bad for Wocky's mom. But if the Wock had been alive, he'd have been cracking up right with us.

The heartbreak was he wasn't, and never would be—ever again.

RESULTS: CALIFORNIA INTERSCHOLASTIC FEDERATION (C.I.F.) SOUTHERN SECTION FINALS
MOUNT SAN ANTONIO COLLEGE, POMONA, CALIFORNIA: SATURDAY, DECEMBER 5TH, 1970

1st	Lopez	San Marino	1 pt	9 minutes 3 seconds
2nd	Soloway	Mission Viejo		9 minutes 19 seconds
3rd	Prentice	San Marino	3 pts	9 minutes 24 seconds
4th	Booboo	La Cañada	4 pts	9 minutes 25 seconds
5th	Martian	La Cañada	5 pts	9 minutes 25 seconds
6th	Echeverria	Chino		9 minutes 26 seconds
7th	Brown	Villa Park		9 minutes 26 seconds
8th	Alphabet	La Cañada	8 pts	9 minutes 27 seconds
9th	Simcic	Orange		9 minutes 31 seconds
10th	Spiselman	San Marino	10 pts	9 minutes 36 seconds
11th	Casey	San Marino	11 pts	9 minutes 37 seconds
12th	Baccellia	San Marino	12 pts	9 minutes 48 seconds
...				
15th	Snooge	La Cañada	15 pts	9 minutes 58 seconds
...				
20th	Rattfink	La Cañada	20 pts	10 minutes 4 seconds

Total Points

San Marino	37 pts	(1st)
La Cañada	52 pts	(2nd)

CHAPTER THIRTEEN

THE TEARS OF A CLOWN

MOUNT SAN ANTONIO COLLEGE, POMONA, CALIFORNIA: SATURDAY, DECEMBER 5TH, 1970
(188 DAYS TO GRADUATION!)

They gave us cheesy-looking trophies for second place in C.I.F. Plastic ones, spray-painted to look like they were gold. The trophy bases were coated with this candy-apple red stuff below a runner who looked exactly like he'd sprinted through a band saw, and then they'd glued him back together, slightly crooked. Mine had a mold mark on his elbow. He balanced on his left foot, leaning forward like some spazz about to fall off his pedestal. His right leg rose, like he'd just kneed somebody's groin, and his golden arm (with no thumb or fingers), delivered an off-balance karate chop. I named this golden trophy doofus "Bob." I'd run twelve-thousand miles in three years of cross country, and all I had to show for it was "Bob."

I planned on hanging Bob from a lampshade in my bedroom with a noose around his neck, in memory of the Jabberwocky.

If you looked up through the trophy bottom all you saw was styrene. It was white, all the way up through the inside of Bob's gold head. Soon, two-hundred watts would burn from the incandescent bulb in my bedroom sending an eerie reddish glow into Bob's skull.

The San Marino trophies looked the same from underneath. David Prentice showed me his. The only difference was the base. David's trophy base was bigger and this weird electric blue, and the thin brass interchangeable reversible metal strip on David's trophy read 1st place. Our red ones all said 2nd. I reversed my metal strip so it said absolutely nothing and ditched Bob in Ivan Alphabet's Corvair to keep him safe.

We'd smiled for meet photographers like we were cows awarded second-place prize ribbons at the L.A. County Fair. Psycho and Rattfink even mooed. David Prentice told me San Marino's team was shocked how well we'd run. We might have beaten them, David said, if the Wocky had been healthy instead of dead. I thanked him for his sportsmanship and kindness, saying I hadn't done the math, except I had.

And then we'd climbed into our cars. Mr. Conrad hadn't booked us any team bus for post-season. They must have told him that cross country didn't matter.

A week later, we'd heard announcements there'd be an assembly at the high school, seventh period in the gym the coming Friday. There, they would let us present our C.I.F.

school trophy to Mr. Conrad, the school activities director. It wasn't a moment we were savoring. Although the team trophy was cheesy, Conrad the Dipshit hadn't earned it. He hadn't even booked a team bus for our championship meet. And that moron was supposed to get a trophy?

We wondered how he'd spin it. Here, we'd placed second in C.I.F., while Harron's winless football players were worshipped one last time. We never got an explanation. Sure enough, there was a pep rally, seventh period. Mandatory. They made us sit up in the bleachers. We were crammed so close together we had to scrunch our shoulders forward, and we could smell where Snoogey's Ban was wearing off.

We hated pep rallies. We usually ditched them so we could run a longer workout. Neal always let us cut out early. But cross country season was over. We had no choice except to come and worship La Cañada football—without the humor of the Jabberwocky's commentary.

I snuck in late. They were introducing Varsity Football's second string. Their names reverberated through loudspeakers and echoed off the gym walls. Booboo sat beside me with our school trophy between his Pumas. On my other side sat Psycho with this giant mayonnaise jar wrapped in tinfoil. It gave off a dull sub-audible hum, and it smelled funky. Something vibrated the foil.

"What's in the jar, Psyche?" I asked.

He brought a finger to his lips. "Ssssh. Don't ask."

"C'mon. What's in there?"

"A surprise."

"You can tell me."

"A contingency in case Conrad forgets our trophy."

"Oh, great. C'mon, Psycho!"

"Pay attention, Martian." Psyche pointed forward. "Conrad the Dipshit's sayin' somethin' you need to know."

"Yeah, right."

Psycho leaned forward, eyes riveted on Conrad, like he was about to give out Candice Bergen's phone number. It was Psycho's way of saying he wasn't telling us his secret.

I sighed.

Conrad, the Director of Student Activities, finished introducing the varsity and now, turned to introduce the entire *junior* varsity, and then the B's and then the C's, and the managers and the water boys and everybody who was trying out for basketball.

The Pep Band played the S.C. Fight Song. The song leaders must have pissed off half the band, because they played it as a waltz. It took the song leaders two stanzas to get their pom-pom act together, and once they did, they looked like they were cheering a minuet.

Heather looked furious. She sat down pouting, picking fuzz balls off her sweater and flicking them, glaring at the pep band. Her lower lip stuck out so far a crow could perch and take a dump there. She stuck her tongue out. Her tantrum was the highlight of the hour.

I looked for Mandy. I missed her smile. I couldn't find her in the crowd.

Conrad turned to Mrs. Zinicola, who introduced the pep squad. Girls in red sweaters shook their bangles and metal bracelets loud as Salvation Army Santas. We glanced at Neal.

He shrugged. We all stared at the clock. Ten minutes to three. Booboo glanced down at our trophy.

Eight minutes to three. School was almost out.

No one had mentioned we'd finished second in C.I.F.

Six minutes.

Mrs. Zinicola sat down.

We turned to Neal. Mister Conrad didn't look at him.

Harron jumped up and started yakking about discipline and football.

Siddown, you stupid schmuck.

Loudspeakers squealed with feedback. We pressed our hands against our ears until the volume got turned down to where Harron's rantings were inaudible. *Thank God.*

Mrs. Zinicola yawned. She snapped a wad of gum before spitting it into her Kleenex. She took out a gold compact and applied pink frosted lipstick in long, sensuous strokes. All the football players stared at Mrs. Zinicola in her tight skirt and her tighter crewneck sweater covered with hearts.

Five minutes to three.

No one had mentioned our C.I.F. trophy. What was the point of winning if they didn't want your trophy?

Psycho grinned. He glanced down at his giant mayonnaise jar. He must have covered it with half a roll of Reynolds Wrap. The jar buzzed with a rumble. My curious cells torqued into overdrive. Psycho slid the mayonnaise jar beneath the roll-out wooden bleachers.

SMASH! CRASH! Tinkling glass.

Uh-oh!

Psycho had dropped his jar. I stiffened. Several heads turned.

Nothing happened. *Bummer!* I paused to take a breath.

Harron babbled into the microphone until 60 seconds later, a thousand horseflies emerged from beneath the wooden bleachers with tinsel glued onto their backs. A squadron of tinsel, flying at random, orbited above the bleachers, reflecting light, swirling and shimmering, doing barrel rolls and loops, getting stuck inside girls' hair, humming, buzzing, biting.

"Eew!" A shriek sounded like Heather's grating voice.

Something about this was pure bitchen!

Slapping arms. Yelps and screams. Someone called out there were wasps. Girls stampeded across the gym floor. Football players laughed out loud. Freshman dangled unconscious flies from tinsel strips like little hypnotists. Glittering plastic arced and funneled toward the ceiling, buzzing, spiraling, reflecting iridescent sparkles. One by one, boys' heads rose toward the ceiling to watch the Christmas tinsel circling the caged fluorescent lights.

Coach Harron was still talking about discipline.

A herd of sophomores were shrieking. "Wasps, hornets, killer bees!"

Students stampeded toward the exits, pushing, swatting, shoving. Harron blew his whistle. *Screeeeeeeeeee! Screeeeeeeeeee! Screeeeeeeeeee!*

Conrad stumbled toward the microphone. Some kid had knocked it over. It didn't work now. He kept shouting the words, "Testing-testing-testing." Half the school pressed and squeezed to escape through double doors while the other half sat laughing in the bleachers.

By three o'clock, our eyes were riveted on Psycho's errant flies when the school bell interrupted Conrad's "testing-testing-testing."

After the gym cleared, clipboard weenies passed out basketballs for hoop practice. We sat stone-faced in the bleachers, staring at our trophy. The last of Psycho's tinsel flies were scurrying out the vents. Ivan Alphabet was arguing with Booboo.

"Screw this school," said Ivan. Ivan cussed so rarely even a laundered verb like 'screw' sounded positively blasphemous. "We win a trophy, and we can't even present it."

"Easy, Ivan," said Booboo. "Don't let this eat you up."

"Why not," said Ivan. "This school hasn't won a C.I.F. trophy in years. You wanna just roll over, Booboo?"

"Ivan, what're you gonna do? We can't *make* people respect us." Booboo pointed out the door. "We even beat those pompous chuckleheads in football, and what happened?"

I shuddered, remembering the Jabberwocky's anguish.

"I vote we superglue our trophy to the front of Conrad's Buick—" said Psycho "—as a hood ornament."

"And your point, Psycho?" I said.

"It forces Conrad to acknowledge us."

"And gets us what?' He'd just have Earl Scheib scrape our trophy off his hood. Momma would even reimburse Conrad for the paint job his car needs anyways. It'd be like givin' him a bonus."

"Well, what do you suggest, Martian?" asked Psycho.

I had to think. The Wock had been our leader. What would he do?

He'd killed himself.

Great! And what had that proved? The *Love Story* guy was right. To teflonistas, life and love meant never having to say you were sorry. But for velcroids it shouldn't mean you that were sorry all the time. That wasn't anything like love. That was a guilt trip.

We'd run our best. We were teammates. Who cared what other people thought? Couldn't we just be proud? We'd made our statement with our running. This was not a time for pranks.

I took a deep breath.

"I say we give the trophy to Neal."

Eyes turned toward me asking questions.

"He's busted up," I said. "He needs it." Another breath. "I was with him the night we found the Wocky's body."

Booboo nodded. Snooge, Ivan, Rattfink and Psycho followed me downstairs. We signed the trophy with felt markers on the bottom to thank Neal. We left the trophy in his office, ran a short five-mile workout and knew La Cañada was too self-absorbed to care.

We told no one it was Psycho who had dropped the mayonnaise jar. But then again, we never pretended to have discipline like Harron did. We just won a lot of races. We'd placed second in C.I.F., and we were proud. And sometime, perhaps a chance would come. A *mitzvah* to honor Wocky.

Wocky's novel—I knew at that moment he wanted *me* to write it.

CHAPTER FOURTEEN

MIDNIGHT CONFESSION
LA CAÑADA HIGH SCHOOL: FRIDAY, DECEMBER 18TH, 1970
(175 DAYS TO GRADUATION!)

The happy hookah-smoking caterpillar thumb-tacked to the walls mocked me as I pondered Mrs. Zinicola's test questions. This close to Winter break, it was too early in the morning to sport measurable brainwaves concerning Alice or English literature. Mrs. Zinicola sat behind her desk, applying lipstick. Holly-berry red, it matched her go-go boots for Christmas. She stared into her compact like she saw the other side.

I closed my eyes. Sounds of Bic pens scrawling on blue-lined paper reminded me of my uncompleted test questions.

Question Number 1: Describe how Lewis Carroll uses Alice to critique Victorian social life and customs.

Answer: Who cares? I don't live in Victorian England. Never did. It's down the rabbit hole with Alice.

I wasn't normally a smart-ass. But it was getting hard to care. Nobody had cared when Wocky died. Nobody cared about our trophy. My job was to go to school, and wear a mask, and hide my feelings, and make sure La Cañada High School got State money for my attendance. Nobody cared.

Except for Mandy.

Mandy! I'd forgotten how much I missed her.

Question Number 2: Discuss the symbolism of Lewis Carroll's Queen of Hearts.

Answer: She was a playing card! What's the symbolism of the friggin' Jack of Diamonds?

And so it went.

It wasn't like me not to study for exams. But now, it seemed a great pandemic of senioritis gripped La Cañada. And I had *stage-four* senioritis. There were no cures or vaccinations. I sat in classrooms cracking jokes and biting nails. A big bad world awaited, and I was getting nervous. It wasn't tests on English literature that frightened me the most during our last Christmas together at La Cañada High.

Not even close.

And it was out of my control.

For teflonistas, like Garry and Heather, the big bad world meant Stanford, Berkeley, U.S.C., or Yale. Fat applications, S.A.T. scores and even fatter checks were mailed out by anxious parents to universities. I wasn't always sure what teflonistas were afraid of. I just overheard them saying they were scared.

For girl velcroids, like Susan Day, the "University of Colorado Boulevard" loomed, the junior college sometimes known as Pasadena City College. We had all heard Susan's parents had pinched back on her allowance. She had two years to get married, or else be sentenced to a life wearing the crummy clothes her day job, selling Kinney's Shoes, afforded her.

For boy velcroids, like me, the big bad scary world meant—war. Parents of teflonistas could still pull strings and score deferments; like Eddie Randall, tight end in football, whose doctor wrote him up 4F (because of asthma) when he owned the high school record for high hurdles, or Kurt Hansen, who used to beat the crap out of me at junior high. His pastor swore he was a conscientious objector.

Crap! Vietnam. After Wock's suicide, I'd totally forgotten. Nam was all the Huntley-Brinkley Report talked about on weeknights. Perhaps, I'd learned about denial watching Mrs. Zinicola. Now I was following the headlines, searching my *Rand McNally World Atlas Imperial Edition* to find out where I was going. Far-off places like Saigon, Khe Sanh, Danang, and Cam Ranh Bay now made their way into my brain along with visions of dead soldiers. People were sending us to fight for places we couldn't even pronounce, while they sent teflonista football jocks to fight for old S.C. Being a year older than my classmates, I'd be first kid off the boat in Vietnam, where unlike U.S.C., no cheerleaders would cheer for us. Plus you could die, which never happened when you fought for old S.C.

Harron had warned me. Charlie Cong could barely wait for me to die. I pictured the Wocky's rent-a-pastor praying at my funeral.

You didn't talk about Vietnam, but it was always on your mind, a cloud of horror that kept sunny California from being sunny. As graduation neared, your cloud kept getting bigger and more frightening. It filled up all of your horizons, left them ominous and blank. You could *die*. Only you had to be a man and keep your mouth shut. So much as mention Vietnam, and any cute girls wrote you off. No self-respecting Republican chick wanted to date a future dead guy. Creepy! And Democratic chicks weren't dating Nazi war pigs. Your odds were better if you told them you were headed to San Quentin.

If you were eighteen, instead of seventeen, you were truly in deep yogurt. People told me not to worry. Their life wasn't on the line. Like that Shirley Jackson short story, my "Lottery" was coming, and I was scared. I was developing a phobia of bags. Plastic trash bags, grocery bags, sleeping bags looked like body bags to me. I imagined myself inside one next to a runway in Southeast Asia, stacked beside my friends like cords of wood.

Another month, and they'd be pulling out my draft number.

A thought crossed my mind. Why should I care if I flunked English? A worm of bitterness gnawing inside my stomach seemed to prod me. What would they do to me if I flunked? Would they send me to San Quentin? Put me in jail? Would they take away my freedom....

...Instead of sending me to Vietnam to die?

I saw the clock. Eight-fifty-five. The bell rang.

I hadn't even answered the last test questions. I handed in my test. I hadn't read *Alice in Wonderland*. I hadn't listened to the lectures. I'd just shook my head, amazed nobody cared the

Wock had died, while I waited, scared spitless, for my turn in Vietnam—to die, or even worse perhaps—to kill.

I glanced at Mrs. Z. For Winter break, they could do nothing. I was a free man. I handed in my test and started laughing. I wanted to race down the corridor, dodging teachers, waving my arms, screaming glory hallelujah, like a kindergartner charging to recess, thinking recess never ends.

I took a deep breath. First, I had to patch things up with Mandy.

In Harron's class, I scribbled the note I should have written Mandy weeks ago. Harron lectured on discipline the day before Winter Break. Hey, it was better than a test. But I wasn't *taking* notes. I was writing one. I struggled to force words out of my pen:

Mandy,
I've been a ~~loser~~ ~~creep~~ total jerk.
Can you meet me? Five o'clock, Christmas Eve, our favorite place.
Please. I'll be waiting. Hope you come. (If you're still willing)
Your sorry friend,
Allen Martin

I folded the paper, gave it to Mandy after lunch, hoping she'd read it.

Mandy smiled.

I didn't say much.

She said, "Thank you."

It sounded like a brush-off. I walked alone to my next class, *praying* she'd read my note. I needed somebody to talk to, someone who'd care.

I climbed the stairs toward my classrooms. I slinked around the corner, and she was waiting by the water fountain, crying.

But she was smiling.

"Allen, I'll be there," Mandy whispered.

I couldn't wait to see her again on Christmas Eve and run again with Mandy by my side.

IMPORTANT NOTICE TO ALL MEMBERS OF THE LA CAÑADA HIGH SCHOOL ACADEMIC STUDENT BODY: Subject: *Temporary suspension of scheduled academic activities for Winter Observances:*

Due to the pending Winter Observances scheduled to occur during the final two weeks of calendar year 1970, the Board of Directors of the La Cañada Unified School District has directed me, on behalf of your High School Principal, to hereby notify you that normally scheduled academic activities at said La Cañada High School will be temporarily suspended for that period of time commencing on the 19th of December, 1970 and reconvening 16 calendar days later, beginning on the 4th of January, in 1971.

During this period of time, all doors of all academic facilities at La Cañada High School will be thoroughly secured and locked by our janitorial staff, and academic instructors will be absent from their posts. Participation in academic activities by members of the student body of La Cañada High School will therefore be impossible during said time period.

As of January 4th of the forthcoming year, at 8:00 a.m., Pacific Standard Time, all students of La Cañada High School are expected to be in their assigned classroom seats, ready to resume scheduled educational activities.

Questions or inquiries which you may have regarding the aforementioned temporary suspension of normally scheduled academic activities shall be directed in writing (in triplicate) to the office of the Assistant Principal and Director of Student Activities at La Cañada High School.

Your strict compliance with the directives of this memorandum is expected.
Roland W. Conrad, M.A.Ed. Assistant Principal and Director of Student Activities

FLINT PEAK, GLENDALE, CALIFORNIA: CHRISTMAS EVE, THURSDAY, DECEMBER 24ᵀᴴ, 1970 (168 DAYS TO GRADUATION!)

The winter wind, when it blew up Glenoaks Canyon toward Flint Peak, carried a chill from the Angeles Crest snow pack. Sitting beneath the tower, Mandy and I held hands. She'd brought wine. Mandy's fingers felt so warm. Her touch was gentle. I wanted to hold her, to hear another person breathe. I was grateful when I'd touched her she hadn't pulled her hand away. After the Jabberwocky's death, I longed to know how people felt. I'd hidden all my loneliness, put on my mask, and crawled inside me.

Mandy squeezed my hand. "I'm glad we're here for Christmas Eve."

"So am I." I squeezed back, grateful she'd shown up.

We sat enjoying the scent of sage and sipping wine. We didn't speak again, until the sun had set, and our arms were showing goose bumps. Mandy asked no questions. Lacking answers, I was grateful. I was afraid of women's questions. Tonight, Mandy let me breathe, allowed my broken soul to heal, allowed me to climb out from the funk I had crawled into.

I'd struggled with what to buy Mandy for Christmas. With Heather, buying stuff was easy. *Paying* was the challenge. If something cost a ton of money, you could be certain Heather wanted it. I still had that crystal unicorn I'd bought Heather for her birthday. Fifty bucks. But it was flawed, and Ivers' wouldn't take it back. Had they given me my refund, Vinnie Skinner would never sell me back those baseball cards. So, my only souvenir left from my childhood was Heather's unicorn, reminding me that I had been a moron. Still, for some reason, I hadn't tossed it out.

Mandy wanted meaning. I'd racked my brain trying to figure out what to buy her. I'd settled on a pair of lightweight running shoes, Onitsuka Tigers that barely weighed an ounce between them.

I remembered the time I'd tried on my first pair.

The tops were nylon instead of leather, so they didn't give you blisters. They felt like seamless silk inside. Somehow, they didn't hold in sweat. When you ran in them, their nylon soles cushioned against the rocks until you felt like you ran barefoot on a cloud. It was the best gift I could think of. I wasn't sure Mandy would like them. If she didn't, she could always take them back.

The sun slipped behind the hills of Griffith Park. Winter winds rustled the toyons and blew grit into our eyes. We turned around, freezing and cold. Sweat circles on our running shirts chilled our necks while the dampness blew away.

Beneath our mountain, shoppers dashed in and out of stores. I imagined they sang Christmas carols and cussed out other drivers. Chamber of Commerce decorations twinkled in greens and golds. Garlands on Glendale Boulevard hung like miniature necklaces across converging lanes that merged at the horizon.

"You like Christmas?" Mandy asked.

"I used to."

She tilted her head. "Used to?"

"As a kid I really liked it." I looked down. "But you grow up, and Christmas changes. I loved it when there was Santa Claus. Santa brought me stuff. He liked me."

Mandy giggled.

"I remember Christmas trees with tinsel and glass ornaments and twinkle lights. I loved that stuff—" I said "—while it lasted."

"Christmas stopped?" Mandy whispered.

"My parents went to church and started fighting. Santa stopped coming. It's like someone at their church wanted him gone. Our pastor told me "Santa" was an anagram for "Satan." We burned fires in our chimneys to ward off Santa on Christmas Eve. But nothing we could do was ever good enough for Jesus."

"Such as?"

"In junior high, back when my parents went to church together, the elders were raising money for their new worship center. They talked my old man into pledging enough money to buy a Cadillac. Said it was his fair share to make sure Jesus got his building. They told us Jesus needed that building. Jesus *died* for their new building, and those old buildings in their parking lot were never any good."

"So what happened?"

"Dad got laid off. A team of lawyers from our church came by to see him. After they left, my dad was shaking. He owed their church five grand, and now, he didn't have a job. Dad took out a second mortgage on our house to pay 'em off. They'd told him God was testing us. We had a duty to come through. He had to prove we were a part of God's elect."

"Elect? So they were Calvinists."

"Yup," I said.

"And you're an atheist?"

"More agnostic. I'm not predestined. Jesus died for only them."

"Goodness, Allen. You make God sound like he's this giant cosmic asshole. Or someone like your dad, who ran away."

I shifted on my seat. "So if Hollywood says 'Love means you never have to say you're sorry,' and Jesus wanted his disciples to be loving one another, that means people in our churches never have to say they're sorry. It comes with being the elect. A perfect system for teflonistas. The smart ones even used it to sell slavery.

I closed my eyes. I'd never put it together this way before. I waited for Mandy to react. Didn't she want to be a nun?

She smiled but didn't let my hand go. It calmed me down. I was relieved she wasn't easily offended.

"I'm not sure churches even know quite what love *is*, Allen," said Mandy. "It's kinda sad, especially when Jesus was a velcroid. Didn't he die for people's sins? When you're wrong, doesn't love really mean you *have* to say you're sorry?"

"Maybe in *your* world." I took a breath. "But not on Planet Teflonista. It's like the whole idea's been hijacked and turned into something fake. Love's all guys talk about these days, but it's turned into something different, Mandy. Love-ins, 'Make love not war,' 'All you need is love.'"

The Beatles' *Magical Mystery Tour* horns blared in my brain. *"L-u-u-u-u-hve, L-u-u-u-u-hve, L-u-u-u-u-hve...."*

"About your theory," said Mandy. "I guess I *want* to be a velcroid; to *give* love and not *need* love, offer grace instead of *dis*grace, to take risks. It's the only way I have to make things better."

"Doing what, Mandy?"

"Loving one person at a time."

"Oh." I might have argued. But I didn't want to lose my only friend. Loving one person at a time was never an option. You were supposed to love mankind. All four billion of 'em at once. Sadly, I had failed to pull it off.

"Jesus was a velcroid," Mandy said again.

I sighed. I'd considered it. "Tell you a secret, Mandy," I said. "A month ago, I asked God for a miracle for a velcroid. Before the Wocky died, I asked to see at least one yucca bloom. They do it once every ten years. It can't be that huge of a deal to make one crummy yucca fill its stalk with flowers."

I pointed to the hillside, toward the clusters of spiny plants, and not a single lousy yucca dared to blossom.

"Maybe the time's not right," said Mandy. "Maybe you'll need it later on."

"'It's not His time.' Great!" I mocked. "It sounds ridiculously pious. What's the point, Mandy? Even Santa brings gifts to children. Is God too busy?"

She shook her head.

"Mandy, I *gave* God a second chance. I asked him to save Ethan. That was the other miracle. Plan B. God didn't do either one."

My heart ached when my thoughts returned to Ethan's disappearance, my poor stepbird, my little feathered velcroid.

And I'd loved him.

Mandy stewed. She stared at the horizon, frowning. "If I could answer all your questions, I'd be God, Allen," she said. "And I suck at being God."

"Well, anyways, Mandy, I brought you something for Christmas."

"For Christmas?" Mandy smiled—wider than I thought a girl could smile. I handed her a sack from Alexander's Market I'd brought with me. Her Onitsuka Tiger box was inside, gift-wrapped in comic strips.

Mandy slid away the ribbon, tore off Dick Tracy and Snoopy, wadded the funnies into a ball, flipped the cover, parted the tissue.

I waited. I was scared.

"ALLEN!!!"

She screamed so loud her echo returned in several seconds from the hillside across Chevy Chase Canyon. Before I knew, she'd laced her shoes up. She was bouncing in them like Tigger on a trampoline. "They're so light. They're so cool. They're just like yours."

I nodded.

"Allen, I love 'em."

I'd never seen a girl so happy. I'd bought all this crap for Heather, and she kept pumping me for more. Chase Manhattan could go bankrupt dating Heather, I'd decided. I'd bought Mandy these stupid running shoes, and she was jumping up and down in them like she'd traded in a sock-monkey for Monty Hall's Corvette.

And then she talked. I mostly listened while Mandy told me how she dreamed of running a marathon. Twenty-six miles, plus 385 yards. There was one in Palos Verdes. She told me she was training. She told me all about her work down at the hospital as a candy-striper, how she'd helped Leta become a Rose Princess, how Mandy wanted to be a teacher on the mission field in Kenya. And then she faced me.

"I have something for you too," she said. "Allen, close your eyes."

I closed them. Besides the wine, I hadn't seen her bring a gift.

I felt her touch me in the center of my back, nudging me toward her, pulling me forward with my eyes closed. I surrendered to her pull. Something soft and almost yearning brushed against my lips, pressed me close. Breath crossed mine. Mandy's breath. It filled my throat, and my neck tingled.

Her lips trembled. They felt like flower petals quivering, wishing me closer, surprising me almost like they belonged there. Mandy wanted to be this nun, but she was kissing me, keeping me warm, and I liked it.

It seemed forever, a simple touch that seemed to bridge two souls, as if neither of us had ever kissed another human being. Except, in my case, I hadn't. I felt like Mandy hadn't either. A warm electric feeling filled my body.

I wanted to hold her for the rest of Christmas Eve, to taste her breath forever, to feel her hands against my back, to smell her neck, to savor the tenderness that pulsed between us, to dance in silence in our bright blue nylon running shoes that matched now.

I pulled her closer.

Being close, we never felt like we were cold. The moon had risen. I opened my eyes.

There weren't as many lights in Glendale. The parking lots were empty. I touched the prickles on Mandy's arms, ran my hands across the goose bumps. I didn't want her catching cold.

Something strange happened. After kissing Mandy, I felt stronger.

I smiled.

We ran downhill. With her new shoes, Mandy was keeping up beside me.

And I felt like we ran barefoot on a cloud.

After she'd dropped me off at home, I took a walk around the neighborhood. Returning home, I found the flag up on our mailbox. There was a note inside, addressed to me from Mandy. An envelope had a sticker on it, a Christmas-tree shaped green one.

"Do not open until December 25th," the sticker ordered.

At 12:01 a.m., I opened up the note.

Dear Allen,

I had this hunch, since Heather said you'd never kissed her, you're afraid—like I am. Nobody's ever kissed me either. Before I become a nun, I wanted to kiss a boy. I was hoping, Alan, you would kiss me back.

I chose you, because I like you, and you make me laugh and smile.

I hope if I say, I love you, you'll respect I truly mean it, even if later I'm called to be a nun.

Love, Mandy

I folded the note into my wallet. Somebody loved me. A real person with flesh and blood. I wasn't some trophy like that Bob thing that twisted beneath my lampshade, like when I'd been on Heather's leash reading Robert Redford fan mags, or like Heather on Garry's leash.

Mandy, for some crazy reason, loved me.

Me!

Okay, it wouldn't last forever. I was facing Vietnam. Mandy wanted to be a nun. What were we doing? Well, for several months, I'd added a human being to the list of other creatures I'd try to love. It wasn't marriage, but what was wrong with basic human kindness? I, for one, could sorely use the practice.

Mandy wanted this, wanted *me*. It would be dumb to turn her down. If I died in Vietnam, I didn't want to die unloved.

If Mandy became a nun, she and her God could still be happy.

I read her note, recalled our kiss.

I smiled at the memory.

It was Christmas, and I already had my gift.

END OF PART ONE

PART TWO

WINTER

Life is the only real counselor. Wisdom, unfiltered by personal experience does not become a part of the moral tissue.
EDITH WHARTON

CHAPTER FIFTEEN

CHAPEL OF LOVE

ROSE PARADE ROUTE, COLORADO BOULEVARD, PASADENA, CALIFORNIA: NEW YEARS EVE, THURSDAY, DECEMBER 31ST, 1970
(162 DAYS TO GRADUATION!)

Not having "dated" Mandy in public, I was nervous about the partying on New Years Eve we'd face on Colorado Boulevard. A zillion cops trying to patrol the streets of Old Town Pasadena were outnumbered by twenty-zillion parties. The air reeked of marijuana. Sidewalks puddled with beer and urine. Hare Krishnas in saffron robes banged on their dirty tambourines. Jesus freaks passed out tracts and hell-and-brimstone Jack Chick comics. A County Mountie rolled down Orange Grove, eyes staring straight ahead, like he was driving through a car wash with no one in it.

For New Year's Eve, Mandy and I had jogged down Linda Vista Avenue, finding a choice spot on the lawn near

Colorado and Orange Grove. It offered good views of the Rose Parade, its floats and marching bands. We'd laid down beach towels in the shadows of the Pasadena Art Museum, where all those Degas ballerinas were impounded. The museum loomed behind us like the big black granite monoliths that show up when *Also Sprach Zarathustra* plays in *2001: A Space Odyssey.*

Even in Pasadena, winter nights were cold. Gusts blew across the snow pack of the San Gabriel Mountains, fell down rocky slopes, whistled over Altadena and chilled our New Year's Eve, biting our ears. Tomorrow was the opening day of 1971, Rose Bowl Day. The undefeated Big Ten champion, Ohio State, faced the Pac-Eight Stanford Indians and Jim Plunkett. Not that I cared. This year I'd graduate to face a war in Vietnam. I had a duty to enjoy life while I could.

Tonight, Mandy's glow could light up Colorado Boulevard. "I'm so excited." She sat beside me, knees tucked underneath her sweatshirt. "My best friend, Leta. Can you believe she'll be a Rose Princess tomorrow?" She smiled.

I smiled back. "Now that you've told me twenty times, I think I can, Mandy."

"It's just—way cool, Allen. Like we've been friends since second grade when we were Bluebirds, and now, she's famous."

"For fifteen minutes."

"Allen, you're so unsentimental."

"I'm just a realist," I said. "Mandy, who was Rose Queen last year?"

"I dunno."

"That's my point." I squeezed her fingers.

"You should be proud of her," said Mandy. "How many Rose Princesses can you name from La Cañada?"

"You *know* this stuff?"

She squeezed back extra hard, crushing my fingers. "Leta's the third. And she's a sweetheart. Don't you dare forget it, Allen. In five years, I'm sending you a pop quiz in the mail. You flunk—" she lowered her voice "—ve have our vays."

I gave a mock shudder. But at that moment, Heather Fairchild, Jenny Watson and Gina Mason had to show up in Heather's marshmallow-white Volkswagen. She screeched her brakes, rolled down her windows. Cars honked and swerved around her. Heather yelled out in a shrill voice. "Barf me out. Oh, eew!" I wondered if she was drunk. She looked angry, even mean. Perhaps, having dumped me, she wanted to keep me in her dumpster.

"Gross!" shrieked Jenny Watson. "I so can't believe you dated him."

"Shut u-uup," Heather said.

Gina snickered, "Gag me."

"She's such a dyke," said Jenny Watson. "What did you *do* to him?" She giggled.

Heather sneered. "I didn't know what he was like then."

"Guess not," Heather's friends chorused.

Mandy's hand shook. Her fingers quivered in my hand. I wasn't sure what to do here. Girl-crap was crueler than any guy-crap. I wanted to take my socks off and cram them down Heather's esophagus, wanted to disassemble her Volkswagen and cram the pieces down a storm drain. Except I couldn't. She was a girl. I sat helpless to fight back.

Jenny and Gina started singing.

Goin' to the cha-pel an' they're...

Jenny Watson and Gina Mason snapped in time to their own taunts. Horns honked. Drunks started singing. Mandy's hand felt like an ice block. Mandy was taller than me, bigger than me. I worried we looked stupid.

Cars backed up down Colorado. Heather's Volkswagen didn't move.

I felt my face flush. Mandy's grip crushed on my fingers. Heather and Gina were cracking up. I wasn't sure what this all meant.

"Don't kiss her, you'll get cooties." Gina slapped her knees. She wasn't funny, but Heather giggled like this was *Rowan and Martin's Laugh-in.*

Veins surged in my neck. Rage churned inside me. I looked into Mandy's eyes, dark with pain.

"I don't like kissing in public," I said.

"I don't either," Mandy said. "But how do we stop this?"

"We give 'em something to honk about." I pressed my thumb against her palm.

She nodded. She understood. My heart thudded in my chest like I was kneeling in the sprint blocks.

I wondered if I was really just a cover for Mandy's lez-rap. Except Leta had said she wasn't.

Heather, Jenny and Gina were still singing.

I closed my eyes. I tasted fear as my lips touched Mandy's mouth. We waited, closed our eyes. Sooner or later, they had to leave. I ran my fingers down Mandy's back and felt her stiffness and her nerves. I massaged her, until her muscles began to loosen and relax, and I felt fingertips rubbing gently on my neck.

At last the singing stopped, and Heather's Volkswagen peeled out. Cars behind her flipped us off, honked their horns, and shouted insults. But we could breathe. Heather was gone. My heart could float back down my throat.

The rest of the evening was a blur of noisy crowds and rowdy drunks. Mandy and I shared our third kiss at midnight New Year's Eve. It was a real one this time. We smooched out 1970, smooched in 1971, and for the first time I remember, I felt secure in someone's arms. It wasn't a performance. We just enjoyed each other's presence. We made a New Year's resolution to run a marathon together. Party horns, noisemakers, air horns and paper blowouts serenaded while Mandy's soft breath warmed the inside of my mouth.

It was 1971. I'd survived another year. For eighteen years, I'd built defenses—until now. I'd been surprised. Mandy liked me. I'd have to tear down all my walls. All my choice sarcastic comments I'd been saving up for months seemed non-essential. I added a second observation to my collection.

Martin's Second Observation:

It is better to be a velcroid than to be a teflonista. Only velcroids have the courage to love beyond themselves. Velcroids offer grace; teflonistas disgrace.

I had a feeling I'd be going to Vietnam before next year. But right now, I had a chance to learn to love.

The street was quiet New Year's morning. Crickets screeched from catch basins. Streets were empty, except for squad cars and discarded cigarette butts. Beer cans and packs of Marlboros littered Colorado Boulevard. I hadn't slept. I'd remembered we were a block from Suicide Bridge. My phobia of sleeping bags and zippers had gotten worse.

Body bags, Suicide Bridge. Maybe God was sending messages. Having lost a classmate, I wondered who'd be next to die. I wondered whose birthdays would be chosen in February's draft lottery. I had an awful premonition they'd choose mine.

For now, I couldn't dwell on it. Why borrow sorrow from tomorrow? Mandy slept beside me. I liked watching her breathe. She smiled. What did she dream about? She always seemed so happy. I wasn't sure how she put up with all my moods, but I was grateful.

It was good to have a friend, especially now.

Soon, Leta would ride past on the Queen's Float. Mandy was so excited. Leta, her best friend, had been crowned Princess for the Tournament of Roses. I was glad it could be Leta. She wasn't self-absorbed like Heather. If Heather had her way she'd be the bride at every wedding, the baby at every shower, even the corpse at every funeral.

Lavender lit the skyline east on Colorado Boulevard. The sun peeked into 1971. Rows of bleachers stretched for miles, crammed into every nook and cranny one could shoehorn between art deco shops and modern steel-frames beside them. Stands filled with spectators. Voices filled the chilly morning. Children and their mothers. Students and their dates.

Mandy stretched, gave a soft yawn, pulled on her sweats inside her sleeping bag and emerged to snuggle beside me.

We sat together on her beach towel while others squeezed in beside us on the lawn. I liked feeling Mandy's warmth. Dew beads glistened in the grass, leaving damp circles on my jeans. Bodies packed in. A wall of people crushed beside us.

Marching bands rang in the distance. "They're coming," a lady whispered. A mile south on Orange Grove, the first banner for the Rose Parade proceeded north. A row of sequined majorettes spun batons and headed toward us.

The crowd around us clapped and rose to watch.

"Look for Leta." Mandy squeezed my hand. "Leta told me she'll be waving from the north side of the Queen's Float." Mandy waved as if she wanted us to practice.

I waved, and we both laughed. People behind us tittered with us.

French horns grew closer. Banging drums. Trombones, Sousaphones and oboes echoed up Orange Grove Boulevard.

Bom-ba-ba-ba-ba-boom. Batons twirled above a banner.

82ND ANNUAL PASADENA
TOURNAMENT OF ROSES PARADE
QUEEN'S COURT

"There she is!" Mandy jumped up, yanking me from our beach towel, squeezing my fingers, calling "Leta, Leta, Leta."

A floral yacht turned, maneuvering east on Colorado. There was Leta in her tiara, her eyes sparkling like sapphires. We blew our New-Years-Eve horns, standing and cheering. We hollered and smiled for Leta.

She blushed, waving from her float. She rotated her waving hand like she was adding invisible light bulbs to marquees that ran the length of Pasadena. She gave a valentine-shaped smile. Seeing Mandy, Leta blew a kiss.

Mandy's eyes lit up like opals, and so did Leta's, like she was glad I'd kept my promise, happy Mandy and I were friends. Leta winked as if she'd just swung by to see how we were doing.

Then, Leta smiled for the cameras and the spectators, for Betty White, for Channel 5, for the CBS Television Network. NBC, ABC, all America saw Leta's nationally televised smile. She rolled away, adding more light bulbs to that infinite marquee, greeting the rest of Pasadena, wearing her glittered gown, smiling for the crowds like Glinda the Good had done for Dorothy and the Munchkins back in Oz. And then she vanished on a long floral conveyor belt.

I watched her drift away, remembering her meeting me after class, the day I'd promised to be Mandy's friend and being embarassed. Leta had never said a word. She rolled away, keeping my secret.

That was class.

She was replaced by Ohio State's float, and then Stanford's, a float from Farmers Insurance, Montie Montana, the McDonald's All American Marching Band. Behind them, drums and horns and flowers blurred past us down Colorado Boulevard. I watched them pass, until the flowered floats were feeling interchangeable, and bands from back east had to wallow through a massive mound of meadow muffins.

We heard that east of El Molino, something broke inside the Queen's float, and they had to call the Auto Club to tow the queens through Pasadena. There was a pause in the parade while the Auto Club hooked up.

Life was like that. I had a duty to enjoy life while I could, before the floats broke down, before the streets filled up with paper cups and horse turds, before America shipped me off to Vietnam.

When I got home from the parade, I walked on eggshells past my mom, who had passed out on the sofa in her robe and fuzzy slippers. She'd gone to sleep beside a wine bottle and a half-filled margarita glass. I saw her cigarettes on the floor. Lucky she'd been too sloshed to light one, or she might have started a fire dropping hot ashes into her carpet. I went upstairs to find a blanket, loaded her laundry into the Maytag and draped the blanket across her shoulders to keep her warm until she sobered. I wondered who would do her laundry if I got shipped to Vietnam, who'd clean her toilet, who'd take her trash out every Thursday.

I opened a can of Starfish tuna, drained the oil into the sink and plunged a fork into the fish to eat my dinner. Mom was snoring. I ambled to my room, sprawled on my bed, stared at the ceiling, at the closet, at naked walls. Six months of school left. Twenty-three weeks. Then graduation. Then Vietnam. I stared at empty walls and felt like I'd never even lived here. My mother insisted I never hang things from the walls of my own bedroom. It gave my room the sterile feeling of an unoccupied apartment. Last time I'd dared to hang a picture from my wall, my mom had freaked. She had this phobia anything framed in glass would fall during an earthquake, spraying shards of glass across the room.

I wanted to call Mandy. Except she'd be at church. And now that Mom had moved the Magnavox into her bedroom, I never watched it. For a brief moment I almost wished I had some homework to numb by brain. The walls squeezed in around me. The contractions seemed more frequent.

I closed my eyes. I tuned in KRLA on my plastic Zenith radio and found out to my consternation Heather had struck again. Disc jockey Casey Kasem read those stupid dedications for the "Sweetheart Tree" shindig he did every afternoon. Sure enough, someone had called in to request KRLA dedicate "Chapel of Love" to me from Mandy. Girl crap could be so much meaner and more vicious than any guy crap. Girl crap seemed to hurt even more than Kryptonite hurt Superman.

I consumed my can of tuna, glad noone could smell my breath. I wondered how many dedications Heather's friends were calling in. I imagined Wolfman Jack, all the KHJ "Boss Jocks," even Doctor Demento being pulled in on the joke, like they'd invited our whole high school to this party out in Hollywood, and every kid in La Cañada was laughing up their sleeves. I dreaded Monday morning. I just wanted to have a friend. What was wrong with that? Did it have to be a joke?

My nose twitched. Something smelled awful, like melting polystyrene. I turned off Casey Kasem and found the gooey remains of Bob, my trophy doofus, sprawled across my bedroom floor behind a table. I'd left the lamp on. Two-hundred watts had superheated Bob's plastic head until it melted in his noose beneath the bulb. He'd escaped. His pedestal with his toes lay by my shoes. The rest of Bob, from the heel up, had snapped off, leaving him footless, and with a black crust where his golden head had melted. The head had fused into the rug fibers. Burnt globs of styrene stained my carpet. *Crap!* Mom would be pissed. I ran to the bathroom and grabbed a washrag. Bob had betrayed me. Turned out he wasn't even good for hanging.

Fumes watered my eyes. I scrubbed the rug like crazy. I'd worried Mom would burn the house down, then nearly done the same myself. I carved a few pieces of Bob out of the pile with my Exacto knife. The scent had soaked into the backing. I tossed Bob into the waste can. Here was another "clue", and omen I'd be going to Vietnam. Three clues, you lose. I'd be dead before 1972. I simply knew it.

Except I wasn't in Vietnam yet. I was still in California, and I was letting that stupid lottery ruin my life. Perhaps I shouldn't waste time worrying about the lottery. I had a month before the drawing. But every day my Vietnam clouds grew in size.

I laced my Onitsuka Tigers, pondering a workout. Perhaps a fifteen-mile run might calm my nerves.

On Monday morning at High School, I kept listening over my shoulder, afraid of all the teasing Heather was certain to dish out. The strange thing was—Mandy and my kiss on Colorado wasn't news. Nothing in January was news. Maybe the deadlines for all those college applications saved our butts, with teflonistas writing essays on how their college educations furthered peace and ended poverty. Perhaps a few even believed it. If they did, I didn't care. Their applications brought *us* peace. They left Mandy and me alone, and we were grateful.

Throughout January, I ate with Mandy, spending our lunches laughing and sharing. A few kids smiled when they saw us. The rest paid no attention. For a month, I was happy. I had a friend who kept me smiling.

January was my calm before the storm.

CHAPTER SIXTEEN

TIME HAS COME TODAY

LA CAÑADA, CALIFORNIA: TUESDAY, FEBRUARY 2ND, 1971
(129 DAYS TO GRADUATION!)

After a fourteen-mile workout, I shook like I had Parkinson's. They'd drawn my draft number while I'd been running, too scared to listen to the lottery. At KPCC they had a phone line you could call and learn your number. I sat quivering on my bed. Long after my trophy from C.I.F. had been discarded, burnt plastic odors of Bob still wafted from my rug. The bare walls of my bedroom closed in to evict me. My handset trembled as if I'd just picked up a jackhammer.

A deep breath. I was so nervous it took three tries to dial the phone.

KPCC put me on hold.

Please not now. The Chambers Brothers kept singing *Time Has Come Today,* the long version, the one that took ten minutes to complete. After the Chambers Brothers were finished, I heard a set by Moby Grape.

C'mon, c'mon, c'mon. Answer the phone, guys.

Some Grateful Dead music.

Answer, dammit!

A woman's voice, at last, answered the phone. "What's your birthday?"

"July 21st."

"Oh, you poor son-of-a-bitch."

Uh-oh. This was a bad sign. My heart crawled into my throat. This wasn't funny. This was my future. This was my *life!*

Ten seconds' silence.

"Tough break, kid. You must have serious bad karma."

"What's my number?" My heart stopped in mid-beat.

"Your draft number is....

...Five."

"Five?"

"You'll be in someone's thoughts and prayers."

Click.

I gulped. I held my breath. *Holy fffriggin' crap!* My heart went dead. I was numb. I held my fingers up and counted them several times. Five. I groaned out loud. Five was my unlucky number. If I'd saved up all of my sticks I'd collected from all my races, I'd have a village of little log cabins built of sticks with little fives on them. For some reason, all along, I'd known my draft number would suck. It was true—my worst fears. I was going to Vietnam.

I closed my eyes, phone still in hand, still hearing the Chambers Brothers playing, seeing a giant number five, like it was flashing on my ceiling. I no more imagined myself fighting in the War in Vietnam than G.I. Joe dancing the hula or Fashion

Barbie playing fullback. It was ludicrous. I was a runner. What could I do in Vietnam; run from rocket-propelled grenades? Chase down Charlie's bullets?

No one understood. My neighbor, whose draft number was 350, told me the only moral choice for me was prison. Prison? What did that solve? Who'd made the neighbor kid the ethics czar? Even kids caught peddling dope volunteered for Vietnam instead of prison. Maybe Muhammad Ali was rough enough for prison, but I wasn't. Getting corn-holed hardly seemed a moral statement. In my case, those giant prison guards were more than twice my size. I hated my neighbor's easy answers for *my* moral dilemmas.

There were C.O.s, conscientious objectors. But my draft board over in Hollywood was so fed up with peaceniks not even Pope Paul could walk away with a C.O. I'd have to hire some high-priced lawyer who cost more than Melvin Belli to convince the Hollywood draft board I didn't really like to kill people. A C.O. slot probably cost as much as Zsa Zsa Gabor's jewelry, *even if* I showed up with stigmata.

Draft numbers. One more way of choosing velcroids and teflonistas. Low numbers meant bad karma; high ones—virtue. There remained three other options; going to Canada, becoming a homosexual or self-inflicted wounds.

A deep breath. Mom wasn't home. One of her friends had taken her shopping. I knew opportunity knocked but once.

I stumbled from my room, out the back door to the garage, removed my shoes and socks. I could fix this thing right now. I stared at my big toes, deciding whether the left one or the right one should take the hit. I imagined taking a tree saw or Dad's rifle—a 44, inflicting the "million-dollar wound," pulling the trigger. I visualized my toe splattering the wall, leaving a red spot on the concrete from a gap on my left foot ugly enough and wide enough to disqualify me from service.

I lowered the garage door. I had to do it. The 44 had last been spotted somewhere underneath Dad's tool chest in an unlocked metal cabinet. I pushed the tools aside. I tossed off some random boards, a pile of rags, a stack of paint cans, and there it was. Cobwebs covered a chipped 48-star-flag decal on the cabinet.

A red spider scurried away. I cleared off ancient webs, opened the latch and smelled the gun oil. Dad's 44 had been sitting there since he'd come home from Korea. I lifted the rifle, sat on the concrete, butting the stock against my shoulder, released the safety. I stared down at my foot. I took a deep breath, closed my eyes. This would only take a second.

One last look. I saw my toenail in the sight.

Sad faces on my toenails begged for mercy. I almost felt tears drip across my cuticles. "Don't hurt us," said my toes. "Please, don't blow us to smithereens. Toes are your friends, Allen." My feet fluttered in fear. "Toes let you run."

I closed my eyes and pulled the trigger.

Nothing happened.

"Crap." I pulled the trigger again.

BAAAANG! The recoil kicked me hard enough to spin me on my butt like one of those spinners you get in Milton Bradley board games. The gunbarrel somersaulted over me, leaving a huge dent in Dad's tool chest. The bullet ricocheted off concrete, leaving a quarter-inch-deep gash. My shoulder throbbed as if a horse had kicked it. I stared down at my foot, expecting the worst.

All ten of my toes wiggled in terror.

A long sigh. I couldn't do it. I was too soft, too sympathetic to even blow off my own toe. What were my chances of killing Charlie in Vietnam?

I stumbled back across the driveway, tiptoeing to my bedroom, shoes in hand, knowing with toes I could still tiptoe, even run. The unhooked handset on my bed now beeped at me with fury. I slammed it down, stared at the phone.

I had to talk to someone. I called the only person I trusted. Mandy answered. "Hello?"

"It's Allen. I need to see you at Flint Peak. I have to see you."

"I'll be there."

I closed my eyes. I was lucky she was my friend.

Having already run a workout, I was exhausted when I finally reached Flint Peak. Mandy was waiting. She'd been waiting twenty minutes. It wasn't like me to be late, but if you added in the miles I'd run earlier, I'd already run a marathon today. I still shook. I kept holding up my hand and counting fingers, repeating the number *five*. How could my draft number be *five?* Why did God hate me?

She held my fingers. Her hand was cold, but it was calming.

"Whatcha gonna do?" She squeezed my hand.

"I dunno yet. I've been goin' over options. When I called you I was considering removing my big toe."

"Allen?"

"It has to be the *big* toe. None of the other toes will satisfy my draft board."

"You're serious?" Mandy laughed, staring at me, head cocked askew.

We sat and watched the sunset. The sun rippled through the horizon. Lights from Glendale and Burbank peeked up Chevy Chase Canyon. The tower lights overhead crackled in the night.

Mandy gripped my fingers. "You're scared, Allen."

"Uh-huh."

"But you aren't dead yet."

"Damn it. Your draft number isn't five, Mandy."

"I know that."

"You don't know half of it. You didn't see how Wock got hurt. We played the football team—in football. Harron called the play. Fifty guys came off the bench and piled on Wocky's knee, leaving him crippled. It was a miracle he ran against San Marino."

A lonely cricket filled the night.

"I figured out why I finish fifth. I'm scared. I'm scared to win, afraid if I do better, they'll want more. They'll pile on. Look what happened to the Wocky or Ethan Frome. You live up to others' expectations until one day—SNAP!—they break you."

We sat apart. I felt fragile and untouchable. Like this whole thing was my fault. It was all about my karma, and I didn't have a clue what I'd done wrong.

We ran down the hill together past the yuccas. My legs wobbled from pain from running 30 miles in a day. I saw Mandy had been training. She had to slow for *me.* She had her heart set on that marathon. If nothing else, I swelled with pride knowing I'd taught her Occam's Razor, taught her to run.

If I could just use Occam's Razor on my life.

I rarely woke up early, but on February 9th, I was wide-eyed and alert at six a.m. The usual mockingbirds, the humming-birds and mourning doves were silent. An eerie quiet settled in. The air seemed dormant, too calm, too still for a February morn....

A low rumble. A rattle, then a jolt. Something snapped. The house shook.

Crap! I panicked, sitting straight up in my bed, staring forward like a marionette doll strung up at attention.

Crashing, groaning, tossing. The ceiling wiggled like a drum skin. Breaking glass. Books fell off the shelves. The ground surged and pulsed beneath me, shaking me, bouncing me, tossing me like a sabot in a squall. A jolt threw me to the floor, and I scrambled to a doorway. Loud cracking timbers, shattering windows. A rumble and a crash thundered from the living room.

I froze in terror. *Holy friggin' crap!*

"Eek!" Mom screamed.

A pause.

I crawled upstairs to find her.

"STAY IN YOUR ROOM," she screamed. "Go back downstairs and hide beneath the covers."

"What?" I struggled toward her. The floor bounced up and down like it was Jello.

"Under the covers. Stay underneath the covers." She hid beneath her blanket like you did when you were five, hiding from monsters. Her voice was muffled, but as loud as any bullhorn.

I scrambled downstairs. Finding a doorway, I heard my mother's screams.

Floors rocked and rattled. Walls wobbled and shook like trampoline skins. A bookshelf tumbled from the wall, spilling dusty books and knick-knacks across smashed tile. A vase of flowers fell off a table. Dishes shattered. Bottles fell from the refrigerator, pouring wine onto the tile where it bled across the grout into the carpet in the family room.

"Mom?"

A loud noise. Diagonal cracks split through plaster around the fireplace. Huge blocks of masonry tumbled through the ceiling. CRASH! A cow-sized hole loomed overhead where the pile of bricks and shingles had fallen through our roof.

Holy crap! "Mom? We lost our chimney."

No answer.

Another snap. Another jolt. My spine froze. *Where was mom?* My neck tightened in terror. An Arcadia door exploded. CRACK! There went the shower glass. There went the window in my bedroom.

A pause. "MOM?"

Another ten seconds of shaking.

Then it stopped....

My breath rushed. I rubbed my stomach, massaging knots of fear inside me. I waited, afraid the shaking might resume.

Maybe Edgar Cayce was right. California was toast. At any moment the whole San Andreas Fault might just unzip, and we'd be underneath the sea, talking to killer whales and sharks while Arizonans drew up plans for new cabanas on their beaches. I waited, expecting doom, afraid the shaking might resume, wondering if my mother was okay.

Silence. I counted seconds. I'd never heard such noisy silence. Ten seconds. Twenty seconds. Mom plodded down the stairs wearing her purple quilted bathrobe and her lavender fuzzy slippers, carrying her nine-transistor Motorola radio. My heart jump-started with gratitude. "Mom, you all right?"

She nodded numbly.

"Mom, I love you."

"I'm okay, Allen," she said. Mom never touched me. Now, she hugged me, shaking like she needed me as an anchor.

"So am I, Mom."

Her fingers tightened around my arm. Her painted nails gouged me. "Thank God, son. Oh, thank God."

She tuned her Motorola to KNX Radio. Reports were streaming in. There'd been an earthquake somewhere north, a 6.7 on the Richter scale. A freeway overpass had caved. There were fires, broken gas mains. Water mains spouted up in geysers. The Olive View Sanitorium had been leveled. The V.A. Hospital had collapsed, and there were people trapped inside. According to Cal Tech, the epicenter was near Sylmar. Sirens whined out of Mom's radio. People were dead in that V.A. Hospital. A pickup truck beneath an overpass had been mashed beneath the freeway. Reporters were adding up the casualties.

An ad cut in for Miller's Outpost.

"Allen," whispered my mom. "Thanks for caring."

We sat waiting for more news amidst a pile of brick and glass inside our living room, holding each other, shaking in socks and slippers. A breeze parted the curtains. A car engine started up outside. The radio announced which school districts had cancelled all their classes. La Cañada Unified wasn't one of them.

And then Mom cried, digging her nails into my shoulders and sobbing. "Allen, Allen, Allen, Allen...."

She'd never called me son. She rarely called me Allen. It felt so good. I was more than just the stupid kid downstairs. She wanted me, needed me. This—I wasn't used to. I felt her heart. It was beating. I'd forgotten her heart did that. Perhaps the earthquake had changed her, the way a clock starts if you shake it. Or now that her wine bottles had been smashed she couldn't pour herself a drink.

I held her hand. I was trying to be strong, to be a son, to be worthy. I wondered who'd fix our damaged house. Who paid for the repairs? Did we even have insurance? But at least I had a mother. I savored every second. Even the fingernails cutting arcs into my shoulders now felt tender. For the first time since November, my mom and I were speaking.

I enjoyed it for ten minutes, before I had to dash to school. I wondered if the school was even standing.

At the high school, I parked my Yamaha in the cage, threw my bike bag on my shoulder and hustled upstairs to stuff my motorcycle helmet into my locker. My normal staircase was blockaded with a maze of yellow tape, spanning across a mess of twisted rebar and broken concrete. I rushed to another staircase. Kids milled around the hallway, amazed and bummed to see our high school hadn't fallen. I was relieved when I saw Mandy. We couldn't talk for long. She was rattled, but she assured me she was fine.

When the bell rang, only ten students sat in their seats inside the chem lab. Mister Copelan, our chemistry teacher, waded through the broken glass. I was surprised they'd even let us in the classroom with all the damage. I studied the mess with morbid fascination.

I'd always wondered what might happen if I walked into my chemistry class and mixed *all* of those chemicals together. Well, this morning I found out. A puddle of brown ooze congealed on the classroom floor tile. The stuff reeked worse than rotten eggs and dead mice mixed together. Black stains covered Linoleum, leaving little fuzzy crystals. The scent of iodine emerged from a closet of broken beakers. Heat had blackened the flooring. A jar of sodium had ignited, leaving brown circles in 9-inch-square asbestos tile.

We held our noses inside chem lab, comparing stories of this morning's Sylmar Earthquake. People whispered and passed notes. We still felt numb. Mr. Copelan and Tony the Teaching Assistant shoveled up debris. Mr. Copelan couldn't teach. There were no beakers in his cabinets. No test tubes, flasks or bottles. Broken glass blanketed his floor.

We whispered while Mr. Copelan hauled a trash can to the dumpster. Ivan Alphabet had lost a tree. A couple kids had lost their chimneys. Garry Jackson and Heather Fairchild had no damage.

It figured.

When Mr. Copelan returned, he'd scrounged a broom and two more dustpans. He asked three students for their help. Luckily, I wasn't one of them. I expected hallucinations from the stench of all those chemicals. Mine wasn't the only headache. Tony the Teaching Assistant staggered outside like he was seriously buzzed.

An aftershock rocked the room. Sara Jensen shrieked. She ducked and covered, hands on her head. She'd always been a little skittish. Mr. Copelan apologized, as if the earthquake were his fault and then excused us, asking us to try school again tomorrow. It was weird. We waited in the hall for a full hour. Second period, Mrs. Z. never showed. By third period, a group of firemen and inspectors combed the hallways. They studied cracks in a concrete stair landing exposing steel rebar. Rumor had it school was cancelled. My next classroom was near-empty. Guys leaving Harron's class informed me today's lecture was on discipline.

That settled it. After an earthquake, I had no stomach for Mr. Harron. Any rumors school was cancelled were good enough for me. I grabbed my running clothes, suiting up to tour La Cañada, curious to see first-hand how bad the damage was.

I ran past blocks of damaged buildings, rows of stores with shattered windows. Houses had ruptured chimneys, broken driveways, fallen fence walls. The radio at the Chevron had the death tally up to fifty. I felt brittle, afraid and fragile. Even Garry'd acted numb. From Foothill Boulevard, I turned up Commonwealth, jogged Craig Avenue to Angeles Crest. County work trucks drove the neighborhoods. Inspectors red-tagged damage. Stucco cracks, even on new homes, left them looking like giant roadmaps.

I wondered what it cost to repair them.

When I got home at three o'clock, a Ford pick-up was out front. I was surprised they'd sent a guy from the insurance company so soon. Some fat adjuster from United States Insurance had stopped by. He introduced himself as Buster. Something about him in his white slacks and company-logo yellow polo shirt made my spine crawl. Here was "Buster the Adjuster," telling my mom our damage wouldn't cover our deductible.

Yeah, right, fat boy. Look again. Start with the big hole in the roof. They probably paid this tub of lard two-hundred bucks a house to clear up easy claims, close them quickly, before some unsuspecting schmuck discovered the damage their adjuster had carefully ignored.

"Missus Martin. Y'all have a two-thousand dollah deductible, ah see." Buster had memorized his script and sounded smoother than a snake and twice as slippery. "Pretty hard to overcome that high a hurdle, even with your chimney, but ah'll give 'er the old college try, Missus Martin."

Mom said, "Thanks."

"What college did you go to?" I asked Buster.

He looked away.

Mom looked annoyed. "It's just a figure of speech, Allen." Her voice rasped with irritation. "I can handle this, okay?"

"Mom, watch out. You're not exactly in good hands here with good neighbors."

Buster pointed at himself. "Ah always try to be fair." His voice oozed across the room, turning my stomach. "Ah take pride in my profession, Missus Martin. Ah might be able to swing mebbe a couple thousand if we work hard at it and mebbe stretch some rules." Buster glanced at Mom as if her script said to act grateful.

"Uh, Mom?"

"Allen, not now." Mom shooed me off. "Shush. Please go outside. I need to concentrate."

"Mom, I wouldn't count on this guy stretching things our way."

"Don't be cynical," she said. "Go outside."

Buster nodded.

I took a long sloooow breath. Where was Dad now that we needed him? I loathed the thought of Buster taking advantage of my mom. I scratched my head. "Be back in ten, Mom. Don't sign anything. Promise me."

"Where are you...?"

Slam! went the screen door. My mind whirled.

I dashed to the garage. I had to hurry while Buster talked. I trusted Buster about as far as I could throw a giant slime ball. I found Dad's flashlight in his tool chest. The garage slab was in pieces. New cracks rambled across our driveway. Concrete foundations had to be brittle too. If there were cracks in our foundation, United Snakes Insurance was gonna pay for them. That oughtta help with our deductible. But first, I had to find them—like in ten minutes before Mom caved in to Buster.

And I knew something about cracks. When I wasn't painting bathrooms, I'd patched cracks in the school basement and covered them over with gray enamel.

I pulled the screen out from the entrance to our crawl space, disturbing dust that had settled there for decades. I wriggled into the crawl well and snaked into the dim underspace. Footsteps thumped across wood flooring in the dining room above me. The shaft of light from the crawl entry seemed smaller every minute. Dust filled my lungs, coated my cheeks, scratched underneath my eyelids. I breathed shallow. The floor muffled the voice of Buster and his routine. In darkness, I prayed Mom wouldn't sign.

I found three fresh cracks between the crawl space entry and the back wall of our house. *Bingo!* The crawling became slower. I squeezed beneath a water main, rubbing my chin against the dust, exhaling until my lungs and chest barely squeezed beneath a pipe. I pushed spider webs aside. I saw a pair of big black widows. I shined my light on them, and neither of them moved. I had to hurry before Mom signed. My knees throbbed from the crawl. I shoved aside a dried up mouse, finding out I traveled faster if, instead of crawling, I rolled to save my knees.

There were five cracks on the rear wall. I found four more on the south wall. There was a big one on the front that let in narrow shafts of light. A girder and joists were shattered where the fireplace had fallen. I found cracks along the mud sill where it had split at the foundation bolts. A puddle of fresh crap stank where the sewer main had separated.

Bastard adjuster. I scurried through dust as fast as I could wiggle, between a maze of pipes and stem walls and leaning piers.

Light. There was the opening. I wanted out of here, and now. I wriggled as fast as I could scurry out the crawl hole.

Coughing up dust, grateful for air, I stood upright in real light. My spit tasted like mud. "Mom!" I panted, staggering down our driveway to our kitchen door, sweating and coughing. "Mom, don't sign...."

Mom screamed, "Allen, what...." She stood inside our back door, arms folded, guarding her kitchen. "Don't you *dare* come inside."

"We got cracks in our foundation, Mom. *Fifteen* cracks. I saw them."

"Oh my...." She walked out onto the patio and drew her hand across her mouth. "Good God, you look like Pig Pen out of Peanuts. Where on earth...?" She grabbed a rag and mopped my forehead, showing me black smears on the terry cloth. "Allen Martin, look how dirty.... Take your shoes off. Where were you?"

"Crawled under the house. Mom, there's tons of damage down there."

"You what?" Mom dried my forehead with Scott towels.

Buster joined us with his standard-issue smile. "Missus Martin, there's no cause for alarm." He touched her shoulder. I was wondering how soon Buster might pat her head. "Most

California houses have some pre-existin' damage. You see, it really don't much matter. In Texas, where ah come from, we build houses on right cindah blocks. So it's fine if y'all have cracks...."

"Do you bolt houses to those cinder blocks in Texas?" I asked. I was steamed, not just from sweat now. "'Cause we bolt foundations here. Except you might not know that if you just flew in from Texas. Ever crawl beneath a house in California?"

Buster ignored me. "Missus Martin, you seem like a fair and decent woman."

Mom tapped her foot.

"An' ah thought we had a deal. Ah get paid to settle claims, fast and fair, ah like to think. But if y'all won't cooperate, that's okay by me. Just know your next adjuster might be a bit more difficult. Ah worked hard just to give you fifteen-hundred."

"Allen, you're filthy. Your face is blacker than a coal mine." Mom was laughing. A good sign.

She turned to Buster, arms still folded. "Thanks," she said. "But no thanks."

"Now repairin' your foundation ain't necessary, Missus Martin."

"Excuse me?"

"This is a single family home. Earthquakes don't damage single...."

"Then why do we buy insurance?" Mom lasered darts at Buster, foot still tapping. I'd never seen my mom so angry when she was sober.

No answer came. Buster the Adjuster had been busted.

Ding! Lights were going on in Mom.

Buster stiffened. "Well don't say ah didn't warn you, Missus Martin." He shook his head. Grabbing his notes, he tidied up his briefcase. "Ah don't have time to argue." He shut his briefcase and spun the lock. "Don't be surprozzed if your next adjuster simply starves you people out."

Buster slammed the entrance door behind him.

We listened, rolling our eyes as Buster started up his pickup and squealed off. Mom stood numb. "How did you know they were such bastards? Where did you learn about construction?"

"I'm a school painter, remember? That's construction." I squeezed Mom's hand.

She nodded before she hugged me. It suddenly felt good to be a son.

I hugged her. She felt tender, almost brittle in my arms. I was grateful we were in this thing together as a family, at least until I went to Vietnam.

A day later, I sat in English, enjoying how Mrs. Zinicola's breasts danced and bounced beneath her pearls and purple turtleneck. I sat surrounded by posters of famous British authors—Shakespeare, Charles Dickens, Lewis Carroll, Emily Bronte. Like my own, their gaze was glued toward the center of the classroom, where Mrs. Z offered her thoughts on Oliver Twist. The authors' mouths turned up in smiles, with the exception of Oscar Wilde, who leered and faced the other way.

Today was chilly. A winter rain pattered a row of open windows. A February shower brought in a clean electric scent.

I'd completed a page of notes on Artful Dodger and Oliver Twist when Conrad the Dipshit opened the door and stuck his bald head through the opening.

"Excuse me, Mrs. Zinicola? I need a word with you outside."

I wondered what was so important. This wasn't just class he'd interrupted. This was Mrs. Zinicola.

She stepped outside.

We waited.

We waited longer.

Heather whispered.

What was happening? Had they kicked Mrs. Zinicola off the faculty? Something worse?

The wall clock ticked off seven minutes while we waited.

She staggered inside, wearing a deer-in-headlights stare, tugging her scarf. She sat down behind her desk, reading a yellow sheet of paper, chewing a pencil, staring out at Oscar Wilde and holding her breath.

Mr. Conrad's footsteps tapered down the hall and turned the corner.

Our eyes riveted on the note. We were all afraid to breathe. Something was wrong. Something awful. Mrs. Zinicola trembled. She sat shaking in her seat. We all wanted to ask what happened, but no one spoke.

Mrs. Z wadded the paper into a lemon-sized ball and threw it, eyes shut, nailing Sara Jansen's forehead.

We sat stunned. This wasn't the Mrs. Zinicola we were used to. Her lips moved in slow motion. Her gaze could bore through concrete walls. Her glossy lips appeared to whisper, but we couldn't quite make out what she whispered around her Eberhard Faber number 2H pencil.

"What's wrong?" asked Sara Jansen, rubbing her forehead.

Mrs. Zinicola glared down at the envelope, blinking her eyes. She stared out at her posters like she was looking for an ally. All of us seemed afraid to meet her gaze.

She looked so shattered. I'd never thought someone so sexy could be shattered. I wanted to comfort her. For a moment, I forgot about her beauty. She'd always been this fantasy, brightening my second period. Now, she was crumbling into pieces right in front of us.

"God Damn him straight to Hell." Mrs. Z. said to her desk. "I swear, if I ever get the chance, someone'll pay."

A minute later, the bell rang. When we walked out, she'd put her head down. None of us had a clue what had been written on that note.

Heather Fairchild scooped the crumpled-lemon ball up from off the floor and jammed it into her purse with no change in her expression.

We crowded around her, outside Mr. Harron's third period class. We all knew Heather never kept a secret.

According to Heather, known as "Radio Free La Cañada" for a reason, The Sylmar earthquake had dumped the Zinicolas' chimney through their roof. Half their swimming pool had tumbled off the cliff near Harter Lane. After the earthquake, Heather figured Mr. Z. had no insurance and was buried to his eyeballs under his mortgage. We'd all heard how Mr. Z had been canned by Yogi Bear after Hanna-Barbara Studios had yanked *Penelope Pitstop*. That meant money problems. Big money problems for Mr. Zinicola, who'd been caught popping a pint a day of No Doze.

Mrs. Z had been concerned. Now she was a widow. Mr. Z. had run his Jaguar off Angeles Crest Highway. He'd crashed a guardrail near Red Box Junction at 100 miles-per-hour. The steering column had run straight through his heart.

In my fantasies, I stepped up to Mrs. Zinicola's rescue. Didn't the Bible say I was supposed to help out widows? I imagined her in her doorway, those wondrous cantaloupe-sized breasts waiting for me, actually glad to see me for a change. We spent pleasant afternoons discussing cabbages and kings before she finally made me dinner. Except, it dawned on me the money I could pull down painting bathrooms didn't add up to the payments on Mrs. Z's Pepto-Bismobile. And she'd be broke if the insurance company ruled her husband committed suicide. And I'd be dead after I went to Vietnam.

I prayed for myself. I also prayed for Mrs. Zinicola.

I wondered if it did us any good.

CHAPTER SEVENTEEN

DEAD MAN'S CURVE

LA CAÑADA HIGH SCHOOL:
THURSDAY, FEBRUARY 11TH, 1971
(120 DAYS TO GRADUATION!)

On Thursday, we'd been sitting outside the classroom for ten minutes when John the janitor helped Mister Conrad unlock the door. Conrad strolled into our classroom. We whispered with speculation. Why was Conrad here? Where was Mrs. Zinicola?

Conrad stood by Mrs. Z.'s desk. He told us to sit down. John the janitor walked behind him with a big brown empty bag. He stripped posters off the walls, securing each poster into a cylinder with a crisp, red rubber band, stuffing them into his shopping bag like giant cigarettes. I waved goodbye to Lewis Carroll, Charles Dickens and Oscar Wilde.

John wrapped an old ceramic walrus inside a half a box of Kleenex. He cleared the top of Mrs. Z.'s desk, emptying her desk drawers. He packed each item like an artifact being shipped to a museum. I glanced at Mandy. John the janitor filled his second bag. Mandy raised her hands and shrugged. John was weeping. Why had Conrad made him do this in front of us?

Conrad's manner didn't help. He paced the room, clearing his throat. "We have a problem," said Mr. Conrad. "Mrs. Zinicola will be taking a leave of absence."

"What?"

"No way," said Tina Sue Delgado.

"What happened?" asked Sara Jensen.

Heather smiled at Sara. "You don't know, Sara?"

"A private matter," said Conrad.

Sara hung her head. I felt for Sara. Save for Heather's gossip, we'd all think Mrs. Z. had died. You could always count on Conrad to be so tight with information he fueled rumors that were far worse than the truth. But of course, that's how Conrad, the Mighty Dipshit, kept his power and kept shy people like Sara in the dark.

Conrad informed us he'd hired a substitute. I looked up, and I saw her; the dreaded Flora Winchcombe walked into the classroom.

"Mrs. Winchcombe?" said Pudge McMasters. "Grrrross. Isn't she dead yet?" We'd liked Mrs. Zinicola. She'd been easy on the eyes. Now, Mrs. Winchcombe was taking over—the flip-side of good karma. If Mrs. Zinicola was too happy, Mrs. Winchcombe was a pit bull, on a bad day, at full moon, with an infection. She was uglier than Bette Davis serving Joan Crawford rats for "din din" in that ancient *Whatever Happened to Baby Jane?* flick. I imagined Mrs. Winchcombe lived in a castle up Angeles Crest where she burned wormwood-scented candles and knitted sweaters for vampire bats.

We sighed as Mr. Conrad stepped outside.

Mrs. Winchcombe opened Mrs. Z's desk drawer, found a piece of yellow chalk. Her lips tightened as if they were being sucked into a soda straw. She toddled toward the blackboard and wrote in script.

Ethan Frome
by Edith Wharton

We were so hosed.

She cackled in her geriatric voice. "This semester, we'll study *Ethan Frome*."

My heart dropped like a brick. I was afraid for several seconds our entire class might slash our wrists in unison.

"Again?" thirty voices groaned in harmony, mine included.

She wrote a date up on the blackboard, Thursday, February 25th. "I expect within two weeks you will all have found a copy of *Ethan Frome* and read at least the first three chapters," said Mrs. Winchcombe.

I wrote the date down on my arm. I wasn't quite sure why. For some reason, I figured the date might be important.

"This is a fine American novel." Mrs. Winchcombe glared at us.

"That's the point," Tina Sue Delgado interrupted. "It's American. We're supposed to be in BritLit, Mrs. Winchcombe. We read that tripe last year."

"'Tripe?'" said Mrs. Winchcombe. "Did you say 'tripe?'"

A death-ray glare withered Tina in her place. It occurred to me all of us were obsessing about dying.

As Mrs. Winchcombe began rambling about the symbolism of Starkfield, I knew my next *mitzvah*, done in the Jabberwocky's memory, was to somehow make sure *Ethan Frome* went out of circulation. I couldn't stand another round of Zeena ruining Ethan's life, a teflonista driving a velcroid toward suicide.

If I got busted, what could they do to me? Send me to Vietnam?

Or was the war the hidden agenda? Why were they teaching *Ethan Frome?* Was Mrs. Winchcombe training all of us to die?

It was a crisis. I hadn't held a meeting of The Society for the Complete Extermination of *Ethan Frome* for seven months. This was entirely my fault. In my club's first year of meeting, I hadn't recruited a single member. Now, the wicked Mrs. Winchcombe had escaped Hades. She'd recrossed the River Styx, the River Phlegethon, the River Acheron, grabbed Charon's coin and plopped it back into her mouth, emerging from hell to inflict our senior class with Edith Wharton's darkest novel.

I stared at Mandy. She looked back. We had to stop Mrs. Winchcombe. The Society needed me, its sole member, to write a plan; an *Ethan Frome de*-marketing plan, erasing *Ethan Frome* from memory. What sort of role model was Ethan Frome? That was the problem being male. You didn't get good stories or good role models. You either got John Wayne bad-asses you had no chance of being, or Ethan Frome losers whose crowning achievement had been to crash into a tree.

Stories for men were broken. *Ethan Frome* needed to go. Small wonder the Jabberwocky jumped off Suicide Bridge after his injury left him crippled, unable to be a bad-ass. Maybe erasing *Ethan Frome* was a *mitzvah*. Since school had started, we'd already had two suicides.

My mind shifted into overdrive. If *Ethan Frome* stopped making money, Charles Scribner would stop printing it.

Bingo!

I racked my brain and wrote past midnight using a marketing plan my old man had prepared for Cap'n Crunch cereal as my model. Mom was snoring in her bedroom. I filled two yellow legal pads with bubble diagrams and brainstorms, sifting through possibilities, boiling down a plan of action that flowed forth from my brain like high-octane gasoline from a Union Oil refinery.

It went like this:

DE-MARKETING PLAN
prepared for
THE SOCIETY FOR THE COMPLETE EXTERMINATION
OF ETHAN FROME
by Allen Daniel Martin

EXECUTIVE SUMMARY:
Immediate action is required to halt the inflicting of Ethan Frome on the consciousness of American youth. The story is disheartening, suicidal and depressing, offering unacceptable

role models for children. A plan to remove this novel from Southern California classrooms is needed now to ensure that by February 25th, 1971, this novel can no longer be found. This document presents a strategy to achieve this. It defines changes to product, price, promotion and place to ensure Ethan Frome vanishes from all high school curricula.

PRODUCT:
The novel sucks. Nobody would read it if it weren't forced upon our youth by teachers across America. The product, as it stands, would be hard to disimprove on. Therefore, no changes to the product are proposed.

PRICE:
Scribner's list price of $1.95 is too low. A new list price of $79.95 is recommended to discourage further sales in California. The price change will be accomplished by intercepting shipments to local distribution warehouses and adding book covers and stickers, displaying the new price. Where possible, jackets should also be added to existing bookstore copies before hiding them behind other books as described below.

PROMOTION:
The book jacket is too colorful. A gray one is preferred, with no printing on the spine, symbolic of the dreariness of Starkfield. Testimonials should be added; back-cover

warnings from other authors alerting poten-
tial readers not to read this book. Blurbs
such as the following are appropriate:

"Stop! Don't buy this. My book's better."
J.D. Salinger,
or
"Total crap." Ernest Hemmingway,
or
"This book blows." Penelope Ashe

PLACE:
The current placement of this book renders the
product too accessible. The only acceptable
placement of Ethan Frome is behind another
book. Copies in all bookstores must be hidden
on lower shelves in sections for unrelated
genres. Booksellers may object to having Ethan
Frome relocated, so agents must act quickly
and unobtrusively. Representatives are advised
to blend in and dress plainly to avoid any
risk of being detected.
Where possible, library copies shall be placed
on teacher's reserve shelves to ensure no one
is allowed to check them out. Other copies
shall be hidden where library staff won't find
them. Utility closets and crawl spaces are
excellent locations.

IMPLEMENTATION:
Immediate implementation of this de-mar-
keting plan is imperative to ensure Ethan
Frome cannot be taught. Agents must ensure

bookstores are no longer permitted to profit from inflicting Ethan Frome on schoolchildren. Under Phase I of this plan, a working chapter of the Society must be established, immediately, in Southern California.

Phase II will implement the program shown above. To avoid capture of our agents, no lists of members will be printed. No dues will be collected. Work will be strictly volunteer and on the hush-hush.

After Phase II is completed, if the membership is willing, under Phase III, the Society will establish chapters nationwide, until Ethan Frome disappears entirely from America's High School education system.

Respectfully submitted:
Allen Daniel Martin

At three a.m., the final sheet of type rolled from my typewriter. I caught four short hours of sleep and woke at seven in the morning. I phoned up Mandy, read her my plan. She said she was excited. I had a member. Our membership had doubled overnight.

I looked down at my arm. The February, 25th deadline was staring back at me. It was time for Ethan Frome to watch his back.

There was one more thing to do. I had to buy a card for Mandy—and my mother. While I was alive, I had a duty to be thoughtful. I wasn't blown to bits yet. A year from now I'd be stuck in Vietnam, where I had doubts that Charlie Cong was selling valentines.

I found a great big card for Mandy at Jundt's Drug. And some flowers for my mother. In the shadow of Vietnam, I might not get another chance to say I love you in a world that didn't say it very often.

I left mom's flowers in the kitchen, placed Mandy's valentine beneath the windshield wiper on her egg-nog-colored Volkswagen and ran away.

By day's end, I had two valentines myself, two more than Charlie Brown. One from my mother; one from Mandy. I held my treasures. Charlie Brown could eat his heart out.

And Ethan Frome was going down. Tomorrow.

On Monday morning, boiling fog behind Devil's Gate Dam gave the air a film-noir feeling Jimmy Cagney might admire. I met Mandy behind the bleachers on the west side of the track. We whispered. No one saw us pour over our plans.

We had a mission. Our lives now had a purpose we'd agreed on. Not like the "meaning" teflonistas dreamed up for college entrance essays. But MEANING. Removing *Ethan Frome* from all high school curricula was a mission any student could relate to.

The *Ethan Frome* emergency had reached such dire proportions we had no choice but to keep our purpose secret. We knew this was a *mitzvah,* a commandment straight from God. Why else would Mandy have an uncle, a San Pedro longshoreman, who had a key that unlocked Charles Scribners's book warehouse? Riddle me that, Batman.

"Super," I told Mandy. "You sure your uncle will help us?"

She nodded, and she smiled. "Ve have vays."

"How 'bout the covers?"

"I have a friend— " she said, "—who's perfect for this assignment."

"Who?"

She blushed. "Trust me, this artist's soooo perfect."

"Who is he?"

Mandy frowned. "Maybe it's a she."

"That doesn't exactly narrow it down."

"Ssssh!" she whispered. I had to trust her. She was my only friend with access to a print shop. She'd covered three of the hardest tasks on our de-marketing plan, printing covers, printing price tags, and unlocking Scribners's warehouse. I had enough tasks on my plate just to deal with the "placement." Copies of *Ethan Frome* were spreading like a cancer across L.A. I had to hide them. With Mandy as my driver, I'd ride shotgun. She was the Bonnie to my Clyde.

Now, the burden fell to me.

I was glad, being a runner, I had efficiency and speed. I'd scoured the local library, finding addresses for all the book dealers in Southern California. I'd drawn up routes on AAA maps, plotting our course to local bookstores. By Monday night, my maps ready, I'd phoned Mandy at home. She'd informed me our covers would come today.

"All right, Mandy. How'd you get 'em done so fast?"

"Ve have vays."

"Can I see 'em?"

"Eight o'clock tomorrow morning."

I couldn't wait. I was pacing across the asphalt at seven-thirty, when Mandy's Volkswagen pulled into the Senior lot.

She didn't even say hello. She just opened up the hood, exposing five-hundred gorgeous book covers printed in stunning death-mask gray. No titles were on the spine, exactly as recommended. The price, $79.95 was displayed on every cover. Admonitions from famous authors had been printed on the back. But the picture on the cover blew my mind.

Here was an ink-drawing of a maniac that reminded me of a cross between Alfred E. Newman and Coney Island's Steeplechase Man. He almost leaped out of the cover on his runaway toboggan. His drooling tongue flapped from his mouth. His ears, back-blown by wind, crusted with icicles. He looked sick, just exactly what I'd dreamed of. The art was magic. Its very presence could make any book look stupid. And on the center of the toboggan, bigger than an eight-ball, a big black circle displayed the number five.

"Nice touch," I said to Mandy.

She smiled a big sardonic grin.

Tree roots branched up from the cover-bottom as if Edith Wharton's elm tree had snapped a photo of *Ethan Frome* less than a second before he crashed. The smile on this guy's face looked like he couldn't wait to die.

We wrapped a cover around one book. It fit like spray paint.

I grabbed my maps. "Let's go." Mandy and I leaped into her Volkswagen. She cranked the engine, and we hauled butt from La Cañada, ditching class. Within ten minutes we were standing in front of Vroman's in Pasadena. We synchronized our watches.

"Three, two, one..."

We worked Vroman's at warp speed. Hustling through the aisles, I carried a copy of the *Sporting News*, last week's edition, from Harron's trash. Within ten seconds, we were in business in the literary aisle. Under W for Wharton were six copies of *Ethan Frome*. With assembly-line presision, six new prefolded covers were dispensed between my fingers from the pages of the *Sporting News*. Mandy caught them, slapping each around a copy of *Ethan Frome*.

A clerk approached. His green nametag said "Hello, my name is Herb."

Crap!

"May I help you?"

"Do you have books on Jackie Robinson?" Before I'd even finished saying it, Mandy was hiding *Ethan Frome* behind a shelf of books on weightlifting.

I followed "Herb" away from Mandy. "We have several in Biography," he said, leading me to the rear door, no more than twenty feet from where Mandy had parked her Volkswagen.

By the time I'd finished saying, "Nope, I've read them both. But thanks," Mandy was revving up her Volkswagen, and the shotgun door was open.

I jumped inside. We sped west, onto Colorado Boulevard.

"A minute and four seconds," Mandy said. "Not too shabby."

"If it wasn't for that Herb guy I could've finished inside a minute."

"Jackie Robinson?" said Mandy. "Way to think there on your feet." She peeled into the lot behind Crown Books.

Like Patrick Macnee and Diana Rigg, we were the *Ethan Frome* Avengers, hitting bookstore after bookstore, slapping gray covers on books, hiding them on lower shelves. Skylight and Dutton's in Los Angeles, Wilshire Books in Santa Monica, Walden's, Barnes and Noble and B. Dalton in every mall. Our operations went like clockwork. We rolled like a well-oiled machine throughout the morning. By noon, we had hit twenty-seven bookstores.

"Tired yet?" I asked Mandy.

"My dear, we're only getting started. This is our *Ethan Frome* Olympics; our marathon."

And we were masters of endurance. By dinner we'd serviced more than 75 bookstores. We grabbed a quick snack, a double-double at In-N-Out Burger, then cruised to the warehouse in San Pedro with our covers. If anyone bought *Ethan Frome,* now it would cost them a small fortune.

By ten o'clock on Wednesday, all of the bookstores west of Long Beach had been serviced. We were on schedule. *Ethan Frome* was going down. I'd spent thirty bucks on gas today, and that was in a Volkswagen. Mandy's odometer crossed 60,000 miles coming up the Harbor Freeway.

"Wanna celebrate? said Mandy.

"Whaddya have in mind?"

"The Pike, the *Cyclone Racer.* I've always wanted to ride it.

"In Long Beach?"

"Mm-hmm. Don't you think roller coasters are romantic?" Before I answered, we were driving up the exit to PCH and she was speaking *sotto voce.* "C'mon, Allen" she said. "Let's give ourselves an hour off."

The gears and wooden framing of the Long Beach *Cyclone Racer* groaned in unison while its cogs hoisted us slowly toward the moon. Mandy pressed against my lap. The ocean breeze whisked through her hair. With my arms around her waist, I felt all of her excitement, her tightening stomach, her heartbeat, her girlish joy pressed on my thighs. Mandy leaned over her shoulder and planted a kiss on me I hadn't expected. The cars crawled higher. The pier looked tiny, like an n-scale model railroad. Gusts of sea spray and the scent of Mandy's perfume filled my lungs. We climbed higher above the surf. It felt so fine holding a woman. Higher. I grinned, wanting to savor every second. It had been worth it, ditching school, just to take this ride with Mandy, never mind our escapade....

The coaster tottered.

I remembered about the elm in *Ethan Frome.*

Mandy screamed into the wind. The bottom dropped out of our seats. We thundered down. Faster-faster. The leather seatstrap pressed my flesh. My heart leaped into my throat. Mandy's hair flew in my face. My arms squeezed around her waist. The rumble of wheels against the scaffold jarred my teeth. Down we flew. Down....

A sudden right, pulling G's at one-hundred miles per hour snapped my neck. The cold Pacific air propelled against my ear, against my cheek with hurricane quickness, our hips pressed against our seatbelts. I imagined we'd just swerved to miss the elm. At least the first one. A rise. A sudden dip. A ricochet to the right. Sea spray stung my eyes. The runaway coaster hurled us screaming over the surf in dizzy spirals. My ears rang. My teeth rattled. I closed my eyes and felt Mandy's fingernails pressed into my forearms.

The coaster careened and spun, threw us out over the surf until dizzy blood throbbed, and my head soared and Mandy's screams turned into laughter....

The *Cyclone Racer* coasted to a stop.

The evening had been burned into my memory.

The next morning, we hit the LCUSD book warehouse, using the skeleton key from Snooge that surprisingly still worked. It was another sign from God. We hid the books inside the crawl space beneath Mrs. Winchcombe's stucco house in Montrose.

On Thursday, we hit a dozen local libraries after school, moving books to teachers' reserves, or hiding them in stacks off limits to students. We worked till ten, hitting bookstores in the San Gabriel Valley until the stores closed, and we were in some store in East San Bernardino.

On Friday, we cut class again and hit the San Fernando Valley and worked up the 101 clear up to Oxnard and Ventura. On Saturday we worked Long Beach and the north end of Orange County, before riding the *Cyclone Racer* one more time.

We were exhausted. We knew we'd done our best.

Random copies of *Ethan Frome* were still adrift in California, but you'd have to drive to Bakersfield to buy one.

It turned out you couldn't find *Ethan Frome* in Bakersfield either. Evidently, there were confederates in cells I didn't know about. The Society for the Complete Extermination of *Ethan Frome* had secret chapters even I, its founder, was unaware of.

The best part was hearing Heather complain the following Tuesday to Mrs. Winchcombe. She'd gone all over Los Angeles and couldn't find an *Ethan Frome* book. She did the whole 'poor me' routine, not knowing none of us had books, until that wicked Mrs. Winchcombe had to *loan* Heather her copy. I seethed. I'd been enjoying Heather's misery. Heather's pain had felt bitchen, so when she wasn't looking, I stuffed her book from Mrs. Winchcombe up my sleeve inside my letter jacket. When the bell rang, Heather didn't note its absence.

That afternoon it went to live in Mrs. Winchcombe's crawl space with the school warehouse copies and the spiders and snakes beneath her floors.

I didn't care now if I got caught. I felt a strange empowering freedom. If I got busted, what sort of punishment could anyone come up with worse than reading *Ethan Frome* and then being shipped to Vietnam? Everything else paled in comparison.

Mandy told me about "Zorro" on the ride to Deadman's Curve. He was expanding our new "Society" state-wide. "This guy's Xeroxing more copies of our cover for *Ethan Frome.*"

"What?"

"Inside every cover—" she said "—he pens his trademark letter 'Z.' Leta's cousin says she saw one at City Lights in San Francisco, and a row of them in Berkeley, at Cody's Books on Telegraph Avenue, in the basement. I called Powell's up in Portland to check it out. They said their *Ethan Frome* stock is depleted."

"No way. Portland?"

"Call 'em yourself."

I looked at Mandy. She wasn't lying.

We rolled our windows down in unison, pumped our thumbs up in the breeze, honked the horn and shouted a loud synchronized "YES!" in perfect harmony, all the way down Los Feliz Boulevard into Hollywood where half of La Cañada High School had been invited to Garry's drag race on Sunset Boulevard.

I wasn't sure why Garry Jackson had invited *us*. Maybe Garry simply wanted a larger audience. Perhaps after the *Ethan Frome* caper we had moved up on the bitchen scale. We shouldn't have; not when the roster for the Society for the Complete Extermination of *Ethan Frome* was secret. There was no buzz around the school, which meant our names hadn't been leaked yet. Even Heather had no clue yet who had made *Ethan Frome* vanish. Not even I knew, for that matter, although

I'd started the ball rolling. Like in those Mission Impossible shows, we now had secret correspondents; active members up and down the coast of California. Someone I didn't even know about had gone and serviced San Diego. Up north, there was this cat who must have started in Santa Barbara and worked his way up Highway 101.

Our hearts raced together. I imagined Zorro galloping, a big red "Z" cutting the sky beyond the stars. The Society for the Complete Extermination of *Ethan Frome* was in business. Zorro was riding into bookstores. His black cape flowed in circles beneath his slashing sword. He reared before each cash register on his big black horse, Tornado, waving his saber overhead until clerks cowered behind the counter, surrendering while Zorro rearranged their bookstore in accordance with a plan which *I* had authored.

Yes!

When finished, he'd doff his black sombrero, charging out the door and down the street to the next bookstore on his map. His saddlebags overflowed with Xerox copies of our cover with his little trademark "Z" he'd handwritten inside the flap.

Zorro: a sign God smiled on our *mitzvah.*

Mandy parked the car a block south of Sunset Boulevard, on Crescent Heights. We walked west toward Havenhurst, where Sunset angled south. Wherever we saw classmates from La Cañada, they waved and smiled. They were beginning to respect us, although our secret wasn't out, like it was written on our foreheads we were doing something cool. A big warm grin, as if the two of us made other people happy, made them laugh, brought them cheer right when they needed it.

It was the first time in my life that I felt even semi-bitchen.

We arrived at Sunset Boulevard just shy of two a.m. Gina Mason and Jenny Watson were telling us Garry'd had a fight. "An hour ago, Allen." We walked west on Sunset Boulevard listening to Jenny. "He's pouring all of his remaining energy into his race." Mandy and I stared eastward toward the starting line.

He revved the engine on his loud cherry-red Mustang. Orange flames surrounded the chrome scoop on Garry's car hood. Beside him, a black GTO driven by some Beverly Hills rich geek idled and sent a growl down Sunset Boulevard.

Both drivers faced the traffic light a mile east on La Brea.

Crowds pressed against the sidewalk, smoking cigarettes and whispering. There were plenty of other drag strips closer to La Cañada. But this was Garry Jackson. Nothing short of legend sufficed for Garry, who'd just replaced the stock 289 in his Mustang with a custom turbo 427.

Now, Garry was ready to race at Dead Man's Curve.

Two pairs of headlights, a mile east on La Brea, glowed like eyes on distant tigers. The GTO from B.H. glistened darker than the Batmobile. With his new spoiler, Garry's 'Stang could have been stolen off a t-shirt, one of those Big Daddy Roth jobs you bought at car shows.

Lines of letter jackets and heads leaned in from the curbs. In our minds, Jan and Dean had stopped tuning their guitars. A hush had settled in, as if the street-racers were afraid to wake the cops.

The silence broke. Engines revved. Mufflers sputtered. Mandy's grip around my hand could crack a walnut.

Dead Man's Curve, it's no place to play.

Green light.

A roar. Squealing tires. Smells of gasoline and rubber. Tread marks chewed across La Brea. Headlights rifled west on Sunset, past Schwab's Drug, toward Crescent Heights. Shifting gears, screaming engines hurt our ears and seemed to lower a half an octave when they passed us. A swoosh of wind whistled in their wake.

Two pairs of taillights shot west on Sunset, converging between sidewalks that pinched down the Boulevard as both cars roared into West Hollywood. Neon blurred behind exhaust. A pair of taillights made the turn.

A skid. A crunch of metal. The second hadn't made Doheny. Garry's Mustang started spinning, cart-wheeling in mid-air, red–white–red–white lights spun like a pinwheel at a circus.

My heart caught in my throat. I'd known Garry since preschool. This couldn't happen. Not to Garry. I now sensed my own mortality. I hated him, but reflexively I sprinted west down Sunset. Mandy chased me. Crowds closed in behind us.

I had to get to Garry—if he was still alive.

The Batmobile vanished down a side street.

Somehow, several paint cans had rolled into the street. Garry must have hit one. You could still see the explosion of mint-green acrylic paint across the westbound lane of Sunset.

We waded through paint so thick my Onitsuka Tigers lost their traction. Columns of mint-green footprints sponged behind us down the asphalt. We had to hurry. The 'Stang was several thousand yards ahead. He hadn't figured on hitting a paint can at 100 miles per hour. Spirals of skid marks left by Garry seemed a quarter-mile long before the tread mark hit the median that knocked a wheel off his Mustang, flipping the car so he cart-wheeled and bounced against an elm tree. The remnants of Garry's car were wrapped around the trunk.

Crap! I took a long breath, sizing up the wreckage.

Garry was staggering straight toward me. I couldn't believe he was alive—with just a scratch across his chin. I heaved a huge sigh of relief. Garry was such a teflonista. He'd made out better than the tree.

For once, he wasn't laughing.

"Fuck," said Garry. He sat down on the curb, put his head between his fists and stared at the debris. His eyes were glazed and watery. His fists were tight and pale. He kept repeating the word "fuck," as if the crash had reduced his vocabulary to his single favorite word.

"Fuck," he said again.

"You okay, Garry?"

Cop sirens howled down to Doheny. Blue and white whirling strobe lights sent out psychedelic auras. Garry dabbed blood from his chin.

"Where's Heather?" Mandy asked him.

"Fuck."

I stared at Mandy. We both stared toward the wreckage. Where was Heather? I could have sworn she wasn't in Garry's car. Maybe she was! I dashed toward the Mustang while the crowds surrounded Garry. My lungs felt seared with gasoline fumes. "Heather?"

All I found was her cardigan in the back seat. The red one Garry'd bought her for her birthday. It was mangled, but there wasn't any blood in the back seat or on the sweater. No sign of Heather or any passengers. Thank God Garry had raced alone.

I wandered back, my heart still jumping. Cops were pushing back the crowds and setting traffic cones and flares. Some were talking to observers. Garry still stared from the curb as if none of us were visible.

"Fuck," said Garry again, closing his eyes.

Mandy squeezed my hand. It surprised me I was glad he hadn't died.

CLIPPING FROM PAGE 14 OF THE SEATTLE POST-INTELLEGENCER
THURSDAY, MARCH 4TH, 1971

POLICE BAFFLED BY DISAPPEARING BOOKS

Police throughout King County are baffled by the sudden disappearance of the novel Ethan Frome from local bookstores up and down the Puget Sound area. Sometime in late February, copies began vanishing. Now, even warehouses can't seem to find a copy. Rare copies have surfaced, bearing a custom cover that has obtained almost overnight currency as a collectable.

"If you can find them you can sell them," said business manager Antoinette Kuritz of Seattle's University Bookstore. "I found a copy in my store someone had stashed behind a cookbook. A guy came in yesterday and bought the thing for $79.95.

It's amazing what people buy. Guy didn't even flinch. They're like gold, but we're concerned they're being stolen."

Local police investigators have yet to find a clue that might shed light on the baffling disappearance of Ethan Frome.

CHAPTER EIGHTEEN

SITTIN' ON THE DOCK OF THE BAY

HEADLINE FROM PAGE 11 OF THE *DESERET NEWS*, SATURDAY, MARCH 6, 1971

SALT LAKE CITY POLICE CAN'T EXPLAIN MISSING *ETHAN FROME* COPIES

HEADLINE FROM PAGE 9 OF THE *DENVER ROCKY MOUNTAIN NEWS*, TUESDAY, MARCH 9

DISAPPEARANCE OF *ETHAN FROME* BAFFLES COLORADO LAW ENFORCEMENT

ANGELES NATIONAL FOREST NORTH OF LA CAÑADA-FLINTRIDGE, CALIFORNIA: SATURDAY, MARCH 13TH
(90 DAYS TO GRADUATION!)

Heather, it turned out, not only wasn't hurt, she hadn't even come to Garry's drag race. She and Garry had had a fight. A huge one, I had learned. A twenty mega-ton MIRV thermonuclear exchange, and she'd stayed home, a move that had saved Heather from extinction. I was surprised she hadn't dumped Garry after he'd lost his wheels. But four weeks allowed no time for Heather to find a better boyfriend, and she needed an escort to the high school senior prom. Now, Garry mooched rides with Heather, who had a Volkswagen like Mandy's. Heather vowed she'd never ride again with Garry at the wheel.

As for me, I pondered a puzzle of my own during my workouts. These Xeroxed news clippings of articles kept appearing in my mailbox, as if Zorro had an interest in reporting his activities. To date, I had no clue who this guy, Zorro, even was. Scary thing was, Zorro knew who *I* was. I'd been thinking about this, running north of Angeles Crest Highway, at twilight, near Wickiup Campground, west of the skinny-dipping hole. My ankles bounced like steel springs along a truck trail through the forest beside a creek at elevations where the pines replaced the oak trees. My latest training binge was practicing at high altitudes. Running at four-thousand feet helped build my heart and my endurance. My lungs burned from the cold. But like those runners in Kenya and Ethiopia, it helped to practice where they didn't have much oxygen. Returning to sea level, I felt as if I'd turbocharged my lungs. It had worked for José Lopez. Why not me?

So far, my regimen *was* working. And so far I had no clue who'd been sending me those clippings on *Ethan Frome.*

Riding back home at sunset on my tiny Yamaha 60, I noticed Mandy's Volkswagen parked on Angeles Crest Highway. *What was she doing way up here? Why did her Volkswagen keep bouncing?* I braked to say hello. An LCHS Spartans bumper sticker reflected in my headlight. I flicked my high beams. Perhaps I wasn't paying attention. All of a sudden I saw my headlamp aimed at....

Heather's.

Naked.

Breasts.

Uh-oh. Crap! Wrong Volkswagen!

Heather pulled a halter across her head and shook her fist. She leaned against her horn. Her glare could torch right through titanium. Muffled screams and whimpers echoed inside of her car.

Garry rose up naked, wiping steam off of the windows. Judging from Heather's glare I feared she might have just lost her virginity.

"Oops. Sorry...."

"Eek. My Gawd. Garry, it's creepy Allen Martin...."

"Relax, Heather." The glass muffled Garry's voice.

"Garry...."

Heather was such a gossip she must have feared I'd share the story. Her face went crimson. I'd rolled my Yamaha to twenty feet away. Heather screamed and revved the engine. Four cylinders screeched above the forest.

"Heather wait. My pants...." Garry was pulling on his boxers.

What was Heather doing? It appeared like she had plans to run me over. I looked in my rear view. Twin-barrel headlights aimed straight toward me.

Yes. That was exactly her intention.

I jumped onto my kick starter and throttled up my Yamaha. I let the clutch out so fast I pulled a wheelie, jerking forward. One-handed, I fastened my Speed Racer helmet as my Yamaha wobbled upright.

Heather's tires screeched from the turnout right behind me. I saw her Beetle in my rear view. She was chasing me, one hand on the wheel, one giving me the finger.

Heather's rear wheels fishtailed down the highway. She was gaining. Four cylinders in her Beetle were matched up against my one. Headlights flickered in my mirror. I felt them crawling up my back like they were reeling in my spine.

She honked her horn. I felt vibration on my jacket.

I changed lanes.

She changed lanes, too.

I changed back.

She changed back, too.

I was doomed.

I saw a forest gate on my left. I veered across Angeles Crest, swerving in front of a truck to take the fire road down to Oakwilde. I swerved around a cable gate. No room for Heather to go around it. The road switch-backed down Dark Canyon to the Arroyo Seco truck trail, where back in Boy Scouts, we'd gone camping by the riverbank. Heather swerved behind me, crashing her Volkswagen through the cable lock. Snapping the wire, she followed the dirt road right behind me.

I gulped hard.

I turned the throttle, kicked the Yamaha 60 into third, tasted the dust, smelled her rage, felt the engine reverberations vibrating up my spine. I cut a switchback to get rid of her, struggling for control, using street tires for traction down a sandy granite hillside. Heather spun around the dirt road. I'd gained some ground cutting the switchbacks. But the road straightened through the forest, and I couldn't outrun Heather without switchbacks.

Like an igloo on little wheels, Heather's Volkswagen closed in on me. Lights reflected in my mirror. She was gaining.

I kicked the Yamaha into fourth, reared back on the throttle. Rocks and acorns beneath my tires jarred my elbows. I fought to keep from spinning out. Splattered bugs coated my face shield. I barely saw the road.

We passed the Oakwilde campsite.

Heather was ten feet behind my taillight.

I heard the Arroyo Seco creek flowing fifty feet in front of me. My brakes squealed. I had no road left. I skidded my bike into the water. A spray of river water funneled in a cone before my tires. The Yamaha had flipped onto its side.

Grit washed through my molars. I got up, lifting my bike. Pebbles had cushioned me when I'd crashed, and I was lucky I wasn't hurt. Water poured out of my helmet in streaks across my face. I was glad there was no current. I dragged the Yamaha across the water, feeling my thighs cramp, feeling the chill soak through my t-shirt.

I bent over to breathe the moment I had reached the other bank. Standing on the shore I kicked the starter. The bike was flooded. Heather's headlights bore down on my eyes. She raced straight toward me.

I'd counted each remaining second of my life, when I noticed Heather's Volkswagen wasn't moving. It had coasted to a stop. It floated. Like a marshmallow in a giant cup of cocoa. She spun her wheels. Nothing happened. She just made a lot of noise and splashed up mud and made her Beetle turn in circles. I'd never believed those ads that claimed a Volkswagen would float.

Heather had just verified the ads.

Totally. Bitchen!

Cones of light from Heather's headlamps rippled beneath the surface. Her car drifted in an eddy. She could not open her doors. If she did, Heather's Volkswagen would sink into the river mud.

I caught my breath. It wasn't every day your ex was at your mercy.

Ah yes. She clawed her nails against her windshield. Her car circled in lazy spirals, like the second hand on the school clock seventh period before the bell rings. Everything happened in slow motion.

Heather screamed. Her breath frosted her windows.

Garry held his Levis up and tried to calm her down. The car tipped when Garry stood and opened a window to climb out. A funnel of water splashed in over the glass.

Heather shrieked. "Garry, sit down. You're ruining my car." Water leaked in through the hood vents. I tried my best to hold my laughter. After Heather rolled up the window, she put her head between her hands and started crying.

It wasn't *my* fault. *I* hadn't asked that crazy psycho bitch to run me over. Moments ago, I had been terrified she'd kill me on the trail. I glanced toward Garry. Having finally tightened his belt around his jeans, he shrugged his shoulders, as if asking me for help.

They were clearly at my mercy. I sat for a minute on a boulder, whistling like Otis Redding on his dock. Removing my shoes, I dipped my toes into the frozen mountain water, watching the Volkswagen float away.

She rolled her window down, caught her breath. "Allen, please." She used her "California nice" voice, so sweet it made your ears bleed. "Allen, please?" Heather smiled. "Just a little noodge?"

Call me a wuss. Not even Heather deserved to drown inside her Volkswagen. I waded toward them, my thighs shivering from the chill. My gym shorts swirled around my legs. I dug my toes in to gain traction against moss and slippery rocks. The snowmelt made my toes feel like Popsicles.

I nudged the car. It glided across the pond surface. I nudged again, rocking her gently. The car drifted toward shore. Heather spun the wheels. Exhaust sputtered from her muffler. A wheel grabbed. A second wheel. Mud splattered in my face. The Volkswagen fishtailed, before Heather and Garry sped away.

Garry looked over his shoulder. A short glance passed between us. He didn't say it but I sensed that he was trying to say thank you.

Heather rolled down the window, stuck her arm out, and flipped me off.

I vowed never again would I be nice to her.

When I got home, I found the draft notice Mom had placed beside my bed pillow, clear proof, after helping

Heather, no good deed went unpunished. It must have come in Saturday's mail. My heart stopped when I saw it. I'd tried to push war from my mind, but there it was in black and white, a crummy scrap of paper, tri-folded on my bedspread, insisting I read it right away. My hands trembled when I saw the message printed on the notice. My throat became a fist, my stomach a knot. One lousy scrap of paper had just ruined my life.

It read as follows:

March 10, 1971
Selective Service
ORDER TO REPORT FOR INDUCTION

The President of the United States,
To <u>Allen Daniel Martin, 5927 Indianola Way,</u>
<u>La Cañada, Calif.</u>

GREETING:
You are hereby ordered for induction into
the Armed Forces of the United States and to
report at
<u>Room 17, 3820 West Hollywood Boulevard,</u>
<u>Los Angeles, Calif.</u>
on <u>13 June, 1971</u> at <u>7 a.m.</u>

Arthur W. Metzger
Executive Secretary of Local Board

June 13th! Who the hell was Arthur Metzger? Some weenie who'd never met me was ordering me to *die.* I wondered what type of perks he got for signing all our death warrants; maybe free drinks and a handshake from the local VFW.

This was my *life* here. I'd spent thirteen years in La Cañada schools waiting for *freedom*. Now, this Metzger jerk was sending me to Nam.

I called Mandy. I drummed the handset. The phone rang a dozen times without an answer. I'd talk to Mom, but stress always freaked her out. I was afraid sharing with Mom might push her back into denial. But I had to. This was my life. I needed somebody to care, someone to cry with. I tiptoed up the stairs.

Mom was sleeping in her bedroom. She was snoring.

A bottle of zinfandel stood empty on her bedstand by her martini glass.

I sighed. Mom wouldn't be talking until at least tomorrow morning. I was pissed. I smelled her wine-breath, felt its weak, exhaled warmth against my cheek. She'd been crying. Perhaps my draft notice hurt more people than just me.

Perhaps, my mother understood my terror all too well.

It occurred to me on Monday, riding my Yamaha to class, we hadn't heard from Buster the Adjuster. Forty days had passed since Buster had offered Mom some token from United Snakes Insurance to fix our damage. They were "starving people out," until we begged to settle claims for next to nothing. We still had holes in our roof where our chimney had caved in. I'd covered shingles over with plywood and a roll of plastic sheeting. When it rained, puddles of scum collected above the film and drooled into our carpet whenever it rained more than an hour. I'd boarded over windows. I'd drawn maps to document cracks inside our footings and our stucco. I was *so* ready for Buster.

But he never returned phone calls. Every time it rained, Buster's insurance gods were smiling. Time was bringing us to our knees. By the time Buster showed up, I'd be fighting in Vietnam, and Mom would tire of having to live beneath that plastic.

A horn honked. I gave a hand signal and swerved my Yamaha 60 past a car stalled in front of me. I turned from Knight Way to Crown Avenue. I planned on lying low myself now that Lieutenant William Calley's Mỹ Lai Massacre had given the Army a status at our high school worse than treason. It was okay if insurance companies ducked their obligations, but any student with a draft card felt America's full wrath. Your draft status bore down on you, like this huge invisible backpack full of guilt, stuffed with fear, topped with their anger and their hatred. You didn't complain. Guys with high draft numbers chocked it up to their good karma. But a low number hung over you like a five-hundred pound cloud. You could die, but you deserved it. Weren't you assisting Nazi war criminals? Weren't you *evil?*

This morning, Claremont College students had come to our high school for a teach-in. A crowd of Juniors circled photos showing Buddhist monks on fire, children's hands burned off by napalm, women with bullet holes in their foreheads. Long-haired protesters whose denim jackets gave off free whiffs of marijuana staked out the cutest coeds for special attention during lunch hour.

"Hey Martian." Someone pointed at me. "Hear you signed up for the Army."

I nodded sadly.

Who'd told them? Arthur Metzger? Did anti-war protesters have spies?

Classmates booed me. Someone spat on me. "He's a war pig. Off the pig."

I hardened my gut, tightened my jaw. It was best if I stayed silent. This wasn't the right time to run away.

"Their blood is on your hands." A pair of college girls dumped buckets of blood-colored water across my head.

Keep walking. I had to tough it out without a word.

Mrs. Fishel, my fifth period French teacher, looked on. An egg splattered against my bike bag. A second hit my forehead.

Red water seeped into my shirt, bloodying the sleeves. The scent of marijuana in people's spit soured my nostrils. Protestors cheered. Guys I didn't even know called out my name. "Fuck Allen Martin. Off the war pig."

Mrs. Fishel tried to stop them.

It was obvious they didn't want to listen.

Garry Jackson came by with Heather in his Spartan Men's Council windbreaker, wondering what was going on. Garry paused. My eyes met Garry's. Two nights ago I'd helped Heather save her Volkswagen from sinking. For a second he saw my pain.

Heather towed Garry away.

I closed my eyes. *Worthless teflonistas.*

"Fuck Allen Martin. Fuck Allen...." Demonstrators chanted, wagging peace symbols on sticks, shaking flower-power headbands. It made me wish I'd been a girl. I was so paranoid of being called a Nazi, I'd thrown all of my brown shirts into the dumpster and bought new tie-dies. You hoped people might be your friends, and then they hated you, spat on you. You couldn't even take a dump without seeing giant silver letters scrawled into the partitions I'd spent all last summer painting.

One-two-three-four.
Help us end the fucking war
Five-six-seven-eight.
No finals if you demonstrate.

Don't change Dicks in the middle of a screw.
Vote for Nixon in '72

More chants came from the demonstrators.

Hell no, we won't go
Girls say yes when boys say no.

I skipped second period. Since Mrs. Winchcombe had started teaching *Ethan Frome* without a book, even the brown-nosers never bothered showing up. Today I didn't feel like joining Mrs. Winchcombe. Nor did I want to hear the protests. I suited up, ran through the showers and ran for seven miles up Lida Street, hoping my sweat would wash the red stains off my skin. I hoped the pain would take my mind off of the war.

In third period, Coach Harron, perhaps the only teacher at school supporting the war, opened discussing today's news flash. Lieutenant Calley had been convicted. When half the classroom stood and cheered, Harron's veins bulged from his neck. His Army Airborne tattoos throbbed with jingoistic fervor.

"Siddown," Harron barked, spraying saliva from his mouth, his flat top wiggling the way it did when he was mad. Little pieces of scrambled eggs from Coach's breakfast machine-gunned students in front rows.

At last the class sat down.

Harron lectured, pacing back and forth in front of us. "Far as I'm concerned, that damn whistle-blower Ron Ridenhour who convicted Lieutenant Calley's a bigger weenie than even Allen Martin here." Coach Harron aimed his crooked finger toward me and zeroed in.

I bit my lip and squeezed my eyes closed until my eyeballs wanted to bleed. My time in high school was running short. I was going to Vietnam. I had to shut this asshole up once and for all.

I raised my hand, glaring at Coach Harron.

"Coach?"

"You gotta problem?"

"Coach, Ron Ridenhour had more courage than you ever will."

A hush fell on the classroom. Things had changed in La Cañada. Now with football season over, nobody cared about

Coach Harron. The war had polarized our school, but hatred of Harron united us.

I was surprised when Garry Jackson raised his hand. "Coach,—" whispered Garry "—what's *your* problem?" Garry glared toward Coach Harron. "I may be going to Vietnam. My draft number's fifty-two. If I go, I'll be defending your right to call Ridenhour a weenie. But I differ with you, Coach Harron. Allen here's all right."

My God. Why was Garry defending me?

"Siddown, Garry."

Garry kept standing. "I'm with Martian."

"He's a faggot."

"You know—" Garry said "— you use that word a lot."

Heather's jaw dropped to her neckline. The rest of us sat stunned. I wasn't sure what gnawed at Garry, but I was ready to applaud. If Garry stood up, so would I. I rose up in my seat. Harron's eyes zeroed on me like a pair of laser death rays. He flexed his arms. I flexed my stomach.

Garry could take Harron if he had to. And if he did, I'd be the first one there to help him.

"I said siddown," said Harron.

Both of us kept standing.

"SIT DOWN."

"That what you want, Harron?" said Garry. "For me to keep my mouth shut while your goons carry out orders like the day we played cross country—in football—and we were losing...?"

"It was an accident."

Classmates' jaws dropped. The clock ticked through the silence.

"I was there, Coach. You ordered us to pile on the Jabberwocky. I'm ashamed of what we did."

"Shuddup, Garry."

The last person I'd expected to confront Harron was Garry; about as likely as Betty Crocker setting fire to General Mills. But Garry Jackson had found a conscience. Something had evidently changed him.

Harron's face turned crimson. He grabbed the globe on his desk, shook it in its stand, until the globe fell from its bearings, bounced across the floor, rolled along an aisle, stopping right in front of Sara Jansen.

Sara stared at it while Garry kept on talking. "Why don't you cut some slack for Martian? He's going to Vietnam to fight. You'll be here in La Cañada making fools out of the Army."

"I said siddown."

"Whatcha gonna do, Harron? Send us all to Vietnam to shut us up? That your dumb idea of 'discipline?'"

"Jackson...."

Garry picked his books up. He stormed out of the classroom.

Harron crushed a paper wad in his fist.

Sara Jansen picked the globe up and stuck her finger into a dent. "Oh my gawd," Sara whispered. "Mister Harron ruptured Canada."

Classmates laughed.

I followed Garry. Harron didn't care. The bell hadn't rung yet. Garry jogged across the street. We found a park bench beneath the canopy of trees at Oak Grove Park. He offered me a cigarette. I didn't smoke, but took one. He handed me a match. I lit the Marlboro, inhaling. I coughed, and Garry smiled.

The bell rang.

Garry blushed before he faced me. "I'm sorry—" he said "—for what we did the other night in Heather's car, and for this morning."

I shrugged. "I didn't mean to crash your party. I thought Mandy...."

"I know. I'm sorry too, for how we treated your cross coun-try team. You guys are athletes," he said. "You guys are good." Course *you* seem to have a soft spot for finishing fifth.

I was amazed. What had happened over at teflonista head-quarters? It was like Garry had gotten fed up and sent in his resignation. What right did he have, saying he was sorry?

I covered a cough.

Except he *was* sorry, and I knew it. "I'm sorry too," I said. "Sorry we didn't have this conversation sooner."

We smoked our cigarettes, listening to scrub jays in the oaks, smelling the sage, feeling the dappled dots of sunshine on our necks. In eighty days we'd graduate. Our time was getting short. Garry Jackson faced the same damn hell that I did.

Vietnam.

"You know what, Allen?" Garry said. "If I had it to do over, I'd let you keep Heather." He grinned. "Fact is—" he tilted his chin "—if you ever feel like trading...."

I looked sideways at Garry. "Give up Mandy? No way."

"Never hurts to ask." Garry shrugged. "I used to like Heather. Now, her brain's stuck in this weird hyper-bitch drive." He scrunched his forehead. "I'd dump her, but I'd ruin her reputation."

"I know." And I knew Garry had a conscience.

We spent our morning on the park bench, swapping La Cañada memories, trading stories through fourth period and lunch hour. Six years at Paradise Canyon Elementary, three years at Foothill Intermediate, four years of high school, soon Vietnam. It was about time we were friends.

And then I knew. The Ron Ridenhours of the world were the draftees, the velcroids. They didn't want to join the Army, but they had to, and they did. And so would I. And so would other men like Garry. As long as there was a draft, I knew the Army would have a conscience to blow whistles on the hard-core, on the Harrons of the world. Guys like Garry, and like me. Perhaps the demonstrators were clueless. But some of us with clues saw good and evil on both sides. And as for me, I was proud to be a velcroid.

FROM THE BACK PAGE OF THE ATLANTA CONSTITUTION

MONDAY, MARCH 22ND, 1971

BOOK BANDIT AT LARGE

The infamous "Zorro," who seems to carry a grudge against Ethan Frome, has hit Atlanta area bookstores with a vengeance. The pattern started in California, hitting West Coast bookstores from San Diego to Seattle before turning east, first hitting Utah, Colorado, Kansas City and St. Louis. This Saturday he targeted Atlanta....

CHAPTER NINETEEN

JULIE, DO YA' LOVE ME?

TEMPLE CITY, CALIFORNIA: FRIDAY, APRIL 9TH, 1971

(63 DAYS TO GRADUATION!)

Leading the last lap of my two-mile race on Temple City's track, my neck stiffened, and I braced for my usual no-kick finish. I'd set the pace through seven laps of jostling elbows, dust, and sweat. I spat and tried to scare up whatever strength I had to finish.

BANG!

Gun lap. The noise and smoke trail seemed to awaken my competition. I was fading. My side cramped up in knots. Booboo, Alphabet and Snooge were in position to sprint past me. I matched them stride for stride to hold them off. Voices chanted from the infield. "Go, Booboo! Come on, Snooge! Beat that little choke artist!"

I dropped my head. I sprinted, straining to hold off pain. Keeping the same cadence as Booboo, I stumbled toward the tape. I hoped I'd somehow hold them off. My sides tightened in agony....

...But my competitors were bigger. Each of their strides stretched inches longer. Making their moves, they matched my effort, step for step. Booboo and Alphabet sling-shotted around me and toward the tape. I fought off Snooge, trying to make my legs move faster to keep my place. I felt needles in my sides. Snooge was breathing down my back. His breath faded. I saw the finish line. I could taste a third-place finish. And then my ankle popped. Pain shot like a thunderbolt up my calf, I stumbled. Something had twisted. I staggered forward toward the tape.

Snooge shot past. Some Temple City giant, Lew Alcindor tall, stampeded past me in the final twenty yards.

"Martian, you choked again," shouted Neal. "Martian, you gutless puke."

Booboo broke the tape, followed by Alphabet and Snooge. The seven-foot giant came in a half step ahead of me in fourth.

I'd finished fifth again. Walking the pain off, I staggered across the grass, grimacing, trying to look as if I hadn't hurt my ankle. I sat down and massaged it. It didn't feel like it was serious. I struggled across the infield, glad my ankle loosened up. But I was furious at myself, angry I still had energy. Why hadn't I spent it on the track? Why hadn't I built a bigger lead? Something kick-proof. I felt guilty. I wasn't retching, wasn't gasping.

Not that it mattered. Our total points had been enough to beat Temple City long before our two-mile race had started. And since in track, unlike cross country, only the first three places counted, it didn't matter who finished fourth or who got fifth.

But Neal stormed across the cinders. His face was watermelon red. Capillaries in his temples bulged like little sausages. "Martian! What kind of stoopid-candy-ass-bullshit stunt was that?" His voice boomed loud enough to carry from Temple City to La Cañada. "Get some balls, you friggin' hamburger. Grow up."

I shrugged. I'd run a good time. Of course, I'd run a stupid race. Maybe subconsciously, I'd decided winning wasn't worth the pain. If, for once, I hadn't puked, it saved some wear on my intestines. I'd be needing those intestines in Vietnam.

Grow up? I wondered. *Why?* So what if I didn't letter! Did anyone wear letter jackets in Vietnam? I jogged around the infield a few feet inside the track. I still had energy for once....

...until it sank in. I resisted, even resented growing up. Every day I was expected to be a man and suck it up, to take responsibility, to be a velcroid, to be tough. But I was starting to figure out if boys were loved, young men were *hated*. Boys were cute. Men were pigs. The writing was on the wall.

"Girls say yes when boys say no."

If ladies said yes when *boys* said no, just where did that leave *men?* If girls said yes when boys said no, who was in charge?

I had thought men got to choose where they were going.

That was a *lie*.

I shuddered. The sun ducked behind the smog. It left a dirty reddish blob to gravitate through the horizon. I longed to run away, but teflonistas always ran, and I despised them. My parents ran away yet neither managed to escape. They were the runaways. I couldn't run away. I had no place to run to.

I had 63 remaining days at La Cañada High, before the Army owned my soul. And I'd be shipped to Vietnam. I had a duty to enjoy, perhaps the last nine weeks of freedom I'd ever see.

It was about time I got started.

The team bus home from Temple City covered twenty miles while I pondered what to do during my last two months of freedom. The bus ride seemed to take almost as long as if I'd run. This time, I was scared. Vietnam was looming. Where was the Wocky when I needed him, or Mandy or Mrs. Z?

A row of juniors in the back seat mooned a motorist at a stoplight, pressing ham against the glass of the back window and making lip-farts. The bus reeked as if a few of those fake farts had been for real. Juniors had fun. What was I doing, being miserable and grumpy? We'd just embarassed Temple City on their home track?

I wanted to hide. I was afraid if someone looked into my eyes they'd see these craters full of fear, plummeting deep into my soul. I envied juniors. Unlike me, they had the luxury of smiling, of laughter. They weren't faced with graduation—and with war.

The driver tuned the radio. The voice of Bobby Sherman

boomed through the bus. Freshman and sophomores joined in mocking chorus, playing sing-along-with-Bobby, waving teenybopper fists in sweeping motions like they were holding onto beer steins. They sang in parody, off key of how they'd be back in September, singing *"Jooolie, Jooolie, Jooolie, do ya' luuuuuh-ve me?"* The verses jarred me. The word *luuuuuh-ve* sounded like half the bus was retching. I had run out of Septembers. I looked around at other seniors, at Ivan Alphabet, at Garry Jackson, at Alan Smithee, Jr. The same stare was etched into every senior's face. All of us were some flavor of scared.

The bus rolled north on Rosemead. At the stoplight at Las Tunas, the row of juniors mooned another motorist. Some lady leaned against her horn, and the bus rocked full of laughter, except for seniors. Come September, we would not be coming back. I'd be in Nam. It seemed you never got permission to be a man. You just grew up. But once you did, then you were stuck—with no way back.

Nine weeks.

The tape across my finish line approached.

The speech I got from Mandy was such an echo of Coach Neal's I wondered if he'd written Mandy's speech.

"Allen, how come you never win?" Mandy shook her head. Her eyes looked sad. "I drove clear to Temple City so I could see you, and you choked. I'm bummed. You looked as though you lost on purpose."

Ouch! I hung my head. The hurt of Mandy's disappointment seared my heart. "I didn't lose on purpose," I replied. "I need to win for you to like me?"

"It's just...."

I looked up. "What, Mandy?"

"...I'd like to see you win once. For a change."

"I never win. Never will. Nobody wants to see me win."

"Nobody? I do. Stop trteating me like I'm a nobody."

"Oh." All of a sudden, I had no compelling answer. Of course, she wanted me to win. Mandy came to all my meets. She *liked* me. I'd been so wrapped-up in myself I hadn't noticed how much she cared. I tried to glance down at my shoes.

She met my gaze, almost glaring at me, eyes filled with disappointment. "'Oh?'" Mandy said. "All you can say, Allen is, 'Oh'?"

"Mandy, I can't out-sprint them. My little legs are just too short."

"Then pick your pace up. Use your first seven laps to build a cushion. Imagine there's some guy waaaaay out in front of you, and let him set the pace."

"I always set the pace. There's nobody in front of me until gun lap."

"Yes there is," Mandy said. "You know you're just like Ethan Frome. You keep looking at the stupid tree in front of you. It's like at the end of every race I watch you crash into it again, again, again. You need to look beyond the tree."

"At what?"

"Make somebody up. You're always staring at Snooge's jersey at the finish line. You even said so. You'll never win a race by staring at other some other person's back. Way in front of you. Make somebody up. Stare beyond them and you'll win."

I had no answer. I breathed in deep. I was too worn out to argue.

When Mandy walked away, I saw her trying to hold back tears.

I stood alone, and I wanted to duck my head beneath my collar.

It tore me up to see her so upset.

IMPORTANT NOTICE TO ALL MEMBERS
OF THE LA CAÑADA HIGH SCHOOL
ACADEMIC STUDENT BODY:

*Subject: Student Compliance
with Uniform Time Act of 1966:*

As required by the provisions of the Uniform Time Act (15 U.S. Code Section 250a) passed by act of the Congress of the United States and signed into law by President Lyndon Baines Johnson effective April 12th, 1966, the Board of Directors of the La Cañada Unified School District has directed me, on behalf of your High School Principal, to require all members of the undergraduate academic student body of La Cañada High School, on the forthcoming Sunday, the 25th of April, 1971, at 1:59 a.m. Pacific Standard Time to set clocks, watches, and all chronometric devices forward exactly one hour to register three o'clock a.m. Pacific Daylight Time, said time which shall constitute the correct legal time at La Cañada High School for the remainder of the 1970–1971 academic year. As a result, the forthcoming weekend shall extend one hour less in duration than has been the customary practice of La Cañada High School students for other scheduled week-end breaks. We apologize for the inconvenience.

Full compliance with the Uniform Time Act on the part of all members of the La Cañada High School student body is mandatory. Failure by any member of the student body to comply with the obligatory provisions of the Uniform Time Act of 1966 will not be tolerated and will be met with the severe disciplinary measures.

At the hour of 8:00 a.m. Pacific Daylight Time on the following Monday, April 26th, 1971, all students of La Cañada High School are expected to be in their assigned classroom seats, ready to resume scheduled educational activities.

Any questions or inquiries which you may have regarding the aforementioned procedure shall be directed in writing (in triplicate) to the office of the Assistant Principal and Director of Student Activities at La Cañada High School.

Your strict compliance with the directives of this memorandum is expected.
Roland W. Conrad, M.A.Ed. Assistant Principal and Director of Student Activities

CHAPTER TWENTY

FIRE AND RAIN

LA CAÑADA-FLINTRIDGE, CALIFORNIA: FRIDAY, APRIL 23RD, 1971
(49 DAYS TO GRADUATION!)

Since La Cañada hosted a senior prom few seniors could afford, our prom had somehow flown above my radar. According to the *Illiad,* the Spartan student newspaper, they would hold our prom this year at the Ambassador Hotel. Someone (clearly not a student) had booked Les Brown and His Band of Renown, whose last hit, I was told, had peaked in 1948. I hadn't known, not being born until mid-1952, but the decision had been made by whomever's parents had booked the band. It must have been some sweetheart deal where someone's parents got free tickets.

Our senior prom, priced affordably at $315 per couple, was open only to the *crème de la crème* of La Cañada. If you were a velcroid, like myself, you could forget about "your" prom, unless you planned to rob a bank to buy a ticket.

Garry was taking Heather. Since he didn't have his Mustang, his old man had made arrangements to fly in Garry with a helicopter. Most of the other teflonistas had to settle for stretch limos. Those who had jobs, like our paint crew, had to settle for staying home. I was resigned to life among the working poor.

On Friday night, I found a package. Mom had placed it on my bed, something soft, like a blanket, wrapped in butcher paper and string. An embossed envelope had been Scotch-taped to the paper behind the twine. I cut the string. I bent the package, crinkling the plastic. My name was on the envelope.

The note inside it read:

You are cordially invited to the
La Cañada High School
FIRST ANNUAL ALTERNATIVE PROM
Time: 7:00 p.m. Saturday, May 1, 1971
Place: High School Gymnasium Second Floor (roof)
Price: Free!
BE THERE OR BE SQUARE
The La Cañada High School Free Prom Committee
RSVP 790-6272

Unwrapping the paper, I found a bubble-wrapped tuxedo, a pair of shoes, and an address card telling where to return the clothing on May 2nd. Mom had assumed I might appreciate this rare gesture of kindness, and I did. My only problem was that Mandy'd be out of town. I'd never heard of this "Free Prom Committee." I searched for a return address, but the sender had only written "LCHS-FPC" in the corner. I didn't recognize the address or the phone number.

The phone rang, and it was Leta, like she'd just seen me on Candid Camera. "Did you get an invitation?"

"Yeah, but Mandy's out of town. Some church orphanage thing in Baja."

"You can still come stag."

I nibbled on my lip.

"Allen, I'm sure that Mandy fully understands," Leta continued. "This is the only prom we get. And she'll have me to keep to an eye on you in case you're worried she might get ideas."

"You're certain she won't mind?"

"Allen, it's no huge deal. A few seniors were bummed out on how we couldn't afford our prom, and I knew Mandy was out of town, and so we thought of you. That's all."

"Thanks," I said, fingers relaxing around the handset.

"I hope you come, Allen. Honest, I really do." Leta sounded sincere. "Well anyways, bye bye, and once again I hope you make it."

"Goodbye, Leta," I said, wondering what options I had, since Mom had shelled out for my tux rental, and Leta'd said Mandy wouldn't mind. I wondered who had planned this.

I dialed up the number.

A stranger's voice inquired if I was coming.

I said I was.

I was excited. This would be fun. My scheduled pity party was cancelled. Someone creative had an excellent idea. A prom for us. A free prom. I was surprised at how I actually looked forward to it.

Les Brown and his Band could eat his money.

I showed up early, at six on Saturday, wishing Mandy had come with me. I feared this whole thing was a joke, but Leta wasn't into jokes, at least not cruel ones. Some total stranger had mailed out proper invitations, set up a reservation service. It seemed too involved to be a prank.

After I climbed up to the roof of the gymnasium through the hatch, I found some rocket scientist in tennis shoes and a zippered J.P.L. jacket. He hoisted a jukebox to the gym roof using come-alongs and pulleys. He asked for help lifting his jukebox. With two people, it came up easy, but I still worried this was some sort of a set-up. We draped a giant orange extension cord over the fence beside the swimming pool. He crawled downstairs to plug one end into a Caterpillar generator on a trailer parked inside the Senior Lot. I jammed the plug into the jukebox. Bright neon colors from the Wurlitzer lit the night. A square of quadraphonic speakers hummed from four roof corners. Although the concrete roof was domed, a 40-foot square flat spot in the center provided a dance floor for our prom. Flashing barricades, on loan from a construction site below guarded the open hatchway in one corner. It was a night for moonlight dancing. Or it might be...

...if any females showed up.

I waited, drumming my fingers on the barricade. The J.P.L. guy talked to some geek wearing overalls down-ladder. Hearing voices, I wondered what the evening held in store. My tux itched around my neck. It was this funky powder blue, and some neck hair I'd missed shaving rubbed the wrong way against my shirt collar. I was about to climb down-ladder to find out what was going on, when some people talking echoed from below.

The voices I could hear put me at ease.

First came Leta, up through the hatch, wearing an orange satin gown. I was surprised she'd come so soon. She'd been a candidate for prom queen. But evidently, she'd decided she would rather be with *us*. Clearly the party was beginning. I looked forward to the evening.

Leta looked prettier than she had riding the Queen's float as a Rose Princess. Next came some guy in a Cal Tech jacket I had never met before and didn't want to. He kept staring at Leta's breasts. Leta kept looking away, rolling her eyes, then glancing toward me, like she was reaching out for sympathy— from me. Through the roof hatch came a third voice.

I recoiled. My heart leaped from its doldrums. It was *Mandy!*

Hearing her steps tap up the ladder, I reached my hand across the opening to assist her. She touched my wrist. I felt her grip around her hand. Tugging her toward me, I tasted scents of a perfume she rarely wore. Her breath tickled and warmed my wrist. I helped Mandy through the roof hatch, feeling her hair sweep past my arm as she ascended to my side.

She shook her hair, and then she took away my breath.

"M-M-Mandy?"

"Surprised?"

"Mandy?" My voice cracked. "Oh my God."

The Cal-Tech dude reached down. He grinned and handed me his orchid, which I pinned onto Mandy's dress. I had been wishing she could be here, but I'd never expected *this*. Her eyes sparkled like brown opals. Her cheeks were glowing brighter than the moon.

Mandy grinned.

Where were her running shoes and hooded sweats and sweatpants? Where were the frumpy clothes that didn't fit her once she started running? When had Mandy become beautiful?

"Hello, Allen," she whispered, while I stood choking on my tongue, feeling the spring breeze chill my spine and wondering what to say. I blushed while Mandy giggled at my side. She twirled in her red dress, sending more perfume past my lips.

Vivid velvet, redder than lipstick, spun into place inside my arms. A single strand of pearls was clasped above a sweetheart neckline. A velvet bow tied off a waist that was more slender than I'd recalled. I smiled. She was here to dance with *me.*

"Why are you blushing, Allen?" she asked.

"Uh—nothing. Just—I never knew you were so beautiful."

Mandy glowed. "Thank you, Allen. You're so sweet."

"And I never dreamed you'd be here."

"You really think that I would miss this?"

Mandy took my hand, and I felt like I was walking with a goddess.

The jukebox played. James Taylor—*Fire and Rain.* We started dancing. Brook Benton—*Rainy Night in Georgia.* The Carpenters—*Rainy Days and Mondays.* It wasn't raining. But the firelight that burned in Mandy's eyes warmed my soul up like a campfire on a cold and lonely evening.

She wore no makeup. She didn't need it after all her miles of running. My heart fluttered in my throat. I was too nervous to talk. Like Herr Von Trapp, I started doubting she was meant to be a nun. I kept remembering the first time we'd come up here to see my bird, the day she'd locked the hatch behind us, and we'd jumped into the pool. She'd made me promise I'd beat the Wocky if she jumped into the water. I had beaten him. I'd actually kept my promise.

"You happy, Mandy?"

"Yes, I'm so glad that I came, that Leta planned this."

We danced to some Chicago, to *Your Song* from Elton John, and to some old tunes from the Platters beneath the stars. Chaparral breezes warmed our evening. I held her close, hearing her laugh, smelling her hair. By ten o'clock, a dozen students from our high school had joined the party.

All have them had ditched the prom.

Word was the real prom had been a monumental disappointment. At last count, they said, the chaperones had outnumbered the students. They said the ice cream was so hard you couldn't cut it with a chain saw, and the cake frosting was evidently made with rancid butter. Leta had been named prom queen, and she hadn't even been there. Heather had been so pissed about it Garry'd left without her. Garry was *here*. Pudge McMasters found a payphone and called friends.

By eleven, there were ninety of us dancing on the roof.

Then it changed. Soft melodies gave way to acid rock and head music. Led Zeppelin—*Stairway to Heaven*. The Rolling Stones—*Brown Sugar*. The smell of alcohol and dope replaced the scent of Mandy's perfume. Empty bottles covered our dance floor. People laughed at stupid jokes and cranked the volume on the jukebox high enough to vibrate beer bottles.

Oh won't you come with me-hee-hee-hee
And take my hand

Mandy had left to find a bathroom. I searched for her and couldn't find her. She had been gone for fifteen minutes. All I saw were classmates partying. Allan Parker had gotten stoned so hard he'd passed out on our dance floor. Kurt Hansen and Pudge McMasters took turns fondling Gina Mason. Doug Wasilewski staggered in circles waving a bottle of Annie Greensprings before he tripped and puked all over Sara Jansen.

And please, please, take my ha-aaaaaaaa....

The music stopped.

Someone below had pulled the cord out from the generator.

Nasal voices barked from bullhorns on the ground below the gym. SCREEEEEE. "All of you kids up on the roof. You can't be up there."

I froze. Below, were *cops!* Five Mountie carloads had snuck up on us. They waved bullhorns from the north side of the gym and blew their whistles. The party reeked of marijuana. The roof was littered with empty wine bottles, beer cans, roach clips, sheets of ZigZag.

My heart jumped into my throat.

Flashing blue lights circled below. A County Mountie faced the roof, pointing his bullhorn at our party.

Static. "COME DOWN NOW!" His bullhorn echoed.

One-hundred students froze. We were afraid we'd all be busted. We stared at each other. Squad cars were positioned below the gym. All of a sudden, the whole party had the same crazy idea.

Ker-splash!

Pudge McMasters had jumped first into the swimming pool. On the south side of the gym, he did a cannonball. He launched water fifteen feet. People inched toward the precipice.

Jenny Watson and Gina Mason closed their eyes and jumped behind him, holding hands. *Splish-splish.* And then, the entire class stampeded, splashes echoing like machine gun blasts as bodies smacked the pool surface. Prom dresses puffed like parachutes. Corsages floated on the pool surface.

Splash-splash-splooooooooosh.

"Allen?" Mandy called my name through the stampede.

I looked to find her. Far below me, throngs of wet and anxious classmates shoved open pool gates, climbed the chain link, jumped and sprinted in all directions across the base-ball diamonds, practice fields, parking lots, and ran into the night. A police car turned on sirens. Their prowl car screeched around the pool and crossed the ball fields, but there were just too many students to round up.

Two cops with Mag-lights poked their heads up through the roof hatch curb behind me. A light beam crossed my shoulder, and I turned.

"FREEZE!" yelled a cop.

Where was Mandy? I was worried. The only ones still up here were Allan Parker (passed out) and Sara Jansen, cleaning her dress with paper napkins.

The cop climbed out the hatch and touched his holster.

A scream. Downstairs, from Leta. "MANDY? OH MY GAWWWWWD!"

What? My gut tightened.

"She tripped before she jumped," somebody yelled. "I think she's hurt."

Leta's voice shook, charged with tears. "MANDY!" She kept shrieking.

"Call for help." a voice called over police radios. *"Someone's hurt."*

"MANDY NO!" Leta screamed. "MANDY BREATHE FOR ME, GODDAMMIT!"

Mandy?

I tried to see. Far below, policemen rushed around a corner. They hurried Leta away in panic and still scream-ing. Five cops surrounded a bright red lump of velvet on the pavement. My heart stopped beating. Mandy's blood covered the concrete. Swirls of red clouded the pool. I had never seen a body lie so still.

Why had I let her use the bathroom? Why had I let go of her hand? She'd tripped and fallen off the gym roof when my class-mates had stampeded? She was lying down there motionless. Leta was still screaming. More cops rounded the corner, stared at Mandy, and yelled, "Don't touch her."

It didn't even look like she was breathing.

"MANDY?" I called out. My heart tightened like a fist. Panic pounded in my forehead. Mandy was hurt! I had to go to her.

"MANDY!"

A big arm curled around my neck, pulling backward on my throat. A huge cop slammed me against the roof gravel. "I said

'FREEZE!'" Two of them jerked me from my seat, half-yanking my arms out of their sockets. Three pointed Mag-lights toward the roof hatch. I was struggling to breathe.

"Sorry, buddy. You're gonna have to come with us downstairs."

All I knew was Mandy *needed* me. My head exploded with adrenaline. Cops grabbed my arms. I wiggled free. I knew I had to get to Mandy. "She's my girlfriend. Let me go." From somewhere I found the strength to outmuscle cops twice my size, dash toward the hatch, grab the top rung, slide downstairs using the stringers outside the ladder rungs like two fire poles. My feet thunked at the bottom a half-beat behind my heart.

"MANDY?" I screamed, dry-mouthed, fighting panic, trying to find her. Two bullet-head cops in shiny shoes were coming toward me with their flashlights. I zig-zagged across the gym floor, dress shoes squeaking on the floorboards. Muddy heel prints led to a circle of blue lights past double doors.

Voices outside crackled through police radios. *"Ten-seventy-eight. Where's that ambulance. We got a girl down. She's not movin'."*

I turned and sprinted toward her. Two cops grabbed me, pressed my face against the gym wall. Again, I managed to wiggle free, terrified Mandy might be dying.

"I think this kid's on PCP." A cop barked out before he waved in reinforcements, five surrounded me with Mag lights. I was staring at a gun, the business side, aimed dead at me.

I felt handcuffs. They snapped shut. Two cops motioned toward the squad car.

"Get in."

"My date...."

"Git your ass inside the squad car."

A fire truck raced into the parking lot, sirens roaring, red lights whirling.

"You can't help her. Get in the car."

Not Mandy. God no. Please take care of Mandy. Make her breathe.

Leta was still crying. Blue lights spun all directions. I wrenched my arms against my cuffs until my wrists bled. Two other prowl cars were full of partiers from our high school. Students were climbing over fences. A squad car screeched south down Oak Grove. A bullet-head shoved me into his squad car across some kid from another school who had passed out. The rear doors slammed. I was locked in with some kid puking in his sleep. Fog clouded my windows. I couldn't hear. For all I knew, Mandy was dead.

MANDY! My mind screamed.

Four paramedics hurried past, wheeling a gurney. She lay immobilized, strapped to white sheets. Blood soaked Mandy's bandaged legs. Mandy's chest was barely moving. They lifted her stretcher into the ambulance.

My hands were cuffed. All I could do was bang my head against the window, twist my arms inside my handcuffs, call Mandy's name while no one listened.

They slammed her shut inside the ambulance. I heard a hurried screech of tires, a lone siren moaning south down Oak Grove Drive. I breathed in deep.

I told myself *they wouldn't do that if she'd died.*

I ached to be beside her more than the cuts hurt from the handcuffs. I felt my blood seep past my wrists. I couldn't move. I couldn't help her.

Her siren faded, and my heart sank. There was nothing I could do.

A cop jumped into the front seat. "Need to take you to the station. You'll get your phone call." His partner next to him said I looked like I was "dusted."

I wasn't. All I wanted was to be at Mandy's side.

The car started. Dirty spots of rain collected on the windshield.

I had never felt more helpless in my life.

FROM PAGE THREE OF THE WASHINGTON POST

SATURDAY, MAY 1ST, 1971

BOOK BANDIT SPREE CONTINUES

The Metro D.C. Area has been repeatedly targeted by the infamous Ethan Frome avenger. Eight weeks ago, the Avenger's spree began in California and has criss-crossed the United States, tracing a giant letter Z across America....

CHAPTER TWENTY-ONE

AIN'T NO SUNSHINE

LA CRESCENTA, CALIFORNIA: SUNDAY, MAY 2ND, 1971
(40 DAYS TO GRADUATION!)

The last person I'd ever thought would bail me out of jail was my old man. But there he was, at three o'clock a.m., wearing his polo shirt, his golf slacks and his ever-present scowl that had been calling me a loser for as long as I remembered. Evidently, he'd come home, or he was talking again with Mom. After we walked out the front doors of the La Crescenta Sheriff's Station, he didn't speak to me, which was fine. With Mandy hurt, I didn't care. He opened the rear door of his new Buick Riviera, and I got in. New car aroma wafted from the car seats. I barely noticed Dad's new wheels. Too much was on my mind. I was scared spitless over Mandy, worried she might be brain-damaged or dead.

Riding east down Foothill Boulevard, I got frostbite from Dad's air conditioner. I had no clue why he'd cranked it up to MAX at three a.m. We didn't speak. You didn't need the English language with my dad. Tonight, he spoke fluent Neanderthal, a series of discontented grunts while my mind whirled with apprehension over what had happened to Mandy. Here, my dad had just come home, had woken up to spring me, and I was too wrapped up with Mandy to even talk. *Where was she? Was she breathing? Could they do anything to fix her?* Not even the cuts around my wrists from wearing handcuffs numbed my fear.

I knew if I asked Dad, he wouldn't know and wouldn't care.

He hung a left on Indianola. He let me off at the front door. I hurried upstairs, threw off my tux, pulled on some shorts, laced up my running shoes, pulled on my shirt.

Before Dad or Mom could tell me I was grounded, I'd raced halfway down Indianola.

I never did look back.

Terror gripped me, and my fear powered my run. I sprinted down Indianola to Foothill Boulevard to Linda Vista. Chilly morning air scared up the goose bumps on my arms. At Colorado, I turned left, racing across Suicide Bridge. I thought of Wocky, of my first ride to Flint Peak in Mandy's Volkswagen. I had no idea whether Mandy was conscious or even alive. I put my head down and got lost inside the rhythm of my breathing. The sting of sweat crossing the fresh cuts on my wrists almost felt calming.

Right on Orange Grove. *Panting.* Left on California. *Huffing.* Seeing Huntington Memorial Hospital, I dashed toward big glass doors.

Inside, my shoes squeaked across the waiting room. I found the desk clerk on the night shift. Her hair was straight and broom-colored. Her big hoop earrings, silver-dollar sized, looked like they hung below ball bearings. She used a half-read copy of *U.S. News* to hide that she was sleeping.

I knocked her magazine aside. Her eyes jumped.

"Wh-wha?"

"Ma'am, I need to—(*breath*)—see a patient." Weariness poured from my lungs, making my voice grate like a hand saw.

"Not tonight." The earring princess glared back at me and frowned. "Read the sign. 'No visitors after eight-o'clock, p.m.'"

"Fine, I'll—stay here overnight."

"You can't stay here."

"Why not?"

"Hospital policy."

"It's a—stupid rule."

She flashed her disapproval.

"Look I—(*breath*)—don't mean to be rude. It's just—I'm scared. Could you just—tell me—tell me if somebody's alive?"

She shook her head and pursed her lips as though she'd wrapped them with a string. She swallowed, and she waited for me to leave.

I didn't budge.

"No, I can't," she finally said, touching the button for Security.

I rocked quietly in front of her. "Please." I searched her eyes until my terror reached in and grabbed her. "Her name's

Mandy. She used to work here as a candy-striper. She was my prom date."

"Mandy Richert?" The woman's mouth dropped lower than her earrings.

"She came here in an ambulance. Hurt bad. My name is Allen."

"Mandy Richert? Oh my Gawd." She stared with horror into my eyes. "She's *here?*"

I gripped the counter to keep from sinking through the floor. "Yeah."

"I used to know her in Orthopedics. I'm Suzanne."

Fighting tears, I wiped the moisture from my eyes. "Look, I'm desperate. Can you just tell me she's alive?"

Clouds of stale coffee reinforced a wall between us. Suzanne stared at me. Then something in her demeanor seemed to yield. She grabbed the phone and said, "I'll try."

A dial tone. She punched an endless string of numbers. "Have we admitted a Mandy Richert?" asked Suzanne. The next five minutes ticked by in slow motion. Suzanne waited on hold. They must have transferred her eight times. Her eyes narrowed. She was shaking. She closed her eyes and said, "Uh-huhhh."

I waited.

"Uh-huhhh." Suzanne nodded with the handset. Her charm bracelet had slid down to her elbow. She drummed her fingers on the handset.

Goose bumps prickled up my legs. Suzanne looked distant and concerned. Laying the handset in its cradle, she composed herself and faced me.

"Oh my Gawd. She's in surgery."

I inhaled so long there probably wasn't air left in the room. I pointed toward a column of blue chairs. "I'm staying until we know." I exhaled a long dry breath and bit my lip.

"I understand." Suzanne nodded, touching my wrist. "If I find out something, I'll tell you."

I found a seat but couldn't sit or even find a way to sleep on rows of chairs with metal arm rests, I was so worried about Mandy.

At least I knew Suzanne and I had done our best. The only thing that I could do right now was wait.

By five a.m. I hadn't slept. I'd given up and tried the floor. I was determined not to leave until I saw Mandy alive. Suzanne had zee'd out at her station, sleeping behind her *U.S. News*. I dared not wake her. I'd need her later. She was my ticket to see Mandy. Worry twisted my stomach into tighter and tighter knots.

Why had this happened to the nicest person I had ever known? Mandy was happy. She was beautiful. Why had she fallen off the roof? It almost seemed God had a mad-on for good people. *God couldn't send her to Vietnam, but there were other ways to off her.*

Couldn't go there. Couldn't afford to. All I thought of was my last race, the disappointment in Mandy's eyes.

"I never win. I never will. Nobody wants to see me win."

"Nobody? I do. Stop treating me like I'm a nobody."

"Oh."

"All you can say, Allen, is, 'Oh'?"

Now, the only girl on earth who'd ever wanted me to win could be dying up in surgery less than 100 feet above me.

"Mandy, I can't out-sprint them. My little legs are just too short."

"Imagine there's some guy waaaaay out in front of you, and let him set the pace."

Waaaaaaay in front of me. Make somebody up. She made running sound so easy, trying to help me. Truth was, I'd never even tried Mandy's advice.

"You know you're just like Ethan Frome. You keep looking at the stupid tree in front of you. It's like at the end of every race I watch you crash into it again, again, again. You need to look beyond the tree."

Look beyond the tree at who? I didn't have a clue. It's just—she wanted me—maybe *needed* me to win. God wasn't listening to my prayers. The only card I had to play would be to win a race for Mandy. It was all part of my *mitzvah* to be her friend.

I had to win.

But the only race remaining in my season was league prelims. I'd be racing José Lopez. And José Lopez was undefeated. The only person I could place in front of Lopez would be...

...God?

And who was I to run faster than God?

The morning sun pried through the curtains in the waiting room of Huntington Memorial. Suzanne's fingers touched my forehead. "Allen," she whispered.

"Wh-what?" I looked up, startled.

"Mandy's out of surgery."

I felt my heart stop. "She's alive?"

"Yes, but she's unconscious. She has a pretty bad concussion."

A long sigh tried to push aside the tentacles of fear that had crept in while I had stayed awake last night. Suzanne sat next to Leta, who'd apparently showed up while I'd been sleeping. The sleeve of Leta's Stanford sweatshirt was wet with tears. I rose and hugged Leta, searching for courage, trying to gather up my wits, surprised at how hard Leta hugged me back. "What'd the doctors say?" I whispered.

Suzanne looked at us and frowned. "She shattered her hip and her right femur. She's still critical."

"How critical?" I asked.

"We don't know," Suzanne replied. "They're not allowing any visitors. They say her life is still in danger. But there's nothing we can do but trust the doctors." Suzanne paused, letting the previous sentence echo in my mind.

Leta stretched and smiled. "I'm on watch now. You look beat Allen. You should go home and get some sleep. Suzanne'll take you in her car."

"Leta, I can't...."

Suzanne opened up her purse and found a Salem. "Allen, I'm getting off my shift. It's ten a.m. You need a ride?"

"I want to see my girl when she wakes up."

"She won't be waking up this morning. You might be waiting here for days."

A long pause.

"She just had hip surgery and has a serious concussion."

I took Suzanne up her offer. It was a chance to make a friend. I might be needing Suzanne to cut through more red tape to visit Mandy when she woke up.

And I was too exhausted to run ten miles home.

COME AND GET IT

LA CAÑADA-FLINTRIDGE, CALIFORNIA: SUNDAY, MAY 2ND, 1971
(40 DAYS TO GRADUATION!)

When my old man met me in the hallway of the house on Indianola, he glared in rage, face redder than a stop sign. He folded his arms across his chest and gave an aboriginal grunt, followed by a, "Where-the-hell-you-been-your-mother's-worried?"

"I'm tired, Dad." I had no strength left. My eyelids felt like anchors. I hadn't slept, worrying my heart out over Mandy, and now I wanted to find my bed. But Dad had raised a head of steam and seemed to want a confrontation. I could tell. His pectorals quivered behind his too-tight Lacoste shirt. He folded his flaccid arms, curling a lip up in defiance. "You'll be a whole lot more than tired once I get through with you," he said.

"Fine let's talk, Dad." I didn't feel much like talking, being tired, but it seemed a better option now than yelling.

"After what you've done, you loser? You've been a screw-up since I met you and I can't wait to see you gone."

"I didn't...."

"Bullshit," Dad said. "Why the hell were you in jail? Why the hell did you take off last night, after I brought you home?"

"Dad...."

"Don't 'Dad' me. What makes you think that I'm your father with your brown eyes. Both your mother and I have *blue* eyes, and the blue gene is recessive?"

"What?" In one short sentence, he'd just explained my entire childhood, why he'd never come to my meets, why his name for me was "Loser." I'd suspected since sophomore year when we had learned about genetics we weren't related, but I'd kept hoping my biology books were wrong.

A long pause, several breaths, and then he whispered. "I'm *not* your father. Or haven't you figured out why I left yet?"

I froze, feeling my heart ramp down to cryogenic levels. Every second on the wall clock seemed to last more than an hour. *Not my father? Then, who was I? What made him sure I wasn't his?*

"And don't go asking about your father. He was a loser, just like you. They found him murdered in Oklahoma back in nineteen-sixty-one."

"Why are you telling me this now?"

His icy glare pushed me away, as though he hoped I'd run upstairs and pack for Vietnam right now.

Weariness flooded me. I had no cope left. My chest crumpled in agony liked someone had just ripped off my head, crapped down my windpipe, then flushed the crap down deeper. Why was he doing this—disowning me? Why did he have to do it now?

"So you're sayin' Mom's a whore?"

"Shut up, Allen. This ain't easy."

"You think it's easier on me? Why are you telling me this crap? Why now? Why are we having this stupid fucking conversation?"

Smack! He slapped me. Again, again. Hands whacked my face like pinwheel blades. "Don't call me stupid."

I staggered.

Ooooof! He kneed my groin.

P-A-I-N!

I crouched in self-protection, guarding my manhood, raising my chin, and felt a hard straight right that cut my lip and knocked me to my knees. "And don't say 'fuck,' you little shit." A kick. Or 'crap,' you little turd."

I licked my lip, tasting the metallic tang of my own blood. I wasn't his son. I was Mom's bastard. He could do whatever he pleased.

I stared into his eyes, a mutt posturing for battle. I sized him up. I measured every single muscle, every ripple. He'd sucker-punched me. But nothing hurt as much as eighteen-years of his rejection. Even the pain down in my groin didn't compare. I felt pain whenever I ran. I staggered to my feet, clenching my fists. It occurred to me I could take him if I wanted to.

I could kill him. I could mash his angry head in.

He was flabby. He might be tall, but he was soft and out of shape. His muscles sagged. His beer gut rolled over his belt, and he had "love handles." I had endurance. I wasn't huge, but what there was of me was muscle. I felt my arms bulge full of blood, tightened my triceps behind my arms. I felt my heart pound in my temples and knew I didn't have to take this. I wanted to rip his bloody heart out, to beat his face into red mush, except—I couldn't.

I'd been thinking I didn't need him, but I did. Mom needed him to help fight Buster the Adjuster. I needed someone to take care of her while I was off in Nam. Maybe Buster and the old man could duke it out while I was gone.

I swallowed my beating, sucking down all the pain erupting inside me, staying silent, saving my rage for my next race with José Lopez.

The old man walked away, not even cutting me a glance. "Stupid shit," he mumbled, easing into his Lazy Boy. "Stupid, worthless-loser, fucking brown-eyed shit."

I answered back. "Keep your words sweet. Some day you just might have to eat them."

"Don't lecture *me,* kid. Not after eighteen years of ruining my marriage."

And then the phone rang.

Mom brought the phone. She stopped mid-stride in shock. Blood streaked from my nose. She stared and touched my lip.

"What happened to you?" she cried.

Afraid to look at her husband, I looked at Mom. And then I lied. "It starts to bleed when I'm excited. There was a fight last night at high school. But really, I'll be fine, Mom."

Her husband looked away.

Mom frowned and handed me the phone.

"Who is it, Mom?"

"Some girl named Leta."

I grabbed the phone, feeling my heart clench like a fist inside my chest. My throat collapsed in fear. "Hello?"

Mom stormed away.

A wavering voice. Leta was nervous. "Allen, Mandy's worse."

"What's wrong?"

A pause. "Allen, it's urgent. She's whispering your name. You have to come here. Allen you need to come here *now.*"

Something inside of me went numb. I walked the handset to the receiver, laid it down without a whisper. I raced upstairs to change.

I threw my shorts on, laced up my running shoes, bounced downstairs in three-stair leaps, shooting like a bullet down the hallway to the living room. I had to see Mandy, see her *now.* Five seconds might make the difference on whether I saw her alive.

Five seconds.

I met my Dad. He was standing in my way. "Where are *you* going?" He glared at me with alien blue eyes.

"My girlfriend could be dying. I have to see her."

"No, you don't."

I lowered my voice. "I'm not your son."

An angry grin wrinkled his lips.

I had no patience left to fight him. I grabbed his elbows, digging my fingers into the pressure points and cramming him against the wall. As his jaw dropped down in pain, I lifted all

180 pounds of him. Adrenaline surged like jet fuel through every vein inside my body.

"Excuse me, sir. I have to leave."

I lowered him, as though my arms had come with big hydraulic jacks. Just as gently as I could, I set him down. "Sir, I'm proud of you," I whispered. "At least you stopped running away."

His arms seemed to exhale with total shock.

"Mom seems happier since you're home. That's why I didn't say you hit me. She needs you, but you hit her the way you just lashed out at me—" I met his gaze, laser to laser. "—You hit Mom, I'll rip your heart out."

His face withered like a two-week old balloon.

"Just remember—" I touched my chest "—your heart."

I closed the door behind me glad to no longer hear him breathing. The soft click of the doorknob could have echoed for five minutes as I tiptoed out the door to run down Indianola Way.

I had one thought on my mind. Get to my motorcycle at the high school, then get to Mandy. And every second mattered.

CHAPTER TWENTY-THREE

YOU'VE GOT A FRIEND

PASADENA, CALIFORNIA: SUNDAY, MAY 2ND, 1971
(40 DAYS TO GRADUATION!)

I hurried to find my Yamaha, my shoes eating up the pavement, down Foothill Boulevard to Michigan Avenue to Oak Grove Drive to the high school. I cranked the key in the ignition, kicked the starter, revved the throttle, jumped into gear and squealed south down Linda Vista to see Mandy. The engine's drone whined in my skull. The leather seat rattled my spine. I leaned left, spinning up gravel, swerving onto Suicide Bridge. Pasadena stoplights blinked from green to yellow to red. I raced to beat them. After less then 30 minutes I hurried through the big electric doors that led to the waiting room of Huntington Memorial.

Leta met me inside. She was pacing back and forth. A stranger sat at Suzanne's station, lost in the latest *U.S. News* with headline stories on MyLai. Leta had just gone to see Mandy, and her eyes were puffed from crying. She sounded hoarse.

I asked, "How is she?"

Leta dabbed tears onto her Stanford sweatshirt sleeve, choking from sobbing. She coughed out, "Follow me."

She led me down a corridor paved with sterile white linoleum, between stainless steel doors, into a Lysol-scented elevator. We rose two floors to Orthopedics, and snaked down antiseptic corridors, past a nursery full of children in a room where painted panda bears were chipping from the walls. We passed a string of empty beds, hung a right before a nursing station, tiptoeing down a corridor painted germ-free shades of gray. We hung a left to face a cold white room where Mandy lay in traction, as if stretched out by that Greek Procrustes guy on a rack of weights and pulleys.

Leta stood outside in tears, while I edged in.

Mandy was sleeping. Her face was puffy like I'd remembered it in September. Not fat this time but fluidy, like they'd pumped it full of Jell-o. Knots of plastic tubing draped from a "tree" into a forearm where purple veins and yellow bruises blotched her flesh.

I kissed her forehead and felt a breath as weak as a butterfly exhaling. I couldn't see most of her body. She was encased in crumpled sheets and wraps of plaster, so thick and fresh I smelled the scent of curing gypsum and felt the heat from where the plaster was still setting.

Less than a day ago, I'd held her, and we'd danced up on the gym roof. Heart to heart. Cheek to cheek, and she'd looked gorgeous. Now, she lay weak and pale as putty. Perhaps, she'd never walk again.

I shuffled toward the window, staring at nurses in the courtyard smoking cigarettes. I had no strength. An overwhelming sense of weakness drained my gut and lowered my shoulders as though a giant sucking syringe had been inserted through my stomach, and someone had vacuumed out my soul, drained out every ounce of endurance, leaving an empty shell of flesh outside a giant aching hole.

"Mandy?" I whispered.

No answer. I wasn't sure I heard her breathing. I couldn't touch her chest beneath her cast to feel her heartbeat. "Mandy," I said.

Again, no answer. I wondered if she heard me.

I closed the door. I didn't want Leta to see me if I cried. I kneeled. I took a lo-o-o-ong breath. If God existed, he was a giant cosmic asshole, worse than Dad, worse than Harron, even worse than Richard Nixon. Every miracle I'd wanted had, in one week, turned to crap. I didn't *get* miracles. None that I'd asked for. I'd just wanted to see a yucca bloom. What was so hard about that? I'd wanted to see Ethan, my little one-legged sparrow, fly away. I'd wanted Mandy to get her wish to be a nun, serving this God who turned everything I asked for into crap if he existed.

Everything.

I wanted to scream at God and ask why he'd disowned me.

"You okay, Allen?" Leta asked walking me back down to the elevator. "You've been so quiet. You haven't said a word." She punched the elevator button. A happy chime rang to annoy me. A red light blinked like it was pointing me toward hell.

Steel doors opened. Leta and I stepped into the elevator. The dropping floor wasn't as bad as the uneasiness inside me. A jerk and opening steel doors. I followed Leta through the waiting room. She found a cluster of ugly chairs, and we sat down.

"I'm scared, Allen."

"So am I, Leta."

"Allen, they know what's wrong with her. Suzanne told me that it's not just broken bones, there's something worse."

"What else is there?"

Leta sighed. "Mandy has this thing called lupus. She's had it for a while, but it's been dormant for five years. And now, the trauma of the accident...." Leta choked. "...the antibodies in her immune...." she swallowed "...system...."

"What?"

"They're attacking Mandy's heart."

I felt blood wash from my face. My heart descended to the floor. I looked at Leta. She was nodding. Leta explained how Mandy had something called Systemic Lupus Erythematosis. What it meant was her immune system had declared war on her heart. The lupus had hovered beneath her radar. She'd forgotten it was there until the trauma from the accident had lit it up like wildfire. Now, her body treated her heart like it had joined the other side, and her immune system had placed it under siege.

Everything went gray. Mandy's hips, her legs, her heart were under siege.

"She could die, Allen. At best I hear she'll never run again."

"No way, Leta." I said. But then I saw Leta's sad eyes, and I felt as though I'd just swallowed a baseball.

"Allen, I'm so sorry."

"Leta, Mandy was my best friend."

"*Is* your friend, Allen.

Her mouth flattened into a horizontal line as though she wanted to express something and feared I couldn't handle it. Leta stared at me, her glare icicle cold. "Mandy could die," she whispered again, and I saw in Leta's eyes what she was asking. "Allen you have to win a race. You have to promise."

"I know, I know."

She stared at me a long time. "Good, Allen," she said. "Good."

I had to win a race. Something was set in Mandy's mind that wouldn't accept it if I always finished fifth, or even second. Second place was still a loser. Mandy longed to see me *win.* She'd always wanted it, nagged me, coached me, even came to all my races. Now, my only fan lay dying. My heart was breaking, and it occurred to me Mandy and I had just one heart between the two of us to share. And it was my little cowardly heart, the one that never won a race.

I couldn't talk. I had to save up every excess erg of energy. I'd need to focus all my anger on my race for Mandy's life. I had to win, so I could stick it up God's ass and my old man's.

Except I couldn't let the world know I was mad until the race. I needed everything I had when I'd be facing José Lopez.

I looked outside....

...And then I saw him. *My sparrow.* I jumped up, dashing out the door and leaving Leta on her chair, shaking her head. There he was. There was Ethan, on the front lawn of the hospital. Hobbling. I saw the band of tape still wrapped around his little leg. He stole a crust of bread and flew away like he was carrying off the burdens on my heart.

For a moment, I almost felt there was a God who'd heard my prayer.

And then a chill. How would I ever win a race with José Lopez?

CHAPTER TWENTY-FOUR

NO TIME

LA CAÑADA HIGH SCHOOL:
THURSDAY, MAY 13TH, 1971
(28 DAYS TO GRADUATION!)

I couldn't sleep. The night before league prelims, I tossed and turned till ten p.m. I took a walk, wondering how on earth I'd ever beat José Lopez. I walked to Foothill, down Woodleigh Lane, up Flintridge Avenue to Berkshire Drive, to Chevy Chase to Figueroa, up the fire road, up, up, crossing gullies where lizards slumbered. I passed the yuccas, up to the tower on Flint Peak where all the lights blinked on and off up on the trusses.

I didn't run this time. I walked until my hands froze in the night. Never again would Mandy join me while I ran. I stared below toward city lights. Flint Peak was back to being mine and mine alone. Who would I share it with if Mandy couldn't walk? She'd been my miracle. My first. First time up here her heart had jack-hammered in her chest. Veins in her temples had bulged like fire hoses. Her heart got tougher every week, until at last she'd had the strongest heart of anyone I knew. So strong, in fact, I'd been worried she could beat me. We'd run hundreds of miles together. Until now.

Now, her immune system was targeting her heart. Something evil attacked her strength. But if I'd strengthened her heart, she'd built mine up too. The root word of *cour*-age wasn't *balls*. Nor was it *guts*.

It was *heart*.

Martin's Third Observation:

Guys boast of having balls, but it's their hearts that we remember.

What had changed? And why? What had happened to our hearts? Why were gonads the hot item when young people needed courage? It was a scary way to go because balls always came with handles, letting other people control you, jerk you around the way that Harron did. And it seemed the latest presidents wanted to jerk me into a war. Wasn't one of them named *Johnson* and other guy named *Dick*?

I gazed below, where Scholl Canyon stood silent. Gone was the noise of horns on dump trucks on the day I had ditched school on Rosh Hashanah, the day I'd picked up my *mitzvah* that brought me Mandy, my first miracle. Maybe there *was* a God. But Mandy couldn't run now. Only *I* could. The only miracle I still had was seeing Ethan still alive.

The only heart I still could count on was my own.

I stared downhill, across the yuccas, toward Pasadena. Somewhere below me, Mandy slept and fought for life. I needed strength to bring her back. Like Ethan Frome, I'd bought into the brand of "nice" that finished last. "HAVE A NICE DAY" printed below a giant sickly yellow smiley.

I had my heart. My heart was good because of Mandy and her kindness. It loved Mandy, hated evil, loved the truth, hated injustice. And now, my heart would have to run the race for both of us.

Tomorrow!

I started running, sprinting, down Figueroa through all the streets of Flintridge. The scent of oak trees whistled past as I raced home to Indianola. I got home at one a.m., knowing I had to keep my word. I'd made a promise. Mandy was sick. Now she needed me to win. Nice guys finished last. I had no luxury to be nice. It was about time that I struggled to be good. To be the best.

The fog lifted. I still imagined Mandy's face, casting a cloud across my mind, and she was willing me to win. I had to *win*. But how? I remembered Mandy's words:

"You know you're just like Ethan Frome. You need to look beyond the tree."

"At what?"

"Make somebody up. You're always staring at Snooge's jersey at the finish line. You'll never win by staring at other people's backs. Way in front of you. Make somebody up. Stare beyond them and you'll win."

I wanted to look beyond them, except nobody was out there.

The next morning, a "Credibility Gap" segment on KRLA news jarred me awake, and was followed by Dave Hull, the Hullabalooer. It was race day. Like every runner, I had a special pre-race ritual. For breakfast, I ate a sugar cookie, a giant carbohydrate H-bomb. Twenty megatons of cane sugar to power me through my day. For lunch, some fruit and peanut butter. Something easy to digest. Nothing too harsh. Nothing to possibly come back up during my race.

Afternoons, I swallowed honey. I had four tubes in my locker. I emptied one big plastic honey bear sixth period. I stuck the others in my bike bag and polished another off after class. Two more honey bears remained. I was beginning to feel the buzz, and it propelled me toward the locker room to suit up.

My mind went through the race strategy Mandy had been preaching. Look beyond Wocky. Build up a cushion in the first part of the race, enough cushion that when they kicked, I would be safely out or range. If I held back, I was near certain I'd be out-sprinted in the finish.

Then the psychology began. You started your mental preparation. Imagining your race, trying to visualize your victory. I imagined José Lopez. I was staring at his jersey. I couldn't do that. Mandy was right. I knew I had to look beyond him. I had to imagine someone faster than even Lopez. For some reason, all I thought of was whatever lived inside of Snooge's locker or the crippled bird I'd rescued with his taped-together leg.

The bird would have to do. Somehow that bird was all I'd thought of. I inhaled another tube of honey. The plastic crumpled in my fist. A hard pucker brought the final ounce of sugar to my throat. One last honey bear remained. I'd need him right before the race.

For league prelims, there were runners in a riot of festive colors, greens and golds for Temple City, Tiger orange for South Pasadena. Blue for San Marino and Duarte; for Bell Gardens, red and white, and then our own school colors, maroon and gold for La Cañada.

Runners warmed up in the infield. Shot putters stretched out in their sweats. Pole vaulters flexed their poles and stepped off paces along the runway, marking their start points. Lines of hurdlers stretched their thighs inside the infield. I sat up in the bleachers staying warm inside my sweats. I sucked my final plastic honey bear like a baby milks a nipple.

Coach Neal found me. "So it's the swansong today, eh Martian?"

I didn't smile.

Neal was chuckling. "Martian's swansong. What a picture." He moved his right hand like he played an invisible violin.

If my eyes could flip him off, I'm sure they would have.

I stared down at my spikes. I couldn't spare the energy. I'd need it for my kick, something I'd never had before. I'd never beaten José Lopez.

No one had beaten José Lopez.

Coach had tried to cut my balls off. But I was counting on my heart. The same heart that I'd been pushing at high altitudes up Angeles Crest, the heart that still loved Mandy pounded harder in my chest. Courage. The word kept pulsing through my brain.

I wasn't sure why I did it. There was a different clipboard weenie for league prelims; not a freshman but some fat fart old as dirt. He asked my name, and I gave him Mandy's surname instead of "Martian." I walked away, blocking out noise. I had to focus on my strategy, on my race, preparing myself for building up my cushion to make sure nobody out-kicked me. I had to find a focus, something far enough beyond me to keep my mind in front of José Lopez.

Spikes dug into the cinders, mine and seven other pairs. Muscles twitched. My heart pounded. I breathed faster, muscles tensing, stomach churning, lungs hyperventilating, waiting for the gun. The gun—the gun—the gun....

Bang!

Eight runners burst out of the blocks.

I had the fifth lane. Ivan Alphabet was in front of me. A staggered start. The first lap of the two-mile, every runner had a lane. They staggerred start blocks on the track so each lane ran for the same distance. In front of Ivan, Booboo and some guy from Temple City kicked up cinders. I kept my arms low. I let my jaw hang, hearing my music in my mind. *Get your ass running.* Steppenwolf. I always ran to the same music. *...Out on the highway....* I stretched my legs, focusing all my strength on running, running, running. I willed Steppenwolf to play faster.

Fire all of your guns, and watch them—explode into spaaayace.

Running. This had to hurt, and I had to smile through it. I dared not waste my energy by frowning. I lowered my arms, closed in on Ivan, who was fading in Lane Six. *Make it look easy*, I told myself. *Make it look simple. Occam's Razor.* I looked at Booboo, stared at his number as if Ivan wasn't there. *Push harder, harder, harder.*

I passed Ivan.

There were seven and a half laps left. I couldn't afford to be a rabbit, but I needed to build up an early lead. I wasn't sure how I'd pass Booboo, except I had to win the race. I thought of Mandy, and of my promise I'd told Leta in the hospital. I dropped my head and breathed in dust, ate smoky fingers of red clay thrown up by spikes from shoes in front of me. I stared in front of Booboo in Lane Seven. I closed in on the Temple City guy up in Lane Eight. Booboo passed him, and so did I, fighting our way around the curve. I dropped my head and stretched my legs. At the end of the first lap, I had to cross the line in first.

Someone's breath came up behind me. From the rhythm, it wasn't Ivan.

Don't be a rabbit. Don't start too fast. Keep a hard and steady pace.

I stretched my gait. Stride-after-stride, each extra centimeter added up. My legs were limber now and loose. *Run through the pain. Think past the others. Loosen your neck and look beyond him.* I passed the chalk after the curve, but José Lopez had shot past me in Lane One.

The extra length of the diagonal might be no more than a step, but it was all that José needed to stay in front of me. I angled toward Lane One.

My sides tightened. *Pick it up now. C'mon, hurt.* I looked at Lopez. I zeroed in on that blue jersey. He was opening a lead. *Look past the jersey.*

Another lap. Two laps down. Six laps to go, and I was losing. I had to close the gap on Lopez and then pass him in the straightaway. I narrowed the lead, running as close as I could trail and not get spiked. Now, the straightaway. This took everything I had....

I sprinted forward. Lopez swerved and threw out elbows, working me that much harder to try to pass before the curve. I closed the gap. A well-placed elbow caught me squarely in the diaphragm, knocking my breath off. Perhaps an accident. Maybe a punch. I dropped my chin, feeling my heart sink, falling back along the curve. Lopez's spikes sprayed sand against my shins. I dared not close in tight until the straightaway by the start line. Just as I hit it, I exploded down Lane Two.

Breathe! Cut in front of him.

He let me go. I shot beyond him. Evidently, he didn't think I'd keep the pace up. I tried to find another runner out in front of me. I focused beyond the pain that was constricting both my sides.

We closed in on the mile. Four laps down and four to go. I had to move *now* to beat Lopez. Like Mandy'd said, I needed distance to keep him from passing me in the kick. Things might get dirty when we reached the final lap.

Look beyond Lopez. Look past him. I almost thought I saw the Wocky, and then beyond him was a jersey. I tried to focus on the name. Moving out, my sides were throbbing. My head pounded like a gong. I couldn't even hear the rhythm of my breathing beneath my pulse. *Catch that jersey.* I hit the straightaway and sprinted toward the jersey, not San Marino's, not the Jabberwocky's; there was another one in front of me. *Look at his jersey.*

Lopez's breathing pounded behind my ear. Hearing the panting, I couldn't look. A single glance could cost the race. We hit the curve. *Up the pace.* He hung behind me to the straight-away. I let loose, and he didn't challenge. We crossed Lap Five.

Three laps to go.

I had a few short strides between me and José. I needed more. I had no kick. My eyes refocused. I made the name out on the jersey. "FROME." I could pass that little sucker. I had to pass him, for the Wocky, for Mrs. Z, for Mandy. I leaned forward and added to my lead.

It got surreal after that. The honey surged into my brain, and a dreamlike runner's high seemed to encase me in its aura. I kicked the pace up. My sides were splitting. It seemed a part of me was dying. Spikes of pain turned in my stomach like I was twisting inside-out. And then I charged. I'd made a promise. Mandy needed me to win. And so did Leta. The track swirled in a long spiral before me, and the guy wearing the "FROME" jersey appeared to be a bird.

Yet he escaped me. After the sixth lap, the breathing behind me faded, and I ran harder. As if I had to race the bird to Ethan's elm tree. I dropped my arms. My vision blurred. My lungs burned and swelled with pain. I passed the goal posts, two laps to go. A half a mile.

Kick! I'd never had one. Some coach was calling from the sidelines. "Kick past him. He's gonna fade." I focused past the bird. Focused everything. Sidelines blurred into green tunnels. I had to catch it. Had to pass it. I had to beat it to the elm tree and set it free.

A pistol fired. Gun lap.

Someone was breathing. I could feel him, like he was stealing all my air. *Look beyond the bird.* My ears tightened on my skull. *Run through the pain.*

A breath behind me.

Run through the pain.

Running. *A breath.* Running. Running.

The bird ascended. Beyond was nothing but a heart the size of God, big enough to love me, love Mandy, our whole high school.

Running. *A breath. A breath.*

A tape cut through my shoulder.

I'd won.

It was the first tape I had broken in my life, and now it stretched across my chest, its paper edge cutting my skin. My legs crumpled. There was nothing I had left out on the track. I collapsed onto the infield, puddled like overcooked linguini, too exhausted, too spent to walk it off. I was still afraid I'd lost. But José Lopez shook his head, clearly amazed. His shell-shocked gaze kept reminding me I'd won.

I writhed on the infield grass. My head throbbed with too much blood. Legs curled and started twitching. I felt too weak to even breathe. "He okay?" Lopez asked Neal.

And then the names came from the loudspeakers. "In third place—Howard from La Cañada."

A golf clap. *Howard? Nobody called Booboo 'Howard.'*

In second place—from San Marino—Lopez.

It was a dream. Had to be. I struggled for a breath.

They were reading Mandy's name. It echoed from the loud-speaker "R-r-r-richert." Every letter seemed embroidered in its static. Teammates clapped their hands. I lay exhausted in the infield, my head spinning in ellipses, grass edges sawing on my cheek, across my forehead, on the flesh beneath my arm bearing the paper cut, the telltale incision from the tape that proved I'd won. Life swirled before me. A spin of faces. Coach Neal's, Garry's, Leta's. I heard my panting, arteries pounding. Needles jabbed against my sides. Dizziness made me feel like I was turning inside out. My diaphragm convulsed, squeezing air out from my lungs like air was toothpaste. When I finally caught my breath, no longer feeling like I'd died, I noticed Heather.

She was screaming in my face. "Allen, you moron. Why do you like her? Is, like, everything a joke to you?"

I glared back. *What was her problem?* But I was too exhausted to answer.

Coach Neal walked between us. He clapped his hands. "Good race, Allen." He walked away. And then he stopped mid-stride. He turned around. "What did she teach you?" His gaze leveled to meet mine. "You learned something from her. How did you *win?*"

Facing Coach Neal, I only smiled and said, "Ask her."

I didn't care. Just eighteen days, and I was out of La Cañada. And I'd won. I'd kept my promise. I had nothing left to do here. Everything I'd ever had I'd just used up to win one race, to win for Mandy. If only Mandy could've seen me win her race.

The world slowed into focus. José Lopez, Ivan, Snooge, half a dozen runners crowded above me in their sweats, looking nervous, as if I'd been unconscious. I looked at Leta Hertz's smile. Her eyes glistened with tears. Even Pudge McMasters and Stan Cunningham were in the crowd and smiling.

Garry Jackson walked over from the shot-put ring. He cupped Heather's elbows in his hands. "Shut up, Heather."

"Garry, stop."

"No, Heather. *You* stop."

I looked at Garry, old memories passed between our eyes; the fact Garry hadn't paid for his red Mustang—Garry's dad had; my "fight" with Garry's friend McMasters, in first grade on Paulette Place; the way Garry had started the food fight; the fact I'd painted Heather's name on all those toilet stalls last summer and hidden go-go boots in the faculty lounge toilet.

We'd all kept secrets. The darkest one, Harron's call to hurt the Wocky had come out, but Garry'd said it to Harron's face. Neither one of us was perfect. But I'd discovered how some secrets can destroy a person's life, while others are the tickets to forgiveness.

The crowd above me stared at Heather, and she bristled. She tossed her hair. "What's wrong, Garry? Are you, like, dumping me or something?"

"Can't, Heather. Wouldn't want the gossip to hurt your reputation." Garry glared back at her. "Think you're way too good for California, don't you. You say we're all made out of ticky-tacky here, but we're still people. Heather, Allen never pretended to be anything he wasn't. He took a girl I used to laugh at and made her prettier than you."

Heather reared up, furious, staring darts. Garry looked at me, nodding across his shoulder as Heather struggled. She was seething, leaning into him, trying to smack him with her purse. Garry rose up, pushing Heather across the infield like a lawnmower.

I was spent, but I still treasure seeing Garry stand so tall.

There'd be league finals in a week. I wouldn't be there. Having put in Mandy's name, instead of mine, I'd been disqualified. My running days were over. And so were Mandy Richert's. I'd kept my word. I wasn't sure if Mandy knew I'd done my part. I'd won a race for her. I'd felt that tape. The paper cut across my arm was as good a badge of honor as any cheesy plastic trophy. Mandy Richert was the only coach who'd shown me how to win, and she had kept her promise too. Our secrets had never left Flint Peak.

One remaining thing to do. I had to thank her.

I ran down Oak Grove, to Berkshire to Linda Vista. The memories of a thousand miles of running flashed before me, running up Lida in the rain, with Ivan Alphabet, with Mandy; the long runs down Linda Vista on the slope above the Rose Bowl. As I crossed Suicide Bridge I heard the Jabberwocky's laugh and saw him shake his long hair and kick the football between the goalposts. Right on Orange Grove, past the spot where I'd kissed Mandy on New Year's morning, where we'd sat and waved at Leta as she passed us in the Rose Parade.

Left on California. I saw Huntington Memorial, where I'd befriended Mandy. The place she might be lying unconscious now.

Leta honked at me from the parking lot, jumped out of her new AMC Gremlin. She sprinted toward me, screaming. "Allen you were fantastic! I can't wait to see you tell Mandy. She'll be prouder than even I am."

I smiled. It wasn't every day a Rose Princess was proud of me.

We passed Suzanne inside the waiting room. She waved, and then we squeezed into the elevator between a pair of wheelchairs. I punched the button for Floor Three. We were the only two inside and the hydraulics on the elevators took their precious time.

"Before we both see Mandy, I want a promise from you," I said.

Leta stared at me. "What's that?"

"You made me promise to win the race. You made me promise to be Mandy's friend. I've been a good friend. My heart's breaking, but I think I've kept my promises."

"So?"

"I need a promise back."

"Name it?"

"You're on the yearbook staff of the *Omega*. A week from now you'll pass out ballots so we can vote on which faculty member we dedicate the yearbook to. I don't know who prepares the ballots. But I need to add a name. John, the janitor."

Leta paused. Wheels turned behind her eyes. A twinkle. A sliver of a smile bent her lips. It broadened into a grin, extending clear across her face. "Oh my gawd, Allen Martin, that's so totally cool."

"We got a deal?'

"Yes! Teachers are sucking up like baby possums. Allen, yes. Allen I love it."

"Promise, Leta?"

"Cross my heart. Hope to die. Stick a needle in my eye," we said together.

"C'mon. Let's go see Mandy."

I almost ran out of the elevator, dodging nurses and random tray carts until we found our way to Room 327, Mandy's room. She was sleeping, still in traction.

I faced Leta. "Come in with me. Mandy was sleeping when we found her. Even in victory, my heart sank seeing her trapped inside her body cast. There were new tubes in her left arm, and she looked swollen full of fluid. A rash freckled across her face like a mask around her eyes. She was shivering; even the body cast had failed to keep her warm. Sides of her face puffed. She looked utterly exhausted.

I squeezed her hand. "Mandy, you okay?"

She nodded, licked her lips.

"Mandy, we won."

Eyes fluttered. She seemed to brighten for a moment.

"He won, Mandy," said Leta. "You showed Allen how to win."

Another squeeze. An unmistakable squeeze from Mandy.

"I knew you could win," Mandy whispered. She tugged me toward her. Her kiss was soft and bore the scent of orange

Jell-o. Her smile was just like on the gym roof. For a moment, I almost thought that she might jump out from the hospital bed and hug me. But she was weak. For five minutes we sat and squeezed each other's hands, and then a nurse came in and said we had to go.

I always think of Mandy; every time I smell orange Jell-o, I still see the smile of pride on Mandy's lips.

Without that smile, I never would have made it out of Nam.

CHAPTER TWENTY-FIVE

OOOH, BABY IT'S A WILD WORLD

LA CAÑADA HIGH SCHOOL: TUESDAY, JUNE 1ST, 1971
(10 DAYS TO GRADUATION!)

RESULTS OF VOTING FOR OMEGA YEARBOOK DEDICATION

TEACHER	SUBJECT	VOTES
Anderson, John	Janitorial Science	365
Zinicola, Audrey	English Literature	49
Fishel, Nadine	French	11
Neal, Michael	Cross Country, Track	4
Conrad, Roland	Student Activities Director	2
Winchcombe, Flora	American Literature	1
Harron, Richard (Dick)	Football, Government	0

IMPORTANT NOTICE TO ALL MEMBERS OF THE LA CAÑADA HIGH SCHOOL ACADEMIC STUDENT BODY EXPECTING TO COMPLETE HIGH SCHOOL CURRICULUM REQUIREMENTS ON OR BEFORE THE SCHEDULED COMMENCEMENT CEREMONIES TO BE CONDUCTED ON THE 10TH OF JUNE, 1971:

Due to the existence of numerous participants in our academic program who expect to complete their requirements for graduation in June, the Board of Directors of the La Cañada Unified School District has directed me, on behalf of your High School Principal, to schedule graduation ceremonies, which shall commence on the concrete patio outside the La Cañada High School gymnasium at eleven o'clock a.m. Pacific Daylight Time on June the tenth.

Those who have fulfilled all requirements for completion of the academic curriculum of La Cañada High School, including full payment of outstanding overdue library book fines, shall report promptly to the La Cañada High School gymnasium at eight o'clock Pacific Daylight Time on said day, wearing full graduation attire, including caps, gowns, tassels, plus a full outfit of clothing beneath said gown, complying with the La Cañada High School Student Body Dress Code. Candidates for graduation will be expected to assemble in alphabetical order and to follow all subsequent instructions. Failure to dress properly, or to follow instructions, shall be met with severe disciplinary measures.

Graduation from La Cañada High School is considered to be a privilege, and students shall conduct themselves accordingly throughout all ceremonies. Horseplay, unnecessary noise or rudeness will not be tolerated, and will be dealt with immediately, using severe disciplinary measures. Students scheduled to offer prayers are admonished that said prayers shall not be addressed to any specific deity to avoid offending students of other faiths and traditions. Students are encouraged to invite their families and/or loved ones to attend graduation ceremonies. However, please advise said families and/or loved ones that any unauthorized flash photography is strictly prohibited throughout all ceremonies to avoid distracting participants. A professional photographer, Unchained Memories Studios, has offered to make graduation photographs available for sale to interested parties.

Throughout scheduled graduation ceremonies, all students of La Cañada High School not assigned to graduate will be expected to be in their assigned classroom seats and ready for scheduled educational activities, with the exception of students in their senior year who have yet to fulfill the requirements of graduation. Said students shall report promptly to the cafetorium at eight o'clock a.m. A movie will be shown.

Any questions or inquiries which you may have regarding the aforementioned commencement ceremonies shall be directed in writing

(in triplicate) to the office of the Assistant
Principal and Director of Student Activities
at La Cañada High School.
Your strict compliance with the directives
of this memorandum is expected.

Roland W. Conrad, M.A.Ed. Assistant Principal
and Director of Student Activities

With only one week left in high school, it was time to clean our lockers. For the first time, the yearly ritual felt almost like our wake. There were no track meets. No more races meant we didn't need to practice. Even Coach Neal had lightened up. Most days we all ditched seventh period; except today, when the time had come to turn in all our uniforms. I'd never wear my number five ever again.

The nylon shorts I'd worn for races were folded on my locker bench over gray La Cañada sweats with yellow crescents beneath the arms. My maroon jersey with my name on it—for some reason they wanted it—went on top. I sat and stared down at the giant number five across my back, the name "MARTIN" in an arch of yellow letters was folded over and laid across the sweats.

I folded a gym towel beneath my pile, and I emptied out my locker, smelling the stench from Snooge's clothespile one last time.

"Careful, Snooge, I said. Somethin' in there could melt your eyeballs."

Snooge placed his sweats into a big brown paper sack, then grabbed a mildewed pair of socks as stiff as plywood, with a toe missing. "It's just a rodent," Snooge informed us.

"Looks like it ate your socks and died," Booboo shot back, removing the mummified skin and skeleton of a mouse and flinging it by the tail to the trash.

A wrinkled shirt stained black with mildew topped off Snooge's sack. One last time we held our noses while he walked out to the dumpster. It was the last time I ever saw that number 18 on his jersey.

Only a hint of locker stench remained among the rust.

Ivan faced me. "How many years at Paradise Canyon had we celebrated the final day of school, beneath the jungle gym?" he asked. From Ivan's pocket, he tossed a compact yellow rectangle my direction.

"A Topps baseball card wax pack?" I grinned at Ivan. "Thanks."

"Any San Francisco Giants in there are mine."

To this day, I've never opened Ivan's wax pack. I like to think every player in that package is a Dodger who now resides in the Cooperstown Hall of Fame.

Booboo, Psycho and Rattfink would be coming back next year. They tagged their uniforms for the cleaners to be laundered for next season. But I wasn't coming back. I was going to Vietnam.

I handed my dirty folded uniform to Clipboard Weenie Number Two.

And then I walked out to my Yamaha—and cried.

High school was over.

When I got home, I found a package on my bed from Calais, Maine. That's what the postmark said. I ripped it open and found a copy of *Ethan Frome*. There was a stamp inside from Unobskey School Library, at the "U. of Maine, Calais." Behind the front page was a marketing plan, tainted with coffee stains and ketchup and folded over around a Shell map of the entire United States. The map displayed a giant letter Z that crossed the country. It began in San Diego, which was circled in red Marks-a-Lot. It passed through Salinas to San Francisco, to Portland, Seattle and more circles. It turned southeast, through Salt Lake City, Denver, St Louis, Chattanooga, Atlanta, Jacksonville. Then it turned north up the entire eastern seaboard to where it ended in a circle around Calais, Maine.

A memo stapled to the map read, "MISSION ACCOMPLISHED."

LA CAÑADA HIGH SCHOOL: FRIDAY, JUNE 10TH, 1971 (GRADUATION!)

I fought back tears at graduation. Other students seemed excited. Classmates exchanged hugs and laughs and memories and cards. The highlight of the ceremony was when Momma chased a freshman across the parking lot and her sharp stilettos sank into hot asphalt. Momma tottered onto her rump, high heels embedded into the pavement. Chunks of gravel and stringy tar stuck to her skirt and to her nylons. Finally John the janitor had to walk out and extract her, carrying Momma to her seat just like a fireman carries a child. She was furious. The Class of 1971 gave John a standing O, and then we noticed Momma's shoes were still embedded beside a Volkswagen. Momma spent the ceremony picking gravel from her nylons. John the janitor spent it beaming like he was every Senior's father.

But then my thoughts returned to Mandy, still in traction in Room 327 of Huntington Memorial. She wouldn't graduate till August. According to Suzanne, they hadn't expected her to live, and yet she'd hung on for seven weeks. The lupus attacking Mandy's heart had turned against her bones. Suzanne had told me about the x-rays. "Things aren't healing right," she'd said. "Mandy will never run again, maybe never even walk." Her last night walking, we had danced. Sometimes it made me feel guilty, but Leta reminded me she'd never seen her best friend look so happy as at her last night at her "prom," before the accident.

Speeches and invocations whirled by in fast-forward, like listening to a speech you'd heard a hundred times before. They called our names, and one-by-one we came to pick up our diplomas from Mister Conrad, who once more found a way to mispronounce my name. We didn't really get diplomas. Those came later in the mail. I got a sheet of yellow paper wrapped in red and yellow ribbons saying the diplomas would arrive after three more weeks of "processing."

But by then I would already have reported to Basic Training. I felt like somewhere a huge clock ticked off my final days of freedom.

Usually, after every victory there was another race. Today I didn't even get a victory lap. You kept on running until you lost. The next war was for keeps. My plane left for Fort Carson, Colorado in four days.

My cap and tassel went into the dumpster. Most boys weren't sentimental. I kicked the starter on my Yamaha, revved up the engine, rolled down Oak Grove, down Linda Vista, Colorado, Orange Grove, California, to the parking lot of Huntington Memorial.

I walked upstairs. Mandy was sound asleep in Room 327. I touched her wrist. She didn't stir. She looked angelic where she slept. I didn't wake her, and if I had, I would have drowned her with my tears. I couldn't bear Mandy remembering me the way that I was crying, to see my fear behind my eyes that I would die in Vietnam. I wanted her to remember me the day I'd won our race. She had gotten me that far, and now the rest was up to me. I wanted to be remembered as a victor, not a coward.

I kissed her lips while she was sleeping and mouthed the words I'd heard so often on the radio from Peter, Paul, and Mary about that jet plane

This time, they were true. I stood there outside Mandy's door.

Whispered:

I hate to wake you up,
and say goodbye.

CHAPTER TWENTY-SIX

LEAVIN' ON A JET PLANE
FORT CARSON, COLORADO: FRIDAY, JULY 29TH, 1971

In Hollywood, you win a big race, and the movie ends right there. After you win, you can live happily ever after. In real life, after you win, they send you back into the fire. Here I was, stuck at Fort Carson in the middle of Colorado after six weeks basic training before Nam. There'd been no parties like my friends' parents had thrown kids at graduation. There'd been no trophies for winning races, not even a post card during mail call. All I got was some old sergeant whose silver tooth gleamed in the sunrise.

He pointed to eight rows of personnel trucks.

"All right, soldiers, ship out."

We shuffled forward. One-hundred-sixty trucks had been sent up from the motor pool. They made us board them in formation. We sat and braved each other's odors with hints of diesel fuel and rubber. A hundred engines started up and left us choking on exhaust. The trucks rumbled toward the highway, leaving the Quonset huts at Carson, and headed north past Colorado Springs.

I watched the guardhouse out of the back gate of the truck. Fort Carson shrank down to a dot, then disappeared. I laid my rifle at my feet. When America shipped off soldiers, they made sure nobody showed up to wave goodbye.

Noisy transmissions in the troop carriers jarred against our spines. The smell of gun oil filled our nostrils while green soldiers, FNG's, "fucking new guys," exchanged glances. Some of us would never see home again. I was scared. Fear was written on every face inside our truck.

The last voice I heard in America, (or the last voice on the ground) was Andy Williams on the radio of the old motor-pool sergeant who drove our truck. He crooned the lyrics to the tired theme from Love Story. "Love means you never have to say you're sorry," I kept hearing over and over as if Teflonistas had decided to drive the Velcroids from America.

Ten minutes later we boarded C-141's at Peterson Air Base. We sat inside, soaking in sweat inside a long steel compartment. They sat us on red webbing that ran the full length of an airplane that already reeked of body odor and farts.

They didn't even give us windows to look outside at America.

A G.I. whispered in my ear. His Gomer Pyle voice had "mentally challenged" written all over it. What I saw in this guy's eyes told me he wasn't coming back. "This is my rifle. This is my gun." He touched his M14 and then his crotch. "This is for fighting. This is for fun." The guy gave off a goofy giggle while we taxied down the runway. Together, we held our breaths, knowing they'd cleared us to take off for Vietnam.

Two months later, I saw the same guy in the bush. I zippered his corpse into his body bag, and we loaded him onto a chopper at Qhang Tri.

END OF PART TWO

PART THREE

SUMMER

There are two ways of spreading light: to be the candle or the mirror that reflects it.
EDITH WHARTON,
Vesalius in Zante

CHAPTER TWENTY-SEVEN

SO FAR AWAY

DA NANG, SOUTH VIETNAM: SEPTEMBER, 1972
(8 DAYS TO FREEDOM!)

The insects in Da Nang were thickest late afternoons when they orbited the ceiling fans like clouds of pissed-off dots. They whirred around the incandescent light bulbs in the hospital, playing chicken with the spinning steel fan blades. The edges of the blades were always covered with their "bug juice," where dozens of their comrades had hit the fan. They didn't talk much. Like a soldier, an insect never cries. I often watched them circle fans on muggy afternoons.

Hundreds of them, ground by boots into concrete below the fans, gave off a stench. In the evenings their odor rolled across our cots. It covered up our farts and even the smell of orange mercurochrome. If the aroma got annoying, we could always sniff our wounds, our rotting scabs, oozing with fungus and infection. Daily, I felt the empty ache where my left foot had disppeared.

Soon, it was evening. Time to prop my head up. Five of us waited expectantly at sunset every day. We had a night nurse. Her name was Carole. At least, that's what Rudy'd told us, before Rudy had faded and no longer had the strength to raise his head. After Rudy got us started, Carole was all we thought about, her forced smile, her sad blue eyes, her auburn hair cut short in bangs, and those tempting nipples pressed against her Army-issue t-shirt.

I wondered if Carole knew she was the high point of our nights. Anywhere outside Da Nang, she'd likely never turn a head. Somehow even the "summer tans" they'd made her put on when the brass came didn't disguise that something pleasant could be found beneath her uniform. We never saw her breasts, but we were happy they were there. They were the only hints of softness in our lives.

She was late tonight. Disappointment was etched deep into several bandaged faces of soldiers who waited with me. We were worried. Had they replaced Carole? Had they shipped her somewhere else or to the States? We whispered to each other in the dark.

At last, footsteps. A soft padding of rubber soles on concrete flooring assured us Carole hadn't left us. Smiles were conjured from my companions. She was coming. Whispers ended and our wry smiles grew wider.

She entered the room and bee-lined straight for Rudy.

She didn't even touch the light switch. Rudy wasn't snoring. Not that Rudy always snored. He only did when he was sleeping. Blood often bubbled in his throat from all the shrapnel in his neck. Lately, Rudy Maldonado snored a lot.

Carole turned him over.

He didn't moan.

"Shit." She slapped him. "Breathe for me, you turkey."

He didn't moan.

"Goddammit, moan for me, you son of a bitch." Carole shook him harder. "Moan, Rudy. Breathe, Goddammit. Tell me where it hurts."

Carole sprinted down the corridor and returned with two big orderlies. They punched Rudy. They slapped him. They shoved paddles against his chest. Both men drove needles into his arms. Men ran from the corridors, clustered. I heard but couldn't see them. "C'mon, soldier. Wake up. Wake up. Wake up!"

"Shit!" voices in unison.

Rudy didn't moan.

The men slid Rudy's body onto a bent three-wheeled gurney that wobbled and squeaked as Rudy rolled away. My heart seized in my throat. I stared silently. Numb. No outward shows of sorrow. None of us even pulled a Kleenex. Had the Army wanted tears, they would have issued them.

At least Rudy didn't hurt now. He was out of Vietnam. He couldn't feel that half his skin was cooked with second and third-degree burns and what was left was filled with jungle rot and shrapnel.

The gurney did its best to fill the silence.

"'S Rudy dead?" It was Callahan. He had seniority and no legs. He'd been here since a month before I got here.

The others nodded, turning heads. We stared at Rudy's empty sheets.

"Poor ol' Rudy," said Callahan. "He never did deserve this shit."

We nodded. Another day. Another death. Another empty bed some amputee would soon be filling. A private in fatigues came in to box up Rudy's things and send some bride in Goodland, Kansas, a framed picture of herself.

An understanding passed between us. We'd been discarded by a country that had no use for us. We read daily in the papers how much they hated us.

But for the first time in my life, I felt somehow I had been lucky. They were shipping me back home. I had a "million-dollar wound." I had only lost my foot, the one I'd chickened out on shooting in my garage in La Cañada.

Now my name was on the roster of the living.

I'd wondered, ditching school on Rosh Hashanah as a goy, whether I also should have taken Yom Kippur off. Ivan had shared a prayer with me his cantor used to sing:

> *On Rosh Hashanah will be inscribed and on Yom Kippur will be sealed how many will pass from the earth and how many will be created; who will live and who will die; who by water and who by fire, who by sword...*

What do you do when given a life you hadn't planned on? I had been afraid I'd die, and now I feared that I would live.

The next day I fasted, gave up bouillon and lemon Jell-o. It seemed too little to forego, when Rudy'd given up his life.

And no one told us, when Rudy died, that it was Carole's final visit, but at that point, we, the living, were too proccupied to care.

I dreamed the nightmare again that night, the awful one about the boot; where I had crossed the empty field to reach a soldier who'd been wounded. It was safer to use the rice paddies and brave their omnipresent leeches. Except a guy out there was bleeding, and he didn't have much time left. Besides I couldn't stand the leeches. The gruesome ritual of peeling them off each other's skin like adhesive tape at nightfall creeped me out.

Sure, there were land mines in the fields. That was why we braved the leeches. The sun had dipped into the eerie evening shadows of the jungle. It being late, I volunteered to cross the field to retrieve him. I was tired and in a hurry. I raced across the clearing and lifted a half-unconscious corporal over my shoulders and kept running. My time was short, and I got careless.

Pop! Something stung my foot. A buddy came to take the soldier while I sat down in a daze. I took my boot off. It didn't feel right. The damn wound didn't hurt until I stared into my boot, at mangled ligaments and tendons.

Toe-popper. I'd tripped one.

I saw my socks, saw half my foot was missing. I poured it from my boot. My toes were wrapped inside a sock. Two arms grabbed me by the armpits and they lifted.

My buddies carried me to the hilltop they called LZ-17. One of them joked about my "million-dollar wound." He wasn't aware I didn't need it. I was the two-digit midget. That's what they called you when your time left was 99 days or less. Seventeen days were all that stood between me and the Freedom Bird to the States once my tour in Vietnam had been completed. It was a number I could grasp, could even count to on my fingers and my toes, at least until my toes had tripped the land mine.

I felt a twinge. They say pain can take a while to kick in. I heard them radio in a Huey. The sergeant stared through his binoculars toward the southeastern horizon.

A chopper.

Half a klick south, five-hundred yards to LZ-17. Corpsmen tied tubing around my ankle to slow the bleeding from the wound. A big guy asked if I could walk. I told the guy, "I'll do my best." The numbness of my wound felt like the buzz after a race. I started walking on the heel stump. Blood soaked the remnant of my socks.

Dizzy.

My fists tightened. Sweat carved gullies down the mud caked on my ankles.

Mandy yelled, Keep your arms low, Allen. It's easier.

I dropped my arms.

Open your fists up. Smile, Allen. It saps less energy.

I tried to smile. Gnats and jungle bugs kept landing in my teeth. I turned the corner, the hardest part. I kept chugging–chugging–chugging.

Come on, Allen. Come on, come on.

I slowed.

Mandy screamed. Come on. You can make it. I know you can. She clapped her hands, and it was almost like she'd telegraphed her energy.

I raised my chin.

Almost there.

I struggled forward.

You're gonna make it.

Running.

I landed in someone's arms, a puddle of sweat. They strapped a harness around my crotch, hoisting me skyward to the copter. The rotor blast hit my face like I had landed in a wind tunnel while straps beneath my crotch pounded my manhood.

They lifted me high above the clearing, my bandage dangling from my foot. With every inch that I was lifted, it seemed the chopper blades grew stronger. Pulses from the blades hammered my upper chest with air blasts. A wingman sat in the doorway holding a blood-stained M16. He was clothed in ammunition belts with several yards of bullets coiled around his flak jacket like snakes.

"Allen Martin?"

I moaned.

"It's Garry. Garry Jackson."

I turned in shock, raising a thumb to acknowledge he'd called my name. At twenty-one, his hair was *white*. Garry Jackson could be fifty!

He cracked a smile.

I did my best to offer a smile in return.

"Ain't this war a bitch, Allen?" he called above the chopper blades.

"No shit."

Mortar fire. A red streak flared past Garry's door. He squeezed his trigger and rained lead across a circle of fields below us. The copter swerved, banging my helmet against the framing of the Huey. Another mortar. Another swerve. Another salvo from Garry's automatic rifle, as I finally felt the pain and shut my eyes.

I came to in Chu Lai. We were surrounded by barbed wire to keep us safe. Garry squeezed my wrist before they loaded me onto a truck. He'd jogged over from his chopper. I'd never expected to see a classmate from La Cañada in Vietnam. Not on this side of the Puddle. Not from a town with so much money. But there was Garry of all people. He glared out at the hillsides. His usual shit-eating grin had seemed a thousand yards away.

"Good luck, Martian. Say hi to La Cañada when you get back."

"You hear from Heather?"

Garry blew a raspberry. "Fuckin' bitch."

"What happened?"

"She's at Yale. She's majoring in self-congratulation. Her last letter, she compared us all to Hitler."

"Bet that hurt."

"This whole war fuckin' hurts." Garry touched my foot. "You and me...." He choked. His voice cracked up mid-sentence. He was crying.

He didn't finish up his sentence. He stood beside my stretcher, wrapped in an ammo belt. Our eyes locked.

"Remember that ton cake you threw at me, and it broke the frigging window," Garry said. He chuckled, and it felt good to see him laugh. "Remember the day—" Garry said "—in Harron's class he ruptured Canada?"

I smiled.

"Laughed my ass off," Garry said. "Matter of fact, get this. I checked out Harron's service record on this computer at Fort

Belvoir. Some war hero. Son of a bitch was four-F diabetic. I shit you not, Martian."

My foot throbbed. My wound called me to attention.

"Laughed my ass off," Garry said and slapped my shoulder. "Laughed my ass off."

I laughed too. Drifted off.

Then I woke. There was a bandage where my foot was supposed to be, and Garry Jackson's obituary was sitting by my water glass. Rudy had found it in *Stars and Stripes*. He'd seen the "La Cañada High." Asked if I knew him.

I said I had. I felt like someone had kicked my heart in.

A day after I'd seen him, an RPG had knocked out his copter. There was even a little picture by his name.

It was almost as if Garry'd known he'd had to die in Vietnam. Like somewhere in Southeast Asoa was this grenade with Garry's name on it. Over the horizon, he could see it on its way, spiraling toward him. Every day it always woke up with one goal—to hunt down Garry, waiting in Charlie's rucksack for Garry's copter. And then—VOOM!—no more Garry. Just shredded metal, blood and bones.

Like brothers, we understood we'd been betrayed. We never said it, but we both knew we were velcroids.

But at least I'd made him smile. We had parted on good terms. I was grateful Garry Jackson had been in Nam to be my friend.

On the battlefield there are no teflonistas.

CHAPTER TWENTY-EIGHT

AMERICAN PIE

TRAVIS AIR FORCE BASE, FAIRFIELD, CA: OCTOBER, 1972

(FREEDOM! WHAT THE HELL DO I DO NOW?)

From the moment our C141 touched down at Travis in California, I knew the place we'd landed wasn't home. We were Stateside. We'd been told there'd be no cheering, no kissing runways, no speeches of being back in the good ol' U.S.A. And we weren't welcome.

While we'd been gone, somehow hatred had become virtuous. America had mutated into something much less friendly. Even the air, the wind and drizzle had smelled foreign when we'd landed.

This wasn't the America we'd fought for.

In Vietnam, I'd often thought about America as her people. Now, we'd learned those people hated us. No thank yous were forthcoming. We had to dream up simple pleasures to serve as proxies for former friends. I looked forward to an In-N-Out Burger and a winter limp up Flint Peak if the soreness in my armpits from my crutches would allow me. I'd joined the Army as a runner and was coming home half-crippled, but I was home. Tough to be bitter when so many hadn't made it. No matter what the evening news said, we'd survived something they hadn't, and we were grateful for small favors. Few surviving soldiers would argue.

Returning from Vietnam, we also faced a battle to contain the silent rage festering underneath our scars. We'd been betrayed. I'd lost a foot. Garry Jackson had lost his life. But few true soldiers spoke their minds. We'd been programmed not to whine, and so we stuffed things. I hadn't even told my mother I'd lost a foot, fearing it might disrupt her marriage to my "father."

The runway thumped our plane harder than usual today. Perhaps the country we had fought for couldn't wait to kick our butts. I grabbed my crutches and stumbled toward the front door of the plane. It was foggy. Blurry truck lights approached a C130 cargo plane behind us. Airmen stacked body bags onto trucks like cords of wood. A death stench drilled through the fog mixed with the smell of rotting blood. One of those zippered bags held Garry Jackson.

Airmen chewing cigarettes seemed indifferent to their missions. C130s and C141s cluttered jet-blasted airstrips. Wings drooped from battered fuselages as though the planes were tired of flying. Even airplanes showed fatigue, like soldiers, never grumbling, just surviving one mission at a time.

An airman shook me. "Smile. You're home, soldier."

Oddly, I didn't feel emotion.

We shuffled forward with glazed eyes, disappointed how the America we returned to in 1972 bore no resemblance to the country we'd left in 1971. There was no laughter. Even the music had turned angry. Songs like *Smiling Faces*, and *Freddie's Dead.*

We assembled on the tarmac, boarded a battered personnel carrier coughing diesel fumes. A sergeant boomed out, "Izzair a Corporal Martin heah?"

I raised my hand.

Some tech sergeant handed me an aerogram that lacked a return address. Its musty aroma and smeared postmarks said it had been to Vietnam and had been forwarded. "Got here yesterday," the sergeant's raspy voice said. "Ya got lucky. Most wind up dead letters."

Damn lucky! Some of us wind up dead soldiers.

I slit the aerogram with my jackknife, shaking, unfolding handwriting:

Allen,
Call me. It's important.
Leta Hertz
(415) 834-5309

I shivered. What did Leta want? She'd only called me once before. About Mandy. I found a phone booth, hands shaking in such spasms I nearly dialed the wrong number.

"Hello?"

"Leta, it's Allen. Got your letter. I'm at Travis. You said to call."

"Oh my gawd." Choking tears back, she promised she'd arrive within the hour.

My heart tightened. I wondered what on earth could be so urgent. "Can you tell me what's the matter?"

Leta hung up, sobbing.

I had a week's leave I could use before returning to Fort Ord, near Monterrey, where Uncle Sam would need to process through my discharge. I worried Leta might have changed, going to Stanford. Was she a Marxist? Would she hate me after I'd fought in Vietnam?

Worse, I worried for Mandy, afraid to ask the awful question that had haunted me, even overseas on muggy nights in Nam. *Was Mandy healthy?* What had happened since the last time I had seen her? I closed my mind and wished to heaven Leta would never come to tell me. After Garry, I was afraid to hear the truth.

A reinforced concrete guardhouse faced the gate outside of Travis. It looked just like all the others in the Air Force. I walked past the M.P. that nodded off behind the glass. "You goin' out there, soldier—" a guard said "—with no vehicle?"

I nodded.

"Bad idea." He shook his head as if he wished I'd reconsider.

I moved forward on my crutches.

And then I saw them, hurrying toward me, knowing I couldn't run away. Ten of them, my age, were dressed in bell-bottoms and tie-dies. One wore a jean jacket with a cannabis leaf larger than my head. A girl spat on my forehead. Her loogie smelled like cheap tobacco. It dribbled down my nose between my eyes.

"Fucking war-pig. Fucking baby-killer. Fucking Nazi."

SLAP!

I froze, muscles tensing, blood stampeding through my temples. Anger flashed, and I struggled to contain my silent rage. We'd been told the raw adrenaline that kept us wired in Vietnam now left us edgy, ready to strike, a spark away from detonation. A slap, a pop, a provocation, a middle finger on the freeway had triggered countless hot-wired soldiers to explode like human time bombs. Surprising some dumb civilian with skills learned in Vietnam could earn a soldier a one-way ticket to Fort Leavenworth.

I wanted to twist her fragile wrist into ligaments and bone meal. She'd slapped me. I bit my cheek, tasted the metal of my blood. I thought of Mandy, breathed in her smile, let her peace release my anger, remembered Garry, John the janitor, the America I'd fought for.

Exhaling, I walked slowly, my foot stump throbbing where scabs healed. I cleared a path between the protesters with my crutches.

The leader taunted me. "Yo, scumbag."

I faced the road. I licked my lips, felt blood trickle across my tongue.

"You think that uniform makes you special?"

Girls clapped their hands. They spat out mantras. "HEY BABYKILLER, PLEASE." I smelled bad dope. They seemed to taunt me to blow my brains out, Ethan Frome style; a special favor, just for them. "SHOOT YOURSELF, NOT VIETNAMESE."

I shut them out. A tour in Nam had taught me English could sound foreign. I clenched my fists, squinched my eyes, sucked in breaths of smoggy air. I pretended the only language I understood was Vietnamese.

A green AMC Gremlin raced toward me.

Thank God, Leta!

The paint had oxidized and peeled on her Gremlin. Someone honked. The rear-window decal spelled out "SNODFART" instead of "STANFORD." The car screeched to the roadside.

Beeeeeeeeeeeeeep!

"Get in."

I turned.

"Allen, get in." Leta'd cut her hair short. She wore glasses, the funky old kind with the rhinestones.

"Hurry. They're throwing eggs. These jerks'll ruin my car."

I scrambled in, buckled my seatbelt, threw my duffel behind the seat and slammed the door. An egg splooshed across our windshield.

She turned the wipers on.

A child was strapped into a car seat in the back, dressed in pink jammies. She was sleeping.

Leta screeched into a u-turn. An egg sailed past the radio antenna. We ran the stop sign. She floored the gas.

Helen Reddy's voice roared from the radio.

We didn't talk much. I was afraid to ask what this was all about. I feard the worst. Something had happened, and it had to do with Mandy. Leta's Gremlin rolled down I-40 through Fairfield, through Vallejo. We crossed a bridge over the Carquinez from Benicia to Martinez. By Richmond, Leta's fuel gage was pinned a quarter-notch past empty, and my heart was feeling lower than even that. We stopped for gas. I filled the tank, scrubbed spattered moths off of her windshield, and ran a tattered rubber squeegee across the egg goop. I went inside to wash the yolk debris and spit off from my uniform. There were no mirrors on the walls. Anything glass had been ripped down. A condom machine was scarred with shiny knife marks and silvered letters. "THIS GUM TASTES LIKE SHIT!" someone had scrawled.

I looked to take a leak, except the urinal was missing. The toilet was heaped with paper towels and feces. I ducked behind the Chevron and found a bush that needed watering.

When I returned to Leta's Gremlin, she was crying.

"Hey, I said quietly, touching Leta's shoulder.

She looked up at me and shivered. Looked away and then looked back." I peered into the back seat, where the baby girl was sleeping.

Leta removed her rhinestone glasses and stared back through her raw eyes. I wondered what was going on between the glasses and the baby.

"What's wrong, Leta? What happened?"

She shook harder now. "It's Mandy." She shook her hair out, opened her car door and sank her head between her fists, muffling sobs. I touched her shoulder. She slid away.

"Allen, I can't believe she's dead."

My heart stopped in midbeat. "Did you say?"

"Yeah."

Numb, I couldn't inhale, couldn't exhale, couldn't think. I hung suspended while I processed Leta's words.

"Dead!" The world blurred. I closed my eyes to hide my pain. *"Dead."* My eyes reopened. Leta's radish eyes stared back at me. I had seen too much of death. How could Mandy be dead too?

Stepping onto weathered asphalt that was reverting back to gravel, Leta padded around the Gremlin, popping the hatch behind the car seat. Numb, I followed. Between diaper bags and suitcases, she retrieved a tattered scrapbook, bound in leather, mildewed, with ragged edges. "Open it," she pleaded, touching my forearm. "I'm worn out from crying alone. I need some company." She squeezed against my arm.

I flipped the cover to see a photo in black and white, cropped with pinking shears. Two girls with milk cartons in front of Palm Crest Elementary. The date, September 1958, was hand-printed beneath the photo. Leta wore glasses. Sitting beside her, Mandy towered above Leta.

But it was Mandy, and my heart raced. She smiled through missing teeth. I flipped through pages of Leta's memories, wanting to share some of their fun. Photos of Mandy and other friends, classroom photos, snapshots from Brownies, clippings from camp on Catalina, Leta and Mandy dressed like clowns for trick-or-treating.

For her sixth grade photo, Leta wasn't smiling. She looked sad, like she did now, shoulders hunched in self-defense. Her chin lowered in resignation, as if she feared facing the camera, eyes frozen as if she felt she might be staring into cross-hairs, a stare I'd seen a lot in Vietnam.

I touched the corner-mount of the photograph, and it flipped onto the asphalt, leaving the snapshot suspended between the three remaining photo corners. "Something happen in sixth grade?" I asked as softly as I could.

Leta shut her eyes.

"It's okay, Leta." I whispered, grateful my voice had sounded gentle.

A nod. Leta kept shaking. "And only Mandy knew what to say. Like every day I talked to Mandy, and she told me I was gorgeous. I'd be okay. I was so glad she was my friend for that semester. I finally gave up and believed her. The way you did and won a race. No one coached like Mandy Richert. No one believed in me like *she* did." Leta blinked back tears. "No one." She blew her nose and wiped her lip.

I trembled when I realized we both were on our own now.

By freshman year in high school, Leta's smile had returned, and she was beaming for Breck Shampoo ads on backs of *Redbook Magazines*. I flipped forward to senior year and saw my face in Leta's album next to Mandy's. Then I was gone. And there was Mandy in her wheelchair, alone. And then on crutches. Then came a walking cane in Kenya, and she was standing with a stopwatch in her fist just like Coach Neal."

"She'd always wanted to be a nun, and this convent over in Kenya let her coach track." Leta whispered, sniffling and turning pages to show a photograph of Mandy teaching athletes to run in front of Mount Kilimanjaro. Teenagers grinned with toothy smiles and their spindly brown legs with their hard rubber-band muscles looked almost gawky. They wore silk uniforms and medals. A Kenyan flag fluttered behind them.

"They were her champions. These are the two who ran in Munich," Leta said.

"The Olympics?"

"Yeaahhh!" Leta swallowed tears. "And Mandy coached them."

In the photo, Mandy stood between her girls holding a stopwatch. She was smiling the same smile I'd seen on the roof of the gymnasium, a smile baby sparrow wide, toughened with a bravery that allowed her to stand tall, despite her injury, a toughness I was trying to learn myself.

"Leta, you're serious? Did she know I used her strategy to win?"

"She always knew that you could win. She never knew that she could *coach* until you showed her."

I felt my breath pass through my lips when I exhaled.

"You might not know *this*." Leta stared right at me. "Coach Neal came around to talk with Mandy right after you left. All summer long they talked while Mandy healed up. Last fall, when La Cañada cross country took first place in C.I.F., I had this chill, like Mandy had taught Coach Neal the same thing she had taught *you*. Except by then, she was in Kenya.

"Yeah." I'd given Mandy something special to take with her. Something good. Something to leave me feeling proud. I needed pride on a day when my world was trying to shame me. Needed it like air.

I allowed myself a smile.

But then my mind returned to the hour I'd lost my foot in Vietnam. I could swear I'd heard Mandy's voice on top of LZ-17. The very moment I'd been pulled into the chopper, I'd felt her with me.

Come on. You can make it. I know you can.

I felt a shiver up my neck. "She died in August, didn't she? The seventeenth."

"What?" Leta turned ashen. She hid her eyes behind her palms. "How did *you* know?"

"Hard to explain. Some day I promise you I'll tell you."

When Leta touched my shoulder I felt her hand tremble. She blew her nose.

My heart shivered, an ache welled in me, an ice block in my chest. I shook my head, hands hardening into fists like giant hailstones. Grief collected in my throat. I looked at Leta's weary eyes.

"I'm sorry," Leta whispered. "I'm so sorry."

I felt empty, as if some hand had punched a hole up through my stomach, grabbed my heart, tearing it loose from all the cobwebs hung inside me. After eleven months of war, I imagined my heart ripping, being yanked out, falling somewhere off the freeway.

Leta paused. The baby girl woke up and fussed. I helped Leta unstrap her. She cradled the baby in her arms, eased it toward her blouse. "Sssh, little Mandy. Mommy's here."

I inhaled. A tiny head with chestnut hair zeroed in on Leta's breast. Miniature lips worked like bellows on Leta's nipple. A flame of hope melted my heart. Quiet gurgles sucked in rhythm through Leta's crying.

"I need another favor, Allen."

I faced the dashboard, feeling self-conscious.

She straightened her glasses. "You had this place, Allen. Mandy never told me where it was. Said she'd promised you she'd always keep it secret. You guys had some kind of a pact. You used to run there, Mandy said."

The memories came washing through my mind, my teaching Mandy how to run, Mandy teaching me to love, how to live and how to win. Mandy was running by my side along the fire road as we descended toward her Volkswagen below us. And we were soaring on our legs, and I was whispering "Occam's Razor," and I could hear her breathing.

And then it faded, and I was crying in the front seat of Leta's Gremlin in a Chevron Station in Richmond, California.

"Flint Peak."

"That's where Mandy wants her ashes spread."

Oh, God. My heart dropped inside my chest. The reality of her death sank in with cruel gravity. Leta straightened her glasses. She had lost her Rose Queen visage. Something had happened.

"You're asking me to show you where it is?"

"Yes, and have a ceremony for Mandy. Give us closure."

I stared at her. A long minute. I searched beyond Leta's wide eyes and saw the well of pain I'd seen the day we'd talked behind the tennis courts. The day she'd lectured me. I saw a pain so deep I feared I might fall in. There were no rails to hold me back.

"That's what I need, Allen," said Leta. "It's what we both need."

I sighed. "Let's go home. You and the baby look exhausted. Maybe you should sleep and let me drive."

I turned the key to start the Gremlin. We rolled south on 101 toward Los Angeles. Towns blurred past. San Jose. Salinas. San Luis Obispo....

CHAPTER TWENTY-NINE

I CAN SEE CLEARLY NOW
FLINT PEAK: OCTOBER, 1972

This morning Leta's Gremlin parked where Lida Street met Figueroa. I was waiting at the fire road to meet her. I lifted her baby and the Snugli and placed both onto my back. The smell of sage soared up the canyon on a dry chaparral breeze like I remembered from my runs up here with Mandy. She was with us—at least her ashes were in a sack in Leta's hand. In silence, we ascended up Flint Peak.

It took longer than it used to when we lumbered up Flint Peak before the sun rose. I plodded with a cane ahead of Leta. Each step throbbed beyond my stump. Missing toes telepathed their absence. The doctors had a name for it. Phantom limb syndrome. Adding insult to my injury my foot stump was now swollen.

It had all sounded so clinical. And no neat little nomenclature sufficed to describe the injustice of it all. Yet I counted myself lucky. Garry Jackson hadn't made it. Fifty-thousand fellow-soldiers had been killed in Vietnam.

I noticed Vietnam veterans never spoke about the war. Only the wanna-be's, the Harron types, believed in things like glory; men who'd never stared down a rifle sight, seen a man and squeezed the trigger, who'd never been caught in friendly fire, who'd never tasted the stench of death. I'd see the posers on local television, in news articles, on street corners. Sometimes I'd ask one where he'd served, and I would listen to his lies. The posers were never sad enough. But maybe that's my fault. Why talk about Vietnam unless I have to? Keep it inside. Maybe the memories should stay in there forever.

Like looking beyond Snooge's jersey, I needed to look beyond the war. Leave Vietnam behind. It's just a tumor on my soul. I turned and waited for Leta to catch up to me.

The baby fussed, and we stopped while Leta nursed. Tiny cheeks extracted breakfast and the child stopped her crying. I faced away, embarrassed I had stared at Leta's breast. I listened while her baby finished feeding. Hard to get used to seeing a classmate offering life after my war tour. Odd, knowing I was a virgin when I'd spent the last year killing.

After a few minutes, she placed the baby in the Snugli, sleepy and warm. Leta faced me. Sighed. "Allen, are you ready?"

She walked uphill. I grabbed my cane, and soon caught up with her and joined her. Today Leta and I'd be spreading Mandy's ashes from Flint Peak. The Jabberwocky, Garry Jackson, Mandy. There were three now. My name had somehow landed on the long list of the living. I'd been whole when

I'd run up here, racing the wind, running with Mandy. Now, I limped.

Still, climbing to the top, I was sad to learn how hard it had become. Mandy's death had left me numb. I remembered her running with me. Each step of Mandy's struggle breathed her strength into my heart.

I'd freed Mandy's heart to run. She had freed my heart to care. Compared to Ethan Frome whose heart was never free, I'd been damn lucky.

Scrub jays squabbled in the elderberries. A year had not resolved their differences. Things seemed mild in La Cañada after a tour in Vietnam. Climbing Flint Peak, I remembered how I'd hated *Ethan Frome*. Had it been more than a year since our Society had convened? Was I the only living member, the way I was, up until Mandy? Ah yes, there'd been more chapters. Someone had even crossed America, carrying out our plan. But like Ethan, I'd survived. I didn't hate *Ethan Frome*, especially now that I was crippled too. I only hated he'd never found the guts to change.

I wanted to set Ethan Frome and Mattie Silver free. The way Mandy had set me free, on this mountain.

By the tower, we opened the bag. Mandy's ashes flew away, swirling in dusty spirals that snowed down on laurel sumacs. For a moment I thought I saw Ethan and Mattie on their sled. As though both of them might slide down slopes of snow you couldn't see. My mind flashed back to high school. I braced for the collision, imagining Ethan Frome's and Mattie Silver's screams.

But Ethan's boot heels seemed to dig into the powder of my mind, kicking a cone of white in front of him. Braking and rising, he tugged on Mattie's mitten until she too rose. Their sled continued down its rut. Empty, it caromed off a tree.

Ethan and Mattie had sprouted wings. Struggling to fly, they swooshed into the air of Sycamore Canyon. Mattie's red scarf fluttered behind her, snapping and crackling. They missed a dump truck, flew past truck scales in Scholl Canyon and sailed toward Eagle Rock.

Goodbye Ethan.

They vanished across the ridge.

So had Mandy. I'd never see her eyes again.

Leta touched my hand. I felt the strength to finally say the words I dreaded.

"Goodbye, Mandy," we both whispered together."

Leta faced me.

She buried her chin into my collar, gently weeping.

I held her, and we cried. I was grateful she was with me.

She was shaking.

I was quivering too.

When Leta's tears had soaked my t-shirt and my own had drenched her blouse sleeve, and we had trembled to contain each other's sobs, we heard the baby. Leta lifted her from the

Snugli, lowered her blouse and let her nurse. This time I didn't feel so ashamed.

Yet I felt as if our tears had flushed the poison from our souls, leftover bitterness from high school, broken hearts, and Vietnam. Crying was exhausting. My diaphragm was aching, but I felt cleaner, like air after a rainstorm.

Leta faced me, eyes bleary. She touched the damp spot on my shoulder, grinned the way fellow soldiers used to smile in Vietnam, the sort of grimace we'd paste on to mask the underlying pain. "Well Allen," Leta's voice choked through her tears. "You kept your promise to me."

"Promise?"

"Behind the motorcycle cage our senior year, remember?" Leta whispered. "You promised me that you'd be Mandy's friend."

I blushed, recalling. "I just remember being grateful you didn't slap me."

"What makes you think I wasn't flattered?" Leta asked. I saw her blush.

I smiled. But right now, I was too numb to answer back. The last of Mandy's ashes had been taken by the breeze.

I'd heard a *mitzvah* was a commandment a person sometimes got from God to do a good deed, a kindness that can flow back to the giver. Although not Jewish, on Rosh Hashanah I'd promised to be a friend, a promise I had done my best to keep.

Now, with the Vietnam War ending, I'd found my name in the Book of Life, and I'd been blessed. I was grateful I had completed my first *mitzvah,* thankful I had called Mandy my friend.

CHAPTER THIRTY

REACH OUT OF THE DARKNESS

FLINT PEAK: MARCH, 1974

I'd met with Leta every month up where we'd sent out Mandy's ashes. I'd moved to Montrose, since La Cañada was too expensive. Leta liked to join me after she moved back from the Bay Area. Until she'd enrolled at the Pasadena Art Center College of Design, I'd never had a clue she was an artist.

For Christmas, I got a portrait she'd done in charcoal from a photo in the *Omega,* our high school yearbook, of Mandy running. And every hike up to Flint Peak, Leta brought her sketch pads. Leta liked to draw, and she was good.

As for me, I studied engineering at Cal Poly Pomona. I decided to take it up to settle a score with Ethan Frome, who'd dreamed of being an engineer and then had never gone to college. I had some help from Uncle Sam in exchange for half my foot. I looked forward to hours with Leta. We often talked about old times. Sometimes she dragged my butt inside the

Pasadena Art Museum, until I found myself on speaking terms with Degas ballerinas.

Leta's daughter walked beside us at twelve months.

Fact was, I hardly noticed I was growing close to Leta until one day, feeling lonely, I took a drive to that museum and told a cast-bronze ballerina how I wished Leta was with me. My foot-stump had now healed. Perhaps my heart was healing too. For now, the Degas ballerina shared my secret and my fear that Leta Hertz, the former Rose Princess was way out of my league.

For spring break, Leta had packed us both a picnic in her hatchback. A basket full of sandwiches and Cokes behind the hatch sat on an envelope of drawings between the wheel-well and the seat. She offered me a Life Saver. I told her I could wait, and she replied she was relieved because the lime ones were her favorites.

I moved the envelope to flatten it, making sure it wouldn't bend or blow away in winter breezes that chilled the fire road to Flint Peak. A set of drawings fell from the opening, pencil sketches, charcoal renderings, a drawing in pen and ink....

...And there it was, the ink drawing of the maniac who'd reminded me of a cross between Alfred E. Newman and Coney Island's Steeplechase Man. He almost leaped out of the paper on his runaway toboggan. His drooling tongue flapped from his mouth. His ears, back-blown by wind, crusted with icicles. He looked as sick as I'd remembered. And on the center of his toboggan, bigger than an eight-ball, a black circle displayed the number five.

"What's this?" I asked.

Leta grinned.

"My God, you drew this?"

"Mandy had me draw the cover."

"No way."

"Guess I'm busted." Leta blushed.

My jaw dropped. The Society for the Complete Extermination of *Ethan Frome* had other members. I'd known that, but had one of them been Leta? I had only one more question.

"Leta, by chance—do you know who 'Zorro' was?"

She took a breath and smiled, as if recalling ancient history. She tipped her rhinestone glasses that by now I'd gotten used to. She laughed. I loved her laugh.

"Remember Mrs. Zinicola?"

"How could I not, with all her miniskirts?"

"When she first heard of our Society, after her husband's suicide, she begged me to sign up. Honest, Allen."

"No freakin' way."

"She wanted to set hearts free. Course, so did Edith Wharton which was the point of *Ethan Frome*. 'If only we'd stop trying to be happy—' Wharton wrote '—we could have a pretty good time.' When I read that up at Stanford, it made sense. I finally got it. But Mrs. Z. insisted everything be happy, happy, happy. Maybe we have to pass through pain to find our freedom, Leta said. "Maybe that's why life can be so rough on us."

"Like childbirth?" I glanced toward Mandy who was walking toward a ridgeline.

"She's pretty. Don't you think?" Leta inquired.

"Rose Princess pretty," I said, looking at Leta's sapphire eyes.

Leta smiled. I'd always wondered who had fathered Leta's baby. For some reason, I'd never dared to ask. We both faced Mandy. Leta gave a smile and touched my wrist. "Haven't you wondered?"

"I've always wondered."

She stared out over the valley. "Guy at Stanford. This professor. We shacked up my freshman year. Said he loved me. Knocked me up."

"You got the 'friends' speech?"

"Yup."

"Why are their *children* called the bastards?"

"Promise me you'll never treat a girl the way that *he* did."

"How'll you know?"

Leta faced me. "Ve have vays."

"Mandy always used to say that."

"Did you know—" Leta said "—people were jealous of you and Mandy? *I* was jealous. Okay, you looked like Laurel and Hardy your first few weeks. But you *belonged* together." She tilted her head the way I remembered from back in high school. "You guys were peanut butter and jelly. I mean the one good thing I did in high school, the thing I'm really really proud of...."

"Was?"

"Bringing you two guys together." Leta grinned. "And the day you won that race, all La Cañada walked tall. We respected you so much. Garry Jackson was in awe. And me—let's just say...." Leta froze, as if her tongue had gotten stuck inside her throat. She stuttered. She stared beyond Scholl Canyon, beyond Los Angeles, past Catalina Island. She ran her palms along her pockets. Her face lost color. Leta shifted. Her pupils widened inside her deep sapphire eyes.

"Leta?"

"Do you know, Allen, I've been in love with you since high school?"

I felt my face flush. "Me?" *What had Leta seen in me?*

"It wasn't easy to keep my secret," Leta said. "Cuz Mandy needed you."

"Oh. My. God." She'd moved here clear from San Francisco to be with *me*.

"You kept your promise. That's why Mandy and I liked you," Leta said. "She had a sense about you. Mandy always knew who she could help, who she could count on."

I stared into Leta's eyes and saw the loneliness I'd seen the day we'd stood beside the tennis courts, and she'd chastised me for welching out on Mandy. I'd forgotten. Too many problems of my own. After Wock's death, I'd been too scared to notice both of us were frightened.

I understood now what had happened both to Leta and her poise. When Mandy died, the flow of kindness filling Leta's heart had ceased. The same with my heart. Two broken hearts, and Mandy wasn't here to heal us.

But *we* could—together, if I found the courage to ask.

Looking again at Leta's eyes felt like facing into a mirror. The pain I'd often seen in my eyes was so obvious in hers. The heartbreak of betrayal. High-school's innocence had left her. How could a former Breck shampoo girl look so lonely? And yet they'd told us that love meant we never had to say we're sorry. Their lie had cost me half my foot. It had cost Leta half her heart. Today, despite my terror, I had to ask a question. If she turned me down, rejecting me might heal her, despite me.

Leta popped a Life Saver into her mouth. She looked tired. I wondered when the last time was she'd laughed. Her hair looked Orphan-Annie frazzled. She'd added a pound or maybe several, but in her eyes, her former sparkle lingered. It was finally time to tell Leta the secret until now I'd only whispered to that cast-bronze ballerina.

"Leta?"

"Mm-hmm?"

"Did you ever read our bylaws?"

"What bylaws?"

"For the Society for the Complete Extermination of *Ethan Frome*. Article Nine, Clause Thirty-Seven A." I cleared my throat. *"When two people are the the last surviving members, and they make each other laugh, and they like being together, it's the duty of the gentleman to ask the lady member to marry him, if he's single.* Which, last time I checked, I am."

Leta looked at me, jaw dropping. "Allen, what about my daughter?"

I whispered, taking her hands. "That's Clause Thirty-Seven B. *He must adopt her as his own, especially one named Mandy."* I grinned.

Leta stared at me, eyes glistening with tears. "You'd love me?"

I nodded.

"You promise?"

I squeezed her palm. "Cross my heart and hope to die, stick a needle in my eye, I love you, Leta. I love your daughter. Plus I keep promises."

Leta tilted her head. "What's Clause Thirty-Seven C say?"

"I haven't written that one yet. I believe that's when the bell rang."

Leta was crying. "That's where it says I'd be a fool to turn him down."

I reached behind her and through her blouse, felt the angle of her shoulder. Her fingernails tiptoed behind my neck. Pulling her toward me she fit like we were pieces of a puzzle. With no armcast in between us, Leta felt like she belonged there, custom-made to snuggle inside my arms. Lips touched mine, moist like flowers. I felt her breath across my nostrils. She closed her eyes, and I closed mine. We melted together in a kiss.

I was dreaming up new clauses we'd need to write into our bylaws, when I noticed I was sucking on her Life Saver.

A voice called. "Look!" Mandy pointed across the ridgeline.

Spars of yucca plants cast silhouettes against the evening sunset. Flowers blazed like candles, flames before a sky the color of burgundy where the evening sun had dropped behind Flint Peak.

I hobbled over to see the child's awe. Ivory petals littered her playsuit. Leta's fingers laced into my own, and I squeezed back.

The Society for the Complete Extermination of *Ethan Frome* would endure.

I faced Mandy and her mother, surrendering my heart. Leta's valentine smile in front of me awaited. I closed my eyes to taste her breath again, to feel her kiss. When at last we stopped for air, a new Mandy made her way into our three-way family hug.

I loved being where I was.

And being velcroids, I just knew we'd stick together.

THE END

DRAMATIS PERSONAE

Characters in *italics* are fictitious. Characters in **bold** were real people or real cultural icons widely known in the 1970s.

Alcindor, Ferdinand Lewis Jr. (Lew) aka Kareem Abdul-Jabbar – 1947-20xx – Basketball center, author, activist, and leader of multiple UCLA championship teams. NBA recordholder whose career for the Milwaukee Bucks and Los Angeles Lakers spanned 20 seasons. Six-time MVP in NBA. Played on 19 All Star Teams. In mid 1971 changed name to Kareem Abdul-Jabbar.

Alexandrowycz, Ivan (Ivan Alphabet) – 1953-20xx - fictitious high school student and cross country athlete.

Ali, Muhammad nee Cassius Marcellus Clay – 1942-2016 – Louisville-born American Heavyweight Boxing Champion who gained notoriety when he went to prison for refusing to serve in Vietnam.

Anderson, John – 1929-19xx – fictitious high school janitor.

Ann-Margret (Olsson) – 1941-20xx – Swedish-American actress and sex symbol known in 1971 for her roles in *Bye-Bye Birdie*, *Viva Las Vegas* and *Carnal Knowledge*. Her numerous USO tours with Bob Hope and others endeared her to many veterans.

Arthur, Michael Patrick – 1951-1970 – fictitious high school student and Vietnam casualty.

Bart, Lily – 18xx-1905 – fictitious protagonist of Edith Wharton's novel *The House of Mirth*, who dies of an overdose after realizing her beauty is diminishing along with her prospects for attracting the perfect man.

Bates, Norman 19xx-1982 – fictitious murderer played by Anthony Perkins in the Alfred Hitchcock motion picture thriller *Psycho*, based on a 1959 novel by Robert Bloch. Immortalized by the famous "shower scene" where Janet Leigh's character is murdered.

Bear, Yogi – 1959-20xx – Hanna-Barbera cartoon character with his own half-hour show, an animated bear inhabiting Jellystone Park and living off of picnic baskets.

Belli, Melvin – 1907-1996 – American lawyer known as the "King of Torts" and by insurance companies as Melvin Bellicose. Belli represented numerous celebrities and high-profile clients, including Muhammad Ali, Chuck Berry, Mae West, Jack Ruby, and ZsaZsa Gabor..

Bergen, Candice Patricia – 1946-20xx – American actress and 1960s sex symbol

Bond, James – 1920-20xx – fictitious British spy and protagonist of Ian Fleming's 007 novels

Bradley, Milton – 1836-1911 – American board game pioneer and publisher. His Milton Bradley Company before being sold to Hasbro sold such popular games as *Chutes and Ladders, Candyland, The Game of Life,* and *Twister.* The Milton Bradley brand went defunct in 2009.

Brady Bunch – American sitcom family that aired from 1969 to 1974 on commercial television.

Braun, Eva Anna Paula – 1912-1945 – mistress to Adolf Hitler. Married to him for the final forty hours of their lives.

Brown, Charlie – 1950-20xx – Peanuts comic strip character who, among other recurring gags, never received a valentine on Valentine's Day

Brown, Lester Raymond – 1912-2001 – Jazz musician and leader of Les Brown and His Band of Renoun for seven decades, who really was booked by someone's parents for our prom, I kid you not.

Buster the Adjuster – 1915-1985 – fictitious insurance adjuster.

Cagney, James Francis (Jimmy) 1899-1986 – American chartacter actor known for playing complicated tough guys in 1930's and 1940's gangster flicks including *The Public Enemy* and *White Heat.*

Calley, Lieutenant William – 1943-20xx – former U.S. Army officer court-martialed for murdering 22 unarmed South Vietnamese civilians on March 16, 1968 in the Mỹ Lai massacre.

Carpenter, Karen Anne – 1950-1983 – lead singer and drummer of Downey-based pop duet, the Carpenters, known for sweet syrupy love songs before she died from anorexia.

Carroll, Lewis nee Charles Lutwidge Dodson – 1832-1898 – British children's novelist, mathematician, and Anglican deacon. Wrote *Alice's Adventures in Wonderland* and *Through the Looking Glass.*

Clark, Penny – 1952-20xx – fictitious La Cañada High School student.

Cong, Charlie – slang term for the Viet Cong in Vietnam

Conrad, Mr. Roland – 1930-19xx – fictitious assistant principal.

Copelan, Mr. Dennis – 1940-20xx – fictitious chemistry teacher.

Crawford, Joan nee Lucille Fay LeSueur – 1907-1977 – Texasborn Academy Award winning actress for her title role in *Mildred Pierce.* She moved from glamour films in the '30s to thrillers in the '40s and '50s to horror in the '60s in a career that spanned six decades from the '20s to the '70s.

Crocker, Betty – 1921-20xx – fictitious character and brand used in advertising campains for General Mills who uses her name on a distinctive red-spoon logo. Voted the second most popular woman in America in 1945 by *Fortune* magazine behind Eleanor Roosevelt. In Golden Valley, Minnesota there is actually a street named Betty Crocker Drive in her honor.

Crunch, Cap'n – 1963-20xx – corn and oats breakfast cereal; manufactured by Quaker Oats Company.

Cunningham, Stan – 1953-20xx – fictitious high school student and football player.

Davis, Ruth Elizabeth (Bette) 1908-1989 – New England-born Hollywood actress who starred in over 100 films in her 50-year acting career. Known for playing unsympathetic characters, and known for her feud with Joan Crawford, Humphrey Bogart claimed she "scared the bejeesus out of him". She is quoted as saying "The best time I ever had with Joan Crawford was when I pushed her down the stairs in *Whatever Happened to Baby Jane?*"

Day, Doris nee Doris Mary Anne Kappelhoff – 1922-2019 – Cincinnati-born singer and actor known for portrayal of young and upbeat female protagonists.

Day, Susan – 1953-20xx – fictitious high school student.

Degas, Edgar nee Hilaire-Germain-Edgar De Gas – 1834-1917 – French impressionist painter and sculptor, known for his impressionistic paintings and sculptures of ballet dancers.

Delgado, Tina Sue – 1953-1997 – subject of recurring refrain on KHJ's Real Don Steele radio program. A woman would proclaim "Tina Delgado is alive. alive!" Nobody knows the meaning of the phrase or the identity of the woman who shouted the words. Also a fictitious high school student.

Demento, Doctor nee Barret Eugene Hansen – 1941-20xx – American disc jockey and radio personality who broadcast at night on KPPC FM in Pasadena and later KMWET. Demento specialized in playing bizarre and unusual novelty recordings from his personal collection.

Drysdale, Donald Scott – 1936-1993 – Hard-throwing Hall of Fame pitcher for the Los Angeles Dodgers. Born in Van Nuys in the San Fernando Valley of Los Angeles.

Dunlap, Mrs. Deborah Jean – 1946-20xx – fictitious high school teacher.

Fairchild, Heather – 1954-20xx – fictitious La Cañada High School student.

Fonda, Peter Henry – 1940-2019 – Actor known for his role in Easy Rider for which he wrote the screenplay. Son of Henry Fonda. Younger brother of Jane Fonda. Father of Bridget Fonda.

Friedan, Betty nee Bettye Naomi Goldstein – 1921-2006 – American feminist and author credited with starting the second wave of feminism. She cofounded the National Organization for Women (NOW) and was elected its first president. In her later years, while remaining feminist, Friedan was critical of extremist writings that denounced and demonized all men.

Frome, Ethan – 18xx-19xx – fictitious Starkfield Massachusetts resident and the main character of Edith Wharton's novella *Ethan Frome.*

Frome, Ethan Jr. – 1970-197x – fictitious bird.

Frome, Zenobia – 18xx-19xx – fictitious hypochondriac wife of Ethan Frome in Edith Wharton's novella.

Gabor, Zsa Zsa nee Sari Gabor – 1917-2016 – Glamorous Hungarian born actress known for profligate spending and sequentially marrying and divorcing nine husbands. Called herself the "best housekeeper in Hollywood", because every time she got a divorce, she kept the house.

Hall, Monty, OC nee Monte Halparin – 1921-2017 – Winnipeg-born host of game show *Let's Make a Deal* in which contestants were allowed to trade what they have in their hands for whatever lies behind one of three doors, knowing behind one of the doors is a new car. During his lifetime, Hall raised over a billion dollars for charities and was elevated into the prestigious Order of Canada.

Hansen, Kurt – 1953-20xx – fictitious high school student and football player.

Hardy, Oliver Norvell – 1892-1957 – Georgia-born American actor and half of comedy duo Laurel and Hardy who were close friends, not only on the screen but in real life.

Harron, Coach Richard (Dick) – 1920-2005 – fictitious high school football coach.

Hendrix, James Marshall "Jimi" nee Johnny Allen Hendrix 1942-1970 – Seattle-born mixed race (African, Irish, and Cherokee) guitarist considered one of the most influential instrumentalists in rock and roll history. In 2005, *Rolling Stone* ranked him as the greatest guitarist of all time.

Hertz, Leta – 1953-20xx – fictitious high school best friend of Mandy Richert.

Hitchcock, Sir Alfred Joseph – 1899-1980 – English director and screenwriter known as the "Master of Suspense" directed over 50 motion picture thrillers including the classics *Rear Window, Vertigo, Psycho,* and *The Birds.*

Hopper, Dennis Lee – 1936-2010 – Actor and director known for his role as both in the movie Easy Rider.

Howard, Aaron (Rusty) (Boo Boo) – 1955-20xx– fictitious high school student and cross country athlete.

Hull, Dave (the Hullabalooer) – 1934-2020 – Alhambra-born L.A. disc jockey on KRLA 1110 AM voted one of the thop ten Los Angeles radio personalities of all time. Began his career working for Armed Forces Radio in Casablanca.

Ivers, Jesse William and Catherine – 19xx-19xx – La Cañada-Flintridge residents and founders of Ivers Department Store chain which had a store in La Cañada.

Jablonski, Andrzej (Jabberwocky) – 1953-1971 – fictitious high school student and cross country athlete.

Jackson, Garry – 1953-1973 – fictitious high school student and football player.

Jackson, Shirley Hardie – 1916-1965 – San Francisco-born American horror writer pioneer whose short story *The Lottery* tells of a village who every year held a lottery to execute one of their villagers.

Jensen, Sara – 1953-1973 – fictitious high school student.

Joplin, Janis – 1943-1970 – Hugely successful blues singer from Port Arthur, Texas with multiple Billboard Hot 100 hits. Lead singer of Big Brother and the Holding Company who broke out after the 1967 Monterey Pop Festival. Died of a heroin overdose.

Kasem, Casey nee Kemal Amin Kasem – 1932-2014 – L.A. disk jockey on KRLA known for his dedications to call-in lovers on the "Sweetheart Tree" segment of his show. Later moved on to produce the syndicated weekly show *American Top Forty.*

Laurel, Arthur Stanley Jefferson (Stan) – 1890-1965 – English actor and half of comedy duo Laurel and Hardy who were close friends, not only on the screen but in real life.

Lopez, José – 1953 20xx – fictitious San Marino High School student and ASF exchange student who is top seed on the Peruvian national distance running team.

Maldonado, Rudy – 1951-1972 – fictitious American war victim.

Manson, Charles Milles nee Maddox – 1934-2017 – Cincinnati-born California-based cult leader of the mass murderer Manson Clan who terrorized Los Angeles in the late 1960s with a series of gruesome murders.

Martin, Allen Daniel – 1953-20xx – fictitious high school student and athlete.

Marx, Julius Henry (Groucho) – 1890-1977 – Manhattan-born comedian and film and television star, known for his spontaneous wit and wordplay. Hosted popular 1950s show *You Bet Your Life.*

Mason, Gena – 1953-20xx – fictitious high school student and friend of Heather's

Mason, Perry – 19xx-20xx – Title character of American legal drama television series (1957-1966) based on mid-century detective fiction involving Mason, a criminal defense lawyer created by novelist Erle Stanley Gardner

McAllister, Billie Joe – 19xx-1967 – fictitious subject of 1967 country music hit *Ode to Billie Joe* by Bobbie Gentry about a boy whose body is found beneath a Mississippi bridge over the Tallahatchee River.

Macnee, Daniel Patrick – 1922-2015 – English actor who played the part of spy John Steed opposite Honor Blackman, Diana Rigg and Linda Thorson in the 1960's espionage TV program, *The Avengers.*

McMasters, Alan (Pudge) – 1953-20xx – fictitious high school student and football player.

McQueen, Terrence Stephen (Steve) – 1930-1980 – American actor known as the "King of Cool" for his portrayal of rebellious anti-hero characters in films such as *The Sand Pebbles, The Magnificent Seven,* and *The Great Escape.*

Mehta, Zubin – 1936-20xx – Indian-born former conductor of the Los Angeles Philharmonic Orchestra from 1962 to 1978 before he moved on to the New York Philharmonic. His father founded the Bombay Symphony Orchestra.

Metzger, Arthur – 1921-19xx – fictitous executive secretary of Hollywood draft board.

Montana, Montie nee Owen Harlen Mickel – 1910-1998 – Rodeo trick rider, trick roper, and Pro Rodeo Hall of Fame member who appeared in more than 60 Pasadena Tournament of Roses parades, waving to the crowd from his silver saddle on his horse Rex.

Morris, Doris (Momma) – 1915-19xx – fictitious acting principal of La Cañada High School.

Morrison, James Douglas (Jim) – 1943-1971 – Florida-born Nietzschean lyricist and lead singer of the iconic L.A.-based band, The Doors. His father, Rear Admiral George Stephen Morrison commanded U.S. naval forces during the Gulf of Tonkin incident.

Mulcahy, Hugh Noyes (Losing Pitcher Mulcahy) – 1913-2001 – American professional baseball player who played for the Phillies and the Pirates from 1935-1947. Also the first major league player to be drafted into military serice for World War II. Mulcahy was known for pitching more games and losing more games than any other major league pitcher of his era, largely because his teammates couldn't hit.

Munch, Edvard – 1863-1944 – Norwegian impressionistic painter known for swirling emotional paint strokes in landmark works such as *The Scream*.

Munster, Herman – 1815-20xx – fictitious Frankenstein-like main character of television sitcom The Munsters played by Fred Gwynne.

Neal, Coach Michael – 1933-2007 – fictitious high school football coach.

Nelson, Oswald George (Ozzie) – 1906-1975 – 1930's Big Band leader from Jersey City, New Jersey who originated and starred in The Adventures of Ozzie and Harriet, a radio and television show about his family. He was known for being extremely paternalistic and authoritarian, even prohibiting his sons, David and Ricky from going to college so the television show would not be cancelled.

Newman, Alfred E – 193x-2019 – fictitious mascot and cover boy for *Mad*, a popular satirical magazine, widely read by boys in the Sixties and the Seventies. The image of Alfred E. Newman actually originated in the 1930s and was used in print ads for painless dentistry and in political ads along with the "What Me Worry?" slogan. Harvey Kurtzman, a cartoonist liked the image and acquired the rights in 1954. By 1956, The newly named Alfred E. Newman made his first appearance on the cover of *Mad* magazine.

Newman, Paul Leonard – 1925-2008 – Connecticut-born Academy Award-Winning actor, director, race car driver and philanthropist.

Nixon, Richard Milhouse – 1913-1994 – Thirty-seventh President of the United States who presided over the closing years of the War in Vietnam. Resigned whle facing impeachment in 1974, shortly after the American withdrawal.

Oakley, Annie nee Phoebe Ann Mosey – 1860-1926 – Ohio-born American sharpshooter and subject of Irving Berlin's 1950's musical motion picture *Annie Get Your Gun.* Famous for her marxmanship in Buffalo Bill's Wild West Show.

Occam, William of – 1287-1347 – English Franciscan friar and scientist known for articulating "Occam's Razor" that the simplest explanation or procedure should suffice.

Page, Bettie Mae – 1923-2008 – American model famous in the 1950s for her appearance in pin-up photographs.

Pig Pen – 1954-2000 – Peanuts comic strip character who always seems to have a cloud of dust around him from being dirty.

Pollock, Paul Jackson – 1912-1956 – American abstractionist painter born in Cody, Wyoming, known for his practice of flinging and dripping paint onto a canvas on the floor of his studio while painting to create the feel of action and motion.

Popeye the Sailor – 1929-20xx – fictitious comic strip and cartoon character, known for eating spinach before fights to instantly become strong.

Poppins, Mary – 18xx-19xx – fictitious magical British nanny based on a series of children's books by P.L. Travers and popularized in the overtly cheery 1964 Disney musical motion picture *Mary Poppins*.

Prentice, David – 1953-20xx – fictitious San Marino High School student.

Price, Vincent Leonard Jr. – 1911-1993 – American character actor who appeared in numerous Hollywood horror films, known for his deep voice and tall intimidating presence.

Racer, Speed – 195x-20xx – fictitious star of Manga originated anime telivision series that debuted in the United States in 1967. The image of Speed Racer (Gō Mifune in Japan) was adapted from the image of Elvis Presley in the American motion picture *Viva Las Vegas*.

Randall, Eddie – 1953-20xx – fictitious high school student and football player.

Redding, Otis – 1941-1967 – Georgia-born American R&B singer songwriter died in a plane crash before his breakout record *The Dock of the Bay*, the first posthumous number one record on the Billboard Hot 100.

Redford, Charles Robert Jr. – 1936-20xx – Santa Monica-born actor and winner of multiple Academy Awards for Best Actor. Known in 1970 for his roles in *Inside Daisly Clover*, *Barefoot in the Park*, and *Butch Cassidy and the Sundance Kid*.

Richert, Mandy – 1953-1973 – fictitious high school student, nun, and women's track coach.

Ridenhour, Ronald Lee – 1946-1998 - Arizona-raised U.S, Army helicopter gunner who gathered eyewitness accounts of the Mỹ Lai massacre and detailed the evidence in a letter sent to

President Nixon which triggered the Mỹ Lai investigations and the conviction of Lieutenant William Calley. The Ridenhour Prizes are given annually to investigative journalists who are honored for their persistence in speaking out the truth.

Rigg, Dame Enid Diana Elizabeth – 1938-2020 – English actress whose portrayal of Emma Peel in the TV series The Avengers endeared her to a generation of Boomers.

Robinson, Jack Roosevelt – 1919-1972 – American professional baseball player who went to high school in Pasadena and broke the Major League Baseball color barrier when he debuted for the Dodgers in was voted Rookie of the Year in 1947.

Roth, Edward (Big Daddy) – 1932-2001 – American cartoonist, graphic artist, and custom car designer who, with his cartoon creation "Ratt Fink" was a staple of the Southern California Kustom Kar scene in the Sixties.

Scheib, Earl – 1908-1992 – Los Angeles based automobile painting entrepreneur who specialized in late night advertising and low-cost auto painting. Known for his late-night advertisements stating "I'll paint any car any color for $39.95. No ups. No extras." At its zenith, Scheib worked in 23 states. The company went defunct in 2010.

Scribner, Charles IV – 1921-1995 – Head of fourth generation of Scribner scions to lead family publishing company, Charles Scribners Sons, which his great grandfather, Charles I had founded in 1846. His company owned the rights to *Ethan Frome*.

Segal, Erich Wolf – 1937-2010 – Brooklyn-born American author, screenwriter, and classicist educator who taught at Yale and Princeton. In 1970, Segal wrote the novel and the screenplay for *Love Story* a tale of an upper class elitist Harvard student who falls in love with a brilliant but middle class Radford student who dies of cancer, leaving him alone. The tearjerker was the

New York Times best-selling novel for 1970 and was the top box-office grossing film of 1971. Its portrayal of elitists proved problematic for Segal who was himself elitist, bordering on megalomania. Segal later said the book "totally ruined me."

Sherman, Robert Cabot (Bobby) – 1943-20xx – American pop singer, actor, and teen idol of the early 1970's. Later became an EMT and officer in the Los Angeles Police Department, retiring as a captain.

Snooge (Nobody knows his real name. Someone told me it was Dave something) – 1953-20xx – fictitious high school student and athlete.

Silver, Mattie – 18xx-19xx – love interest of Ethan Frome in Edith Wharton's novel of the same name.

Skinner, Vinnie – 1956-20xx – fictitious neighbor kid.

Smithee, Alan – 1968-2000 – pseudonym used in motion picture credits by members of the Directors Guild of America who felt a project they had worked on was so awful they refused to have their name associated with it.

Tracy, Dick – 1931-20xx – Fictitious comic strip policemen, a staple of newspaper funnies from 1931 to the present and now the oldest continuous running newspaper comic strip in the county.

Unser, Robert William (Bobby) – 1934-2021 – American IndyCar driver and winner of multiple Indianapolis 500s.

Watson, Jenny – 1953-20xx – fictitious high school student and friend of Heather's.

Wayne, John nee Marion Robert Morrison – 1907-1979 – Iowa-born motion picture star and graduate of Glendale High School. Known for starring in numerous Westerns and patriotic World War 2 films.

Welk, Lawrence – 1903-1992 –North Dakota born band leader and accordionist whose televised "Champagne Music Makers", sponsored by Geritol, was targeted toward an audience born in the early 1900s.

Wharton, Edith nee Edith Newbold Jones – 1862-1937 – American novelist, short story writer, and designer who wrote of the New York aristocracy exposing the lives and morals of the Gildied Age. Her works included *The Age of Innocence, The House of Mirth,* and *Ethan Frome.* She was the first woman to win the Pulitzer Prize in literature.

White, Betty Marion – 1922-20xx – Illinois-born American actress whose television career spanned eight decades. Among her many achievements, she co hosted the annual Rose Parade for nineteen consecutive years.

Winchcombe, Mrs. Flora Dora – 1900-1999 – fictitious high school English teacher who has presumably taught Ethan Frome *to high school students since it came out in 1911.*

Wolfman Jack nee Robert Weston Smith –1938-1995 – Raspy-voiced American disc jockey who broadcast live from Mexican border-blaster station XERB with a 250,000 watt nighttime signal allowing him to be heard throughout the Southwestern United States.

Zinicola, Mrs. Audrey – 1942-20xx – fictitious high school English teacher.

Zorro (Don Diego de la Vega) – 1919-20xx – fictitious romantic fiction vigilante character created by Johnston McCulley appearing in books set in colonial California.

1. Allen is eighteen years old when we meet him. Would you describe him as a man or a boy? Why?

2. Allen notices that Mandy would be cute if she were thinner. Why? What makes him push aside his initial disdain and realize this?

3. Coach Neal says, "You're so damn alienated you might as well go live on Mars, you freak. Every race, you start out well, and then you choke. Get some courage. Get some cojones. Get some balls. Maybe then someone'll want you as a friend." Discuss the impact the words of a parent, teacher, or coach can have on a young person and a time such words had an impact on you.

4. Allen says, "I didn't run to win, but ran to vanish…" Why would he want to vanish? And is his solution to his problems healthy or unhealthy? Discuss a time when you might have wanted to vanish and why you felt that way and discuss how you handled it.

5. The hierarchy in high school determines each student's status. How does this change once high school is over? In what ways does it still impact us?

6. When he all but ignores Mandy in the school hallway, Allen succumbs to peer pressure. Do we ever really push past that need to belong or the concurrent tendency to succumb to peer pressure? In what ways does it manifest as we get older?

7. Allen says, "I'd been hiding pain so long pain had become my anesthesia, helping me forget I was a dickwad." What

are some reasons we hide our pain, and what happens when we do so?

8. What kept Allen from making his friendship with Mandy public? Then, what allowed him to do so? We all sometimes react and respond to situations in this way. What does it say about us?

9. Allen is functionally abandoned by both of his parents. Which abandonment might have more impact and why?

10. What effect would Allen's relationship with his mother have on him? Discuss your relationship with your own mother and what impact it had on you.

11. Mandy and Allen become friends. Discuss what friendship means to you and what the most important quality of friendship is.

12. Had you heard of Occam's Razor? What are some ways that we allow our thoughts to complicate our lives?

13. In Chapter Seven, Allen offers to teach Mandy to run, eliminating all unnecessary motions. What were your feelings being with Allen and Mandy this time while they ran together?

14. What do you think of "Martin's First Observation" that there two types of people, Teflonistas and Velcroids and Teflonistas never have to say they're sorry? Do you agree or disagree? Can you think of some examples of Teflonistas in real life?

15. When Allen says to Mandy, "Maybe I'd make Ethan Frome good instead of nice, what does he mean? What is the primary difference between the two?

16. When the janitor tells Allen to, "Keep your words sweet, kid. Some day you just might have to eat them," what does he mean?

17. Discuss the development of Allen and Mandy's friendship. What role does she assume in his life, what need does she fulfill?

18. What was missing from Allen's school when Jabberwocky died? Discuss a situation you have been in where you were made to feel alone with your emotions, and discuss how this impacted you.

19. At one point Allen says, "Girl crap could be so much meaner and more vicious than any guy crap." How do girl crap and boy crap differ?

20. What changes for Allen once he knows his draft number? And in what ways are the changes positive and negative? Discuss an event in your life that dramatically changed your attitude and perspective.

21. "I never win. I never will. Nobody wants to see me win." This seems to be Allen's mantra. What drives this attitude?

22. How long do you think Allen knew about his relationship to his father? Or was what his father told him actually a surprise? How would such knowledge affect you?

23. Why does Allen use Mandy's name in the race?

24. How is the Allen we see at the end of his senior year different from the Allen we met in Chapter 1? Where in the story did you start to notice a change in Allen?

25. Allen is simultaneously terrified and stoic about being inducted into the army, about having been drafted. What other feelings might the young men drafted to serve in Vietnam have felt?

26. How is the Rosh Hashanah theme of Chapter Four revisited in Vietnam in Chapter Twenty-Seven? What is the significance of Rosh Hashanah to Allen?

27. Several times Allen says, "We'd been betrayed." Why and how did America betray its Vietnam vets? And to this day, what impact did that betrayal have on the people who fought in that war?

28. What is the ultimate irony of how the protesters treated returning soldiers? Why do you think the attitude towards the military has now changed?

29. How were kids in 1970 – 1972 different from kids today? How are they the same?

30. Even from the worst of circumstances we can often take away a gift. What gift does Allen take away from his time in Vietnam?

31. Why is Allen obsessed with Ethan Frome? What does he take away from his obsession – and how does it change over time?

32. Do you think the author likes or hates Edith Wharton's writing?

33. Leta says, "Maybe we have to pass through pain to find our freedom." Give an example of this happening in your life.

WITH GRATITUDE

TO DECEASED MEMBERS OF OUR LA CANADA HIGH SCHOOL CLASS OF 1971 THANKS FOR THE MEMORIES!

David Amescua, Rick Bauer, Gregg Berkey, Marijane Binkley, Marilyn Black, Dan Bosche, Reed Bradish, Dan Brown, Bill Bungartz, Sylvia Castaño, Pete Christos, Michael Collins, Curtis Condon, Chris Cox, Mark Ehrenreich, Cindy Flick, Jack Fredericks Fredricks, Kathleen Galleher, John Giberson, Ben Goulden, Bruce Graham, Kent Hellenga, Dan Hoagland, Lynn Hoeven, Christina Holmes, Scott Honsberger, Steven Hufstedler, John Iverson. Michael Jaidar, Greg Jensen, Sue Johnson, Karen Kile, Cyndy Kirsten, Dennis Kraus, Thomas Langbehn, Gayle MacGregor, Jim Nichols, Steve Roberts, John Rudy, Trinka Sandquist, Curt Smith, Bill Springer, Ray Thompson, Mike Tobias, Dorrie Zulli

ACKNOWLEDGMENTS

If I thanked everyone who in some manner contributed to this book, the names would fill a dozen pages. I am truly very fortunate. But there are seven individuals I wish to thank profusely for their patience, wisdom, guidance, and contributions to this book.

1. To Dennis Copelan, author, who helped me crystalize the story.

2. To Louella Nelson, author, teacher, and writing mentor.

3. To Janet Simcic, author and critique group leader, who kept nagging me to publish this one too.

4. To Maddie Margarita, author, and the foremost cheerleader for authors in Orange County, California, who convinced me that my writing didn't suck.

5. To Gwyn Flowers who masterminded the artwork and the cover.

6. To Antoinette Kuritz, publicist and La Jolla Writers Conference founder, who helped to get the word out on this book.

7. Finally, to my wife, Sharon Phinney, who has stuck with me for over forty years.

ABOUT THE AUTHOR

D. J. PHINNEY is an Air Force veteran and a licensed civil and mechanical engineer who has been responsible for design and construction of more than $100 million in water and wastewater infrastructure in California and Arizona.

A Southern California native with a passion for history and construction, Mr. Phinney turned to writing fiction, following the Northridge Earthquake, when a death threat from an insurance company helped him see fiction as a sneaky way to write about the truth.

The Society for the Complete Extermination of Ethan Frome is his third historical or period novel set in old Southern California. When not writing, Mr. Phinney divides his time between Irvine and La Cañada-Flintridge, California.